RUNESCAPE

LEGACY OF BLOOD

LEGACY OF BLOOD

TITAN BOOKS

RuneScape: Legacy of Blood
Print edition ISBN: 9780857687579
E-book edition ISBN: 9780857687593

Published by Titan Books
A division of Titan Publishing Group Ltd
144 Southwark St
London
SE1 0UP

First edition: June 2012

10 9 8 7 6 5 4 3 2 1

The names, characters, logos, symbols, designs, visual representations and all
other elements of RuneScape are trade marks and/or copyright of Jagex Limited
and are used under license.

Visit our website: www.titanbooks.com

Special thanks to the entire team at Jagex, and especially to Claire Byrne, Mark
Ogilvie, Paul Broadbridge, Wendy Rosenthal, and David Osborne.

Did you enjoy this book? We love to hear from our readers. Please email us
at readerfeedback@titanemail.com or write to us at Reader Feedback at the
above address.

To receive advance information, news, competitions, and exclusive offers online,
please sign up for the Titan newsletter on our website.

A CIP catalgue record for this title is available from the British Library.

Printed and bound in the United States.

1

"We shouldn't be here."

Gar'rth ignored the speaker and stepped from the shadows of the castle's high walls. Above him—far above—the early evening sky seemed a dull reflection of the realm below, mirroring the morbid cityscape with all its gray shades of despair and poverty.

He took another step, but this time his servant's strong hand clamped down on his arm.

"My lord, it is dangerous. Even for you." The older man glanced around nervously. "The other lords of Morytania might not know you. Or if they do, they might not care.

"What's more," he continued, his voice lower, "*she* may be there." He tightened his grip. "If the Mistress of Darkmeyer is there then it won't be safe for anyone."

"Remove your hand, Georgi," Gar'rth replied firmly. "I need to see for myself."

Their eyes met.

"But if something happens to you, my lord, it's your father to whom I will answer," the elderly werewolf protested. "The ghetto's

inhabitants will already have been rounded up. In the passion of
the tithe, the Vyrewatch might mistake you for one of the humans.
And if Vanescula comes to feed…"

The hand remained, and Gar'rth saw fear in his servant's
expression—fear that made him bold.

"I am no ordinary citizen of Canifis," he said, baring his teeth. "I
have in me the blood of kings. Vanescula will know that, too.

"Besides," he added, "am I not her newest entertainment?"

He felt Georgi's hand relax. With a sigh, the white-haired man
lowered it.

"And you shouldn't worry about my father, either. Somehow,
I think he wants me to experience this." Gar'rth smiled bitterly.
"Most likely he thinks it will make me stronger."

Georgi shook his head and his craggy, narrow face softened.

"And what of your mother, Gar'rth?" he whispered. "When you
were a newborn here, she made me promise to protect you as best
I could if ever you returned to Castle Drakan."

"Then I will not ask you to break your promise, Georgi. If you
want to honor her memory then you can still protect me. But not
from Tenebra, nor from Vanescula. You must protect me from
myself, from what I might become if I take an innocent life.

"Go home, Georgi," he said, sighing. Then he spoke firmly. "I
command it." Gar'rth turned quickly and stepped away, following
the path that led from the castle toward Meiyerditch's widespread
ghettoes. As he walked he removed his right glove and reached to the
inside pocket of his fine coat. The tips of his fingers found what he
sought—a clipping of human hair, tied with a string, taken in secret.

Where are you now, Kara? he thought. *And what must you think
of me?*

Such thoughts ended abruptly as he approached an immense gate
set in black stone. His keen eyes, to which natural darkness was no
veil, picked out the small postern door on the gate's right side.

Reaching deeper into his pocket he seized a single key, which he had begged from his father only the day before. He had thought it would have been laden with conditions, or denied him altogether. But Tenebra had handed it to him with just an enigmatic smile.

Still wondering at his father's motives, Gar'rth unlocked the postern door and stepped into the darkness that lay beyond.

The stench of the ghetto affected Gar'rth more than its sights and sounds. In such a place as this, he realized, his inhuman senses worked against him.

I cannot so easily pretend I am apart from them, he thought. *Away from the misery and despair.*

He shook his head and forced his way on, past black buildings to his right and left, each several stories high. They stretched away until his gaze was interrupted by another immense black stone wall to the south. Although he couldn't see them, he knew there were other walls to the east and west. The streets reminded him of rabbit warrens, or pathways for cattle.

Cattle to provide the vampires with their blood tithes.

Gar'rth glanced up to the dark heights above, and as he watched a winged figure suddenly darted across his view, flying south.

He blinked, thinking that he might have imagined it.

But two more man-sized figures followed in the path of the first. Soon, he knew, the tithe would begin.

I'm sorry, Kara.

He gritted his teeth and snarled angrily, his left fist clenching with a strength that made the leather glove squeal.

A startled cry, so faint that it would have been missed by any human, made him instantly alert. His gaze shot to the left and his black eyes opened wide, easily penetrating the darkness of a nearby alley.

It was a young girl—alone, barefoot, and dressed in rags.

He took a step closer, and entered the narrow passageway.

As he did so, the girl scrambled away from him, her breathing quick and her eyes terrified. Her ribs showed under the rags, and her thin arms spoke of desperate hunger.

She is probably eight or nine, he realized with sudden clarity. *About the same age as Kara was when Sulla slew her family.*

From the south, Gar'rth felt a warm breeze caress his clean-shaven face, too weak to stir his long coat but powerful enough to stir his appetite.

The wind carries with it a flavor I know too well.

"You must hide," he gritted urgently. "Now. They will be coming."

Boxed into a corner, the girl didn't move.

"Do you understand me?" he asked. "Others of your people have understood my words. Do you?"

Now the breeze picked up, and the scent grew stronger. He felt his mouth grow dry and his stomach ached. The breeze became a wind, and his long coat whipped behind him. As he turned he could hear the screams carried on its growing violence.

He had no time left. Nor did she.

Gar'rth strode forward, ignoring her cry as she threw an arm across her face to block the sight of him. He took her wrist in his left hand while his right clawed at the ground, where the wall rose from the alley. Ancient stonework crumbled under his desperate digging.

Moments passed, until there was room enough. Roughly he pushed her into the alcove he had created, ignoring her cry of pain as her body smashed against the hard stone. Then, working quickly, he piled the remnants of the broken masonry over her.

At once she realized what he was doing, and helped. The last thing he saw of her was a faint smile.

It lifted his spirits. In allowing her to think she had a chance, he had won some kind of victory over the oppressors.

Stepping to the alley's mouth, he turned into the blood-flavored wind, and headed south.

The wind turned into a gale as he neared the center of the human enclave. It became a roar as Gar'rth felt the change coming on, his instincts tempted by the iron smell carried toward him.

He paused and shielded himself behind a corner. Frantically he reached again into his coat pocket, this time on his right side, withdrawing a strange wooden sheath in his gloved left hand. It made him shudder. This was a splitbark sheath, an enchanted wood that kept the power of the weapon inside from affecting him.

Yet it was his only hope now.

I must resist the change, and this is the only way to do it.

He unsheathed the two-pronged dagger from the splitbark covering. The effect was instant. The scent on the wind vanished, and all sound was muffled. The shadows seemed darker and his vision less acute. Perspiration moistened his brow.

The creature inside him ceased its raging.

Gar'rth groaned and leaned against the wall. The wolfsbane dagger had done its work. He felt weak, and he shivered for a long moment.

But he was his own man again.

Quickly he returned the blade to its enchanted sheath and tucked it into his coat pocket. As he took a deep breath the symptoms passed quickly. Knowing now what to expect, he prepared himself for the sweet scent on the wind, and continued on.

Yet when he turned the corner the wind was slackening, and the scent of blood was noticeably absent.

2

The two Vyrewatch saw him as soon as he approached the square.

Each stood a head taller even than him, a height that would dwarf all but the greatest human. Their broad bodies and thick arms told of an unnatural strength, and yet when they moved there was no ripple under the gray reptilian skin. Fangs as long as a finger protruded from their mouths, and their eyes glowed with a red light.

Protruding from their shoulders through crafted armor, their great wings were folded behind them. Both creatures carried a long spear.

Gar'rth decided that a bold approach was most likely to succeed.

"Do you know who I am?" he demanded.

The nearest one advanced, its taloned feet clicking on the paving. Behind, the second one spread its wings and crouched. Without a sound, it leapt into the air, passing the first and coming to land behind Gar'rth.

"I asked you a question," he repeated, louder this time. "Do you know who I am?"

Neither answered.

He turned sideways in an effort to keep both in view when they moved. A dull blur from his right was all he saw as the spear swung toward his face. He raised his arms instinctively to block the incoming pole.

Crack!

Gar'rth's legs were swept from under him by his second attacker's blow as the incoming pole he had sought to block passed overhead, missing his face by a hand's width alone.

The two vampires circled him, each spinning their spears in lazy circles in their clawed hands. Gar'rth sat up and pulled off his gloves.

"I am Tenebra's son and heir," he said angrily. "Challenge me at your own peril."

Again neither answered.

Behind the Vyrewatch to his right lay the square, in the middle of which clustered a group of ragged people. His plight had caught their attention. Some watched with curiosity. Others, he noted grimly, turned away, indifferent to the drama that was unfolding.

They've lived with such brutality for all their lives, he thought. Then the vampires stopped spinning their spears, both at the very same instant.

Gar'rth didn't wait for them to move first. Instead, he leapt up and charged at the nearest—the one on his right. As he ran he willed the change, summoning the werewolf half of his heritage. Fur thickened on his body, his features distended into the form of a snout, and claws emerged from the tips of his fingers. Loose-fitting clothes allowed the transformation to go unhindered.

At the last moment he leapt high, thrusting his bare hands forward to gouge the face and throat of his foe. He hoped the change would prove startling enough to buy him a moment's advantage.

Yet the Vyrewatch showed no hesitation at Gar'rth's changed

state. The creature crouched and lashed out with its free hand, seizing Gar'rth's wrist in mid-leap.

The grip was impossibly strong, as if stone had encased his wrist. The moment it was secure the vampire pivoted on its back foot, allowing Gar'rth's momentum to turn it.

"No!" he cried.

The creature swept Gar'rth around by his wrist, and then released him.

Hard stone broke against his back as he impacted the wall of the nearest hovel. He fell to the ground, gasping for breath. As he pushed himself up, his hand closed around a piece of broken rubble.

He leapt to his feet once more, and had covered half the distance to his enemy when the second Vyrewatch hurled its spear. The pole found its mark in the ground between Gar'rth's legs.

The werewolf tripped and fell forward, straight into the oncoming fist of his nearest enemy. The force of the blow doubled him over.

Yet still he was not beaten.

With all of his strength he brought the stone into the face of the vampire. It broke upon impact, jarring his hand painfully and scattering shards. But the vampire didn't flinch.

"That's impossible—"

Its hands lashed out. One took Gar'rth around the throat while the other tore at his coat. His world grew hazy and his strength faded as he was forced to his knees. When he spoke, he wheezed the words.

"No, no—not that," he gasped, sensing a familiar baleful influence. "Not now." As he weakened the vampire held up the wolfsbane dagger it had taken from the inside of his coat, unsheathed. Then, its curiosity seemingly sated, it dropped the weapon and reached forward again, pulling something else from his pockets.

"No!"

Now the vampire held the blonde strands of Kara-Meir's hair. It took a long sniff of the object, its red eyes never leaving Gar'rth's face.

"Give that back," he growled. "Give that back or I'll—"

For the first time the Vyrewatch made a sound.

It *hissed*. Then it dropped the blonde strands onto the dirty pavement.

Gar'rth was wrenched to his feet from behind by his second attacker. Still feeling the dagger's power upon him, there was nothing he could do as his face was smashed mercilessly against the wall. He felt his nose break with a *crunch*, and his top lip split open. Instantly black blood poured from the cuts, and he tasted it in his mouth.

Stunned, he was lifted like a toy and thrown into the square, bouncing off the rough-hewn stones before he scraped to a stop. One of his attackers grabbed him by the collar and dragged him up, then forced him to kneel.

Both of his foes stood behind him, each placing a hand upon one of his shoulders, applying an insurmountable pressure. Again they were unnaturally silent.

"What do you want from me?" he muttered through his swelling jaw. One of the vampires grabbed his hair and yanked backward, forcing him to look up.

He blinked away the blurred shapes and focused. He was near the center of the square now, and the people—a hundred or so—clustered all around, their faces downcast, their skin anemic and gray. Here and there he saw smears of blood on the ground, and in the shadows lay the unmoving forms of the few who had resisted.

Among them were women and children.

More Vyrewatch arrived, until a half-dozen or more had gathered. One human, a bearded man with a grim face, caught Gar'rth's eye.

"Why don't you try to fight?" Gar'rth said, and the act of speaking sent needles of pain through his face. "You could—*arrhh...*"

The vampire on his right squeezed his shoulder until his bones crunched. He grimaced in pain, gritting his teeth. When he looked for the bearded man again, he was gone.

They have nothing, he realized. *Yet still Drakan's minions take.*

The humans were formed into a line. At the front, where a single Vyrewatch held a woman, there was a strange, tubed device that fed into one of many barrels. He tensed as the vampire bent its head to the woman's throat. She moaned weakly, at first making no attempt to resist. When she did finally struggle, the creature only gripped her more tightly, its claws piercing the flesh of her arms.

Then the iron taste of blood entered the thick air and teased his lips.

Suddenly the vampire drew back, and Gar'rth saw the crimson slick on her neck. His eyes narrowed and he felt his heart quicken with excitement.

No, he protested silently. *I will not give in. I will not.*

He closed his eyes and breathed out.

"I will not," he whispered.

Suddenly his head was pulled back roughly. Then a clenched fist slammed into his cheek, forcing his eyes open in surprise. The Vyrewatch who held his right shoulder pointed toward the tithe.

Gar'rth nodded grimly.

His vision sharpened as the pain in his face dulled to a throb. The vampire still held the woman, but now the tube had been fastened to the wound at her neck. As the minutes passed, the woman visibly slackened, held by the undead monstrosity behind her. Finally, after her blood was drained, she sank to her knees with a faint sigh where she flopped like a boneless creature upon the ground.

But the tithe-master had forgotten her already. He gestured to the next in line, a young man with a shaven head who stepped anxiously forward. As before, the vampire leaned forward to puncture his vein before tapping it with another tube that led into the infernal device. This time his victim remained utterly silent.

And I can do nothing but watch, Gar'rth thought.

On and on it went. The next one who resisted was taken aside. A trio of the creatures nipped and clawed at him, each bite taking a piece of flesh and eliciting cries of pain. Finally they overwhelmed him, blocking Gar'rth's view. His screams ended as quickly as they had begun.

After that example, mothers led their daughters forward, fathers their own sons. A second queue was formed, then a third.

All submitted willingly.

As the queues grew shorter, the pile of bodies grew larger. None were left with the strength to stand. Instead they lay upon the cold ground, unmoving, their bodies as white as maggots. Some, Gar'rth was sure, were dead, taxed too much by their undead masters.

Yet for all the bloodletting, the Vyrewatch had not been wasteful. Every drop was harvested with an efficiency that was uncanny.

Did you enjoy the show, Soft-Heart?

Gar'rth jumped. The words had been so real in his mind.

"Tenebra?" he said aloud. "Is that you, Father?"

He tried to stand, but his captors' grip was unyielding.

No, Soft-Heart. I am more. Infinitely more. And hungry. Always hungry.

"Who are you?" Gar'rth cried through the pain. "Where—"

A commotion rippled through the Vyrewatch in the square. The two who held him suddenly backed away and seized their spears, hissing tensely. Others moved to surround the barrels that contained their precious blood, as if to fend off some attack.

He felt a presence then. It clutched at his throat and tightened his chest. His very body seemed to be wishing itself into silence, as though afraid of being heard and discovered.

Then a sound reached him. Yet not a sound.

Laughter. He heard it in his mind. *Far away and cold. Mocking the living and the dead alike. It must be her,* he thought. *Vanescula herself. Mistress of Darkmeyer.*

Gar'rth gasped at the air and struggled to his feet. He wondered if he had the strength to run, and knew instinctively that it would do him no good. Before him, the tithe-master hissed loudly in complaint. From a canister at its belt the creature unraveled a document and held it up toward the black sky.

Again, he heard the laughter.

"Please..." a voice croaked from among the taxed humans. Gar'rth watched as a middle-aged man heaved himself to his knees and prostrated himself before the heavens. "Please, dark mistress. I beg you. We have no more... no more to give."

The tithe-master turned suddenly and ran only a few steps before leaping into the air, its wings beating furiously to give it lift. All around the square every one of the Vyrewatch did the same, each with the same sense of urgency and fear. After only a few seconds he was left alone with the taxed.

Vanescula. He felt certain he was right, and he knew he had only one chance. *I have traveled beyond the holy river. I am Tenebra's son and heir. There is indeed much to interest her.* Gar'rth stood his ground and steadied his nerves.

You are as arrogant as your father, Soft-Heart. The words were conveyed with a drumming into the very depths of his brain. He winced involuntarily. *Leave me now,* they continued, *for this night I feast. The appetizer you left for me under the wall was well chosen, but fear not, for something of her remains for you.*

"No!" Gar'rth muttered. His words seemed hollow. "Please, no..."

We shall meet again. Soon.

The man who had begged suddenly screamed. Gar'rth watched as he jerked to his feet and flailed uncontrollably in the manner of a man having a fit. A crimson sweat moistened his pale face.

"Pleeeease, mistress…" His voice became a high screech. The crimson sweat became a film of blood, and only then did Gar'rth notice how the other taxed humans were likewise afflicted. All of them. They groaned and wailed as their blood was torn from their pores, at first hanging in the air, then swirling upward in a red mist.

Upward toward the source of the presence.

Gar'rth summoned the courage to peer through the red haze that surrounded the roof of the square's tallest building. And there, in the midst of all, she stood.

Vanescula Drakan, flame-haired and pale.

He had heard rumors of her, of course. Growing up in Canifis, where the werewolves feared their vampire overlords, Vanescula was foremost among their nightmares. Some legends said that just to see her was death, while others claimed that she had consumed the very life of the swamp itself, turning it into a dead and darkened place.

Gar'rth watched as she summoned the blood of her chattels, leaving them as dried husks, their blackened corpses twisted at grotesque angles, violated even in death. The crimson storm closed around her, becoming darkly vivid before disappearing altogether.

Go home, Soft-Heart. Despite the carnage, the voice remained calm. Nevertheless, it caused him to wince. *I am sated for now. Go home. Go home.*

Then there was silence.

Gar'rth looked for Vanescula, but she was gone.

Drunkenly, he staggered backward. The surreal nightmare he had been forced to witness left a great emptiness inside of him. Part of him wanted to jump in among the dead, to join them and rid himself of the terrible guilt that he had survived the slaughter

I am sick of this world and its evil, he despaired inwardly. *More so because I know I cannot stop it.*

Suddenly he lurched against the same wall into which he had been thrust. There, beneath a smear of his own blood, he vomited. After a few moments the heaving subsided, and he stood, his entire body shaking.

Gathering himself, he turned away from the dead and walked, one faulty step after another, back the way he had come. He paused first to pick up the wolfsbane dagger and return it to its splitbark sheath, and then again to retrieve his gloves.

Of Kara's golden hair, there was no sign.

His mind was numb as he made his way north, and from numbness it fell into despair.

Then he remembered.

He ran, full of purpose, hope wrestling with fear inside him.

Gar'rth found the alley where he had hidden the girl, and when he saw what Vanescula had left, he sank to his knees.

The walls of the alley were covered with blood—an impossible amount, it seemed. Her body was ripped and torn, like a doll discarded by a mad dog.

Suddenly anger erupted inside of him. He punched at the wall, the aged stone crumbling under his clenched fist. Only after his knuckles were cut and black blood dripped from gashes in his torn skin did he stop.

Wearily, and in pain, Gar'rth stood and made his way back toward the castle.

3

We must hasten! The city is near."

The officer leading the ragged column raised his arm and gestured forward, perhaps hoping his action could inspire new strength in those he had been sent to protect.

Behind him, the wizard in the blue robes made a bitter face before turning his head to address the blonde-haired girl who rode behind him.

"Kara, can't we have a break for a moment?" the wizard asked. "The horses are near to collapse."

Kara-Meir shook her head. She tried to speak, but found her lips were dry, her throat parched. When she did manage to form the words, her tongue felt swollen and tired.

"No, Castimir," she said. "Captain Hardinge is right. We cannot be more than an hour from Varrock now. We must report to the king…" She stopped, and narrowed her dark eyes, focusing on the exhausted wizard. "We must tell him what we know.

"Do you understand?" she finished.

Castimir nodded. He massaged his bandaged left hand and then patted the nearest saddlebag. The mysterious book she knew to be inside gave a deep *thud* as his right hand beat against it.

"After this journey, I won't have the strength left to speak," he replied. "We haven't stopped once since we left the River Salve."

That wasn't strictly true. What remained of King Roald's embassy to Morytania—under the guard of a dozen soldiers of Misthalin—had stopped more than once to change steeds. Still, Kara's body ached painfully, and she was growing more fearful by the mile of the time when she would be forced to dismount and stand before the king.

She glanced over her shoulder. Each of them bore signs of the horrors they had shared.

Immediately behind her rode Gideon Gleeman, the jester to the court of King Roald Remanis the Third. The tall man was slumped forward in his saddle, his breathing laborious. The wounds given him by the undead Vyrewatch had formed into distinct scabs on his long gray face. His thin black hair whipped in the wind.

He looks broken, she thought. *Something inside of him has reached its limit.*

"Gideon, are you all right?" she asked.

The jester's hollow eyes focused on her. He gave a near-imperceptible nod and closed his eyes for a long moment.

Guthix knows why the king sent him with us. He shouldn't have come at all.

Next came Sir Theodore Kassel, valiantly trying to ride with his head held up. Uncompromising to the point of stubbornness, he refused to admit his fatigue, which he would consider a dereliction of his sacred duty. When he saw Kara's stare, he gave a resigned smile.

Quickly, she guided her horse aside to let Gideon pass by, and only when she was level with Theodore did she speak, her voice quiet.

"When we go before the king, Theodore, I think I should do the speaking."

His handsome face darkened.

"I see, Kara," he replied. "You still intend to keep Gar'rth's identity secret from the king." He sighed. "I agreed at the riverbank because I was as surprised as anyone by what he had written, but now I have had time to think.

"I believe the king should know," he continued. Theodore pushed his hand back through his fair hair, and then looked her in the eye. "We cannot count on Gar'rth, Kara. He told you so in his letter. And then he—"

The young knight stopped short, and looked away.

"And then he betrayed us," Kara finished for him. "Is that what you think?"

Theodore nodded.

"He gave us his word that we wouldn't be prevented from leaving Morytania." The knight looked back, and Kara followed his steely glare over the head of the dwarf Doric, toward Arisha and a wild-looking man who rode at the barbarian priestess's side. The man's horse neighed, and he looked in sudden danger of falling until Arisha took his reins and calmed the beast.

"How many people did Karnac lose coming out?" Theodore pressed. "Gar'rth gave us his word, Kara." He stared at her sadly, without any of the triumph she might once have expected. "At best it was worthless, and if not that, then it was treachery."

He rode on, yet Kara held back, unsure of what to say.

Because he is right, she thought. *He gave his word, and it was broken.*

Doric drew alongside her. The squat figure grunted as he watched Theodore ride away.

"Gar'rth might not have had a choice, you know." The dwarf turned his head and gazed at her impassively. He held his reins in both hands, his knuckles white, and Kara wondered if he had done so for their entire journey.

That doesn't make it any easier, though, she thought.

"Jerrod tried to force him to embrace Zamorak," Doric continued. "But now that Gar'rth has returned to Morytania, I don't see how he will be able to resist his father's efforts." His gaze sank toward the ground. "I am sorry, Kara. Truly I am, for there was much in him that I admired." Letting loose with one hand, he reached up and stroked his beard.

"Was?" Kara said, her voice louder than she had intended. She glanced around, then looked back at him. "He isn't dead, Doric."

"No, Kara," he admitted. "Gar'rth isn't dead. But we may want to think of him as such. If he yields to the chaos god's influence, then he won't be the friend we knew." He reached forward and grasped her wrist. "I'm sorry, Kara, truly I am."

She nodded.

"But you have forgotten one thing, Doric." She leaned close and spoke in a whisper. "Gar'rth is half-human. He can fight it. I *know* he can."

The dwarf sighed deeply.

"Would you be willing to bet your life on that, Kara?"

She turned away without replying.

But as she looked at the road ahead, winding down through the gentle hills and small woods that vanished beneath the gray stone walls of Varrock, she caught sight of a small crowd that barred the way. Quickly they ran forward, a motley bunch without discipline, armed with scythes and rusted axes.

Behind her, she heard a horse ride up.

"Who are they?" Karnac asked in a thick accent he shared with the others who had escaped from Morytania.

"Peasants," Lord Despaard answered. The military leader of the embassy made the word sound like a curse.

"Angry peasants," Arisha observed.

Kara counted at least thirty of them as Captain Hardinge arranged their escort into a thin line.

"Lancers at the center," he said. "On my command, ride straight down the road at a trot. The embassy will follow on your heels." He paused, one hand in the air, then thrust it forward. "Advance!"

"Why would people fight one another?" Karnac asked. Kara heard fear in his voice.

So much has changed for him, and too quickly, she realized. *Living in the land of vampires and werewolves, his foes have been inhuman. He has not seen how man can treat his fellow man.*

She goaded her own horse as Arisha led Karnac's steed forward at her side. Now they were close enough to hear the cries of the mob.

"Can't we talk to them, captain?" Theodore asked. "Surely there is no need to employ force?"

"Misthalin has changed since you crossed the river, Sir Theodore," Hardinge replied. "You shall see. And I have orders to ensure that you reach Varrock safely." He turned to address his contingent. "Now, *charge!*"

Eight strong soldiers rushed forward, the lancers concentrated at their center to force their way through the mob as Kara might have used her knife point to pry open a walnut. She rode close behind, a sick feeling inside of her that turned to relief when she saw the peasants part before them, leaping to either side of the column.

"Death to King Roald!" one of the rabble cried.

"The true king is coming," another shouted, "and he will bring death to us all."

Within moments they cleared the mass, but the calls continued.

"The prophecy must not be ignored." The voice was that of a woman. "We neglect it at our peril. King Roald is a false king!"

Captain Hardinge broke away with three of the escort and moved to guard the embassy's rear. Only when they were safely away from the angry mob did he call for the riders to slow.

"What is this about, Hardinge?" Lord Despaard asked angrily. "Never have I heard such treason from the likes of them! You should take your men back and cut them down."

"A sentiment I share with you, my lord, but my orders were to locate the embassy and bring you back as soon as possible." His expression was grim. "There are daily reports coming in of unrest throughout the countryside. People have been harassed and killed, and there have even been attacks made against the king's property. Granaries and stores have been burned, and agents of Zamorak are abroad, coordinating these atrocities.

"No, my lord," he continued. "It is not safe for travelers to be wandering Misthalin these days."

"Then what of those who follow us?" Arisha shouted suddenly. "What of the survivors who came out with us, or of Pia and Jack? They have no horses to ride through a mob!"

The priestess's words ushered in an uncomfortable silence. Captain Hardinge wore an ill look and rode again to the front of the column.

"She asked you a question," Castimir said indignantly as he passed. Kara saw his right hand twist and noticed a small ball of paper drop from his sleeve into his palm. "I would advise you to answer."

Captain Hardinge shot the wizard a look of contempt.

"Or what, wizard?" he countered. "You will melt my sword, as you did Captain Rovin's when you protected an enemy of the realm?

"Yes, I know you well," he continued, "and your threats will not deter me." He gave a grim smile. "Nor will I deviate from my duty. The people are rebellious, and even the death of the monster has done nothing to calm their nerves. I will not add to the chaos by betraying my king. Besides, your friends have a small guard with them. With luck they should reach Varrock without incident."

Kara gritted her teeth. They had been forced to leave Pia and Jack in the company of only six mounted guardsmen, and accompanied by an exhausted group of survivors. She pictured them as she had last seen them, sitting together on a farmer's wagon with Albertus Black's wrapped corpse between them.

Pia is stubborn, in her way, she thought. *I should have insisted she come back with us—both her and Jack—but she was determined to honor Albertus by staying with him on his final journey.*

Her thoughts melted away as she heard Doric speak.

"You said the *Wyrd* was dead," he said. "How did she die? Who killed her?"

Captain Hardinge shared a surprised look with his men, laced with ill-concealed mirth.

"You don't know?" he replied. "Well, Varrock is near. All your questions will be answered there." The officer snapped his reins and the column advanced again.

"Just remember, all of you, that Varrock is not as you left it."

As the embassy drew near the great gray stone walls in which the eastern gate stood open, Theodore saw at once how many more of the city guard were present. Above him, archers eyed them with a distrust bordering on hostility.

"We left Varrock to cheering crowds," Castimir murmured, "and not more than two weeks ago." The wizard gave the knight a mirthless grin. "We were heroes then, weren't we?"

"It's not about you anymore," Captain Hardinge remarked. "When the *Wyrd* was killed people rejoiced for a short time, and then the attacks started." They entered a square and he gazed grimly across at the faces of the crowds. There were more people in Varrock now—more even than in the run-up to the Midsummer Festival when the city had swelled with visitors. Witnessing their arrival, some cheered while others glared angrily. Isolated fights broke out here and there—far more than could be controlled by the king's men.

We have been through so much, in such a short space of time, he thought. *The Midsummer Festival, where I bested the greatest knight in Misthalin, Gar'rth's encounter with the Wyrd, and then our embassy to Morytania. Lady Anne...*

He felt his heart quicken at the thought of her.

"Those who follow Zamorak have stirred things up no end," Captain Hardinge continued. "They terrorize the 'peasants,' as you called them, who already live in fear of the prophecy."

"Prophecy?" Karnac responded. "What kind of prophecy?"

"It was made by the High Priest of Entrana a century ago," Kara explained doubtfully. "It tells of a true king crossing the river, and the lands becoming one under his rule. A land of the living and the dead."

Karnac paled at her words.

He has just escaped that very sort of existence, Theodore mused. *And now it threatens to pursue him, taking from him the very freedom paid for by the deaths of so many.*

"The king will want to speak to you about it, Master Karnac," Captain Hardinge noted. "You who have lived all your life in Morytania, in the shadow of the vampire lords, well, you are a rare asset to us here. Your experience and knowledge cannot be wasted." Karnac just stared at him wordlessly.

They were in front of the palace now, facing the entrance to the north of the square. The great, squat stone building was crowned by a peculiarly short tower in its center, King Botolph's Tower. It had been erected more than a century ago as a means for the paranoid ruler to live free from assassins, for it was accessible by only a single passage and tight spiral stairs.

Theodore gave a last look round behind him, and when his gaze landed on four statues at the square's center, standing amid a great fountain, he halted. Beneath one, a woman knelt in prayer.

He gasped suddenly, a recollection hitting him.

He heard the voice of his friend, Father Lawrence, who had guided him in his first few months in Varrock, and who had once told him about those very same statues.

"That one was Tenebra, who was the king's heir at the time he went to war. He was just twenty, slightly older than you when he led his father's nation against Lord Drakan. From what I recall, there wasn't enough of his remains to be recovered."

"Theodore! Theodore, are you all right?" Kara's voice cut through his surprise. He turned his head, ignoring the familiar shooting pain that tormented his back. The rest of his party were near the entrance to the palace now, while he had remained behind.

Gideon Gleeman rode back to sit alongside him. His face was tight with the pain of his wounds, and he wore a cold stare.

"That is Tenebra," Gleeman said, nodding to the statue. Theodore heard undisguised hostility in his words. "One of our greatest heroes, the heir-apparent to Misthalin a millennium ago. We sing ballads about him now, of him and the beautiful Ailane, and of the tragedy of their love, cut so short by war."

The kneeling woman stood and bowed to the statue before taking a few steps backward.

A hero. Theodore looked to his friends, first to Kara, grim-faced and silent, then to Castimir and Arisha, and finally Doric, who was nodding his head slowly.

A true king.

How will Varrock react when they learn the truth? He knew the answer instinctively. *It will tear the nation apart.*

"We have no time for this," Despaard warned. "Come on!" His words broke the spell, and quickly they rode in through the walls to the palace grounds. Messengers appeared in front of them now, and somewhere a horn sounded.

Inside the great baileys on either side of the palace building, there stood large tents where regiments of soldiers were being drilled. Archers practiced relentlessly, young soldiers were instructed in martial skills, and the sound of the blacksmith's hammer chimed a fateful tempo.

War is here, Theodore knew. *King Roald is leaving nothing to chance.*

He caught Castimir's worried gaze as they neared the inner wall of the palace, and shivered.

But then, neither is Tenebra.

They passed through the inner wall and onto a paved courtyard where servants took their reins and an excited messenger bade them make haste. The knight grimaced against his body's protestation as he slid from his saddle. He walked awkwardly to the top of the eight stone steps that ran the width of the portico, to where a distinguished-looking group of men waited in the shadows.

I am exhausted, he thought, trying his best to appear otherwise. But any thought of fatigue was driven from his mind as the crowd parted and an old, white-haired man stepped forward, leaning precariously on a walking stick. His eyes widened behind the spectacles he wore.

"Theodore!" he cried. "Oh, Theodore, thank the gods you have returned." His gaze worked its way across the knight's companions. "And Kara and Castimir and Doric and Arisha and… and Gar'rth—where is he?" The old man looked suddenly lost.

"And Albertus," he continued. "Where is *he*?" His voice softened and he looked uncertain on his feet. Theodore took his arm. "Where are they, Theodore? Where are they?"

"I'm sorry, Ebenezer," the knight replied. "Gar'rth lives still, and is unharmed. He remained behind to guarantee our liberty." His words twisted in his throat. "But Albertus…"

Kara moved to stand at his side. She took Ebenezer's left arm in her own and gazed at him in sympathy.

"I'm sorry, Ebenezer," she said. "Albertus is dead. He died a hero's death. Truly. His body is being brought to Varrock by Pia and Jack—for we managed to save them, at least."

Lord Despaard was beside them in an instant.

"Come," he said briskly, earning him a frown from Kara—which he ignored. "We have no time for grief. The king has gathered his advisors and needs to hear our account. All of you, come on!"

Theodore motioned for a page to take Ebenezer's arm, to make certain he did not fall. He gave the alchemist's hand a gentle squeeze, then amid a small crowd he followed his friends through to the king's throne room.

4

Theodore had been here many times before, yet now the atmosphere was changed. It was colder, tenser. A cacophony of voices filled the space, and no respect was being shown for ceremony.

The voices ceased as Kara-Meir forced her way through the throng that stood before the throne. King Roald Remanis gave her a cool nod. They exchanged greetings, and then an old man standing beside the king spoke irritably.

"Tell us what you have learned," he snapped. Then he pulled a black bearskin fur cloak around his thin shoulders tightly, as if preparing to brace himself for the news.

That cloak will do him no good, Theodore mused darkly.

"I will speak for us all, Papelford," Lord Despaard said. "I was the leader of the embassy to Morytania, and I am trusted by all in this chamber for my long years of service to the crown."

Theodore listened to the account with interest, gazing around the chamber at several familiar faces. Sharp-featured Lord Ruthven, who had accompanied the embassy to the holy temple of Paterdomus, stood with his hands clasped together, his eyes never leaving the speaker. Nearby stood a brown-robed monk of Saradomin with a round face, Father Lawrence, who gave the knight a discreet smile. Two of the men, however, stood with a permanent frown shadowing their faces.

The first was Aeonisig Raispher, King Roald's religious advisor and a fanatical priest. The other was Captain Rovin, whose sword hand still remained bandaged after Castimir has used his magic to protect Gar'rth. *That all seems like so long ago,* Theodore thought. *We have all been through so much since.*

But the one face he looked for most of all was not present. There was no sign of Lady Anne.

"Our horses were spooked by an apparition, and most fled only a few hours after setting out from Paterdomus," Lord Despaard said. "Our werewolf guide believed they might have reached the temple but I am doubtful—"

"They did return." Captain Rovin interrupted Despaard, and gave an uncharacteristic smile. "Sir Theodore's mare and Castimir's yak among them." Theodore heard Castimir gasp at his side, and recalled how upset his friend had been when the yak had fled, carrying with it his precious books.

Rovin narrowed his eyes and looked at the wizard, suddenly grim, his bandaged hand clenching.

"They are still at Paterdomus, for Drezel could not spare the men to send them back just yet. But they are well."

"That is one mystery explained, then," King Roald said. "We believed the embassy had perished for a time. Continue, Lord Despaard."

"It was in Canifis where the embassy became forfeit, and our lives endangered. The youths Pia and Jack were there, taken by a werewolf and imprisoned. The night they were to be sacrificed, Canifis was attacked."

A murmur of surprise broke out.

"Attacked? By whom?" Raispher asked impatiently. "Who would be stupid enough to attack a town of werewolves?"

Karnac stepped forward angrily, his fatigue momentarily forgotten. He pushed Lord Despaard aside to stand squarely in front of the king.

"It was my people," he murmured. "And we are not stupid, nor are we mad. Not a one of us. We were *desperate*. We grew up in the ghettoes of Meiyerditch, harvested for our blood in the tithes. And we would try anything, *anything*, to be free of that place and its inhumanity."

Karnac took a step closer to the priest, until their faces were only a hand's width apart. Raispher blanched and tried desperately to look away, but Karnac would not let him.

"You ask who we are? I will tell you." Karnac's head jutted forward, and Raispher gave a small shriek as he stepped back, in danger of tripping in his heavily laden robes of office.

"We are the Myreque."

A stony silence filled the throne room. King Roald gazed at Karnac intently for a long moment.

Finally, he nodded.

"Then there is much you can reveal about the land beyond the river. To us, Morytania is a realm known more by legend than fact. Isn't that so, Papelford?"

The old man in the bearskin cloak nodded.

"It is, sire, despite my attempts over the years at discerning fact from fiction. Long have I feared that the task might fall to my apprentice to complete what I have started, for there are still many years' labor ahead. This man's knowledge is a great gift.

"But please, Lord Despaard," he added, "tell us what happened next in Canifis."

"The Myreque started a great many fires, and in the confusion the embassy was split," Despaard explained. "Some of us went south with the attackers, while Kara, Castimir, Theodore and Gar'rth were captured. Gideon and Albertus, too, were taken." The nobleman turned to face his companions.

"Perhaps it is best if I let you carry the story on, Kara-Meir." She nodded, gathered her breath, then spoke to the king.

"Very well," she began, "but first I must ask a question of my own, sire. Pia and Jack are under my charge. They stole a horse from your stables and fled foolishly to Morytania, and were lucky to escape." Her eyes fell. "Such an offense warrants a death sentence, I know, but in these times, such an escape from Morytania will prove that our enemy is fallible. It will hearten the people.

"I ask you to grant them pardon," she said.

King Roald looked to Despaard, who gave a thoughtful nod.

"Very well, Kara-Meir," said the king. "You will have to make payment for the horse, however." The king's hands tightened on the arms of his throne. "Now tell me more of the embassy. What happened after you were taken?"

"Thank you, sire, but there really isn't much to tell," Kara answered. "For we were kept in a magical sleep until we were woken…"

Theodore sensed her uncertainty.

How much can she tell them? Dare we reveal the truth?

He found himself stepping forward.

"Sire, I think we have something to add to this account," he said, never once looking in Kara's direction. "But I think it would be best if the court was cleared, so that we may speak with you in private."

Several voices cried out in disagreement, until Gideon Gleeman, the king's jester, raised his arms and begged for silence.

"I agree, majesty," the jester said. "Sir Theodore's words show wisdom." Gideon stared at the king, who quickly nodded.

"Very well," he said. "Captain Rovin, please clear the room." Despite the protests, he moved to do so, until he came to Ebenezer, pale and quiet, sitting on a bench.

"What of the alchemist, sire?" The captain seemed unwilling to lay a hand on the white-haired old man.

"He will stay," the king instructed, "for he has news of his own to impart, on which the embassy might be able to shed light."

When Theodore spoke again, he did so to a vastly reduced audience. Only the king, Ebenezer, Papelford, Lord Ruthven and Captain Rovin remained of their audience.

"Our enemy is not Lord Drakan, sire," he said. "Not at this hour, at least."

He saw Kara glare a warning at him.

"Then who?" Lord Ruthven commanded.

"Tenebra," Theodore replied in a voice so low it was almost a whisper. Then, stronger: "It is Tenebra, my lords."

King Roald's eyes narrowed, and he frowned.

"What do you mean? Who is this Tenebra?"

Doric gave a strangled gasp and stamped his metal-heeled boot onto the stone.

"He's talking about *the* Tenebra!" the dwarf said, doing his best to avoid shouting. "Your ancestor. The one who everyone thought died a thousand years ago. He's alive, in a way… he's a vampire now, see? And he wants his throne back."

"Tenebra?" King Roald stood slowly, his face pale. "This cannot be. He is one of our greatest heroes—the man who would have inherited the throne had he survived the Battle of the Salve." The monarch covered his mouth with one hand, and he was shaking.

"Tenebra," he muttered again. "*This* is our enemy?"

Doric gave Theodore a quick look, then glanced to Kara and nodded reassuringly.

"Aye. *That* Tenebra," he sighed.

"But he's a hero," the king repeated. "He's a legend…"

"And he is coming," Castimir added. "On our flight from Meiyerditch we observed three immense contraptions. We think they are bridges that he can use to span the Salve."

"My lord, there is the prophecy," Lord Ruthven interjected. "The Wyrd alluded to it in her murders, and if it truly is Tenebra, then it all makes sense. For who is a truer king than he?"

"But he still has to cross the Salve," Arisha said. "The power of Saradomin remains strong enough to bar the undead."

King Roald turned to the alchemist.

"Perhaps it is time you shared the results of your research," he said. Ebenezer looked confused for a moment, as if his thoughts had been far away. But his gaze focused, and he cleared his throat.

"After you left Varrock I took it upon myself to examine the Wyrd's kidnappings and killings," Ebenezer explained. "Six children, all under one year of age, have been taken. All of them show a birthmark above their hearts, each different yet each shaped like one of the seven marks found upon the altar of Saradomin in Paterdomus.

"Then there is the seventh child," he said, "a girl called Felicity, now under guard in the palace, kept in King Botolph's Tower."

Ebenezer looked sourly at Captain Rovin.

"Felicity, might I add, is the one who was saved by Gar'rth. If it hadn't been for him, all seven of the children would be missing." He turned to address the entire group. "What would happen then, I am not sure, but Reldo is busily helping me study as best he can."

Papelford snorted in derision.

Ebenezer frowned.

"You should not doubt your apprentice so, Master Papelford," he said. "He is able, and he—"

"Yes, yes, yes," Papelford crowed bitterly. "Continue, alchemist, and get to the point." Ebenezer frowned again, and before he could comply, Theodore spoke.

"Gar'rth believed the Wyrd was sent by Tenebra," he lied

carefully, for Gar'rth had been told so by his father. "He thinks it was her task to somehow pollute the Salve enough for Tenebra to attempt a crossing. And he was sure that the kidnapped children were never taken to Morytania—that they are still here, in Misthalin somewhere."

"So the links fall into place," King Roald mused. "We must be ready then, for when he comes. Our first priority must be to ensure that Felicity is kept safe, for if her kidnapping had been the Wyrd's task then surely Tenebra will send another creature to finish it." He paused a moment, then peered directly at the knight. "Is there anything more to add to your account?"

A silence settled. Theodore looked to his friends, and then back to the king.

The truth of Gar'rth's heritage can be of no benefit here. He shook his head slowly.

"I do not think so, sire," he said.

Gideon Gleeman coughed. He caught Theodore's eye and peered intently.

"Are you… are you quite sure of that, Sir Theodore?" he asked, and he turned. "Or you, Kara-Meir?"

A cold chill froze Theodore's stomach. He recalled the jester's hostile stare in the square, and suddenly he understood.

He knows!

How could he possibly know?

"There is nothing else I wish to add, Gideon," Kara said amicably before he could speak. She looked to the king. "Save, I suppose, to return the sword Kingsguard to you, sire, now that I have retrieved my own blade. Here it is." She unsheathed the sword slowly and placed it delicately before the throne.

Gideon bit his lip.

"No, Kara-Meir. I was not referring to the sword that King Roald lent you for the embassy." He stared hard at Kara, who frowned back.

She will not back down, Gleeman, Theodore predicted. *You have misjudged her.*

"There is something I wish you to confirm," he pressed. "About Gar'rth."

Kara stepped back, and was immediately flanked by Doric and Castimir, with Arisha standing nearby.

"Nothing?" Gideon sighed. "Well then, I suppose it falls to me.

"Majesty," he said, turning toward the throne. "There is another truth here that these people keep from you. Even Lord Despaard doesn't know of it. They have done so not for treason's sake, but out of loyalty to a comrade who has saved their lives—and mine.

"It is about Gar'rth."

Kara stiffened, and her eyes widened.

It seems we underestimated the jester, as well, Theodore realized.

"Gar'rth is Tenebra's son," Gleeman finished quietly. "He is half-werewolf and half-human, descended from the same stock as you, my king. And that is why he was so important. That is why Jerrod was sent from Morytania to take him home."

"How do you know this, Gideon?" Kara demanded. "How *could* you know?"

The jester shook his head.

"I am sorry, Kara, and to all of you, truly I am. But I serve a master higher than mere fellowship, even one forged by the dangers we have shared." He walked to the king's side and turned to face them. "It was an easy matter for me to take Gar'rth's letter from your saddlebag and read it. That is how I know."

Kara staggered momentarily under the weight of his betrayal. Theodore took a deep breath, and spoke.

"It's true," he said simply. "Yet it makes no difference, does it, sire?" He put his hand on Kara's shoulder and looked back at the king. "You said yourself that if ever he returned he would not be welcomed. That he would be tolerated, forced to live away from others and never be allowed to take a wife. Those were your words, so how now does this truth change anything?"

"Those were my words, Sir Theodore Kassel," King Roald said quietly, his eyes burning. He stood in anger. "But in this hour I require absolute loyalty. The kingdom is seething. Agents of Zamorak sabotage my property and assail my people. And if, if it were ever known that Tenebra himself has returned from history, to lead an assault against me…"

The king turned his back upon them and stared at the south-facing stained-glass window. For the first time Theodore noted what it depicted—Tenebra, fighting and falling against the hordes of monsters that Lord Drakan had unleashed in another time.

"I need to know I can trust you," King Roald said, turning to face them. Behind him, the sun shone brighter, the contrast hiding the monarch's face in shadow. "Very soon you will be more famous than ever. Heroes who first saved Falador, then ventured into Morytania and returned to tell of it. I would have you use that fame, to help pacify my worried people."

His gaze intensified.

"But *can* I use you? Can I trust you?" His voice rose in anger. "Why shouldn't I lock you up for lying to me?"

Kara stepped forward. She looked quickly to Theodore, her gaze sympathetic, before addressing the king.

"You can trust us, sire," she said, her voice steady. "Gar'rth will come with Tenebra. He may very well have embraced Zamorak, for that is a possibility that cannot be ignored." Her face fell, then she looked up again. "But I know Gar'rth, sire, as does no other—not even Ebenezer." Her voice rose and threatened to crack. She took a deep breath as she looked the king in the eye.

"I know him so well because he confided to me many of his most intimate thoughts, fears and aspirations, when we became lovers in The Wilderness."

• • •

Castimir heard Theodore exhale sharply.

To his right, Doric mumbled something in his native tongue, the words meaningless to the wizard but clearly filled with surprise.

Before anyone could speak, the door at the far end of the throne room opened. They turned to see a man with a thin gray beard enter, a green-tinted monocle perched in his right eye. The familiar face made Castimir uneasy.

Fully a dozen soldiers followed in his wake. The old wizard stopped just a few steps away from him.

"Castimir," he said frostily. "I am glad to see you returned to us safely."

"Master Aubury." Castimir gave a modest bow to his superior from the Wizards' Tower. "I have much to report."

"There will be time enough for that." Aubury stepped past him curtly and approached the throne. Without a word he handed King Roald a scroll, tied with a blue seal.

The diplomatic symbol of the Tower, Castimir recognized. *Words from the greatest wizards in the world. Is this about Morytania? Have they found something?*

The king broke the seal and read quickly, his eyes sometimes breaking from their journey and looking to the faces of the embassy. To him in particular, Castimir thought.

From the king's side, Captain Rovin stepped over to him. He looked at Castimir's bandaged hand and smiled grimly.

"I hope your hand hurts as much as mine, boy."

The young wizard ignored the comment, instead moving closer to Arisha.

"What's going on?" she asked him quietly.

"I don't know," he replied. "But that is a missive from the Tower." She leaned closer and whispered in his ear.

"Could it be about the books you took?" she asked. "They might have found them on the yak."

"I doubt it," Castimir said, forcing a smile. It was a false confidence though. "Those aren't important enough for a monarch to deal with." He fell silent when the king spoke.

"Is there no other way?" Roald asked. "I am loath to allow this at such an hour, when there is unrest enough. It will not be perceived favorably."

Aubury tilted his head.

"I understand that, sire, but things are more complicated than they seem. I am afraid this must be done, and done immediately."

The wizard gave a nod to Captain Rovin, who smiled slyly.

"Very well," King Roald sighed. "Kara, Sir Theodore, you will both be needed in the days to come."

He waved them forward, and as they stepped closer Castimir saw how Aubury's men had spaced themselves out, a loose cordon behind them. At the throne's side, Papelford and Lord Ruthven moved away several steps. On the other side of the throne, to the right, a guard ushered Gideon and Lord Despaard back, along with Ebenezer and Karnac.

That left only Castimir's closest friends. Theodore and Kara with their backs to him, Doric and Arisha off to his right.

He felt a sudden chill.

We're isolated, he realized. *And surrounded.*

Captain Rovin appeared at his side, eyes blazing angrily into his.

"I owe you this," he whispered.

"I'm sorry—?"

Rovin backhanded the wizard across the face with his clenched fist. Castimir cried and staggered, the shock more potent than the physical pain. He heard swords being drawn and then the king's voice, booming an order.

"Hold, Sir Theodore," he cried. "And you, Kara-Meir. This

business is not your concern. It is the business of the Tower."

To his right, Castimir heard Arisha scream.

Rovin followed in with a brutal kick, doubling Castimir over, then grabbed his left wrist and twisted, causing him to scream. Kara was shouting, the words lost over the thundering in his head.

This is the throne room of King Roald, he thought wildly. *This can't be allowed to happen!*

"Burn me, would you?" Rovin spat into his face as the man's knee pounded into Castimir's stomach. "Burn me to help an *animal* escape justice!" The knee smashed in again.

Castimir gasped.

"Arisha—" he grated.

He twisted his right wrist sharply and waited for the pebble-like runes—contained in their paper wrapping—to land in his palm.

But it was not to be. He felt a tickle as the paper brushed his thumb and fell free. Then another hand seized his right arm and pushed it behind his back as a second man forced him to the stone floor, sitting squarely on top of him.

"Help me," he cried.

"Look about you, Castimir," Aubury said coldly. "They cannot help you." The senior wizard knelt before him. "They dare not help a *criminal.* For that is what you are. When word came of your yak's return, I journeyed to Paterdomus, for the monks there were not eager to rifle the property of a wizard. I found what you had hidden from us. You have stolen from the Tower and tried to keep knowledge for yourself.

"You know our history and the seriousness of that deceit. In our circles, such actions are unpardonable. You will be tried by a court of your betters, and if found guilty, you will burn."

Castimir was heaved to his feet, held by the two guards. Aubury's men surrounded his friends, their weapons ready.

"Theo?" he said. "Help me!"

The knight stepped forward, his sword half-drawn. But even as he did so Aubury's guards moved to bar him, and Captain Rovin gave a gruff laugh.

"Do not intervene, Sir Theodore," Aubury scolded. "Castimir will need witnesses for his trial, and your honest reputation will be tested there. Your friend cannot afford any mistake you might make here today, else he will have few to speak in his defense."

Theodore hesitated.

Through blurred eyes Castimir looked to Kara.

"Kara, please!"

She turned to King Roald, who sat, unmoved.

"You cannot possibly permit this," she protested. "He is a hero of your realm—a hero you will need in the coming days."

"It's outrageous," Ebenezer contributed, his face shocked pale.

Captain Rovin laughed again. Clearly he was enjoying himself.

"Hero, is he?" he said harshly. "Like you lot?" He raised his bandaged sword hand and looked back to Kara. "Anyone can be a hero, these days. Even the likes of Sulla."

Kara gasped.

"What's that supposed to mean?" she asked.

"You didn't know?" he replied. "Who do you think slew the Wyrd? It was Sulla, the man who killed your parents." Rovin's grin grew even wider, and was laced with irony. "He is here, now, in the palace. Another *hero*." He spat the last word as if it tasted sour.

Castimir felt his wrists being bound together behind his back. His sleeves were pulled up and secured above his elbows.

Aubury is taking no chances, he realized bitterly. *He knows all my tricks, knows how I hide my runes.*

His head was pulled back as a gag was looped around his chin. For the first time since Rovin's surprising attack he caught a glimpse of Arisha and Doric, away to his right. The dwarf lay still on the flagstones, three men holding him down. Doric gritted his teeth as their eyes met. Further to the right, Arisha was held between two men. Her head was bowed, her silver tiara had fallen from her brow, and her dark hair hid her face.

"Don't make us force you, boy," the man holding the gag whispered in his ear. "Captain Rovin wants the excuse to hurt you some more. Now, open your mouth and I promise not to bind it too tight."

As the gag was pulled up to Castimir's mouth, Arisha threw her head back and looked at him. Her face was bruised and bleeding. Her eyes burned in anger.

Castimir screamed.

He jerked his head back, his skull crunching against the man's nose with the satisfying *crack* of breaking cartilage. The gag slipped to the floor as he heard the man swear.

Red rage ruled his world now. With a madness he launched himself backward, the two guards giving ground but keeping their hands on his arms. Through the anger he saw Rovin advance, he heard Arisha scream as she struggled anew, and turned to see her bite at the face of the man nearest her. The man struck her chin with his elbow and her body went limp, sagging like a damp scarecrow.

"What have you done to her?" Castimir roared. "I'll kill you—"

Rovin was near now. The short man drew his hand back and delivered a punch to Castimir's jaw.

The wizard felt his teeth loosen. Suddenly he slumped, the madness over. When he blinked, the world was blurred through a gray mist, the shapes and colors multiplying, unfocused. Above, Rovin drew back to hit him again, and instinctively he cringed, shut his eyes, and turned his head aside.

Then there was the king's voice, shouting over all others, shouting something to Rovin, commanding him.

The blow never came.

When he opened his eyes again, the world returned to focus. Rovin had backed off, breathing deeply, a look of satisfaction on his face. To his right, Arisha lifted her head again, the fire in her eyes undimmed.

As the rushing of his blood faded in his head, Castimir heard Aubury speaking.

"…when his pet barbarian is finished with her exertions, then let her be, but make sure she doesn't bite you again."

Arisha leaned back and spat toward the wizard. Aubury sidestepped and her effort was wasted. The two men holding her arms pushed her to her knees.

"No doubt a dignified gesture among your primitive people," Aubury mused. "It's quite pathetic to remember that only a hundred years ago the world trembled under your genocidal crusades. You have fallen so very far so very quickly."

"Enough, Aubury!" King Roald commanded, his face set as stone, his eyes narrow. "I have given you what you asked for, as is due the Tower in affairs of the wizards, but I will not have you spark a diplomatic incident. Take your thief and leave us be.

"Now."

The young wizard was pulled upright by the ever-present guards.

"Castimir!" Arisha shrieked suddenly.

I won't forgive this, Aubury, he promised as the gag was forced into his mouth. *I will remember this.*

"Castimir!" he heard her shout again. She was straining wildly against the grip of the men who held her.

But then he was pulled backward and out of the throne room, the sound of Arisha's sobs scarring his memory.

I won't forgive. I won't forget. It's a promise.

5

"I still don't understand."

The woman frowned and looked sideways at Pia.

"Why would anyone steal from another person? You have so much here." She looked over the wagon's side to the wooded hills to the south. "It's so *green*, so fertile." Her hand fell to her swollen belly and she sighed.

"Does it hurt, Mary?" Pia asked. "Can you feel the baby move?"

Mary smiled.

"Every day," she admitted. "And it's a pain I delight in feeling. In Morytania, it's just as likely that my first-born would have been taken from me at birth, as a sacrifice. But we are free now, thanks to Karnac and your friends." She looked to the sleeping figure who sat opposite them in the wagon. "And to the gnome. Without Master Peregrim, none of us would have escaped."

She fell silent, and sadness clouded her features. The young girl knew why.

Pia looked back eastward along the road they were traveling, to the second of the three wagons. She hid her own grim look from Mary.

Eleven survivors out of two hundred. Such a tiny number.

Suddenly the gnome gave a deep snore, so loud it woke him with a start.

"Huh. Are we there yet?" the diminutive fellow asked.

"No, Master Peregrim. Not yet," Mary said, more happily now. "But as soon as Varrock comes into view, I will wake you with my shouting, for we have legends of the city, even in the ghettoes. Legends of just kings and brave knights and—"

And vengeful gang-masters and determined ambassadors, Pia thought, ignoring Mary's optimistic account of a city she knew didn't exist. Certainly, it was not a Varrock she recognized.

Instead, she looked at the white cloth that covered the body of Albertus Black.

I will try to be a better person, Albertus, she promised. *For your sake, and for Vanstrom's.*

"No, the world this side of the river is like nothing I had ever imagined," Mary continued, suddenly sobbing. Tears rolled down her cheeks. "There wasn't one tree in the ghettoes, not one patch of grass. Not a one! No life other than us. You can't imagine."

She leaned forward and wiped her eyes with the back of her hand. Her sobs woke the final passenger who shared the wagon, lying next to the gnome.

Jack's eyes opened, and he smiled wearily at Pia, his exhausted pale face unusually hopeful. Her brother had been looking more like that ever since they had met Kara-Meir, when she had taken them under her protection.

We will go back to her now, Pia thought. *I will trust her this time. She risked everything for us in Canifis. Her, and Vanstrom...*

Pia felt her stomach grow cold.

"Tell me, Mary, what did you know of Vanstrom Klause? I only knew him for a few days and yet..." Her voice grew faint and the older woman looked down at her with a sympathetic smile.

"I know your look, Pia." She smiled in understanding. "He was a good man. But I think you know that, don't you?"

Pia felt her face redden.

"He showed me great kindness after our capture," she replied. "He knew I was a thief, yet he accepted me without question. And he gave me hope. Somehow, when he was near, I wasn't afraid anymore." She wiped her own tears away.

The wagon rolled on in silence for a long minute. Pia let the afternoon sun warm her face, looking to the west, over the driver's broad shoulders. Her eyes scanned the near horizon, where at the crest of the rising road stood a single man by the side of his armored horse. It was a lone knight.

She wasn't worried, though, for there were three guards who rode up front and three more who followed.

Besides, she told herself, *the danger is across the river. Not here.*

"Tell me more of Vanstrom," she murmured, closing her eyes to enjoy the sun.

"He was a charmed man," Mary said. "He had escaped the purges and tithes in a neighboring ghetto, and taught us much about the vampire overlords. His skills and experience came to the attention of those who fought back."

Mary paused for a second and gathered her breath, and when she spoke she did so with growing pride.

"They called themselves the Myreque. People made fearless by the endless deprivations. People who had suffered so much that they were immune to torment."

Pia opened her eyes and waited for Mary to continue.

"Vanstrom ended up working with the Myreque. He accepted increasingly dangerous missions and became a legend in his own way.

"Later on, when we were at Hope Rock, I was told he had led an expedition deep under Meiyerditch, to recover a weapon we call the Sunspear. A weapon that can hurt them. A weapon they will *fear*."

"And did he find it?" Jack piped up eagerly. Pia smiled, for it was good to see her brother talking again.

Mary shook her head.

"You will have to ask Karnac when we arrive in Varrock. His brother went with Vanstrom, and if they did find it they kept it secret. Even Karnac may not know."

Jack shifted his weight and stretched his legs. From his belt pouch he withdrew a glass-like shard the length of Pia's finger and toyed with it absently. Mary watched him do so, her face thoughtful.

"The woman who gave you that, Jack, did she ever tell you anything about herself?"

"The spirit lady?" he replied. "No, but when she summoned the creature she used me somehow. She said she needed me to help her do it, and when she did it, I felt…" Jack made a sour face.

"I felt like I was burning. All over. Not in a hot way though, but cold, and it was as if I could *control* that coldness, as if I could have frozen the whole world." He looked warily at the shard in his hand. "It made me feel very powerful, and very afraid. I'm not sure I want to feel that way, ever again."

"Then put the shard away for now, Jack," Mary told him. "But you have an affinity for magic. That much is obvious. In Meiyerditch, you would have been considered blessed."

Jack dropped the shard into the pouch, where it tinkled as it came into contact with the others.

"Perhaps I could have worked with the Myreque."

"Perhaps," Mary said. "Someone of your gifts I think—" She was cut short as the wagon stopped. Pia looked over the pregnant woman's shoulder to the road ahead. The lone knight had mounted his horse and drawn near. In response the three guards at the front had advanced to meet him.

"What's happening?" Jack asked nervously.

"Hush," urged the driver. "I can't hear if you talk."

Pia stood up in the wagon and strained to listen. The men were too far away for her to make out the words, but the tone was not encouraging. One of the guards gestured angrily, and another lowered his lance point.

Instinctively she reached for the small knife on her belt.

"Don't worry," Peregrim whispered. Pia cast a quick look at the gnome. "I'm sure it's not—"

Someone screamed.

"…the Boar!" a guard cried in warning.

Pia's head shot round.

The leader of the escort fell from his saddle, headless. Behind him, the rider in blue-metaled armor held his bloodied sword aloft.

The lancer prepared to charge. Pia watched as the man urged his horse on with shouts, but the animal seemed frozen. With a sudden spurt of speed, the knight rode past the lance and brought his sword edge across the man's throat. Then, as if released from some spell, the lancer's horse galloped away in a frenzy, carrying its dead master with it. His blood misted in the air around him.

The knight and the final guard closed, exchanging sword cuts, the clash of their blades acting as a catalyst to Pia.

"Come on," she urged her companions. "We should go. *Now.*" She heaved Jack up and pointed to the south, to the nearest tree line. "Into the woods." They leapt from the wagon as the three rear guards passed them, charging to attack the knight. Master Peregrim flashed a smile.

"Four against one now," he said. "Those are odds I'd favor, if I was a gambling man."

But Pia didn't slow. She knew she was missing something. After all, why would one knight attack six armed men and three wagons full of refugees?

Jack ran, too. Mary followed with a grimace. The refugees in the remaining wagons copied their example, some running to the trees to the north as well.

Pia looked back to the crest of the road as the mystery knight lunged, his sword skewering an opponent in the shoulder. As the guard pulled away with a scream the sword was withdrawn and reversed, the edge biting into his face.

He didn't scream again.

Meanwhile, the three guards from the rear closed upon their attacker. Pia held her breath. At her side Jack called her name, and she heard Mary carry on into the wooded cover.

Three mounted men against one, she thought, *not even Sir Theodore—or perhaps even Kara—could fight them simultaneously. Not in such a situation.*

Flames roared from the shallow dip to the right of the road. They engulfed two of the three guards and their steeds, while the third swung wildly to his left. A second later he cried out as two arrows thudded into his chest.

"Oh, gods…" Pia wheezed.

"Come on, Pia," Jack whispered loudly. "We must hide."

As she turned to join her brother another scream reached her. Those refugees who had headed north to the trees found themselves confronted by several armed men.

If they hid in the northern cover, then they are likely in the south, too! She opened her mouth to scream a warning to Jack, who had already vanished ahead of her. Yet even as she drew breath a sharp *crack* sounded close above her.

An arrow quivered in the bark of the oak, just a fraction above her head. Pia leapt forward, uncaring of the cuts that the thick vegetation dealt her. She forced her way forward for several breaths before pausing to listen.

Thrumb… thrumb… thrumb…

The beating of her heart, blood rushing through her ears and her throat, pumping so fast her head ached.

She breathed out slowly, willing the furious beat to calm. Someone nearby moved, behind her. *Someone trying to be silent.* She turned her head, eager to listen for the attackers. *Could it be Jack?*

A bird chirped somewhere above. A squirrel fled across a branch to a neighboring tree, while overhead the sun shone through a thousand different perforations in the swaying canopy.

"None of them escaped to the north!" a man shouted from the road. "But at least three got into the undergrowth here. Perhaps more. Shall we go in and find them?"

"No, don't bother," another answered angrily. "We have what we came for, anyhow. The old fox will be pleased enough."

"Perhaps young Rudolph will want to set fire to the woods? That would make sure of the witnesses."

"Hold your tongue, fool! He will not waste one of his precious runes on starting a forest fire. We have what the old man wanted, and we will make our way back to Varrock. Come, we cannot waste a moment."

A horse neighed and the speakers moved away. Pia knelt. For several moments she remained absolutely still, breathing slowly through her open mouth to quiet the sound.

Crack!

Cold fear clenched her stomach. She spun to confront the sound, her hand coming up with her drawn knife—

"Jack!" She gasped, halting the blade a finger's width from his shocked face. "Never do that to me again. Do you hear? Never!"

Her brother lowered his face in dismay at her rebuke, yet Pia's shock turned to happiness to see he was unharmed. Quickly she hugged him.

"It's all right," she said.

"I think we are safe now, Pia," he answered. "I heard them talking. I think they've all gone." Jack made to crawl back the way Pia had come, but she stayed him with a firm grip.

"Keep still, Jack. And keep quiet," she whispered. "They might be baiting us, like the guards used to do in the market in Ardougne. Remember that?"

Jack nodded in silence, then he moved back to sit by her side. It was hot in the undergrowth, and insects of all kinds crawled on them as the moments wore on.

After an eternity seemed to pass, the undergrowth to their right shook. Something large forced its way through to the edge of the road, breathing heavily.

"It could be Mary," Jack suggested. "We should warn her to stay back." He attempted to stand, but Pia seized him tightly. The sound fell silent.

"It's too late, Jack. If it's her she's at the roadside by now."

Jack nodded and she relaxed her grasp, but still she held him in her arms, ready to shield him in an instant.

Another moment passed in silence. She tried to recall how many refugees had taken the northern escape, only to be caught and murdered. Had it been five of them? More? Master Peregrim and Mary had made it to the woods with her and Jack, she recalled. That left nine others unaccounted for.

Oh gods.

"Hello?" It was Mary's voice, calling from the road. "Is anybody there? Pia? Master Peregrim?"

Jack gasped and turned a fright-filled face to Pia.

She signaled for him to remain quiet.

"Pia? Jack? Anyone?"

The sound of an arrow hissed through the air.

Mary screamed. A cry of torment that shouldn't have been possible for any human to make.

Oh gods oh gods oh gods... no no no...

"Pia! Oh, oh Pia, no!" Jack wept, biting into his sleeve to silence his sobs as Mary screamed again.

Pia clutched Jack to her, her arms squeezing him as tightly as she could. She pushed her face next to his and felt her hot tears drip onto his cheek.

"I love you, Jack," she whispered. "We're safe. That's what matters. We're safe, we're safe. Nothing else in the world matters. Nothing."

But when Mary screamed for the final time, Pia knew that her words were a lie. And as the day turned into darkness, neither of them dared move.

6

"I would have paid good coin to have been there!" Sulla said triumphantly. "Kara-Meir returns from Morytania, only to have her wizard arrested and to be told that I, the slayer of her family, am considered a hero!"

The laughter that followed his words threatened to become uncontrollable. His one good eye watered and his body shuddered. A goblet of wine poised on his stomach, held uneasily between his two prosthetic hands, lurched to one side and spilt onto the floor.

Despite this, his joy continued unabated.

Not even the fact that Kara-Meir took my hands can upset me now. Not today. Everything I plotted has come to pass. Varrock will need Jerrod, and to get him they will need me.

He forced himself upright in the chair, crawling back with his elbows, and stared at the three who sat before him. None shared his mirth. Mirroring their expressions, he nodded gravely, trying hard not to laugh again.

"And Gar'rth was not with them," he mused. "I told Lord Ruthven that such would be the case. Someone in Morytania went to a great deal of effort in sending Jerrod after him, so it was obvious that once he returned to the place of his birth, they wouldn't let him go a second time." His right eye focused on the woman under the chamber window, her green dress illuminated by the afternoon sun. He felt her contempt across the distance, and smiled as he stared at her long enough to make her uncomfortable.

"Take your eye off her, Sulla," a well-manicured young man said coldly.

Sulla ignored the demand.

"Well, Lady Caroline?" he asked the dark-haired girl. "Shall I do as your suitor begs?"

The woman sighed, her mouth opening to reveal a gap in her front teeth. It was something of which Sulla had grown fond.

"You would be well advised to do as Lord William dictates, Sulla," the last of the three individuals said, anger seething in her voice. "You are no hero! You are an outlaw who is fast running out of time."

Sulla could not help but turn his attention to the speaker of the angry words. Lady Anne. Always her. Passionate, beautiful, too easily driven to anger. He had tired of her already.

"We'll see about that," he hissed to the blonde-haired woman. "But you and I have a problem, for now Sir Theodore has returned from Morytania with all his limbs intact. No doubt you will be off to fling yourself at him again." He enjoyed her burning stare and sighed. "But let us hope he never finds out about us, hey? After all, the king himself promised me the wife of my choice. And I chose you, if only because you hate me so! Still, for a Kinshra knight you would make an ideal spouse."

Lady Anne's blue eyes remained unmoved.

"You were never a Kinshra knight, Sulla," she said. "You were a butcher. An animal who lived to torment others." She smiled unexpectedly, an expression which puzzled him. "Do you know

what they say at court these days? About you?" She took a step
toward his chair, somehow threatening. "They say the Kinshra are
distancing themselves from you in every way possible. They hate
you, Sulla. The new lord of the Kinshra, the Lord Daquarius, has
sent word throughout The Wilderness to any who fled after your
inept leadership. He is allowing them to return—for in his eyes,
those who deserted a leader as mad as you acted rightfully."

Lord William nodded at her side, stroking his trim black beard
thoughtfully.

"It's true, Sulla. The Kinshra are apparently trying to restore any
honor they can to their knighthood, after the damage you did.
And rumor also has it that they are sending an envoy to press for
your extradition." William smiled wickedly. "No doubt they are
preparing the torture chambers that you yourself set up under Ice
Mountain. Ironic, really, don't you think? Hmm. I wonder if you
will scream to Zamorak, calling out for mercy when they put you
on the rack? Or perhaps it will be the Pear of Anguish?"

The young man winced at the thought.

Sulla held his tongue before replying. There was much he wanted
to say, to discover how much they *really* knew.

*Someone who frequents my chamber—perhaps one of these three
weak fools—is a Kinshra spy,* he thought. *And both Lady Anne and
Lord William seem to know much about the Kinshra.*

He lowered his gaze, feigning concern.

"Zamorak doesn't offer mercy, Lord William," he said slowly,
then glanced up to look the nobleman in the eye. "I would have
thought you knew that?"

Lord William tilted his head.

"Zamorak is the god of chaos, Sulla. Chaos itself is neither good
nor evil. It is not kind, but neither is it cruel. Chaos simply is a
force in nature—a necessary one. One that is often beneficial." He
shook his head. "It is a far different canon than that blasphemy you

follow, preached by the renegade Bishop Lungrim and the Charred Folk. There is no sanity in those words."

Sulla growled. "The blood of Saradomin's flock was used as wine, their cries our choir," he snarled, and grinned viciously. "There is beauty in Zamorak's teaching, boy. A beauty you can never learn until you have killed or maimed. Beauty..." His eye fell on Lady Anne, who held his gaze. He smiled in delight, for a new game sprang to mind.

"Theodore will refuse you, Lady Anne," he said with relish. "He has no choice. He is a Knight of Falador now, and he is married to his order. Of course... there might just be a way. Perhaps if he loved you enough."

Interest grew behind her blue eyes.

"Yes, it's possible," Sulla continued. "The boy would have to disavow his order, however, and he would only do that if he were madly in love with you." He wrinkled up his scarred face and grimaced at her. "But you're not worth it, truth be told. And from the way people regard you at court, you are a favorite of King Roald's. I wonder why? Others do, also." Sulla smirked. Lady Caroline moved to her friend's side and took her arm in her hand as Anne's face reddened.

"No. It can't be, I'm afraid," Sulla continued. "He could never love you enough, for your reputation isn't as chaste as it should be. That is the price an independent woman pays."

Sulla readied himself for her outburst, but nothing came. She breathed steadily, still in control.

"Of course, I *can* help you," he continued, undeterred. "There is a man I know who specializes in potions." He winked slyly. "Love potions, for example."

Suddenly Lord William laughed.

"Love potions, Sulla? You've been reading too many fairytales." The nobleman ran a finger across his family crest, a silver brooch fashioned into the shape of a fox caught in mid-leap. "And besides, the use of such potions would make a mockery of anyone's love, would it not? If Lady Anne did use one on Theodore, then it would be coercion.

"To coerce one whom you love, to remove their free will, is hardly an act of affection." William turned his eyes to Lady Caroline and smiled briefly. "Love must be earned, Sulla. It cannot be wrested by force or guile."

It was Sulla's turn to laugh.

"For one who has not yet seen his twentieth year, you are wise indeed, Lord de Adlard. But I suspect your wisdom has its limits." He delighted in the doubt that flickered across the young man's face. "You are intelligent, certainly, and very well read, yet I suspect you have never raised a hand in anger. Most certainly you have never fought for your life, and you cannot know the truth that such a victory adds to your own existence."

William's eyes narrowed. Encouraged, Sulla continued.

"In a city like Varrock, where martial valor is encouraged among the young, this must make you different. Suspect, perhaps. Untrusted." He blinked once and held his eyes closed for several heartbeats. When he opened them again he saw how William stared, his eyes glaring.

"Held beneath contempt by many," Sulla whispered. "Cowardly."

"Don't listen to him, William," Caroline urged, her hands reaching out to close on his arm. "Please. He does this often. It is the only sport he has as he awaits his fate."

Her words were lost as the nobleman shook her off and stormed toward the door. Sulla smiled as he caught tears in the young man's eyes, and he laughed as Lady Caroline ran after him.

"You should be wary of making an enemy of Lord William," Anne said quietly. "He comes from a respected line. His grandfather was chancellor, and a rather adept one, too." Her eyes grew cold. "And one day he might very well take up the same position. Even if not, he will likely become a powerful force at court—perhaps powerful enough for you to fear."

"Would you enjoy watching me die, Lady Anne?" he responded. "Could one as beautiful as you really delight in the wretched death of another?"

"Not usually, Sulla. I confess that." She smiled broadly, her white teeth gleaming in a predatory fashion. "But with you, I am prepared to make the exception."

Sulla said nothing for a long moment. He watched as Anne stepped to the mirror to make an imperceptible adjustment to the silver ferronnière upon her forehead, its diamond glinting as she did so. Finally, he breathed deeply.

"You mock an ill creature, Lady Anne," he said. "One who would do you a service. For I alone can give you Theodore's love."

She hesitated, still looking into the mirror.

"I'm not interested in your love potions, Sulla."

"Lord William has only read of them in fairytales," he persisted. "The truth is that they can only work if the imbiber already loves. So if Sir Theodore loves you, then the potion would simply exaggerate that emotion. It cannot create it."

Anne turned, her expression one of poorly muted curiosity.

She wants to learn more, but she doesn't want me to know it.

"You know much about potions, Sulla."

He nodded.

"I do," he said. "I have used them several times, though never love potions, for I had no need to make anyone love me. Why would I, when I could take whatever I wanted by force?" He smiled at her horrified expression, then continued.

"You should also remember that you will be saving Theodore's life. As a Knight of Falador, he will always charge headlong into danger. That is his duty, and sooner or later he will meet someone stronger, or more cunning, or a dragon with three heads who will gobble him up!"

He stretched idly.

"There is a man I know, one of the very men who helped me to kill the Wyrd. His name is Mergil. He lives in Varrock, though I don't know where. Herblore and botany are his specialties. It won't be hard for one of your contacts to seek him out."

She stared at him for some time before speaking.

"I won't rise to your bait, Sulla. Lord William speaks truly."

"Then you will lose Sir Theodore, and he will die, Lady Anne." He closed his eyes and sighed. The wine had made him tired.

When he opened them again, Lady Anne had gone.

Sulla slept uneasily. He dreamed of the last time he had seen Kara-Meir, when she had challenged him to personal combat, just over six months ago. In his mind, his hands—the very ones the she-wolf had severed—clenched the hilt of his sword.

He woke, inhaling sharply. He wasn't alone. A shadow moved in the mirror, something black, from behind him.

Sulla sat up in his chair, expecting to feel the tip of a blade drawn across his throat or plunged into his back. He turned with a roar.

An elderly maid stared at him without moving.

"You," Sulla rasped. "Knock before you enter my quarters, crone. Else I'll have the skin off your back!"

The scrawny woman said nothing. With undisguised disdain she knelt and took the fallen goblet from the shadow of the chair leg.

Sulla reclined once again and regarded her grimly.

"I don't want you anymore, crone," he muttered. "I want a younger maid. Something more pleasing on the eye. I'll have a word with your master."

Suddenly she looked up, her face impassive.

"You are not a guest in this palace," she said flatly. "You are a prisoner. You are a prisoner who plays games with my lady and her friends. It is ill-advised. And I have no master, for Lady Caroline is the one I serve."

She stood and left the goblet on the table at Sulla's side.

"Aren't you going to refill it?" he asked, nodding to the bottle of wine that sat next to his cup.

"Can't you manage it?" the woman taunted.

Sulla growled.

"What is your name, harpy?"

"It is Lucretia," she answered. "And you should know that any taunt you heap upon my mistress will be paid back tenfold." She turned from the window and looked back to him. "Do you understand? It is not a wise man who makes enemies of those who feed and clothe him."

She turned her attention to his bed then, carefully drawing up the sheets. As he watched, Sulla's mind ran in circles.

Could it be her? Could the maid have planted the message? Lucretia moved forward to straighten the pillows. Her hands touched the fabric—

"Wait!" Sulla snapped. She stopped and stood as he continued on, calmer than before. "There is no need of that, kind woman, for soon I shall rest. And you are right. Only a fool insults those he needs." He laughed mournfully and held his arms up before her, the prosthetics dangling lamely. "But look at me. *Look at me.* Do I not have a right to be angry? Have I not suffered enough? I cannot even build a fire to keep my crippled body warm."

Lucretia stared coldly.

She's hard, this one. He shivered suddenly.

"Do you really want a fire?" Lucretia asked critically. "It's warm enough in here."

Sulla shook his head.

"Not for me it isn't. Not for me."

The old maid grunted and approached the fireplace. As she prepared the coals and set the wood Sulla looked back to the pillows on his bed.

That was close, he thought.

The fire lit, Lucretia left the room. The goblet remained empty, but Sulla was secretly pleased, for he had won his victory. He stood and moved to the bed, throwing aside the pillows. Beneath them he found a single piece of white paper, with a single black mark drawn upon its surface. It was a warning from the Kinshra, a notice to say that his life would shortly be taken.

He held the paper between his prosthetic hands and moved to the growing flames, lowering its corner into the blaze. Very quickly the paper caught fire. Sulla dropped it into the crackling tongues and stepped back.

Ebenezer the alchemist, Lord Ruthven, Captain Rovin, Lord William de Adlard, he thought, reviewing the list in his mind. *Lady Anne and Lady Caroline. Now the maid, Lucretia. Any one of them could have done it.*

He bit his lip uncomfortably.

The scent of the burning paper was lost amid the stronger fumes of the coal. Sulla smiled grimly as the final corner of the paper curled itself up. So intent was he, he didn't hear the door open. There was an audible *click* as it shut.

He turned his head. Captain Rovin stood there along with two men, one of whom he knew to be Lord Ruthven. The third man stood back, his hand clenched around a two-pronged dagger the like of which Sulla had seen before. Recently.

"Well, Sulla. You were right." Lord Ruthven advanced, his hawk face an unreadable mask. "As you predicted, Gar'rth did not return from Morytania. And we will need a werewolf's knowledge sooner, rather than later."

Sulla smiled in the shadows.

"Now the embassy has failed, you mean?" he said. "Now that Kara-Meir's pet wizard has been arrested, and I am considered as great a hero as her?" He laughed cruelly. "You need a man like me here, Lord Ruthven. And you can trust me, more so than those young whelps who claim to be heroes."

The look on Ruthven's face was filled with doubt.

"You *know* me," he continued. "You know that I worship Zamorak. You know I enjoy causing pain. You know that I am, in my own small way, a monster." Sulla paused for a moment, staring at each man in turn. Captain Rovin wore a bemused smile. Lord Ruthven was frowning. But the unknown man with the knife made him uneasy. He was tall and lean and armored in worn black leather, his rugged face conveying no emotion.

"I mean, what do you really know of them? Have you ever seen Kara-Meir kill, for instance?" Sulla smirked. "I have. She enjoys it, even more than I once did. You cannot trust her." He held up his prosthetics. "And besides, I'm unlikely to kill again."

Lord Ruthven nodded.

"But it's not the physical danger you pose, Sulla." He nodded to the third man. "Simon here could cut your throat with ease, have no doubt of that. But he is not going to. His job is to make sure that Jerrod comes in. And you are going to help him do it."

Sulla swallowed nervously, and hoped they hadn't noticed.

"And then?" he said. "What have you decided on for me? Once I do as you ask, will Simon then dispatch me?"

Lord Ruthven smiled coldly.

"No, Sulla. We will stick to the bargain." He blinked, then continued. "You will leave the palace, to make contact with Jerrod in the city. When you return, you will come with him, and bring the documents you have used to exercise your... influence over others.

"Jerrod will not be harmed, for we need his knowledge of

Morytania and those who plot against us. From that moment onward you both will be kept in gilded cages, your every need satisfied."

It was Sulla's turn to laugh.

"Are you so sure of that?" he asked. "Jerrod likes eating children and maidens. Somehow, I don't think King Roald would permit him that."

Captain Rovin gave a discreet shrug.

"No one will care if the occasional thief or murderer goes missing from the king's dungeons, Sulla." He held a bandaged hand up to his face, and stared at it closely. "Who knows? Perhaps he will even have the opportunity to eat a blue-robed wizard."

Sulla doubted Castimir would be given to Jerrod, but he smiled all the same.

"All are mere details," Lord Ruthven muttered. "But soon you will leave this palace to enter Varrock. I should warn you not to try anything foolish. The guards will be watching for you. You stand no chance of fleeing the city."

The old man's cold stare bore into Sulla's single working eye.

"There is no safer place for you than the palace of King Roald," he added.

Sulla nodded and gazed down at the fire. The note had completely gone now, but its threatening message remained stained on his mind.

No safer place in all the world, he thought bitterly.

He looked up to see Simon's unchanged face regarding him with indifference, the two-bladed dagger balanced in his hand. Then Sulla had to hold back an impulsive grin.

But nothing is forever, Lord Ruthven.

7

The only light came from the pool, radiating upward in shivering waves from the ripples that ran across its surface. Gar'rth looked again at the watery image and frowned.

"Do you see now, my son, how weak our descendants have become?" Tenebra stood at his side. The vampire was clothed in a black cloak that seemed composed more of shadow than fabric. When he moved, he did so without a sound. Only his pale hands and face were visible.

Gar'rth gave his father an uncertain look.

"You doubt the pool's veracity," Tenebra mused. "That is wise, but the pool shows the truth." The heir to the throne of Misthalin stroked his centuries-old jawline and nodded toward the water. "But how can a man of his rank, of our blood, sink so low?"

Gar'rth nodded without thinking as he looked down. The image in the pool showed King Roald and Ellamaria, who had previously disguised herself as a woman of noble birth to confront the king about the kidnappings and slayings in Varrock. Her subterfuge had led to the creation of the embassy itself.

His fist balled in sudden anger, scabs tearing on the cuts there.

If not for her, he thought, *I might still be across the river, with Kara.*

Enviously he watched the couple share an intimate embrace. King Roald laughed, soundlessly, as if he had forgotten all the cares of running his kingdom.

Again, the anger grew.

Your cares were enough to send me back to Morytania. And now you frolic, King Roald.

Have you forgotten me already?

Gar'rth tasted black blood in his mouth and sucked his bleeding lip. He was aware of Tenebra's eyes upon him, the violent red behind his father's pupils showing brighter than before.

"You must not… you must not do that, my son." Tenebra's tongue moistened his lips. "Even with your werewolf blood, you cannot understand the hunger my kind feels. Despite the long centuries, it is an urge I cannot fully control."

The vampire tore his gaze back to the pool at their feet.

"But look," he continued. "King Roald would mix our bloodline with that of a peasant woman. This alone is enough to justify his abdication."

"Or his death," Gar'rth whispered.

Tenebra turned to him and smiled.

"Yes," he hissed. "His death would be justified." Gar'rth felt a grip upon his shoulder. "Death at your own hand, for if you wish to sit on the throne of Misthalin, what better way to reclaim the crown? Prize it from his dead hand, my son. Show the world the gods favor you in his stead."

In the pool, Ellamaria stood and departed. Her actions implied some urgency, and Gar'rth's curiosity grew.

"Can you follow her?" he asked. "Can you show me where she is going?"

Tenebra shook his head.

"No. The pool cannot view just any subject. There must be a distinct connection with those upon whom I wish to scry, be it a shared experience, a blood link, or a strong emotional attachment. Or, better still, a sample of skin or hair, such as those I took from your friends while they slept."

Tenebra made a motion with his hand and the image changed again. Gar'rth saw the long, worn face of Gideon Gleeman, staring thoughtfully into a child's cot. Near the entrance to the rounded room stood two armed guards, and the windows were barred on the inside.

The image of the injured jester, with the scabs on his face, turned Gar'rth's stomach.

"I gave my word that my friends would not be stopped leaving Morytania. It was a promise you made to me." He paused to draw breath and summon his courage. "And yet it was broken."

Tenebra shook his head.

"The word we gave was not broken. It was another who wished to stop your friends from leaving." The vampire's eyes took on a cunning look. "Someone you have met only recently, perhaps."

Gar'rth turned his head aside. He hadn't told Tenebra of the events in the ghetto. He hadn't wanted to give him the satisfaction.

And yet he knows. Should I really have expected otherwise?

"Vanescula?" Gar'rth said. "But why would she wish to stop them?"

The vampire smiled.

"To frustrate my plans, perhaps," he replied. "She doesn't know the particulars, but that doesn't prevent her from interfering. It is knowledge she yearns for, probably more than the blood of the living." He turned back to the pool. "But the last key still remains, in the form of the baby Felicity."

When Gar'rth looked again he saw that Ellamaria had joined Gleeman.

"It is ironic, Gar'rth, that it was you who heard the Wyrd's song the night she tried to take Felicity from the palace. If you hadn't prevented the abduction, then all seven of the children would be in my hands now." Tenebra gave a disingenuous smile. "But you did, and the Wyrd is dead. Our enemies in Varrock are beginning to understand that we need her. So I sent something else back with your friends. Something that will assure my success."

Gar'rth's heart froze. His mind whirled as he recalled watching his friends' desperate escape on the balloon *Hope Soars*— Vanstrom's sacrifice to cut the mooring line, the Vyrewatch attack which had caused them to crash just a mile before the Salve, and the subsequent pursuit of the werewolves which had led to the slaughter of many.

Miraculously, of their original party, only Albertus Black had perished.

Gar'rth looked to his father quizzically.

What have you done?

Tenebra smiled, as though he had heard Gar'rth's thoughts. Then he turned his gaze to the wounded jester and snorted dismissively.

"What weak servants my descendant has. When I rode to battle a millennium ago, in the service of Avarrocka, I had at my command some of the greatest heroes of my time. Men who would gladly sacrifice their lives for their beliefs." His voice grew bitter. "Yet the memories are dim, imperfect. It was all so very long ago, and I have lived many different lives since then. After what *she* did to me… No creature should suffer as I did then, at her hands."

Tenebra lowered his head.

"It is better that I don't remember."

"But I would like to know," Gar'rth said after a moment's silence. "I would like to know how you, as heir-apparent to Misthalin, sworn enemy to the undead, came to reside here, in command of magic that no human mage has ever wielded." He stared, uncomprehending. "When you were taken captive at the Battle of the Salve and brought here, why did they not kill you? Why did they allow you to live as one of them?"

The vampire's eyes flared angrily.

"As I said, boy, it is better not to remember." He turned back to the pool. "Now," he instructed impatiently, "it is time for you to try again. See if you can locate Kara-Meir, for your attachment to her is strong."

"What is the point to this?" Gar'rth countered. "If we manage to cross the Salve and triumph—"

"Don't dare to refuse me!" Tenebra whirled on him quicker than the eye could register. The vampire's hand took him around his throat and lifted him easily. "I am offering you tools that no king has ever possessed. With them, and with my guidance, you will rule as no monarch has before. Ever." He sneered and released his grip.

Gar'rth fell, wheezing, his hand held to a bruised throat.

"But you would not understand," his father continued. "You *cannot*." Tenebra calmed. "Your short life has not given you the vision to see beyond the end of a single day, let alone manage the affairs of mankind." He stepped back and gazed into the shadows that surrounded them. "Whereas I have watched the follies of men for hundreds of years. I have seen petty wars erupt and sow the seed of greater conflicts. Needless death and devastation, plague and fire, all misfortunes that have been exacerbated by humanity's own weakness.

"By its stupidity."

Gar'rth felt Tenebra's eyes fasten upon him. His courage fled. As the vampire spoke, his skin grew cold.

"And only I possess both the strength of will and the means to bring such pointless existence to an end, to craft a new race, one that I—through you—will guide. Now, stand, and try the pool again. See if you can find your precious lover."

"We were never that," Gar'rth rasped.

But still, he did as his father commanded. He stood over the pool, and instinctively reached inside his coat pocket.

But the lock of Kara's golden hair was gone. He had nothing left of her now. Nothing save his love.

He closed his eyes and thought of her face, her skin tanned from long hours of walking under the open sky. He remembered her smile with its teasing affection. And he remembered the sometimes-troubled look in her dark eyes, when they sat over the fires at night. She would stare at him, and say nothing for many hours.

Thinking about me, perhaps, he thought. *Wondering if there could be any chance for us.*

"Good!" Tenebra cried unexpectedly. "Look. Open your eyes and look. See your friends, for having found Kara you have found them all."

Gar'rth did as instructed. And he gasped.

In the pool the wavering image of Kara had appeared. She stood at the head of a wooden table, along one side of which sat Theodore and Ebenezer, facing Doric and Arisha. The priestess had a hand held over her face. Of Castimir there was no sign.

He knew instantly it was the inside of King Roald's palace, for he recognized the yellow standard that hung behind Kara's shoulder.

She was shaking her head angrily. Theodore seemed to be arguing with her.

"How do I know what they are saying?" Gar'rth asked.

Tenebra shrugged.

"It is the limits of the magic. You cannot hear them, but with practice you will discover that you can often interpret the words by watching the movements of their lips."

"Can you do that now?" Gar'rth demanded. "What are they talking about?"

"Your wizard friend, I think."

Arisha lowered her hand and for the first time Gar'rth saw her bruised face. The image wavered violently.

"Keep calm," Tenebra hissed. "Or you will lose her."

"Arisha has been injured," Gar'rth muttered. "And sometime since their return to Varrock. *Urrghhh—*"

Gar'rth winced as a lancing pain pierced the back of his eyes. His vision blurred and the image vanished beneath the rippling waters.

Tenebra sighed.

"What happened?" Gar'rth asked, rubbing his hand over his eyes and blinking quickly to clear the fog from the room.

"You are a novice at the art of scrying. It requires concentration of a sort you have never had to summon before. Your mind is not used to its toll." He shook his head. "Not yet."

"Bring them back, please," Gar'rth pleaded, eliciting a frown from his father. "I need to see. What has happened to them?"

Again Tenebra shook his head.

"You must harden your heart, Gar'rth. That is why I sent you to Canifis in the very first place—so you would grow up to be as strong as each task requires. So you would be inured to death, and injury, and the pain of others, as well as your own.

"And to keep you from Vanescula's reach for as long as possible." Tenebra peered coldly. "I hadn't counted on you resisting Zamorak's influence, and I certainly never expected you to run away, let alone escape Morytania." He turned aside in contempt. "You have been tainted by compassion, but once I have removed the cause, you will realize your true potential."

Gar'rth stared with hatred at his father's unguarded back.

Could I even hurt him at all? he contemplated furiously, his heart racing.

"Kara-Meir will require special attention." Tenebra rubbed his hands together slowly, thinking deeply. "Together, you and I will make her nightmares a reality—"

Without warning Gar'rth leapt, urging the change as he hurled himself through the air. He felt the hair erupt from his skin and his nails harden into claws as his jaw distended. Then Tenebra's black cloak was before him, and he reached out to seize his father about the throat.

Tenebra spun, impossibly fast. The vampire grinned in delight and waved his right hand, as though he were wafting away an unpleasant odor.

Gar'rth's momentum died as he stopped in mid-air, his claws a finger's width away from his target.

"How?" he gritted. "You have no runes—"

A rush of cold air chilled him, despite his half-transformed state. It hurled him backward until he ended in a clumsy roll across the flagstones, coming to rest at the wall's edge.

As he rose to his knees, he no longer felt the rage. It was as if the cold wind had sobered his mind.

Tenebra laughed. It was a wicked sound that slowly trailed away. Finally, he clapped.

"Perhaps your experience in the land beyond the river was not in vain," he said. "At least you have conviction, and as king you will need that. You have courage, too." The vampire's smile died and Gar'rth readied himself for more punishment. Instead, Tenebra simply frowned. "But there is foolishness in you. And a quickness to anger that your enemies will exploit."

With each word, Gar'rth felt the sting of tears gather in his eyes. His father advanced slowly.

"Here in Morytania the strength that made you so special among normal men is no longer a currency of any great value. You must feel weak, my son." Tenebra paused to stand above him. "Impotent." The vampire lowered his right hand to Gar'rth, palm up. "Frustrated."

"I feel all of those things," Gar'rth said bitterly. "And I hate you for it. You, and no other!"

Tenebra's hand did not waver.

"Your hate will pass," he said. "You will soon see what a far greater destiny I have planned for you. A destiny untainted by the weakness of compassion."

Gar'rth closed his eyes and clenched his jaw.

"My words will come true, my son," Tenebra uttered. "Soon, you will embrace Zamorak—as must all who share the blood of Canifis. Yet you will still possess the ability to choose. Don't you see what I have given you, Gar'rth? You will have the strengths of the werewolf, yet your mind will be your own, for you have inherited your humanity from me.

"I was born a human a thousand years ago, yet the gift of vampirism cannot be passed down from father to son. Not by me." Tenebra's voice was strangely comforting. "You, my son, are unique in the world. I have spent years fathering children this side of the river, yet only you have showed the promise.

"Now, take my hand. Rise."

Gar'rth opened his eyes and stared at his father for a long moment. Tears blurred his vision, yet the hand remained held out to him, palm up. With a slight hesitation, he took it. The cold emanating from the undead flesh caused him to wince.

Tenebra smiled as Gar'rth stood.

"Today you will do something about the frustration you feel so acutely," he said. "The Vyrewatch plan to butcher several dozen inhabitants of a ghetto, all in the belief that they are part of the Myreque trying to escape from their miserable home. You might be able to save their lives if you can warn them in time. They will make for a tunnel under a wall, and that is where the ambush will occur. Reach them before and they will be safe."

"I don't understand," Gar'rth said. "Why would you do this for me?"

"Because you need to see that while a man has limits in what he can do, a king has none. It is a lesson you will have to learn, in order to claim your birthright."

So, it's another test, Gar'rth thought.

Tenebra let Gar'rth's hand fall. He turned and gestured behind him, to the doorway. There Gar'rth saw a single figure standing among the shadows, shadows to which even his vision was no aid.

"Who is that?" Gar'rth asked.

"He will guide you to the ghetto," the vampire replied. "He knows the streets like no other. He is one of the Myreque, captured recently, yet one who is of far more use alive than dead." Tenebra beckoned and the figure—a man—advanced.

And as he neared Gar'rth's mouth fell open, for it was the face of a ghost.

"You!" he cried. "But I thought you were dead. I saw you fall—"

"Aye, I thought so too—for a moment." The bearded man dared a smile, though his face was beaten and bruised. "But it takes more than a fall and a few werewolves to kill Vanstrom Klause."

8

The world was shrouded in shadow that exaggerated the ancient battlement upon which Gar'rth and his companion stood. It seemed unnaturally still in the ghetto's twisting alleys, far below.

"How much longer will we have to wait?" he muttered.

At his side, Vanstrom grunted.

"It's been two hours at least," Gar'rth pressed.

"Are you nervous?" Vanstrom asked. "After what you told me about your last experience with the Vyrewatch, it would be expected."

"I am more fearful of Vanescula," Gar'rth said. "Even *they* fear her."

Vanstrom shot him a grim smile.

"Then they are not so stupid." The bearded man gave him a long look, suddenly hard. "You said you saw me fall from the balloon then, on Hope Rock. But how?"

"Tenebra has a scrying pool through which he watches the world. He showed me." He peered down into the shadows, his gaze shifting from rooftop to rooftop. Nothing stirred. "He can even

look across the river into Varrock, into King Roald's own chamber
when he so wishes."

Vanstrom shuddered.

"Think of what secrets he must have been privy to, over all the
years. Perhaps he has watched them for centuries." He laughed
grimly. "Imagine what a human lord would give for such power."

Gar'rth smiled, his mind a burning recollection.

*Yes, King Roald, what would you offer to hold the power I am
given by your ancestor? Would you heap one injustice atop another,
ignoring the protests of your conscience as the ends justified the
means? As you did with me, sending me to my death.*

Or worse.

He felt Vanstrom's hand on his left shoulder and gave a startled
jump.

"Did you see anything else in the pool, after my fall?" the man
asked. "Did any of the others get out?"

Gar'rth exhaled and nodded.

"Yes, Vanstrom. Yes they did. Kara and all my friends escaped,
though not without injury." He lowered his head. "Albertus Black
died upon the riverbank of Misthalin, though. He was ill and
dying before he set foot in Morytania anyhow. He should never
have come."

Vanstrom squeezed Gar'rth's shoulder firmly.

"He was old, but he was a good, brave man. If Varrock breeds
men like him, men of such conviction, then it is a blessed realm
indeed. You must not pity anyone who died in such a way,
Gar'rth. Here, in Morytania, such a life would have been utterly
impossible."

He withdrew his hand.

"But what of the others?" he asked. "What of Pia and her brother?
Are they safe too? And the others who escaped with them?"

Gar'rth nodded.

"Pia and Jack made it across the river, thankfully, but I don't know what occurred after that." He paused. "I fear many of your people perished in the attempt."

"Gods," Vanstrom hissed. He was silent for a long moment. "Nevertheless, with each of us who escapes Drakan's clutches, word of our plight will spread. Perhaps, one day soon, a king from across the river will stir, and take up arms against the undying one." His face darkened and his eyes narrowed. "But there is still something I must know. About you, Gar'rth.

"You came across the river as one of the embassy. Yet you remained here, and I find you at the Black Prince's very side, dressed as nobility. Tell me honestly, Gar'rth, who are you?"

Gar'rth looked into his face.

My friends trusted him, and he was prepared to sacrifice his life to enable them to escape. The bearded man, wild and beaten, held his gaze. *I can trust him, too.*

"Tenebra is my father, Vanstrom." He paused as the man's jaw fell and his eyes gaped wide. "I only found out very recently. I am half-human, half-werewolf, sired by a man who abandoned his own humanity long ago.

"Yet the ideals my friends taught me are those I choose to follow. I am not like others of my race, for Zamorak's hold over me is far from absolute. And I would slay Tenebra at once, if I could." It was his turn to take the startled man by the shoulder. "I will not lie to you. It is hard. My life is a constant battle. Often I relish the thought of violence and blood. Often I dream of it, of inflicting pain on those I love most, and yet... I refuse to do so. I have rejected everything my father believes in.

"I will not be like him."

As he stared into Vanstrom's wounded face, he noticed that one of the cuts there was leaking blood. Once the smell of it would have spurred something primal, but here, on the still battlements, he felt no such thing. He didn't know what to think of it—whether to hope or fear.

Perhaps, he thought, *I have had so much of the smell of blood that I have tired of it.* He was about to speak when Vanstrom's face lit up in excitement.

"There!" he hissed, pointing.

Gar'rth followed his gesture to the ghetto below. Several people had emerged from the side of a building. Very quickly the small gathering grew in size, as others clambered out through an entrance hidden in shadow.

"We must intercept them before they try for the tunnel under the wall," Vanstrom urged, eyeing Gar'rth suspiciously. "If, of course, what your father said is true."

Gar'rth said nothing to express his own lingering doubt. He nodded and they raced down the battlement's steps that led to the ghetto below. Getting to the group before they reached the wall—where the Vyrewatch waited—would challenge even one of Gar'rth's speed.

He ran as fast as his human form would allow. Halfway down, Vanstrom swore.

"No!" he cried. "Gar'rth, it is the Vyrewatch. We're too late!"

Gar'rth stared. From the terraced rooftops above the silent gathering, winged vampires dropped like predators. His heart was pounding and his stomach twisted in horror as over the distance the screams reached his ears.

The Vyrewatch themselves made no sound, and their silence only made it more obscene.

"None of them will escape," Vanstrom moaned, covering his face in his hands. "Not a one of them. Tenebra said the ambush would take place at the tunnel, not here! Curse your father for his word!"

Gar'rth felt himself nodding in agreement. Twice now his

father had promised him something, and twice now his words had been lies.

"We can do nothing here, and we could be seen," he said urgently. "Come, Vanstrom." He pushed him before him, up the steps, away from the killings.

They were near the top when a sudden image flashed through his mind, so vivid that it seemed real. He saw himself tightening his grip on Vanstrom's shoulder, pushing him over the edge. He heard his screams as Vanstrom fell, then the satisfying *crunch* of bone and muscle as he hit the stone far below.

"What are you doing?" Vanstrom demanded. The fright in his voice woke Gar'rth from his vision. He shook himself, and when he looked, he realized that he *had* tightened his grip on Vanstrom's shoulder, that he had forced him toward the edge.

He let go in shock.

"I'm sorry, Vanstrom," he muttered. "I wasn't thinking."

The bearded man gave him a curious look, turned, and ran ahead, while Gar'rth remained for a moment to get his breath and steady his nerves. When he looked up to the battlement again, Vanstrom had gone.

"What's happening to me?" he whispered.

Isn't it obvious, Soft-Heart?

The ache began in the depths of his brain. The smothering presence he had felt only once before he felt again.

"Vanescula?" he said aloud, his voice low. "What did you do to me?"

Mocking laughter erupted from behind him, lower on the stairs. Gar'rth spun.

Just a few yards away, Vanescula Drakan leaned against the battlement wall, her bare right arm stretched behind her head, her long pale leg thrust out through the slit in an ankle-length black skirt. Her face was polished alabaster, her luxurious red hair framing her head.

He staggered in surprise.

"Careful, Soft-Heart, careful," she chided. "It wouldn't be very fun to have you fall. No doubt you can imagine *exactly* what it would be like." She smiled. Her large oval eyes widened, a blood-red burning in their depths. "Like the sound the human would have made when he hit the stone… quite exquisite."

Gar'rth moved away from the stairs' edge. He sat awkwardly, never taking his eyes from her face.

A beautiful face, he thought, *an impossibly beautiful one.*

Vanescula tittered. She turned her head away from him, exposing her neck. She let the top of her dress slide from the edge of her left shoulder. Her skin was flawless. His head ached from sudden desire tempered by fear.

"You are far more civil than your father, Soft-Heart." She sighed and looked back to him. "He fought me for years after his capture. Refused me. Me!"

"Stop," Gar'rth mumbled weakly. "Please… please stop. My head… it hurts."

"I know you hate him," she continued. "I know you fear him. And here, in the place of your birth, you feel so weak. So impotent. So unable to change anything, always the pawn of others.

"I can help you."

Gar'rth grunted.

"You mean to make me your own pawn, princess. To use me against my father, against my own blood."

The red in Vanescula's eyes flared for an instant. Her smile vanished, then reappeared. But it was different.

"Am I so very transparent?" she asked, licking her top lip with her red tongue. "But you are right, of course. It wouldn't be fun otherwise. To turn a child against a parent—there is rarely any better sport."

Gar'rth mustered all of his strength, and stood.

"I will not serve one monster in place of another," he said. "If you wish to take my life, then let us waste no more time, princess."

Surprise rippled across her face.

"Are you really that foolish, to believe that death would end your torment? Your father died a dozen times in his imprisonment, in excruciating circumstances beyond any torture that any human king could contrive. He begged for death a thousand thousand times before I granted it." Her red lips parted in a sinister smile. "And then I brought him back. Again, and again, and again. For I would not permit a mortal to defy me. He would break before my will, as all men must."

Her eyes held Gar'rth's.

"As you must. As you will." She stepped toward him and cupped his jaw in her hand. "Here, Soft-Heart."

She leaned forward and kissed him.

"That is my gift to you, Soft-Heart. My blood mark. It will grant you protection from all but the greatest vampires, and it will shield your mind from those who can see. Like your father with his scrying pool. Like the Vyrewatch.

"Like me."

Gar'rth staggered as his mind cleared. It was like breaking through the surface of a river after being held under too long. When he blinked and looked again at Vanescula, she seemed different. Somehow less real than before.

"I have given you a freedom, Soft-Heart. Freedom even from me." She smiled wolfishly. "It will be interesting to see what you do with it."

She stepped from the wall and to the stairs' edge, where she gave Gar'rth an amused stare. Then she stepped into empty space.

When Gar'rth looked into the void, she was gone.

He took a deep breath.

I can trust no one here, he thought. *No one. Everyone has an agenda.*

He turned his eyes back to where he had last seen Vanstrom, unsure of what to do. Then he ran up the steps, debating whether or not to return to Castle Drakan.

When he reached the top, a high-pitched whistle reached his ear. In the darkness to his right, where a second, higher wall cut across the very battlement he stood upon, built to divide the ghettoes, he saw a wave. Somehow Vanstrom had climbed the higher wall, the height of at least three tall men.

Gar'rth broke into a run. As he drew nearer he saw that the wall would not be easy, even for one of his werewolf heritage. The surface was glassy smooth—each crevice had been filled with a resin that prevented any handhold.

"So, what did the demon have to say?" Vanstrom called.

"She wants to use me against my father," Gar'rth replied. "She even gave me the means to resist his magic."

Vanstrom said nothing, but Gar'rth felt his gaze.

"You can trust me, Vanstrom. I came with Kara and the others. I chose to remain so they could leave here safely."

"Then why not return to your father now?" he replied. "I have work to do. The Myreque must be told of the massacre and warned that the tunnel is no longer safe."

"Then let me come with you." He saw Vanstrom's puzzled expression. "Tenebra has taken me, to some degree at least, into his confidence. And if I remain here, with you, then he will waste valuable time trying to locate me—time that will allow our friends on the other side of the Salve to prepare for his invasion. They will need it, too, judging from my experience in King Roald's court."

"Very well," Vanstrom said. "Climb up."

Gar'rth removed his gloves and studied the wall. Wishing not to appear weak, he leapt upward, his fingers grasping the tiniest curves in the brick as his feet flailed below to give him a push.

Slowly but surely he ascended. It was only when he was a hand's length from the edge that his grip failed. He felt himself slip and gave a desperate cry.

Vanstrom's hand lashed out, seizing his right wrist. The wild man heaved, not up, but to his left, toward the edge.

And beyond it.

Oh, gods!

"Wait, Vanstrom! Wait!" He couldn't keep the fear from his voice. There was no way he would survive a fall that far into the ghetto below. No way.

"Wait?" Vanstrom laughed cruelly. He dragged Gar'rth farther to the right, where there was nothing below but empty space. "I will wait, but only long enough for you to pledge something to me, werewolf. I want your promise—sworn to Zamorak Himself."

Gar'rth gritted his teeth, and craned his neck back to look into Vanstrom's eyes. Without blinking, he held the man's stare.

"I do not follow Zamorak, Vanstrom," he replied. "I have resisted his will my whole life. Kara and Theodore and the friends I met across the river showed me a better way."

"Then swear upon her then—swear upon the soul of Kara-Meir." Vanstrom scowled down. "But remember, wolf, the gods are always listening. If you break your oath to me, then she will perish. Do you agree?"

Gar'rth nodded.

"I do. What is it you would have me swear?"

"I want you to promise me that when the time is right, and when you can, you will slay your father. Promise me that." Gar'rth felt Vanstrom's hand relax slightly. "Promise me that or die."

Gar'rth let several heartbeats pass before answering.

"Very well," he said finally. "It is something I have already tried to do, Vanstrom, but I lacked the means. Yet you have my word, my oath. If I can do so, I will do it, for the lives of many people precious to me depend upon it. I swear it upon Kara-Meir."

Vanstrom frowned down upon him. Then, with a sudden shake of his head and a growl of exertion, he heaved Gar'rth up to the edge of the wall and over.

Gar'rth hid his head in shadow, relieved beyond words. He was tempted to kiss the stonework, so solidly reassuring beneath his feet.

"You're a strong man, Vanstrom Klause, and a hard one too," he said. "I thought you were going to let me drop."

When he looked up he saw Vanstrom regard him coldly. The big man gave him an icy smile.

"I had planned to," he admitted. "For no one escapes Vanescula's clutches unless she wants them to. Besides, one fewer of your blood in this land would be a good thing, and it would surely confound Tenebra's plans if his heir was to die."

"Then why didn't you let me fall?"

Vanstrom looked quickly to his right and left before replying.

"Because you are different from others of your race. I can see that. And if you did die, then I wouldn't know what Tenebra was planning, would I? Now, come on, we must make haste."

Gar'rth followed on his heels, passing over the place where the massacre had occurred.

"Where are we going?" he called out, running hard to keep up.

"Where are we going? *Ha!*" Vanstrom laughed as he ran, showing no signs of exertion. He turned to Gar'rth and grinned manically. "We are going to find the Myreque, and they are going to give you what you need to fulfill your oath—the means to slay your father."

9

Theodore held the blunted sparring sword in his right hand as he lunged against his opponent's shield. The man shifted his weight to brace for the impact, and the tip was turned aside, leaving Theodore open.

The man's sword came up to take advantage of the opening. Just as he moved to strike…

Nothing. Theodore stood without moving.

"Sir?" the man said. "Is everything all right?"

Suddenly aware, Theodore shook his head and stepped aside.

"I have much on my mind, Edmond," he said. "Continue your training with Philip—he seems recovered from his wounds now." He motioned, and a scarred onlooker, Philip, stepped into his former position. Moments later both men were thrusting and parrying, their actions lightened by the good-natured insults they exchanged, the sounds of their combat filling the gymnasium.

Yet Theodore heard little of it. His nerves had been drawn tight, ever since the embassy's return. Subsequent events had only made it worse.

"Sir?" A country-accented voice spoke from behind. He turned to find a young man. "Lord William is here to see you."

Theodore nodded.

"Thank you, Hamel. Bring him over."

His sixteen-year-old aide hastened to the doorway where the nobleman stood, and escorted him over. As he did so, the youth's club foot hindered his walk. But if he noticed, William did not show it.

"Good morning, Sir Theodore," the young noble said jovially as Hamel retreated beyond earshot. Theodore only nodded again, unable to match his friend's enthusiasm.

"I see your humor has not improved since yesterday," William commented, and he smiled cunningly. "Perhaps I can help, for Lady Anne has returned from her mysterious errand—some business on behalf of her father, I would imagine. Not that I can blame her, really. Any excuse to get away from Sulla."

Theodore nodded again. He hadn't yet seen Anne—not since his return from Morytania. And she hadn't made any effort to seek him out, either. It made him wonder.

"Does she wish to see me, William?" he asked, uncertain as to whether or not he wanted to know the answer.

The young nobleman looked surprised.

"I believe she does," he said. "Yes. Absolutely. She told me she wants you to visit her tonight." There was an uneasy silence, and then William spoke again, his tone serious. "Do you know what will happen to Castimir?" he asked. "Do you know what you will say tomorrow, at the trial?"

Theodore sighed.

"No, I don't," he replied. "I have racked my brain for inspiration, but I am as uncertain now as I was when this all began." He bowed his head. "The truth is, Castimir *did* keep information from the Tower. He didn't steal it—not strictly speaking—but he broke their laws, nonetheless." He glanced sidelong at his friend. "Tell me, William, should I lie for him?" he asked, searching for guidance. "Would you?"

"He is your childhood friend, Theodore," William responded. "He has saved your life more than once. Do you really need to ask me that?"

Theodore smiled grimly.

"It has always been so easy for you, William. You have all the answers." He clenched his fists. "But if I lie, they will know, won't they? They are wizards, after all. And to lie goes against all I stand for—all that being a Knight of Falador stands for!"

His attention was drawn by a sudden clamor as Edmond submitted to Philip's final attack. The two men bowed to each other, and shook hands before clearing the way for another pair of combatants. Soon, the crash of steel was heard again.

"Has there been any news of Kara?" Theodore asked.

William shook his head.

"She went with Captain Hardinge and twenty men of the palace guard, leaving as soon as we heard the news. Theodore..." His voice faltered. "I think we must be prepared for the very worst news. Several bodies were found at the site of the massacre, and though Pia and Jack were not among them, I fear for their safety. Surely they could have made it to Varrock by now."

"Yet you know Kara, William," the knight said. "You know how stubborn she is. She will not stop until she finds them, or their bodies."

William sighed and nodded. When he spoke again, he weighed his words carefully.

"When Castimir was arrested, in the throne room—" He hesitated. "People are saying all sorts of things. And when you left, you and Kara didn't speak. What happened in there? What did you learn in Morytania?"

Theodore laughed bitterly.

"You know how I feel about Kara. You have known that since the very day I arrived."

William nodded.

"In the throne room, she said that she and Gar'rth had been lovers." Theodore felt his heart beat forcefully, and his eyes stung. "Gods…" he said. "Then afterward, among our friends, she claimed that she had lied to the king."

"Lied to him?" William frowned. "But why?"

"She said she wanted the king to think Gar'rth considered her of great importance—even more so than before." Theodore shook his head. "It means she will be needed in the days to come, for she may be able to exploit the affection our enemy feels for her."

"I don't understand, Theo," William said. "Gar'rth is your friend, isn't he? I certainly counted him as one when he came to Varrock."

The young knight nodded.

"There is much I haven't told you, William. Much I cannot tell you, for we were forbidden from doing so." He looked straight toward the combat, away from his friend. "Things are moving too fast, William. Since we returned everything is just… it all just feels out of control.

"I don't know what to believe," he said. "There is nothing I can do."

Before Lord William could reply, Hamel came running.

"It is time, sir," the boy said. "The priestess will be waiting." Theodore gritted his teeth and Hamel hesitated. "You did ask me to tell you when it was time, sir."

The knight nodded.

"You are quite right," he said. "Forgive me. And thank you."

He turned back to William.

"I am going to meet Arisha in the eastern bailey. She wants to know what I will say in Castimir's defense." He grimaced. "To lie, or not to lie," he remarked quietly.

William frowned.

"That is no question, Theo. The real one is simple," he said. "Will you do honor to a friend who has saved your life, and the lives of many others? Castimir is a good man. He deserves your support. He has earned it."

But as Theodore strode away, he knew it wasn't that simple.

The bells of the church sounded the eleventh hour. Ebenezer tried to count the chimes, but the sound was distant, faint to his old ears. He turned his head to listen better, leaning on his stick as he shifted his weight.

"He's coming, Ebenezer," Arisha said warily.

She is without hope, he thought. *She thinks she knows what Theodore will say.*

As do I.

The knight walked quickly toward them without smiling. He gave them both a brief bow.

"Thank you for coming, Theodore," Arisha said. "I think you know why I want to speak to you."

"Of course," he answered. "You want to know what I intend to say at Castimir's trial." He held up his hand to stop her before she could respond, and when he spoke, he did so quickly. Desperately, Ebenezer thought.

"The truth is, I do not know *what* to say. I don't know what form the trial will take. Will they ask me questions? Will I have to account for Castimir's actions after the Siege of Falador? I just don't know."

Ebenezer nodded in understanding, but Arisha's face darkened.

"Yet you will defend him, won't you?" she asked. "You will tell them that he is no thief."

Theodore's eyes darted away.

In Theodore's eyes, Castimir is a thief, the old alchemist mused.

"He *did* withhold knowledge from the Tower, Arisha," Theodore remarked, speaking as if the words left a bad taste in his mouth. "Knowledge that was rightfully theirs."

"But he did not *steal* it, Theodore," Arisha responded, her usual composure vanishing. "Surely there is a difference!"

Ebenezer shook his head, and spoke up.

"Not from the Tower's point of view, Arisha," he said. "To them, knowledge must be shared between all within the Tower. It was the hoarding of knowledge between wizards that led to the burning of the original Tower—as well you know—and among them the hoarding of knowledge is now considered a very grave crime."

"So what would you have me say?" Theodore asked desperately. "How can I lie when Castimir's own actions have so utterly condemned him?" The knight grabbed Arisha by the arm and Ebenezer heard his voice break. "I love him like a brother, Arisha. I do! You know that. But what story could I invent? What words could I say that would mask his actions?

"There are none," he said, and he pulled his hands away, clasping them to his head.

"He even wrote a *thesis* based on the books, for Saradomin's sake! A thesis that couldn't fail to come to the attention of his masters." He looked at her. "There is no lie I can invent that can account for that."

Arisha fell silent. She caressed the bruises upon her face.

"Couldn't you tell them he purchased the books after the Siege of Falador?" she asked "There would have been so much confusion in the city after the war—"

"They would know I lie," Theodore replied. "The wizards who are sitting in judgment will be among their most powerful members. For all I know, they could read my mind."

"No, Theodore," she replied, scolding him. "That is a myth—it is not true. You know the history of my people. A century ago we fought the wizards and drove them near to extinction, all for their blasphemous use of the runes. There were more of them, and they were far more powerful than they are now.

"If they had possessed the power to peer into our minds, then we would never have been able to defeat them."

"I agree," Ebenezer remarked, and he smiled ruefully. "I trained as a wizard in my youth, though I wasn't very good at it. Nevertheless, there was never any mention of such an ability." He shook his head. "More likely it is a ruse promoted by the Tower, to further their own myth of invincibility.

"I think many of their claims are false these days." He smiled. "Though I would never tell Castimir that."

Theodore's face brightened slightly, then he looked at Arisha.

"You have proven yourself as cunning as anyone I have met, Arisha," he said. "And I owe Castimir my life. Pray, tell me what *you* think I should say."

Arisha sighed and ran a finger over her blackened right eye. For several moments she remained silent.

"I haven't been allowed to see Castimir, so I do not know what he has already said," she finally admitted. "If he has said nothing, then we have a clean slate from which to start.

"The fact can't be hidden that he received the books in Falador, after the war," she continued. "But it might be said that he didn't know their true nature—that they were the books of Master Segainus. Not for certain, at least. And not if he came upon them by accident, or if some plunderer sold them to him."

Theodore's face screwed up in doubt.

The boy is capable in many things, Ebenezer observed, *but not this. It is the antithesis of everything he seeks to be.*

"I will have to see what they say tomorrow, Arisha," Theodore replied, his voice low. "If I can help him, I will do so. I promise. But we must consider the possibility that I may not be able to convince them." He peered at her again. "We must have a second plan, based on that chance."

"I have one in mind," Arisha said bitterly, "but it is an unlikely solution. No, Theodore. Our best hope is for you to convince the judges."

The knight's doubtful expression grew.

"I will do what I can," he said. "I can promise no more." Without another word, he turned and left them alone.

After a long moment, Ebenezer could not restrain his curiosity.

"Do you really have an alternative?" he asked. "I can think of none."

Arisha smiled, and there was cunning in her expression.

"I do," she said. "And it's actually a very good one. After Castimir's arrest I returned to the stables, to his horse. The book he took from Canifis was still in his saddlebags—he planned to retrieve it later on. It is similar to those he kept hidden from the Tower, and what is more, there are sections of it written in the common tongue. It might even serve as a way to translate the unknown text." She brushed her dark hair back over her shoulder and glared in triumph. "I would be willing to exchange it for his life."

"Why not do that now?" the alchemist asked incredulously. "And why not tell Theodore? The Tower obviously places a high value on these books. Surely they—"

Arisha raised her hand.

"Let us first see how the trial goes," she said. "It might be that we do not *need* to yield the book—not at all. That will depend entirely upon Theodore's words, and he is a bad liar at the best of times." She smiled grimly. "If he knew we had this alternative, he would lack the impetus to fabricate a tale, and his fiction would be transparent.

"Besides, I can't yet offer them the book," she said, "for I do not currently possess it."

"Don't possess it?" Ebenezer couldn't keep the exasperation

from his voice. "If you don't have it, then where is it?"

Arisha massaged the bruises upon her face, wincing slightly. "I owe Aubury for what his men did to me. It is an indignity I won't forget." She rubbed her blackened eye again, and when she moved her hand Ebenezer saw passion burning in her eyes.

"I don't have it, Ebenezer, because it is currently being copied—word for word, page for page—by two scribes I found in the city, the very day of Castimir's arrest. I offered them exceptionally good terms for their work, as long as the copy is both timely and—above all—accurate.

"They don't possess the knowledge to understand what they are transcribing," she added. "But if we have to hand it over, then Castimir will still have his copy."

Ebenezer couldn't help but smile at her cunning. She brushed her hair back once more and grinned in response.

"I couldn't permit Aubury to win everything, after all," she said. "Could I?"

10

Night had fallen in Varrock, yet still Theodore could not find peace.

In the hours following the meeting in the bailey, Arisha's words lost their power. So faded his commitment. Now, whenever he thought of Castimir's trial, he was more unnerved than ever.

He needed something to occupy his mind.

So it was that he found himself outside the door to Lady Anne's quarters. He raised his hand to knock on the door, but as his knuckle touched the wood his strength failed, resulting in a barely audible *tap*. He breathed out and knocked again, this time clenching his fist until his knuckles were white.

Rap-rap-rap.

After a moment, the door was unbolted from the inside and pulled open.

Lady Anne stood alone, framed in the doorway. Their eyes met under the dim light of the torches that lined the passageway.

She is so beautiful, he thought.

"My lady," he said quietly. His throat was dry.

"Sir Theodore," she replied in little more than a whisper.

His heart beat faster. He couldn't help himself from striding forward. His arms wrapped about her waist as she, too, advanced, her head pressing against his shoulder. Theodore breathed in, noticing the delicate smell of strawberry-scented perfume.

"I thought I would never see you again," she said. Her voice broke, and she sobbed. "I thought you would die in Morytania, and I hated Kara for making you go with her. All the time you were gone, Sulla taunted me about you."

"*Shhh.* I have come back," he whispered, cradling her. "I was unharmed. There is no need for you to cry anymore. Not now, not ever again." He felt tears come to his own eyes.

Why am I crying? he wondered.

Her touch felt so right to him, so natural that nothing about it could ever be wrong—of that he was certain, no matter what the holiest preacher would say from the whitest pulpit.

"Come," she whispered.

She guided him into her room, lit by many candles, and he heard the door close behind him. Blood roared through his body, thrilling him. His actions weren't his own, for a deep instinct had taken over, and he rejoiced in it.

"I love you, Theodore Kassel," Lady Anne whispered in his ear. "Stay here tonight, with me."

I would so love to do so, he thought. *But...*

"I cannot, Lady Anne," he said. "Not tonight. My friend is imprisoned, and he depends upon me tomorrow at his trial. I cannot sleep easily knowing that. And it would be very wrong for me to do so, given his plight." He lowered his head and kissed her neck, just below her right ear.

She gasped joyfully.

"I never want to risk losing you again, Theodore," she murmured, her left hand grasping the back of his head, her fingers running through his hair. "Please, stay. Please..."

He held his breath, then let it out.

"I cannot," he whispered, straightening. Her face looked up into his, her blue eyes filled with tears. "I would not cause dishonor to your name."

She frowned delicately.

"It is my honor, Theodore, to spend as I choose. And a man like you, a man as *good* as you…" She blinked, and a tear ran down her perfect cheek. "You would be *honoring* me. And besides, no one else would know."

"Yet I would know, Lady Anne. That is enough for me." He stepped back and held her shoulders at arm's length. "You are beautiful, Anne, beautiful beyond words. And right now I do need someone, someone to listen to me and to… to tell me everything will be all right."

She stared at him curiously, then she sniffed back a sob and took his hands in hers.

"My poor brave knight," she said without teasing. "I am here, and I will listen. I will listen as long as you want, to whatever you wish to say. And I will tell you, too—I will tell you a thousand times that everything will be all right." She pulled him to the bed and sat down. Following her instructions he laid his head down on her lap. He had never felt anything so good as her fingers brushing through his hair.

"I will tell you that everything will be all right," she whispered in his ear again. "And it will be, because we love each other, and no one can destroy what we have. No one."

A tear fell upon his cheek.

"Now," she said. "Tell me whatever you wish. I am here for you, my love. I am listening."

For how long he lay with his head upon her lap, he could not tell. The words poured out of him, and never once did she interrupt him. Nor did she cease stroking his hair.

Finally, he fell silent. After he had remained that way for several minutes, she spoke, and her voice was firm.

"It *will* be all right, Theodore," she said. "I promise you that. But you must stop punishing yourself. You seek something that is beyond the reach of any man, yet you will not let it go."

"What is that?" he murmured, lost in the pleasure of her touch.

"You strive to be a hero, Theodore," she replied. "You strive to live your life based on ideals that are *beyond* impossible." She bent down and kissed him on his forehead. "You are the noblest man I have ever known, sir knight. But if you continue to pursue such absolutes, then you will be driven to madness, or death."

She lifted his head from her lap and stood.

"Would you like a drink?" she asked, and her voice caught again, though slightly. "You must be thirsty after all your talking."

Her form was dim in the darkened room. The candles she had set out had long since burned low, and the only light came from a lantern that hung in the next chamber. Her shadow moved to a table, and he heard the gentle splash of liquid as it cascaded into a glass.

She appeared over him, holding two glasses, a goddess of mercy in a white silk dress. She held one of the glasses out to him.

"Here," she said. "Drink."

"Thank you," he said, taking it. Perhaps it was a trick of the gloom, but her eyes seemed unusually wide. "I really mean that, Anne. Thank you. I needed to talk to someone who cared, someone I... someone for whom I have the highest regard."

He grinned, hoping she would do the same. But she remained stoic, taking a sip from her glass, and he found himself looking at her more intently than before.

"Someone whom I love," Theodore whispered. "That person is you, Anne."

He raised the glass in preparation to drink when she halted him with a sudden cry.

"Theodore, wait!" she said, and then her voice softened. "Do you mean that... what you said? Do you *really* mean it?" She sat down next to him, her free hand resting on his wrist, preventing him from lifting the glass any farther.

"I do, Anne," he said. "I really do."

Again he tried to raise his drink, but Anne's hand remained in place. He looked down at it, briefly, and then he heard her sob.

She was crying.

"Anne?" he whispered. "What... what's wrong?"

"I want you," she began. "I want you to *go*, Theodore. Now. P-please, it is for your own good!"

He sat motionless, stunned.

"Anne, tell me—"

Suddenly she lashed out. Her free hand caught his wine glass and sent it flying from his grasp. It shattered in the shadows.

"Anne!"

"Go, Theodore—please go."

Reluctantly he stood.

"I will go, if that is your wish," he said, though his heart told him to stay. "But I don't understand, Anne. I thought that what I said was what you wished to hear."

She nodded as her sobs shook her body. Then she opened her tear-filled eyes and smiled over her crying.

"It is, Theodore," she said. "B-but you don't know me. There is far too much you don't understand."

"What?"

"P-please, please just go."

Theodore stepped back and watched her for a moment longer. Then he nodded. Without another word he strode to the door.

"Theodore, wait." Anne's voice was strained. As he turned he saw her take a hurried drink from her wine glass. She stared into his eyes and took a second great gulp. Then she stood and ran over to him.

"I love you, Theodore, more than you know." She held his face and kissed him on his cheek. "Please remember that."

Saying nothing more, she ushered him out into the passageway. Before he could turn, she closed the door and bolted it.

Theodore stood in silence, listening. But there was nothing to hear.

11

The world was twilight under the trees, for the afternoon sun could not penetrate the canopy above.

Kara-Meir focused on the trail ahead, her dark eyes examining as much detail as she could find. At her side, Captain Hardinge shifted uncomfortably.

"We'll lose them for sure in this light," he muttered bitterly. He'd been angry since the first sight of Mary's corpse. It was a feeling she shared.

I must be detached, she thought. *I must not let my passions get the better of me.*

"I won't lose them again, captain," she answered. "I can't. Not after bringing them back from the land of the dead. I gave them my word I'd protect them, and I won't leave here until I find them."

Dead or alive, she thought. But she refused to say it.

"The king might not like you gone for too long, Kara-Meir," he answered. Kara snorted.

"The king has other heroes he can call upon," she replied. "Sulla, for one."

Hardinge wisely kept his silence.

Sulla. She closed her eyes momentarily as she recalled Captain Rovin's triumphant face, just moments after Castimir's arrest. *Somehow I will finish what I started with him.*

When she looked again, her eye settled on a broken branch, level with a tall man's head. Pia and Jack's trail had been characterized by a meandering clumsiness through the wood, where haste had been more important than concealment. Blocked from going forward, paths taken would sometimes turn back on themselves.

All signs indicated that they had been pursued.

"How long a head start do you think they had?" her companion asked.

Kara had thought very hard on this key point.

"They stayed at least twelve hours within sight of the road," she said. "They remained quiet, and absolutely still all that time. Perhaps they expected help to arrive sooner, but evidently it did not. They probably heard Mary dying, only yards away."

Kara gritted her teeth, then continued.

"But when they moved, at night, that was when their unknown tracker discovered them."

Hardinge looked doubtful.

"How can you possibly tell that they moved at night?"

Kara smiled.

"It's a logical assumption, for one. Wouldn't you, if you were hiding from your enemies? But the evidence is clear enough. When they left their den they went in the dark, without a light. Their tracks are uneven, close together, indicative of people feeling their way. But the proof came when their tracks turned back on themselves, after encountering that impassable briar."

"How so?"

Kara sighed.

"In daylight, we could see the briar long before we reached it.

Yet their tracks led right up to it. Therefore, they had no way of seeing it until they ran into it. Hence, it must have been dark when they did so."

The man nodded, and he looked impressed.

"You are an able hunter, Kara-Meir."

"I grew up for a while in a village near Ice Mountain. My father was a woodcutter there. It was a wild place that I recall more in dreams than in memory now, but I remember the lessons I learned about hunting." She pursed her lips. "Strange, but after Sulla slew my family, the first thing to fade was the memory of the people who died, not the sights or the smells. Perhaps my mind was trying to protect me from harm."

She shook her head, to clear it. Then she looked to Hardinge.

"I am far from the most able hunter, captain," she said. "In my experience, that praise belongs to Gar'rth. Had he been with us now, we would have found them already."

The thought of Gar'rth stirred her.

I have dreamed of him recently, every night—him and Theodore, fighting over me. She shivered at the thought. *Gar'rth, evil and vicious. Theodore, noble and white, defeating the werewolf and rescuing me, always.*

She grimaced at the thought of the lie she had told to King Roald. She had said it only to convince him that she would be useful in his war. Yet it was a lie she knew had caused Theodore great pain. Later, when she had revealed the truth, his expression had spoken volumes.

He had not believed her.

The breeze stirred the canopy, and the twilight lightened for the briefest instant.

"Come," she said, "let us see what that broken branch tells us. It seems too high for either Pia or Jack to have made."

The two hastened along the trail to where she indicated. Kara examined the broken limb for only a few seconds before pushing aside the branches below.

There!

"A footprint, captain. A perfect footprint. And it is no doubt the print of our enemy—look."

"Is that the print of a rider's spur?"

Kara nodded.

"None of the escapees were wearing a spur. It has to be one of the attackers. Come!"

With renewed determination she took the trail up once more. For three hours they traveled south.

So many twists and turns, she observed. *They must be terribly panicked! Or worse...*

The afternoon progressed to early evening. Kara pulled ahead of her companion, and gave a muted cry of triumph. Hardinge ran to her side, standing upon a small hillock overlooking the trail ahead.

"What is it?" the captain asked.

"The spur print again, several times, one atop the other. Some quite deep."

"So he stood here for a time?"

Kara nodded.

"Perhaps he waited here last night," she offered. "And there is more. Look." She pointed to the shadowed ground where several white feathers lay caught among a spider's web. "And this also." Her finger shifted to a point just ahead of the spur print. Hardinge strained to see.

"Wood filings," Kara told him, picking one up and holding it in a ray of fading light for him to see. "Wood filings and feathers. What does that indicate?"

"A bowman," he said. "He waited here, pruned his arrows, and filed his sheafs." Kara nodded. "But where next? We cannot be far from Lord Ruthven's estates—most likely we are already upon them. Soon the forest will end, and we will be among his northern fields, where there won't be any cover for your friends."

"How far away are the fields?" Kara asked. Hardinge looked around.

"We can't be far from the end of it now. We've traveled south far enough to be only a few miles east of Saradomin's statue that we passed on the road. The forest end can't be more than a hundred yards that way." He pointed over her shoulder.

Kara turned and headed in the direction he had indicated, seeking the end of the trees. Abruptly they thinned, allowing more of the sunlight to penetrate. And then, quite suddenly, she found herself at the forest's edge, overlooking a wide expanse of green fields divided by low stone walls. They carried on for two miles or so before a second forest cut them off.

"Surely they will wait for darkness before crossing that?" Hardinge whispered.

Kara nodded.

"I agree," she said. "There is no sign of their trail here, so they must have holed themselves up, as they did before. Pia and Jack might be no more than a hundred yards from us, even now, waiting for nightfall.

"Hopefully our mysterious archer can't locate them, either," she added.

"What do you want to do, Kara?"

She thought for a moment, urging herself to be calm.

"We *could* try to scare the archer off. If he is alone, as we think, then together we could shout for Pia. If we raise enough of an alarm, he might mistake us for a larger search party and withdraw."

"You don't sound too hopeful," Hardinge observed.

"I think our chances of success are slim," she admitted. "Neither of us is armed with a bow, so he would have the advantage if we gave ourselves away." She looked into the young captain's eyes. "A very dangerous advantage, too."

"So we wait, and hold that plan as a last resort," he said. "What do we try in the meantime?"

"If we cannot track Pia and Jack anymore, then let us take up the trail of their hunter. We know he waited on a hillock previously, perhaps to view more ground. Would he do the same here?" She nodded. "I would, if I was a bowman readying an ambush. So, where is the high ground that overlooks these fields?"

Hardinge pointed.

"I think it is to the east. The land rises to a ridge there. That would be the best place to look." He peered out over the fields, and looked doubtful. "But Kara, it might be a mistake for both of us to go. It might be best if I waited here, for if Pia and Jack do run out at dusk, then there is a chance I could call them back. They should recognize me from our brief meeting at the Salve."

Kara stared skyward. Dusk was no more than an hour away. Quickly she drew her sword halfway from its scabbard before letting it slide back in. She did the same with her long hunting knife.

"That might be best," she agreed. "If it gets dark, you will not be able to see as well as I, and in the forest you could easily give yourself away." She saw his expression and shot him a smile. "I have an unfair advantage. After Sulla destroyed my village I was rescued by dwarfs from Ice Mountain. I grew up in the darkness of their caverns. To me, the night under the stars is clear as day."

Hardinge smiled back and bowed.

"Very well, Kara-Meir. I shall wait here until dawn, or until Pia and Jack reveal themselves. If I hear the sound of battle I shall follow the tree line and come when I may." He held out his hand. "Good luck."

She took the hand and shook it tightly.

"You also, captain. And I thank you for your help in this, whatever its outcome."

• • •

Kara retraced her steps at a brisk jog, aware that with every second the darkness grew. She had little time.

She returned to the hillock where the archer had waited. To the east, the land did indeed seem to rise, but the trees were thinned to the degree that there was no obvious trail to follow.

She sighed as she thought of what best to do.

If my prediction is correct, and he has taken the high ground, then it doesn't matter by what trail he has gone, she reflected. *It just matters where he is.*

Aware that she could easily miss some sign in her haste, but feeling the pressure of passing time, she took the path of least resistance and made directly for the ridge. Soft humus bedded her booted steps, swallowing a dried leaf she was careless enough to tread on, hiding its rustling sound.

Finally, crouching behind the thick bole of an ancient oak, she waited, forcing herself to listen.

Minutes passed.

The world darkened.

Please, Pia. She clutched the bark under her tense fingertips. *Please know patience this night.*

An owl hooted in triumph as it took a mouse from the ground, a bat's wing fluttered by her ear, and the trees sighed in the calming breeze.

Patience, Kara. It is the hardest skill to learn, yet the most important. She silently repeated the words her foster father—the dwarf smith Phyllis—had told her when she had been young and so full of anger, always rushing to avenge any perceived slight, be it real or imagined.

Patience.

She closed her eyes, anticipating the forest's sounds, breathing with it, searching for anything out of the ordinary.

Thump-thump-thump.

It was the repeating of the sound that drew her attention. It did not fit in with the forest around her.

Kara drew her hunting knife. Remaining crouched, she thrust it into the soft earth at the foot of the oak and withdrew it slowly. She smiled. The blade was dark with mud. No moonlight would reflect off it.

Thump-thump-thump.

She rose. The sound was off to the south, near the forest's edge. Her eyes examined the ground around her, evaluating the best route across. Only when she had found one that suited her best did she take a step.

Thump-thump-thump.

She stole ever closer to the source. The ridge rose before her, and as she crested it, she stopped behind a tree that grew upon its edge. Hardly daring to breathe, she waited, listening.

Thump-thump-thump.

She smiled grimly.

It was a horse, not ten feet away, looking gray in the dim light. The animal was tied and muzzled, yet its front hoof beat the earth. Beyond it a darker horse waited, also muzzled.

But there was no horse on the trail. It would have been impossible to take such an animal through the forest. Impossible for me to miss, as well.

One man must have tracked their prey, while another had rounded the forest with their steeds. It was the only explanation.

Kara gripped her knife tighter. She felt for the wind. Thankfully it was blowing away from the horse and toward her. There would be no danger of the animals picking up her scent and giving her away.

She made her way back around the tree, passing behind the

horses. Nearing the forest edge, she found what she had sought.

Two men stood with their backs to her, scant yards away. The taller shadow to the left was the archer, for he stood with his bow ready. Before him were three arrows, their heads embedded in the earth, ready to be strung at a moment's notice.

The man shifted his weight slightly as he stared over the rolling fields that stretched out below. As he did so a dull metallic *clunk* gave away the presence of his spur.

"We cannot miss them tonight, Martin," the unknown man whispered. "The old fox was very specific in his orders. He wants *no* loose ends."

The archer, Martin, spat at the speaker's feet.

"Then why don't you or your master curse them with your painted pebbles?"

Kara grew cold.

A wizard, she realized. *I've never actually fought a wizard. I cannot play any games with that one.*

"Oh, don't be so sullen, Martin. Runes are very rare things," the mage responded. "Not to be wasted." Then the wizard snickered. "Though I must admit, I did enjoy snaring those horses when the guards bore down on our unholy knight. It is a victory Zamorak can be proud of."

Suddenly Martin grabbed the nearest arrow. He moved forward, stepping out from the trees, and stared somewhere off to his right.

From far away, Kara thought she heard a shout.

"It's them!" Martin hissed, stringing his bow.

Kara leapt forward. Her knee drove into the wizard's spine as her right hand covered his mouth. At the same time she drew her left hand in, bringing the sharp tip of her knife into his throat.

The firm resistance of his windpipe softened, and she heard the air exhale wetly from his wound.

But she needed to be certain. She pulled him back and jerked her knife hand savagely to the left, twisting the blade as she did so. The wash of hot blood over her wrist and face told her she had severed his jugular.

The wizard flopped back soundlessly against her body as she drew him atop her, ensuring that his flailing limbs were beyond the reach of anything other than air.

Twang.

"I missed!" Martin cried. "Get the horses! We will need to ride them down—"

Kara-Meir dumped the wizard's corpse at her feet the moment the archer turned. Martin stared in amazement, and she held his gaze, freezing him as she drew her left arm back.

The bloodied knife left her hand and spun, end over end.

It missed his face by a hair's breadth and passed over his shoulder.

He smiled evilly.

"You missed," he said. "I don't know who you are, but you will suffer for what you did to my comrade." He grabbed the nearest of the remaining two arrows and readied his bow, never once taking his eyes off her.

"You can surrender, Martin," Kara said confidently. "If you do that, I will not hurt you."

Martin laughed scornfully.

"I've no fear of that," he replied. He lifted the arrow into place and pulled back the bowstring. "What…?"

The string was slack in his hand. It had been severed by Kara's knife.

She smiled her own wicked smile.

"I didn't miss," she said. "Now, will you surrender, or do you want me to hurt you?"

She threw back her cloak and drew her sword a foot from its scabbard. "Just give me a reason," she begged. "Please. For what you did to Mary."

Uncertainty flashed across his face, clear even in the gloom.

To him I am just a girl, she realized. *And he is becoming desperate.*

Kara drew her blade fully and stepped forward. The green-tinted metal flashed as Martin reached for his own long knife, exactly as Kara had anticipated.

He screamed as the sword severed the thumb and two fingers on his right hand. He fell to his knees and yelled at the sky as blood pumped from his injury.

"Now, your other hand."

"No… N-no. P-please."

Kara gritted her teeth and held the point of her sword to his throat.

"Your other hand. Hold it out. Now. Or I will take something more vital."

"Please," he wept. "P-please… I beg you."

"You are a murderer and a coward. And I will make sure you can do nothing of this kind again. Your other hand. *Now*." To spur him on, she allowed the blade to break skin.

Martin obeyed. His left hand shook uncontrollably.

"Wh-who are you?"

She raised her sword.

"I am Kara-Meir," she said. "And this is for Mary."

Her sword flashed down.

Martin screamed.

Captain Hardinge found her just a few moments later. Pia and Jack were behind him, both worn and pale and so exhausted as to be near dead on their feet. But otherwise they appeared to be unharmed.

Seeing her, they both lurched forward. She embraced them in a hug.

"Who are they?" Hardinge asked of the two men. The bowman

was curled up on the ground, moaning and holding his arms to his chest.

Nearby the horses fidgeted nervously. The dark one snorted.

"The man missing most of his fingers is Martin. He is—" she smiled grimly, "—or *was*, an archer. He killed Mary, and he will hang for it." She kicked the mage's body. "I don't know who he is, and Martin is too shocked to speak."

Hardinge turned over the body of the slain wizard, to view his face by the light of the moon. She thought she heard him inhale, but he just stared.

"Do you know him?" she asked.

Hardinge nodded. He put a hand over his mouth, and looked as if he might be sick.

"You know his cousin," he finally muttered. "Sir Theodore's best friend in Varrock."

Kara froze.

"Best friend?" she muttered. "Who?"

"Lord William," the captain said. "This is Lord William de Adlard's cousin." Hardinge shook his head. "There's nothing to indicate that Lord William was involved in the killings, of course," he added, "but nevertheless, it won't sit well at court."

The chattering of Jack's teeth stirred Kara to action.

"Let us return to Varrock," she said. "If we leave now we can be back in time for the morning sun." *And Castimir's trial too,* she thought. She stared back to the two horses that remained tethered nearby. "We can drop Martin off with your men, captain. I suggest we go now."

"And the body?" Hardinge nodded at the corpse.

"Leave it," she said. "It's the same courtesy he offered to poor Mary. Perhaps we will find some guards willing to come and retrieve it. But right now, our concern must be for the living. Pia and Jack need food, water and dry clothes."

Hardinge gave her a discreet nod as Kara dragged the failing Martin to his feet.

To her eyes, it looked like a nod of uncertainty.

And it made her feel uneasy.

12

Naked, Castimir was chained in complete darkness.

His hands were bound in thick gloves specifically designed to stop any dexterous use of his fingers that might contribute to the casting of a spell. Likewise he was kept gagged. The metal chair in which he sat pressed into the bruises where he had been beaten. His arms were chained above him, and always he was cold.

Terribly, terribly cold.

Time was lost on him. He wasn't sure if he ever slept, and if he did, his nightmares were no different from the horror of the waking world.

Sometimes the darkness would give its permission for a torch to enter its domain. Two men who never spoke would come and clean him where he sat. They would remove a stopper from his bespoke gag and pour bitter soup into his hungry mouth, his head tilted back to make sure he swallowed.

Whenever they did he wondered if it were poisoned.

Sometimes he wished it had been, for when they departed, he was left alone again with the darkness.

I cannot stand this, he despaired. *I will submit to anything you want me to say. Please, please just make the darkness go away.*

Please, Arisha… please be strong.

But the darkness did not answer.

I am not strong, he would say wordlessly, again and again and again. *I am not strong, I am not strong, I am not—*

The darkness never even listened. Or if it did, no doubt it found amusement in his suffering. Hunger. Cold. Fear. For how many days those were his only companions he did not—could not—know.

Finally, the light came again.

It hurt his eyes, and when the stinging finally subsided, he gazed into the face of the man who had orchestrated his humiliation. The man who was responsible for what had happened to Arisha.

"Your trial will commence shortly," Aubury said, walking behind him so he could not see. "You are accused of hiding knowledge from your betters. It is more than obvious you are guilty." The senior wizard walked around to face him again. "But you will be honored, for Sedridor himself has journeyed from the Tower to pass judgment on you. And with him comes Grayzag. It is he who has insisted on keeping you so uncomfortable." Aubury looked at his feet. "This isn't something with which I agree."

Grayzag, the Summoner? Castimir breathed deeply through his nose. *If what people whisper is true, then he should be here in my place.* The cold turned colder.

Aubury removed his monocle and breathed upon it.

"Few indeed are those who have been judged by such mighty men. None are wiser in all the world." He rubbed the monocle with the edge of his sleeve. "I hope that will comfort you when they pass their judgment." He looked into the shadows, out of range of the torchlight, and motioned with his head.

The two men who had fed and cleaned Castimir advanced and

knelt at his feet, busying themselves with his ankle restraints.

"It is time, Castimir," Aubury said, his voice low. "Time for you to face the consequences of your deceits."

One of the men stood and forced a black hood over his head. The darkness returned.

Castimir shut his eyes and forced back the tears.

And he prayed.

They wrapped him in a robe, fashioned so that his hands were held behind his back.

For several painful minutes he was pushed and pulled by his two silent guardians, guided up steps, along passages, and through low doorways. The temperature changed and he heard a distant birdsong, then he was thrust into a coach.

As they lurched into motion, Castimir tried desperately to listen for passing signs of life, to gauge his whereabouts. But it was pointless. All he heard was the hoofbeats of the horses and the clatter of the wheels.

Finally the horses slowed, then came to a stop. The coach door was opened and from outside he heard a large gate being pulled shut.

One of the men prodded him in the back while the other pulled his arm. He followed submissively.

They haven't burned a wizard for decades, he thought. *And they can't burn one now, can they? At this hour, with danger so near?*

He sobbed silently beneath his hood. He knew too well the arrogance of the Tower. They *would* burn him—because they were weak, with a perverse logic that it would only make them appear strong.

As he was guided up a narrow flight of wooden steps his sobs became moans, his footsteps ever heavier. He grabbed hold of the rail at his back in an effort to prevent his being taken any farther.

He was punched in the back for his trouble, and dragged more roughly than before.

The pain, however, gave him clarity. He remained silent now.

A creaking wooden door was opened above, and Castimir imagined for a second that he could hear Theodore's voice raised in argument, only to be silenced by the reply of another.

They have called him as a witness, Castimir thought, *as Aubury threatened to do. Oh, Theodore, anyone but you. They will run circles around you, for truth means nothing to them.*

His head fell in despair.

They stopped, and though his legs could hardly hold him, he was forced to stand upright. For how long, he did not know. Several times he thought he heard Theodore's voice again, often sounding anguished. But he could not make out the words.

Finally, a door was opened and Aubury's voice sounded.

"Bring the accused," he commanded. "Chain him, and remove his hood. Keep his gag in place."

I cannot let Theodore see me so weak, he thought, summoning whatever courage he could. *I will not cause him embarrassment.*

He was dragged into another room and guided up a step. He felt rough hands turn him around, then he heard the rattle of chains as they were fastened to loops in the back of his unfamiliar robe.

The hands that held him were gone, and the hood was finally removed.

White daylight flooded his eyes. He winced as he turned his head to one side. To his right, he saw Theodore's outline, standing in burnished armor. As his eyes adjusted he noted his friend's grim expression.

He looked away, and saw three robed men who sat on a platform that raised them above all others. They were positioned in front of a set of high windows, so their features were obscured by the glare. They were looking down upon the court.

Only seven persons were present, himself included.

A wizards' court, he knew. *Probably the same court where Salaman the Black was condemned, over a century ago. Will I be remembered as he is?*

His eyes focused and he looked again to the three men.

He recognized Aubury, scowling, seated on the left. Next to him was a pale-faced man with a straight brown beard.

Sedridor, he knew. *The greatest wizard in all the world. Quiet and unassuming, always busying himself in his private study in the basement of the Tower.* The man's face reflected neither hostility nor anger, but Castimir felt the intensity of his gaze.

Last there was Grayzag, wearing a brown beard and dressed more finely than his peers, with garish red and black trappings coloring his gray robe. He rose from his seat, staring with open hostility.

"Well, Castimir," Grayzag said. "It appears you have been less than honest with us." The master wizard nodded to one of the men who stood nearby. "Remove his gag. He may want to offer up some poor excuses before he burns."

The man moved to obey. As he unbuckled the straps, Castimir glanced at Sedridor, and was surprised to see a look of distaste as he gazed at Grayzag's back.

Is there conflict between them? he wondered fervently. *Is there some way I can use it to my advantage?* It was a dim hope, he knew, but he was at the point of grasping at straws.

For the first time since his imprisonment, the gag was removed. Castimir's mouth ached, and his jaw felt as if it had been dislocated.

"Speak, boy," Grayzag said, his voice booming. "Tell us how you plead to the charge of theft?"

He tried to answer, but no words would form.

"Shall we take your silence as an admission of guilt?" Grayzag asked, his voice mocking.

Aubury tilted his head.

"I fear the gag may have crippled him, Master Grayzag," he said. "We may have been too hard on him in his imprisonment—"

"I do not think so, Master Aubury," Grayzag answered, cutting him off. "This wretch sought to hide valuable knowledge from us. Knowledge that would allow him to build upon the very skills we taught him. And having done so, challenge our authority—perhaps even seek to usurp us.

"Now, boy, how do you plead?"

Castimir moved his jaw as much as he was able. Slowly, sensation returned.

"N-not... not guilty," he said. The words came as little more than a whisper. "Not guilty, master. I would never oppose the authority of the Tower."

Grayzag frowned. Taking advantage of his silence, Aubury stood and spoke.

"The knight has spoken on your behalf," he said. "His words were... interesting." He looked toward Theodore, and Castimir followed suit. But Theodore stared at the floor, and wouldn't meet his gaze. "Some here refuse to believe him."

Theodore turned then, and stared hard at the three men. Grayzag smirked at the knight's discomfort. Aubury raised an eyebrow.

"Perhaps you would care to add something further, sir knight?"

Castimir watched as Theodore took a deep breath, and nodded to him, his eyes sympathetic.

"We're waiting," Grayzag said.

"I have known Castimir all my life," Theodore began. "He was my best friend when we grew up in Rimmington. He helped me learn to read, and taught me stories of life beyond the confines of the manor in which I was born. He encouraged my desire to become a Knight of Falador, and I in turn encouraged him on his path to the Tower." His face darkened and he turned to Castimir again. Their eyes met.

"Perhaps, in hindsight, that is something I wish I could take back."

"Very few of us can read the future, Sir Theodore," Master Sedridor murmured. "It is foolish to punish yourself for something you did in good faith, based on trust in your fellow man."

Theodore acknowledged the wizard with a slight bow.

"Since then," he continued, "Castimir has saved my life on more than one occasion. Without his skills—which you in the Tower have so aptly taught him—I doubt very much if any of us would have escaped from Morytania. He is famous now, a hero, and a credit to the Tower. And he is a good person. That must be..." Theodore's fist clenched and his words grew passionate.

"That *must* count for something!" he concluded.

Grayzag snorted.

"You claim you are his best friend?" he said. "You say that he has saved your life—on more than one occasion?"

Theodore nodded vigorously.

"Absolutely," he responded. "It is the truth. I stand by my—"

Grayzag cut him off with a wave of his hand.

"If you are so indebted to him," the wizard said, "then we must question your own motives. As a Knight of Falador, you are sworn to truth, or that which you *believe* is the truth." Grayzag's taunting smile caused Theodore to wince.

Keep calm, Theodore, Castimir willed. *He's trying to goad you.*

"You are a man of duty, as well," Grayzag continued, and he nodded toward Castimir. "If a wretch such as this could convince you that you owe him your life, then you would feel a duty to aid him whenever you could. Is that not so?"

Theodore frowned.

Keep calm, Theodore, don't let him—

"Isn't that true, Sir Theodore?" Grayzag shouted. "Do you owe Castimir a life debt, that your honor binds you to repay?"

Theodore's face reddened.

"Yes, yes, of course it is," he said. "But I fail to understand—"

"So you admit it," Grayzag crowed. "You admit that your honor dictates that you will help your friend, by whatever means. Even if it means lying here today. Tell me, *Sir* Theodore, under such circumstances, why should we trust *anything* you have to say?"

Theodore's entire body shook. His face went red with anger. He gasped and looked quickly to Castimir. He mouthed a single word.

Sorry.

"Sit down, Master Grayzag." Sedridor's words were not to be refused. "You too, Sir Theodore. Sit now." Then the head of the Tower turned to face the accused.

"How do you explain the facts as we know them?" he demanded. "How *did* you get the books, and why did you not surrender them to us immediately?"

Castimir's mind whirled. None of the tales he had rehearsed in his mind answered all the arguments set against him. He felt his face redden in guilt.

"I—I am no thief," he uttered timidly.

Silence fell. After a moment Sedridor nodded dispassionately.

"Now, it is the time of judgment," he proclaimed.

Two small polished marble balls sat in front of each wizard— one black, the other white. Following Sedridor's lead, Grayzag and Aubury took them both in their clenched fists, hiding them from Castimir's view. One of the aides, the same man who had unfastened the gag, worked his way over to the desk and passed an urn between the judges. Three *clinks* sounded as each man dropped a marble into the vessel. Otherwise, all was silent in the court. Finally, the man approached Castimir. His eyes were fixed on the wizard.

Taking a breath, he upended the urn.

Thud-thud-thud.

Three polished balls fell to the wooden floorboards. At first he could not look.

He heard Theodore curse, and finally he sought across the darkened wood for them. He found it hard to focus, hard to see them.

Then he knew why.

"No... N-no," he gasped.

All three were black.

"You are found guilty, Castimir," Sedridor said. "As I think we all knew. The question that remains is of your punishment. Life, or death."

Castimir bowed his head, emotion welling up in him. A sob escaped, and then another.

All I have worked for, all I have loved, he thought. *It is all ended. Everything.*

He wept loudly, feeling Theodore's gaze on him as though it were a hot knife. But he had nowhere to hide.

"Raise your head, Castimir," Sedridor instructed. "The moment of your judgment is at hand."

Castimir did as he was commanded and saw that the three wizards had walked to the side of the room, to stand in a group on his left. Sedridor stepped forward.

"The runes will speak your sentence." Sedridor opened his palm and held a curious pebble toward him. Castimir, though familiar with it, could not help but look. The rune stone was gray, and on its smooth surface was painted a white skull with two bones crossed beneath it.

Death.

Sedridor closed his fist and offered his other hand.

"But there is also life, here, Castimir. Should even one of us vote for that, then you will be spared. But you will be expelled from the Tower." Sedridor's fist unclenched to reveal the rune nestled in his palm. The scales of justice were visible on its surface, painted in a bright blue.

"Let's be about it," Grayzag snapped, motioning anew for the urn. He grinned at Castimir as he held up his hand, balancing a single rune between two fingers. A death rune.

Castimir shook his head.

"P-please," he uttered. "Please don't—"

Clink.

Grayzag dropped the death rune into the urn. Aubury's face darkened as he witnessed the torture, but he said nothing. Sedridor's gaze was unreadable.

Then he too held out his hand as the urn was offered. He kept his choice hidden from Castimir, and still the wizard's face revealed nothing of his decision.

Clink.

Castimir lowered his face and wept anew.

Please, have mercy, he begged silently.

Finally, Aubury stood over the urn. Castimir raised his head to look at the old man through his blurred eyes.

"Please…" he muttered.

Aubury's mouth straightened in determination. He turned his eyes away as he opened his hand over the urn, the rune hidden.

Clink.

Sedridor nodded to the urn's carrier, who stepped to the center of the room. Castimir saw Theodore behind, his face hidden in his hands.

"Theo," he said, his voice strangled. "Theo, you can't let them— you can't…"

The knight heard his words and looked up. His eyes were red and his face was contorted in anger. Then he closed his eyes and lowered his head again.

"Theo!"

Thud.

The first of the runes had dropped from the urn. Castimir stared across the darkened wood to find it.

"No…"

For it was a death rune.

The carrier angled the urn slightly. Castimir couldn't tell if he was taking delight in prolonging the process.

Thud.

Death. Again.

"No! No no no no no," Castimir raged at his chains as he wept. "I am a good man," he cried. "I am not a thief! I am not, not, *not.*"

He closed his eyes and drew an exhausted breath.

Thud.

Castimir kept his eyes closed. Across the room, Theodore gave a strained gasp.

"Who?" Grayzag muttered angrily.

Castimir opened his eyes and searched the floor. His heart was pounding hard enough to bruise his ribs. He moaned softly as he sought for the final rune.

"Where? Where is it?" he gasped.

"It is here. By my foot," Sedridor said. "Look."

The master wizard tapped his right foot on the dark floorboard.

And there it was. The blue scales of justice face up.

A law rune.

Castimir's strength left him in that instant. He fell, his hands still chained at his back, gasping. And laughing—laughing as he had never done before. And he wept. He wept because he would live, because the last few days would shortly be a memory. He would hold Arisha again, and he would breathe the air at her side. It no longer mattered that he would never again hold a rune, or summon the strength to unleash its power.

Only one thing mattered.

I will live. I will live!

13

The moments that followed were swept away as Castimir was taken by his two silent guardians and thrust into a black coach. He didn't say anything as Aubury got in and sat opposite him, for he wasn't in any mood to talk to the man. The courtyard gate was opened and the horses neighed as they were driven forward.

Tears of relief still rolled down his face as he gasped for air. He found a water flask that had been left at his feet. Picking it up, he drank greedily.

They passed the markets, where the traders were setting out their wares. He hadn't realized it was so early in the morning still. At the city's wells lines of women and children waited patiently to draw water with which to cook their breakfasts.

"What will you do now?" Aubury asked slowly. Castimir looked at the man who had ruined him, and an odd sensation swept over him.

He began to grin.

I don't need him anymore, he thought. *I don't live by Aubury's rules.*

"I'll think of something," he replied, feeling strangely confident. *I do not need money,* he realized. *I have Gar'rth to thank for that.*

As they traveled, however, a pang of regret hit him. Thoughts of Gar'rth, of Theodore, Arisha, and all of his friends brought to mind the experiences they had shared. He would no longer experience life as he had—he would be without the respect and deference he had been shown by peasants and nobility alike.

His confidence began to fade.

"Can there ever be a chance of me coming back?" he asked Aubury. "To the Tower?"

The man tilted his head.

"None whatsoever."

Castimir cursed silently and looked out through the window. Theodore was riding just ahead, and as the wizard peered at him, he glanced back. The young knight's expression seemed oddly guilty.

"What did Theo say in there," he asked without moving his gaze, "when you questioned him?"

Aubury let a moment pass before answering.

"He tried to help you, I suppose. In the only way a man like that could." He hesitated before continuing. "In truth, he was no help to you at all. In the end he told us all we needed to know to make our decision." The wizard shrugged. "Perhaps he tried to shape the truth on your behalf, I don't know. But regardless, it was the truth.

"I think a man such as he believes that honor begets honor. That one kindness will deserve another. That the 'truth will out,' so to speak." He watched Castimir for a long second and then rubbed his gray beard. "Pitiful, really. Quite pitiful."

Castimir lay back in his seat and regarded Aubury silently, remembering what the man had done to Arisha. His anger overcame his relief.

"Where are you taking me?" he asked after a time.

Aubury smiled cryptically.

"Your days of working for the Tower are over, Castimir. We all know that. We all accept it." He removed his monocle and rubbed it on his sleeve. It brought back unpleasant memories of Castimir's time in the darkness.

Aubury's darkness, he thought savagely. *I still owe you.*

"However, Castimir, your days working as a mage are only now beginning."

"What?" Castimir was taken aback. "What do you mean?"

"The Tower hasn't taken an active role in the world for many years, Castimir." Aubury's eyes focused on him sternly. "You know that—and you know why. We don't have the runes anymore.

"But a place like Varrock, so close to Morytania and The Wilderness, is of great importance to us," he continued. "What's more, monetary contributions from the crown are what keep the Tower viable." Aubury blew on his monocle again and held it up to the light of the window. "Under such circumstances, well, let us just say we need to prove our worth."

"How do you accomplish such a thing, without placing yourselves at risk?" Castimir asked, a touch of derision in his voice. "And how does it involve me?"

"Renegades!" Aubury replied. He put his monocle back to his eye with a smile. "Varrock is a magnet for adventurers, among them many self-proclaimed magic users. There are even a few *female* ones, would you believe? Like the enchanting Turine, who helped Sulla destroy the Wyrd." He peered at Castimir, a new light in his eyes. "Managing them is what I do in Varrock." He smiled smugly. "The Tower knows of it. They even understand the need for it.

"We are a *political* power these days, Castimir, not magical— at least not in any meaningful way. The people still revere us, of course, mostly thanks to our glorious past. But those days

LEGACY OF BLOOD 129

are dead and gone. The barbarian crusade drove us to the edge of extinction, and much of our knowledge was lost." Aubury frowned. "Perhaps forever."

"And so you use others to fight your wars," Castimir muttered. "You play upon your reputations as keepers of great secrets. No doubt kings are impressed with that, and mages who operate without the Tower's consent are cowed enough to cooperate."

Aubury nodded.

"It only takes a little magic to convince a king that we have a lot," he admitted. "Yet we are not just frauds, Castimir. We still *do* possess power, but it is a remnant of past times.

"And this will be to your advantage," he added. "You should see it as a grand opportunity. No longer will you be bound by the traditions and ceremony of the Tower. You will be free to do what really matters in the world."

"And what is that?"

"The king has called a meeting to discuss the Zamorak insurrection," Aubury said. "You will be free to help your friends with their investigations, spending as much time with them as you like." He smiled rudely. "Even with Arisha."

He treats us as if we are pieces on a board, Castimir mused, raging inwardly. *As if he is playing a game.* But he kept his tongue.

"Oh, don't frown so, Castimir," the older wizard said. "Your barbarian pet is made of stern stuff. The people of the tribes aren't weaklings." He looked through the window to where Theodore had fallen behind, then snorted in disdain. "She certainly has more backbone than *that* truth-besotted fool. I didn't dare ask for her as a witness at your trial, you know, for she would have had enough conviction to lie, and to do so most effectively."

Castimir glanced out at Theodore and couldn't help but feel let down.

Does he put his duty, his honor, ahead of my life? It was a question he couldn't answer. And a part of him didn't want to, for deep down he knew. The more he thought about it, the more his disappointment turned to anger.

The coach rolled to a stop in front of an unassuming brick-and-plaster structure.

"Ah, we are here," Aubury announced. "My home." He glanced at Castimir and smiled. "It's about time we got you out of those rags and into something more suitable. Something an adventurer might wear. Come!"

He opened the door and stepped down. Castimir followed.

"There is one thing I must know, Aubury," he said, "the law rune. That was… that was yours?"

Aubury smiled in a way that reminded Castimir of a friendly uncle.

"Yes, Castimir, it was." He winked. "Your crimes were serious, but your new role was already decided. Master Sedridor and I had already agreed upon it. He only voted for your death in order to placate Grayzag—knowing that I would grant you life. As I said, it's all politics with us in this day and age." He frowned as he withdrew a key from his pocket. "Now, come!"

Aubury stepped up to the front door as Theodore reined his horse to a halt. Castimir waited for his friend to dismount.

"Ah, Sir Theodore," Aubury called before either could utter a word. "I have told Castimir how helpful you were at his trial. How your honest assessment swayed our undecided minds."

Theodore shook his head.

"It wasn't like that, Castimir, it really wasn't."

Castimir remained silent.

I know you, Theodore. I know you better than you know yourself.

Theodore smiled hopefully. Castimir couldn't recall seeing anything so pathetic.

"I couldn't lie, Castimir," he said. "I thought I might try, but I couldn't—" Theodore's smile vanished. He looked awkwardly to one side. "I *tried*, Cas... really I tried." He exhaled loudly and then clenched his fist. "I was there, wasn't I?" Anger tainted his words.

Finally, the knight took Castimir's arm in a firm grip.

"Say something, Castimir. Please tell me—"

"I *know* what you said, Theodore," Castimir growled, tearing his arm free. "My career was ruined today, partly because you hold your own precious honor in more value than my life." He watched as a pained look appeared on the knight's face. It gave him a sudden sense of power, and it felt good. "How would you have felt if our roles were reversed, Theo? What would you have said to me if I hadn't bent the truth, ever so slightly, to allow you to remain a Knight of Falador?" His eyes burned.

"You didn't even *try!*" Castimir yelled. "Not for me, not for your best friend. That's what hurts so much!"

Theodore's face fell. Castimir saw the tears in his eyes, but still he wanted more.

"And if your honor is so precious to you, then why did you not go to the Tower as soon as you knew I had the books?" he demanded. "Why didn't you do so then, six months ago, if you were so convinced that what I was doing was wrong?"

Theodore winced.

"I'll tell you why!" Castimir hissed, his arms waving. "You didn't do it because your honor wasn't in danger. You could turn a blind eye, and as long as no one asked, you could pretend no wrong had been committed. But when I was found out," he said, "and when you were called as a witness, only then, only *then* could you *refuse* to lie. For the danger of being caught was too great." His tears flowed freely now. "Only then—when everything I desired was called into question, when my very *life* was at stake. *Only then!*"

Theodore lifted his head. His face was blanched white, his eyes red. He sucked in his lips, and slowly shook his head from side to side.

"It's not true, Castimir," he said quietly. "It didn't happen like that."

"You're a hypocrite, Theodore. A damned lying hypocrite! You and all of your knights, with your righteous honor. Kara thinks so too, after you used her as bait in Falador. She's never forgiven you for that."

"Please, Castimir—"

The young wizard gestured angrily.

"Go away, Theodore. Just go." He turned and walked to stand at Aubury's side. Then he paused and looked back, and when he spoke he did so coldly. "I will return to the palace this afternoon. Tell Arisha to expect me."

He enjoyed the knight's pain.

"Castimir... Cas," he said. "Please—"

Before he could continue, Castimir followed Aubury through the door, and shut it behind him.

14

Doric waited at the top of the spiral stairs as Ebenezer wheezed his way up the narrow well of King Botolph's Tower. The dwarf stared at him for a brief second before speaking, and the alchemist thought he saw a flicker of concern pass over his rugged features.

"Just let me get my breath, my friend," he whispered as he reached the penultimate step. Doric nodded, then stepped into the room and looked around him.

"More prison than any nursery I ever saw," he muttered. "Bars on the outside *and* inside of the windows, so tight a child's hand couldn't fit through. The chimney has been blocked off, and no doubt there's a guard hidden halfway up it." He rolled his eyes. "Probably a legion, in fact."

He smiled as a dark-haired woman rose abruptly from her chair, which was situated at the side of a baby's cot.

"Surely you understand why," she said sharply.

Doric's eyes widened, and he reddened.

"Good morning, Lady Ellamaria," Ebenezer said cheerfully.

"May I be so kind as to beg a seat off you? My legs are not what they once were."

Few things are, he thought bitterly. *Ever since the Wyrd's attack I have been fatigued, as if ten extra years have been added to my age.*

Ellamaria's expression softened and she beckoned him forward.

"Of course, my friend. Please." She gestured to the chair at the side of the cot. "Take mine."

He shuffled forward and sank gratefully into it.

"Did Felicity have a good night?" he asked.

Ellamaria nodded.

"Gideon Gleeman saw to it that she never was alone. She rested comfortably, and never once cried out. Her mother, however, is beside herself, for she can't understand why she isn't allowed to visit her daughter."

Doric moved to stand at his friend's side, and stared down into the cot.

"If what we suspect true," he said, "if the fate of the River Salve depends upon keeping her out of the enemy's hands, then the king is right to be so cautious. For a desperate mother might not think or act wisely." The dwarf shook his head. "So much depends upon her that he cannot afford even a moment's weakness. King Roald must be a rock in this hour—not a thing of blood or heart."

Ellamaria nodded. Her eyes misted.

"He knows, oh, how he knows. But you are right, master dwarf. He is a king, not a man." She looked into the cot. "And we must all do our duties as best we can, to help him make the wisest choices, however demanding they may be." Her face grew angry.

"Sometimes I don't believe the people of his realm understand that," she continued. "These riots, and the reports of sedition, all brought about by the prophecy! They don't know how well they live in Misthalin."

Ebenezer nodded.

Yet how quickly you have changed, my dear, he mused. *It wasn't long ago that you broke the laws to disguise yourself as a noble. The people were on your side then. Perhaps, being so close to the heart of power, you have seen the burden a crowned head must carry.*

He turned as Doric spoke up.

"You are right, my lady. I have seen how people live in Morytania." He frowned. "It is a shame that so many this side of the river think that the harsh truths are only legends. If they could see for themselves, then they would appreciate King Roald all the more."

"You speak wisely, Doric." A man's gravelly voice came from the stairs. "Such thoughts have occupied my mind, as well."

Lord Despaard, cloaked as ever in his black tunic, strode into the room.

"For the people to understand, first they must know the truth," he continued. "Gideon Gleeman is sitting with Karnac, and writing down all of his experiences in the land beyond the river. It will reveal the realities of Drakan's realm, and add enormously to our knowledge of the place."

"Has there been any news of the refugees?" Doric asked. "Has Kara sent word?"

Lord Despaard shook his head. He thrust his gloved hand back through his gray-peppered black hair.

"There has been nothing yet," he said. "Karnac has been driven to the edge of despair by it."

"Can you blame him?" Doric said.

"No," Despaard said. "No, I cannot."

"And what of Castimir?" Ebenezer asked. "What news is there of the wizard?"

Despaard frowned.

"Theodore has returned, and he was quite upset. He is with Lady Anne." Despaard smiled slightly. It didn't suit his face, the

alchemist observed, and it didn't last. "As for Castimir, I gather he
will be present at King Roald's gathering. He may be here already."

Doric grinned widely, and Ebenezer felt his heart leap.

"Then Castimir is…" he began. "Is he free? Has he been
exonerated?"

Lord Despaard shook his head.

"The Tower has reassigned him, master alchemist," he said, and
Ellamaria looked confused. "As I understand it, he will be working
under Aubury's guidance."

Doric snorted.

"Aubury?" he said derisively. "Arisha is going to be thrilled to
hear that news."

"Hearts of stone, Doric," Ebenezer muttered. "In such an hour as
this, we must be rocks, just as we expect of the king." He strained
to his feet and cast a paternal look into the cot, where Felicity slept
soundly. The mysterious birthmark on her chest was hidden under
a white blanket.

"And now, we must be off," he said. "Let us see what will be
revealed at the king's gathering."

Ebenezer's aching limbs were forgotten as he followed Doric into
the throne room. People spoke in excited whispers, and an electric
tension infused the atmosphere.

"Kara-Meir has returned," Lord William whispered as they found
their places to the right of the yellow carpet that ran in a straight line
to the king's throne. "She has found Pia and Jack, and some others
have been rescued, as well. Master Peregrim was found, and two of
Karnac's refugees. They have all been brought back here."

The tramp of booted feet sounded on the stone. Kara-Meir
appeared, with a red streak over her face.

"Is that—is that blood?" Lord William stammered as she
approaches.

Kara blinked once, her face unreadable. She stared coldly at William and then, without a word, she made her way to Captain Rovin.

William huffed.

"What did I say?"

"Leave her, lad," Doric instructed. "It looks like she's had a fight on her hands. Sometimes the temper gets hold of you in a moment like that, and it can take a while to calm down." He winked. "You know what I mean."

William looked doubtful. He grasped at the silver fox, the sigil of his house.

"No," he said. "No I don't."

Rovin's eyes were wide as he listened to Kara's whispers.

"Is the captain staring at me?" William asked faintly.

Before anyone could respond, more people entered the throne room. Ebenezer turned as someone stepped next to him, closer than was necessary. Grumbling, he looked up.

It was Castimir. At his side stood Arisha. Gone were his blue robes, and there was no sign on his fire staff. Without intending to, Ebenezer stared curiously. The priestess saw his expression, and gave a brief smirk.

"You look like a vagabond," Doric observed with a chuckle, and it was clear from his expression that he was pleased to see their friend.

Castimir wore a studded-leather brown jerkin, beneath which Ebenezer saw a long-sleeved burgundy shirt. A black belt was coiled about his waist, with two daggers hanging from the left side. Over his shoulder he carried a satchel that rested against his right thigh. His feet were booted, and the trousers he wore were hard leather.

He looks more like an archer than a wizard, Ebenezer thought.

"What happened to you?" he asked. Then he smiled. "Did

someone knock you on the head?"

Castimir didn't return the smile. He gazed across the carpet toward Kara, where Theodore had joined her. The knight saw him and turned away.

Castimir kept staring.

"I am no longer of the Tower, Ebenezer," he said frostily. "I have been expelled. I am forbidden from wearing the blue robes and, in theory, from using magic." He patted the satchel, however, and Ebenezer thought he heard the *chink* of rune stones.

"Is that safe for you to have?" he asked.

Castimir nodded.

"Apparently Varrock uses rogue wizards all the time. Freelance mercenaries and adventurers. I am one of them now." He pointed as Aubury entered the chamber, following in the king's wake. The chatter died as Roald advanced to his throne. "The Tower *knows* about it, Ebenezer. They even support it," he whispered. "They have done so for years."

The king took his place upon the throne, where he was illuminated by the morning sun that shone through the stained-glass windows. Raispher stood to his right.

"Before I take counsel with my closest advisors, I wish first to address news of the insurrection." King Roald glared at the assembled courtiers. "I know that most of you find their attacks abhorrent, and condemn them," he said. "But not all feel the same."

Ebenezer felt his heart beat faster.

"Some of you, I am led to believe, have even had a hand in the uprisings."

Lord William moaned.

Gasps and cries issued from the crowd.

"Silence!" Raispher bellowed. Despite his intensity, he seemed inexplicably pleased. "Silence for his majesty!" The Saradominist priest bashed his golden staff upon the ground, only to find it muffled by the yellow carpet. Saving what dignity he could, he angrily stretched out his hand and brought it down again, ensuring that the staff impacted upon the flagstones.

This is the last thing Varrock needs now, Ebenezer thought.

"It is true," King Roald said, his voice loud to be heard over the din. "Not all practice the religion of Saradomin. Some worship Guthix, and others—an influential minority—worship Zamorak." He paused as the murmurs died out, then continued.

"The worship of Zamorak *cannot* be tolerated," he said. "Not in this hour, as our enemies are gathering. The attacks against my people and my property are carried out by his worshipers.

"I know this beyond the shadow of a doubt."

King Roald stood.

"Granaries have been burned. Wells tainted. Seditious messages painted on walls. Prominent citizens have been harassed, even assaulted. Let me be clear. Let me be very, very clear."

He stepped down from his throne and walked several yards along the carpet. His face reddened behind his beard.

"If any of you—*any* of you—are found to be involved in these activities, then I give you my word that I will take everything you possess. Your properties." King Roald turned in a wide circle to stare into the faces of the assembled. "Your estates. Your castles. Your peasants. Even your *children.*" He held up his hand and pointed a finger skyward. "And then you will suffer a death such as no man or woman in Misthalin has suffered in decades. I promise you this."

King Roald breathed heavily, and with a grim look he returned to his throne. When he neared, Raispher stepped forward and whispered urgently in his ear. The king nodded, then turned back to address the onlookers.

"With immediate effect, and by royal decree," he said, "I am reinstating the Inquisition of Saradomin, to be headed by Raispher.

Anyone suspected of a hand in these attacks will answer to him."

The king sat, and the court erupted. People shouted, some cried, one or two even wept.

"This is madness. Utter madness," Lord William hissed, and he trembled. "Raispher is mad, yet now he has got what he always wanted. Real power."

King Roald remained motionless, his eyes fixed.

15

As the room emptied, Kara-Meir watched one man more intently than any other. To her eyes, Lord William de Adlard looked genuinely fearful.

Yet so do many others, she realized. *And it's not difficult to see why. Raispher. A weak man given absolute power.*

When the priest departed, everyone gave him as wide a berth as possible, seeking to avoid his unwelcome attention. Through it all, Raispher beamed.

He stands taller and more fanatical than ever, Kara mused, and she shivered at the thought.

Near the entrance to the throne room, she saw Lady Caroline embrace Lord William. His face was whiter than usual, and they both looked bleak.

With good reason, she thought. *No good will come of this, especially now.*

Then the doors were shut, and only a select few remained behind with the king. Theodore stood at her side, his features sullen, while across the carpet Castimir stood with Arisha. Aubury gazed at the priestess, who occasionally returned his look with a cold stare. Ebenezer retreated to a chair by the wall, his legs shaking as Doric guided him down. The only other person who sat was Papelford, the ancient librarian, swallowed in his great bearskin cloak.

"Is the main entrance sealed?" Lord Despaard called to Rovin. The captain nodded as he took his place next to the throne.

Kara watched as a side door opened, off to her right. Reldo entered. Gleeman and Karnac followed. Behind them came Lord Ruthven, who locked the door with an iron key.

"We are all here now," King Roald said in a low tone. "We are the only ones who know the true nature of the threat. No one outside this room knows that it is my own ancestor who seeks to usurp us." The king glanced at Aubury. "You have been informed, haven't you?"

"I have, sire, thank you." Aubury bowed. "And Master Sedridor himself is currently in Varrock, as I believe you know. I have shared the details of the threat with him, as was your desire."

King Roald nodded.

"Very good," he said. "The help of the Tower will be needed in the days to come." He looked from person to person. "Tell me what we have learned since our last meeting."

For a moment no one spoke. Then Lord Despaard stirred.

"Sire, I believe we are making a mistake with the Inquisition. It will cause those who don't follow Saradomin to take up arms, at a time when we need the support of every citizen." He bowed his head. "Is there any chance you will reconsider?"

The king shook his head.

"I would rather have ten foes arrayed openly against me, than have one remain unknown," he said. "There can be no middle ground in the fight to come. It is a hard choice I have made but, for now, it will suit our purposes."

"Very well, sire." Despaard stepped away from the throne. Then

Captain Rovin spoke up, and Kara felt his eyes on her.

"The latest atrocity these insurrectionists have committed is an attack on the Morytanian refugees." He paused, then continued. "Only five survived." She heard Karnac gasp as if he had been stabbed.

"W-who?" he stammered. Kara stepped forward.

"I found Pia and Jack," she said. "Master Peregrim, the gnome pilot, was found by Captain Hardinge's men, as were two others. All were exhausted, but they are relatively unharmed, and are here now. Lady Caroline's maid, Lucretia, is helping with their recovery, as too is Sally."

"Mary... what about Mary?" Karnac asked. Gleeman's hand squeezed his shoulder. The jester had never looked so worn, so broken, as he did then, Kara thought.

She winced.

"I am sorry, Karnac," she said. The man's face seemed to cave in. He hunched over and sobbed uncontrollably. "But she was the very first to die. She would have done so, I think, without being aware of it, so quick and fatal was her injury."

Guthix forgive me for that lie, she thought. *But the poor man has been through so much.*

"Why did they attack the group in the first place?" Doric growled. "It makes no sense. A column of refugees, under official guard. What's the point? What's to gain?"

"Some of the bodies were heaped onto a cart and burned," Captain Rovin reported. "Others were mutilated. All, I think, were robbed of their valuables. But Kara told me that Pia heard two of the men talking about finding something—something they seemed to expect. She did not know what, though."

Kara nodded.

"And the man I killed, the wizard—" she held Rovin's gaze for a moment, "—he had been ordered by his master, whom he called

'the old fox,' to make certain there were no witnesses." She stamped
her foot angrily. "There *must* have been a reason for the attack."

Silence fell for a long moment, then Despaard spoke.

"I will take some of my men and ride out there today," he said. "It
might be we can find something, now that the attackers have gone."

Captain Rovin shifted his weight from one foot to another, and
then addressed the king.

"We have a prisoner, sire," he said. "A man called Martin. But in
order to make him reveal what he knows, we might need to resort
to torture."

"That is forbidden against citizens of Misthalin," Ebenezer said
from his chair. "Surely we cannot—"

"Do it," King Roald commanded. "Place his fingers in the
screws—or any other part of him, for that matter—but find out
whatever you can." He glared angrily. "This man, Martin, has slain
my people. He has forfeited the right to call himself a citizen. He is
an enemy of the realm now."

"Make him scream," Karnac said bitterly. "Make him *scream*."

Despaard bowed his head and frowned. Ebenezer moaned.

Torture and an inquisition, Kara thought. *Just yesterday Misthalin
was an enlightened realm.*

"Very well," the king muttered. He frowned at the floor for a
moment, and then looked up again. "Where do we stand with our
inquiries concerning Felicity and her relation to the River Salve?"

Reldo stepped forward. The young man had aged visibly since
Kara had seen him last. His eyes sat on two black, puffed cheeks,
his hair unkempt and uncared for.

"I have been told of all the embassy has discovered," he said.
"And I believe I have found something that could help us if the
Salve fails." He held up a small book in his palm. Kara noticed how
Papelford suddenly became more animated. The old man strained
to see.

"This book tells of a tradition in which the kings of Misthalin used to participate." He smiled wanly, his thin beard lifting as he did so. "Upon a monarch's coronation, each new ruler would make a pilgrimage to Paterdomus. There he would submit an offering to the river, in acknowledgment of its power and the fact that the security of the realm depended upon it. The offering is described as *essence,* given to the king by the Wizards' Tower, and blessed by priests of Saradomin.

"Legend has it that this essence strengthened the Salve and helped to keep it pure."

Kara frowned.

"Essence?" Papelford snapped, a look of disdain on his face. "Is that all you have to offer? What is this *essence*?"

Reldo shook his head in defeat.

"The records do not say," he admitted. "But the illustrations seem to indicate a stone tablet of sorts, about the size of a dinner plate."

"*Bah!* Young fool." Papelford stood and turned to the king. "We are placing too much emphasis on legends and myth. Such things will not help us." The old man's wizened face furrowed. He gave a sudden, deep breath.

Lord Despaard stepped closer behind him.

Ebenezer also stood. The white-haired alchemist spoke up.

"It is all we have!" he shouted across the carpet, glaring openly at Papelford. "Your own efforts have been woeful. When the Wyrd's attacks began, it was all you could do to conceal the corpses in the palace crypt." He advanced, his face wrathful. Doric walked beside him.

"You are too old for this game, Papelford," Ebenezer chided. "You are confused, have made mistakes." The alchemist sighed. "I am sorry. I am. But it needs to be said."

"Mistakes?" Papelford gurgled. "I have not made a single mistake. Not one! I-I *defy* you." Papelford gritted his teeth in anguish. "Name one," he whispered. "Name just one."

"You told me in the crypts," Ebenezer countered, "as we examined the still-fresh corpses of the Wyrd's victims, that Lady Elizabeth had been killed several months before. The truth is that she was killed at least a year ago. It was the others who came later."

Papelford glared in hatred.

"A mistake anyone can make," he hissed, "especially at my age. Time moves by ever quicker, the older you get—"

"But you should not have made it, Papelford," Ebenezer asserted. "Not the man who was in charge of the investigation." He looked back to the king, and Kara saw the monarch nod, just once. "Since then you have impeded Reldo. You have barred him from using your most precious tomes.

"I know what it is like to grow old, Papelford," the alchemist continued sadly. "My faculties are not what they once were, either. But we who are so fortunate to live this long must face the truth. I am sorry." He lowered his gaze to the flagstones. "I don't think you should continue in your position as librarian."

Papelford's face blistered. He turned angrily to the king, but as he did so he tottered and fell face down. His cane snapped beneath him.

Kara ran forward as Despaard bent to his aid.

"Get away from me," the librarian gritted. "Get away—

"My king," he continued, looking up. "I served your father, and your grandfather! You cannot be so merciless as to take away my books… not my books."

The sound of the old man weeping weighed heavily on Kara's conscience. The room was silent but for his sobs. King Roald bowed his head.

"The alchemist is right," he said. He forced himself to look at the pathetic man at his feet. "You have served my family well over the years, my old friend. But I fear you need your rest now." Papelford wept and put his hands over his ears. But the king continued. "You will keep your position at court, should you wish to do so, but the Society of Owls needs a younger advisor." He turned to face the apprentice. "Reldo, this is the hour of your ascension. Let us hope you meet the standard Papelford has set."

Reldo nodded solemnly.

Despaard and Rovin escorted Papelford back to his chair, where he retreated into the bearskin cloak, his face ashen and still.

"Perhaps Aubury can enlighten us as to the essence's whereabouts," Arisha offered calmly, "since the Tower was the source of it." She brushed a hand over her fading black eye, and waited.

Aubury gave a cough.

"Essence?" he murmured, looking down. "Essence. Hmm." He nodded. "It *could* be a reference to rune essence, I suppose." He looked up to stare into the king's face. "The existence of rune essence has not been proven, though," he said. "Many think it is from this substance that our runes are crafted—"

King Roald held up his hand.

"Spare me the tall tales, Master Aubury. I know full well that no runes have been crafted in nearly a hundred years."

Kara gasped.

No runes crafted for a century, she thought. *No wonder Castimir treasures them so.*

Aubury staggered. His mouth gaped open. Suddenly his monocle slipped from his eye and shattered on the stone.

"That's... that's not true," he wheezed. "It's not—"

Castimir smiled grimly.

Arisha looked on in triumph.

"Whatever the truth is, Master Aubury, I do not care," King Roald snapped. "My kingdom is tearing itself apart. Answers are needed. *Now.* Regardless of its nature, can this essence be found?

Do you in the Tower possess any?"

"I do not believe so, sire," Aubury replied. "If any did exist, then it must have been lost, or consumed when the original Tower was burned by the barbarian heathen in the seventieth year of this age." He peered angrily at Arisha. "Your people and their insane crusades—three-quarters of a century on, and we still suffer for their ignorance."

"My people have much to answer for," Arisha acknowledged with a puzzling smile. "But it was not my kin who sacked the Tower. It was other wizards—those who followed Zamorak. Until that time, wizards of all religions worked side-by-side, until their jealousies destroyed them." She stepped close to Aubury and the master wizard shrank back.

"You destroyed *yourselves*," she whispered. "You did my peoples' work for them—with your ignorance and your lust for power."

"Enough of this!" King Roald commanded. "It brings us no closer to solving the problem." He looked again at the wizard. "Where can this essence be found?"

Aubury gave him a grim look.

"Th-there is none left," he stammered.

Once again, Arisha smiled.

"That may not be entirely true, sire." She turned to face the gathering. "I am a priestess of the tribes. In sharing our tales, we also chronicle our deeds. Among the legends are the crusades we launched against the wizards and *their* heresy, for Guthix commanded us to prevent the wizards from perverting the nature of essence.

"Stories tell of our victories, for they were many. My people learned to hunt the sorcerers. We knew their limits and their weaknesses. We learned about the runes—"

Arisha looked back to Aubury and sneered.

"—and *essence*," she added. "We took what they coveted, and what wasn't destroyed, we hid."

It was Castimir's turn to gasp.

Aubury's head shot up.

"You… y-you know where it is?" he asked.

Arisha smiled more broadly than before, and Kara felt as if she had been struck, for she had rarely seen anything so cold.

"I don't know where it is," Arisha said. "But I know how to find it." She leaned toward Aubury's ear. "And you will *never* know." Her finger jabbed the old man's chest. "Never. Because of what you did to us. To Castimir and me. Because of your *ignorance.*"

She stepped away and moved to Castimir's side.

"The problem we face, my king," she continued, "is that the essence will not be given up willingly. Among my tribesmen, I alone have walked in Morytania. I *know* the evil we face—they do not. Therefore, I will go to them, and ask for their aid. But they might not give it."

"Your quest is too important for one person," King Roald remarked. "Take others with you, like Sir Theodore, whose fame is widespread. Like Kara—"

"No, sire," Arisha told him, her hand raised. "If too many accompany me, it will raise suspicions." She nodded. "I will go, and I will take one other with me.

"You, Castimir," she said. "You will escort me to my tribe, and from there wherever we must go. Will you guide me?"

He nodded silently.

With an animal cry, Theodore stepped forward.

"You must allow me to accompany you," he said, and he knelt at her feet. "You don't know what lies ahead." The knight looked to Castimir, and there were tears in his eyes. "Please, Cas…"

"No, Sir Theodore," Arisha said. His face twisted in emotion and his head fell. "We must do this alone." She rested her hand on his shoulder and knelt opposite him. "And you *will* be needed here, brave knight. I am certain of it. We must divide our forces wisely."

She stood and addressed the onlookers.

"We will leave tomorrow, at dawn."

King Roald nodded.

"Then you will go with my blessing," he said. "And with a king's warrant that will compel all to give you aid. I shall prepare it immediately." His face darkened. "Let us pray that it will be enough."

16

Kara-Meir returned to her quarters to wash. She desperately needed to sleep, but she forced herself back downstairs to lunch.

She found the room her friends had commandeered as their own. Theodore sat at the table, staring into a bowl, and poked at the soup with his spoon. Nearby, Doric was topping up his glass from a keg that had been gifted to him by the city's brewers. The black liquid pumped into his glass from the tap, thick and heavy.

"Aha, Kara!" he said, grinning. "Would you like a dwarven stout? You probably haven't had one of these since you left Ice Mountain." The dwarf tilted his head toward Theodore. Then he rolled his eyes and made a face.

Kara understood.

"Too early for me, Doric. Besides, I'm famished—a pint would just give me a headache."

She moved to the buffet table, cut herself a slice of ham, then took some bread and a cup of water. Standing at her side, the dwarf spoke.

"Theodore's been like that all morning," he murmured.

"Something to do with what he said at Castimir's trial. Perhaps you can liven him up."

She nodded, returned to the table, and moved to sit opposite the knight.

"Is Castimir not eating lunch?" she asked while buttering her bread.

Theodore put the spoon down and peered at her bleakly. There was an awkward silence, and just when she thought she would need to press, he spoke.

"Cas thinks I let him down," he said. "At his trial. He thinks I should have lied to help him keep his position." He lowered his head and shut his eyes. "I couldn't do it."

"I went in there with a story prepared," he continued, "to try to get them to dismiss the charge of theft, but I..." He grimaced, and his voice broke. "Sedridor just stared and stared. He hardly spoke. Grayzag shouted and tried to trap me." Theodore looked up, and his eyes were red.

"I have always believed that the truth counters any lie, Kara," he said. "You have known that since the first time we met, when I was forced to lie to you to draw Finistere out." He clenched his right hand. "Because of that lie, people died in Falador. And today I have destroyed all that Castimir has ever wanted.

"Where is the good in those things, Kara?" he asked. "Where?"

He raised his fist and smashed the tabletop. Kara caught her goblet before it fell.

"You're too hard on yourself, lad," Doric said. "No one died in Falador because of what you did. Their deaths were the work of others. And no lie could have hid Castimir's guilt."

Theodore remained silent, but his hands clenched in anger. Kara didn't know what to say. She had never completely forgiven Theodore for his actions in Falador, but now, looking at how he suffered, she felt for him.

She reached over the table and took his hand in hers.

After a moment, the knight nodded in appreciation.

Suddenly the door shot open. Gideon Gleeman burst in, a look of madness in his eyes.

"There you are, Kara. I am glad I have found you. It's the Kandarin ambassador." The jester's long face darkened. "Sir Cecil wishes you to surrender Pia and Jack to his authority, so that they may be sent back to Ardougne to be hanged for murder."

Kara's back stiffened.

Can't I have a moment's rest? she thought angrily.

"But they are Kara's servants now," Doric observed. "Sir Cecil cannot claim them."

Gideon nodded.

"That may be true, but still he persists." His head dipped to one side. "I think he pursues the matter purely out of spite." He paused, then continued. "There might be a better way, though."

"Tell me, Gideon," Kara urged.

"You could offer King Lathas some form of payment," the jester answered. "He has been known to forgive sins in exchange for donations that sponsor public works. Whether he agrees or not, it would force Cecil to contact his government. A reply could take weeks."

Kara smiled.

"Then go and offer it to him on my behalf, Gideon," she said. "If I am faced with the pompous old fool, I'm liable to say something I will regret." Gleeman bowed, and turned back to the door. As he did, she called after him.

"And Gideon…" she said, prompting him to turn. "Thank you."

Evening fell, and Kara busied herself by cleaning her sword. Her chamber was lit by starlight coming through the open window. She found the dark relaxing, and the task of oiling the blade—with its repetitive *swish-swash* of her cloth—calmed her nerves.

In the room adjoining hers, Pia and Jack both slept soundly, as they had all day. Two candles cast a soft light. Peering through the open door, she watched them for a moment, and smiled before returning to her blade.

Sitting on her bed, she guided the cloth down the face of the long sword, delighting in the cold of the adamant metal and the green shine of the reflected light.

She won't be long now, Kara thought to herself. She turned the blade over and ran the cloth up and down the new face.

Swish-swash.

Footsteps sounded from the passage outside her quarters. Kara stood and, still holding her sword, made her way silently past Pia and Jack. Then someone tapped lightly on the door.

Kara opened it, her sword ready.

Seeing it, Lady Caroline gasped in surprise.

"Oh!" she said softly. "Y-you wanted to see me?"

Kara smiled.

"Yes," she replied. "Please, come in." She waved the sword dismissively. "I didn't mean to frighten you."

Caroline entered, and Kara closed the door. The candle flames were buffeted by the movement, and the shadows jiggled as they settled.

"First, I would like to thank you for lending me Lucretia," Kara said. "She has been invaluable, and has helped me in caring for Pia and Jack." Kara nodded to the sleeping children.

Caroline smiled, the gap between her front teeth charmingly prominent.

"She is wonderful," she agreed. "But sometimes I find her a little scary. My mother insisted that she serve me, yet she *can* be a bit of a dragon. I think Sulla found that out to his cost."

"Sulla?" His name brought a scowl to Kara's face. "I meant to ask—where is he being kept?"

Lady Caroline looked at the sword and then back to Kara.

"I do not know, for just yesterday Lord Ruthven had him moved. Lady Anne and I have been told we will no longer be required to... *entertain* him." She smiled again and her eyes blazed in delight. "Are you going to kill him, Kara?" she squeaked. "Are you? Can I watch? I've never seen anyone killed before." Suddenly she looked sad. "Mother says I have a weak stomach for that kind of thing."

Kara had to bite her lip to prevent herself from laughing. She took a deep breath and guided Caroline through to her bedchamber, pausing only to take one of the candles with her.

"It's better that we speak in here," she said. Casting a look back at Pia and her brother, she kicked the door shut with a gentle tap of her foot. "What does your mother think of you and Lord William, then?"

"Oh, so you know about it? Well, it's not a secret anymore, I suppose." Her voice lowered. "But I haven't told my mother yet."

"Wouldn't she be pleased? William is from a good family, and he is a decent man... isn't he?"

Caroline nodded.

Kara waited.

Tell me about William, she thought. *I killed his cousin last night. How far does the rot go?*

Caroline looked again at her adamant sword.

"Can I—can I hold it?"

"Of course." Kara guided her hand to the hilt. Caroline lifted the blade in one hand, gritting her teeth. The blade shook.

"It's heavy," she gasped, setting it down upon the bed.

"I suppose I am used to it," Kara told her. "But you were saying something... about William?"

Caroline's face brightened.

"Oh, yes," she replied. "He is a good man. He's kind and sensitive and clever…" Her voice trailed off.

"But?"

"But he's *Lord William!*" Caroline sighed. "I do love him, Kara. Really I do. But William is treated with suspicion by many at court."

"Why is that, Caroline?" Kara knew she was getting close.

Caroline bowed her head.

"He's different," she whispered. "And he isn't devoted to Saradomin, as most are at court."

"Who does he follow, then?"

Caroline sniffed and lifted her head to reveal large eyes wet with tears.

"You know, Kara," she said. "You know…"

"Zamorak," Kara muttered. "Is that right?"

Caroline nodded as her sobs gained strength.

"I can't believe it," Kara remarked. "He is not a violent man in any way. And he is friends with Theodore. Unless—" Her eyes narrowed. "Is he only pretending to be friends with us, Caroline? Is he one of those who stand behind the insurrection?"

Caroline gaped in surprise.

"William? Gods *no*, not him. He would never hurt anyone. And he speaks highly of Theodore. In f-fact…" Her sobs interfered with her words. "I th-think he admires him. Sir Theodore is someone he would like to have been, but never could be."

"What do you mean by that?" Kara frowned.

"It's something he told me once, Kara. I don't know anymore."

The bells of Father Lawrence's church rang the hour.

Caroline stood.

"I have said too much. Far, far too much. It's time I left." She stared at Kara, her face begging. "Please, Kara, please don't tell anyone. If Raispher finds out, he will take William to the lowest dungeon and… oh, Kara!" At that, she wept uncontrollably. Kara put a hand on her shoulder. It felt awkward to her.

"There was a reason I needed to ask you, Caroline," Kara said. Caroline continued to weep. "I killed William's cousin," she said. "Just last night."

The shuddering stopped. Caroline took her hands away from her face. She frowned.

"Y-you, you did *what?*" she gasped, and she glanced at the sword.

"I killed his cousin, last night. He was one of the Zamorak insurrectionists, Caroline. He participated in the attack on the refugees." Seeing how agitated the young woman was becoming, Kara lifted the glass jug at her bedside. "Perhaps you should take some wine—"

Caroline growled in anguish and lashed out. Kara stepped back but the jug was knocked from her grasp. It hit the rug at her feet and broke into pieces with a muted *crash* as Caroline fled from her room and then out through the main door of her chambers to vanish in the passageway.

Kara thought of Theodore.

"I told the truth," she whispered to herself. "And another person has been hurt." She crossed to the outer door and bolted it tight. As she turned, she saw Jack's weary eyes upon her.

"Kara?" he asked wearily. "Who was that?"

"Lady Caroline, Jack," she answered. "We had an argument. Go back to sleep."

Jack nodded. As soon as his head touched his pillow his eyes closed. Kara blew out the candles and went to her bed. The jug and its mess could wait for morning.

When she woke she was covered in sweat. She sat up and threw off her blanket, letting the breeze from her window cool her.

She had dreamt. And it had been a good dream. A *very* good dream.

A dream about Theodore.

Kara tried hard to remember it. She recalled Theodore's embrace and his kiss, and the glorious anticipation that had thrilled her body. Hints remained, but the details eluded her. Nevertheless, the dream hadn't been tainted in any way by Gar'rth's presence.

Tainted, she thought suddenly. *Why should I feel that way?*

She licked her lips and found her mouth was parched.

I need a drink, she decided. *A drink of cold water.*

Kara pulled off her shift and threw on her trousers and wool shirt. Remembering the broken glass jug, she reached in the dark for her boots and slipped them on over her bare feet.

Her night-attuned eyes navigated around the broken jug that lay in the shadows beneath her bed. The rug beneath it had absorbed much of the impact, and she found that it had broken into two large pieces. She took them up in her hands and crept toward the outer door, opening it a hand's width.

Something was wrong. The passageway was dark, and the smell of smoke signaled to her that the torches had very recently been put out.

All of them, at the same time? Kara grew suspicious.

Silently, she eased open her door and listened.

Clunk. Clunk. Click.

The sound came from her left, from Arisha's quarters. Or outside of them. Kara held her breath and ducked her head around the side of her doorframe.

A hulking shadow stood at Arisha's door. It pulled its hand back, a key in its grasp.

It has just unlocked her door, she realized.

Then the figure, a man, drew a dagger. Silently he pushed the door open and stepped inside.

Instantly Kara ran forward, the pieces of the broken glass jug angled in either hand. She burst into Arisha's anteroom to see the man push back the door to the priestess's bedchamber.

He's big, she realized. *I can't take any risks.* Without hesitating she hurled the heaviest glass piece. Even as it left her hand, she continued to run forward, veering to the man's left.

Crash!

The glass exploded on the doorframe just to the right of his head. He shouted and turned, raising the black dagger to the source of the sound.

It was exactly the action Kara had anticipated. Exactly the action she had hoped for. She came from his left, behind him, so that he didn't see her until it was too late.

She brought the remaining glass splinter up into his face. It struck him beneath the jaw and Kara felt it *crack* against the top of his mouth.

"Urrghhhh—"

The attacker dropped the dagger and fell through the open door into the bedchamber beyond.

"What's going on?" Arisha's voice demanded from the darkness.

"An assassin," Kara replied, without taking her eyes off the man who flopped at her feet. "Creeping into your bedchamber."

"Have you killed him?" Arisha asked.

The man gasped once more, and then lay still.

"I think so," Kara replied. She kicked him with her foot. There was no response. "Yes."

"What's going on?"

At the sound of a third voice, Kara looked up sharply.

By the gods!

Castimir lay alongside Arisha. The priestess was poised to move, but he just rubbed his eyes.

"I'm sorry," Kara started. "I didn't know—"

Arisha threw off the blanket and stood naked before her.

"Don't be foolish, Kara. Now is not the time." She turned. "Castimir, get some light. Kara, go and close the door to my quarters."

The priestess strode past her into the larger room. She pulled on the traveling shirt that she wore beneath her blue robes. Then she pulled on her trousers.

"The door, Kara," she hissed. "Before someone sees the body."

Shaking her head, Kara obeyed. When she turned back, a faint glow lit the bedchamber. A second later Castimir swore.

"What did you *do*, Kara?" His words were strangled.

"I killed an assassin. He had a knife—"

"You killed a *guard*, Kara. One of King Roald's men."

"What?" Arisha gasped, then she ran back to the bedchamber. Kara did the same.

The dead man lay at the foot of the bed. He had stumbled back before falling, and now a great pool of blood spread in a growing circle from his throat. Castimir held back his black outer garment. Beneath was the emblem of the palace guard.

"I have seen him before," Kara realized. Her stomach twisted in horror. "He was one of Captain Hardinge's men, who escorted us back from the Salve."

"Are you… are you certain he was an assassin, Kara?" For the first time there was fear in Arisha's voice. Kara nodded.

"He had a key to your rooms. In his pocket. Why would a guard have a key to an honored guest's room?"

Her mind raced. Should she have called out first? If she had done that, she might not have been able to overcome him—not with two pieces of a broken glass jug.

Castimir rummaged in the man's pocket. He pulled out the key.

"Someone wanted you dead," he told the priestess.

Arisha nodded.

"Then we cannot wait till dawn. Our horses must be made ready and rations gathered. It's two days to the River Lum and my people at Gunnarsgrunn, so we can travel light and replenish ourselves there. Cas, do you have the king's warrant?"

He nodded grimly as he stood.

"You will only have a few hours' head start," Kara warned. "Even now, somewhere in the palace, someone might be waiting for news of your death."

"Then every second counts," Castimir added. "We must get ready."

Kara stepped back from the bedchamber and opened the door to the passageway. She stared out for several seconds.

It was empty.

Quickly she stole back to her room and woke Pia and her brother.

"I need you," she said. "Something bad has happened. Something terrible. Can you saddle a horse?"

Seeing the doubt on Pia's face, she moved quickly to her own bedchamber and returned with her satchel. She reached inside and pulled out a finely crafted gem.

Pia's eyes widened.

"There is a boy who sleeps in the stables, most nights. He works there. Give him this and get him to help you. I need three fast horses—two saddled and one to act as a beast of burden. And Castimir's yak, too. That's a hardy beast. I will send Sir Theodore to help you in a moment, but we *must* be quick."

Pia nodded and stood. She took the gem, rammed on her boots, and ran to the door. Fearfully Jack watched her go.

"And you, Jack," Kara said. "I have need of you, as well. Go to the kitchens." She emptied her satchel over the small desk that stood in her room. "Fill this with bread, meats and apples. Water flasks, too. Enough to keep two people for three days. Do you understand?"

The boy had already pulled on his shoes and stood waiting when Kara turned back to hand him the empty satchel.

"Do you understand, Jack?"

He nodded.

"Do I get a jewel, too?" he asked.

Kara smiled. She picked a small one from the desk.

Thank you, Gar'rth, she thought. *It was a useful gift you made to each of us, to make us rich.*

Jack took the ruby in his hand and ran.

Then Kara went into the passageway, and closed the door behind her.

17

Gar'rth stood at the window and waited, his breath fogging the air. He tried hard to remember how long it had been since Vanstrom had held him above the drop, only his strong grip preventing him from certain death.

A human's grip, he thought. *Just that, preventing me from falling.* The image of the ghetto below his feet, of obscure shadows made obscenely sharp by the hovels, made him shiver.

He looked skyward. He had yet to see proper daylight here. Always the clouds were low, only ever gray or black, impossibly thick and unmoving. Even the power of the sun was vanquished. When he had caught sight of it, it was like a torch seen through smoke, so brief as to be imagined.

So distant to the inhabitants of these ghettoes as to be a legend, he thought. *I could never have imagined such misery.*

Down in the street a man in ragged garments remained where he had been for the last hour. Like all of the inhabitants, he was worryingly pale.

A short distance away, a barricade created an artificial dead end.

To Gar'rth, Meiyerditch seemed an impossible city, divided into sectors, where ruined hovels housed the populace in dwellings that made the poorest peasant in Misthalin seem like a king.

Not a single tree had he seen. Not a blade of grass. The only animals were stray dogs and cats and the occasional unfortunate gull that flew in from the sea, somewhere far to the south.

He stretched his arms and crossed them over his chest. He, too, was dressed in rags, so he could pass through the streets without attracting undue attention. They had stolen them as soon as they came down from the wall, and he had kept them. They would be perfect for the night's activities.

Gar'rth gazed out at the street below again. The man still hadn't moved.

"Come on," he whispered in frustration.

Either the man read his thoughts or heard his words, for suddenly he looked up and gave a nod. Gar'rth heard the clatter of running feet, and several figures ran around the corner to the door of the house. He heard the door open, and the tramp of feet on the stairs outside his room.

I am in your hands, he thought. *Again.*

The door burst open as Vanstrom entered. Two men followed, while behind them others waited on the landing.

"Here," Vanstrom exclaimed. "I have told them everything about you, Gar'rth." He nodded to the first of the men. "This is Ben Strainge." A broad man stepped forward and gazed intently at him. He gave a grunt and then stepped back. "And this, Gar'rth, is Karnac's brother, Kendrick."

The second man advanced, breathing heavily.

"I don't know any Karnac," Gar'rth whispered, fearing some trickery.

Vanstrom nodded.

"Of course…" he said apologetically. "Of course you don't, for you never met him. Karnac led the community at Hope Rock. He led your friends to safety."

"Is it true?" Kendrick begged. "Is it? The gnome's stunt was a mad one."

Gar'rth smiled.

"It is true. My friends, and some refugees from Hope Rock, made it across the river."

Kendrick gasped and held his hand over his mouth. Outside the door, the men listened in silence.

"Th-they made it?" Kendrick stammered. Tears rolled down his cheeks. "Across the river?" His lip trembled with excitement. "Then it's possible! Escape is possible!"

Kendrick sobbed suddenly.

"Tell me, tell me please, of the outside world."

Gar'rth smiled again, but before he could reply Vanstrom spoke.

"Later, Ken. We will have time for that later. But now we must help Gar'rth. He has the opportunity to destroy a great evil, as I have explained to you all. He just lacks the means to do it." The man clasped Kendrick's arm tightly. "We must give him the Sunspear."

Silence fell. Kendrick nodded and the swarthy Ben Strainge gritted his teeth.

"We have already discussed this," Vanstrom hissed. "You agreed to try and recover it. If Tenebra is felled, then think what effect the Black Prince's death would have among our people!"

"Yes," Kendrick agreed. "You are right." His eyes fell on Gar'rth and remained there for a long moment. "The world is changing quicker now than it has ever done before. In the northern sectors the Black Prince—this Tenebra—builds great artifacts for a coming war. Thousands of souls have been pressed into his service. As ever, the witch queen Vanescula watches and plots and plays her deadly games, vying for power with her siblings.

"And for many a long year we have had no news of the great

architect of all our misery, for nothing has been seen or heard of Lord Drakan himself." Kendrick blinked once, and Gar'rth felt as if he had been released from some spell. "Now visitors come from across the holy river, from the lands of legend. A land of forests and fields, where life flourishes. And we must give our all to aid them."

Kendrick turned toward the doorway.

"Ivan? Ivan, are you there, boy? I need you to be lucky tonight. And you have more luck than anyone I've ever met, save Vanstrom here."

A boy of no more than twelve years appeared. He seemed pathetically small to Gar'rth. He brushed back his black hair and bowed solemnly.

"It's Saradomin's luck, sir," he said humbly.

Kendrick grinned.

"Your faith does you proud, boy. But make sure the Vyrewatch never hear you mention His name, or they will kill you on the spot for such a blasphemy. Now, run to the lights. I need the bait tonight."

Ivan bowed again before vanishing down the stairs.

"Bait?" Gar'rth whispered.

"Aye, bait," Vanstrom muttered. "The Vyrewatch patrol the ghettoes every hour of every day, and we need to cross into the northern sector, under the wall. We will be caught moving in such numbers as this, unless we have bait." His mouth hardened in a line. "Bait for them. People too old and weak to fight can help in other ways."

Gar'rth shivered when he recalled the tithe-master and his kin, carrying out their horrific business.

"They *volunteer* to be tithed?" he asked incredulously.

Ben Strainge snarled.

"They volunteer for more than that, werewolf. They will most likely be killed today. The bait will cause a riot, and that means the Vyrewatch will respond with lethal force. Remember that, when you next stand at your father's side—remember that old men and women who haven't the strength to fight but who still possess the will have given their lives for you. Do not let them down!"

Gar'rth found himself nodding as he thought of the sacrifice that these unknown people would soon make.

"It's time!" Kendrick whispered in excitement. "The lantern in the sentry window has been lit. Ivan has got through with his message." Kendrick tugged his beard and smiled. "He's got luck on his side, that one, no mistaking it. He could kiss Vanescula and still walk away with all his limbs.

"Now, come, the bait shall act soon, and we must use the time they will grant us. Come!"

Gar'rth felt Vanstrom's hand push him in the small of his back. Without hesitating, he followed the small group down the stairs and out into the dark of the street.

Eight of them left the house, and upon Ben Strainge's advice they split into three separate groups.

"People are not allowed to gather in numbers," Vanstrom explained as they walked onward, their faces down. Gar'rth mirrored their actions, and several times he heard the beating of great wings overhead. He didn't dare look up.

It wasn't until they found their way barred by another of the immense walls that Gar'rth heard the screaming.

"It's the riot," Vanstrom explained as the groups gathered together again at the foot of the wall. "It will keep the Vyres busy for a good hour or so—plenty of time for us to pass into the northern sector."

Gar'rth wished he could make himself deaf.

"Blindfolds," Strainge ordered. Six of the eight men had their eyes covered. Gar'rth did, too, so only Ben and Kendrick could see. The blind joined hands and were guided in a chain for several minutes.

"No one member of the Myreque knows all our ways," Vanstrom said, "for if ever such a person would be captured, then our whole organization would be laid bare."

"That's not quite true, Vanstrom," Strainge murmured from up ahead. "You know more than most. And Hallow and Calsidiu know still more."

"Who are they?" Gar'rth asked.

"Our leaders," Ben replied. "In a manner of speaking. We are a loose organization, and Calsidiu explains it best. 'The Myreque are made of ropes, the vampires of stone. If a rope breaks, we can retie it.'"

"It means we're flexible and can act independently when the need arises," Kendrick added. Then he said, "Right, we're here."

The column stumbled to a stop. Gar'rth listened as a key rattled in a lock. A door was opened.

"Duck your heads as you go under. Especially you, Gar'rth."

He did as advised, yielding to Kendrick's guiding hands. The door was closed behind them.

Echoing sounds. The drip of water, and something else…

He breathed deeply through his nose.

Mold. Death.

Gar'rth felt the man in front of him tighten his grip.

"The ground is uneven here," Ben told them. "Soon we will have to wade through water, chest-high. Stay together."

The passage twisted and turned, and several times Gar'rth felt a draft of air on his skin. At times the echoes varied, signaling a wider space or a smaller one.

"The water," Kendrick warned. "It's deep and cold and it lasts for a good few minutes. Come on."

Gar'rth stumbled forward as Kendrick's hand guided him down a step. His right foot was swallowed by water that ended at knee height. He gasped at the coldness. Another few steps and the water was above his waist. One more, and it was above his belly. Ahead of him the men groaned or swore, but splashed onward.

"I hate water," Vanstrom muttered from behind him. In the cold, Gar'rth couldn't help but agree.

"What is it that we seek down here?" he asked. "What is this Sunspear?"

"It's a weapon. A weapon to kill vampires," Vanstrom replied. "We tried to retrieve it years ago, after it was hidden in the caverns beneath the city by those who fought the undead long before the Myreque were organized. Its presence became a folk tale among the ghettoes." He stumbled in the water and swore.

"Quiet!" Strainge hissed.

They carried on for several minutes. Finally, Gar'rth could no longer remain patient.

"So why is it down here?" he whispered. "Why was it sent to the caverns?"

"It was used, apparently, to kill a member of the Vyrewatch," Vanstrom replied, his voice low. "After that the vampires sacked the ghetto in retaliation. It was decided to hide the weapon away until it could be used for a greater purpose."

"And it's safe down here?"

He heard Vanstrom laugh.

"Safe from the vampires, I think. But not safe in any normal sense. It was sent here to keep it out of reach of those members of the Myreque who wanted to use it. But you, Gar'rth, you can get close to Tenebra." Vanstrom squeezed his hand. "*You* can deliver the killing blow."

Finally they waded out of the freezing waters, but that provided little relief. Cool air chilled Gar'rth's skin under his soaked rags.

"We are in the northern sector now," Kendrick said. "You can remove the blindfolds."

They were outside again, and Gar'rth opened his eyes to see

another ghetto, similar to the one they had just left. They stood in a large crack that opened onto a large culvert running beneath the wall.

Kendrick advanced with two others. They slid down the side of the culvert, climbed the other side, then walked swiftly to the nearest hovel.

Strainge waved Gar'rth forward. Vanstrom was at his side.

"Give it a few minutes," he said, "then you'll be next."

They waited until Straange gave the signal, then slid down the slope. Quickly, Gar'rth helped Vanstrom to his feet and together they followed briskly in Kendrick's path.

"Don't look up," Vanstrom whispered as they found cover. The beating of wings passed overhead. From far away, the sounds of fighting could still be heard. And the screaming, though there was less now.

"Must be the last of the rioters," Vanstrom said. "If they climbed onto the rooftops, the sound can carry over the heights."

Thump!

A body landed nearby. The figure turned on its side, its face the image of agony. Gar'rth saw that it was an old woman, her legs crooked and broken from her fall.

"Help me!" she said, writhing and moaning in pain. "*Please!*"

Gar'rth felt Vanstrom's hand tighten on his wrist.

"Don't," he hissed. "She's been carried over the wall from the riot. She's not our business. *Come on.*"

Before they could move, one of the Vyrewatch landed above her. Gar'rth watched as the vampire readied its long spear. Without thinking he stepped forward. He heard Vanstrom curse as the vampire lifted its head toward them.

The Vyrewatch gazed at Gar'rth. Then, it lowered its spear and knelt.

"What have you done?" Vanstrom whispered.

He didn't know.

"It's her gift, Vanescula's mark. It must be," he mumbled to Vanstrom.

From the crack in the wall, the rest of Strainge's men caught them up. They gave Gar'rth a suspicious look before passing him.

"You can do nothing for her, Gar'rth," Vanstrom advised. "Her injuries are too evil. A quick death is best for her."

"Please…" the woman murmured. "H-hide me." A pool of blood had gathered beneath her head. Her legs were twisted and useless.

Forgive me, Kara, he pleaded. *Please understand, there is more at stake here. Far more.*

Blinking back his tears, Gar'rth turned his back on the woman and ran. Vanstrom was at his side.

"It was the only choice you could have made," he said.

But Gar'rth didn't reply.

As the woman screamed and the sound of a spear parting flesh reached his ears, Gar'rth wished, once again, that he could make himself deaf.

18

An hour later, the small group gathered above a trapdoor in the darkened basement of a hovel. A rusted ladder descended into the blackness.

"We won't be able to use our lantern. There are things down there that hate the light," Strainge advised. "We should send the wolf first." Since witnessing the Vyrewatch's actions, his hostility had grown—a feeling they all seemed to share.

"Very well," Gar'rth replied. He stared into the gaping darkness and blinked. When he looked back up, they were all eyeing him expectantly.

"Go, Gar'rth," Kendrick said. It was more demand than urging. "Your eyesight will be better than any of ours. I will follow."

He tested his weight on the first rung, then slowly lowered himself down. The air in the shaft was cold, and the scent of putrid water offensive. He climbed, counting each rung, and then slipped suddenly as the one he had expected his foot to find was missing.

"Watch out," Gar'rth called up. "The tenth rung is missing."

He pushed himself away from the wall and looked down as best he could.

The eleventh was missing, as well. And there was no sign of the bottom.

Three times more he found missing rungs and, on one occasion where several were gone, he had to lower himself by using the ladder's sides.

If we have to come back up this way, then it will prove hard, he realized grimly.

Finally, his feet impacted against solid rock. He waited to allow his eyes to adjust. Above him the ladder rattled as the members of the Myreque descended. He kept his right hand clasped to the ladder's rail, fearful of letting it go. With his other hand he felt around. After a moment of groping he realized that he stood in an alcove which faced out into a far wider expanse. Yet even his eyes could barely see anything beyond the length of his arm.

He was about to speak when something caused him to hesitate.

There was something near. Whatever it was, it was foul. And it was *waiting*. He remained still until Kendrick reached the bottom.

"It's too dark for me to see anything," Gar'rth whispered. "And there's something... out there. Can you feel it?"

Kendrick put his hand on Gar'rth's shoulder and stood in silence. Above them, the ladder shook continually as the men made their descent, slowly and in as much silence as they could. To Gar'rth, the noise was alarming. There would be no hope of concealing their presence.

"There are things down here, Gar'rth," Kendrick replied in a hushed voice. "Evil things. The weapon was placed down here deliberately, so it would be impossible for one person to retrieve it. That is why there are so many of us." His hand tightened.

"Now, Gar'rth. We must go straight out into the chamber. There is a pool about twenty strides from us. When you get to it, follow its edge to the left. There is another alcove there with a crack in the wall.

"Come on, Gar'rth," Kendrick hissed as Vanstrom reached the bottom.

"I can't," he said. "Not yet. There is something there."

Kendrick gave him a slight push forward. As he did so a breeze wafted through the chamber and his ominous feeling subsided with the onset of the fresher air.

"Come on!" Kendrick said again. He gripped Gar'rth's shoulder.

Reluctantly, Gar'rth stepped out, counting his strides. When he reached fifteen he slowed and reached his foot out to test the ground. On the seventeenth stride the tip of his boot splashed into water.

"Left then," Kendrick urged, never taking his hand away.

Gar'rth turned and headed left, still in utter darkness. His right foot sank a finger's depth into moist ground, and made a sucking sound as he pulled it free. Soon, his outstretched hand found hard stone.

Kendrick paused and took his hand off Gar'rth's shoulder for the first time. He knelt at Gar'rth's feet, his face suddenly visible in a faint green light.

"Luminous mold," he explained as he placed a lump of the substance in the mud. "Not enough to see by, but enough for those behind to follow. Ben will plant one when he gets to the bottom of the ladder. It will make the way back easier." He stood. "Now, we have to duck under the wall. Be careful here, for in the cavern beyond there may be danger."

"Where is the Sunspear?" Gar'rth whispered as he stepped into the alcove and groped the wall, looking for the hole.

"It's in a chest in the cavern beyond, hidden under a stone slab—"

Kerrang!

"Agh!"

Someone cried out from behind them as the snap of rusted metal and the clang of a loose rung falling down the shaft echoed throughout the cavern.

Gar'rth froze.

Kendrick cursed.

"Ben!" someone cried. "Ben, are you all right?" From above, faint and far away, Gar'rth heard Strainge answer.

"The ladder *broke!* I slipped!"

The echoes died as men muttered in the darkness.

Gar'rth shut his eyes and listened.

The sound of water rippling, the fading ring of the metal bar. At the same time he inhaled, taking in the scent of his surroundings. *Blood in the air,* he detected. *It wasn't there before.*

The same feeling that had unnerved him when he first stood in the alcove struck him again. Only now it was stronger.

"Kendrick, we can't stay here," he whispered.

He opened his eyes and stepped back into the chamber. The sound of the water grew more violent than before.

Perhaps there is something in the pool?

He felt Kendrick duck past him and search for the crack. Suddenly he looked at the glowing mold, only a yard away.

The green light sheened off something wet that crawled past.

Click-click-click.

He felt Kendrick grab him and pull him back as somebody screamed from the direction of the first alcove.

"Something's got my leg!" the unknown man cried.

Gar'rth could smell the blood now. Fresh blood that overcame his senses. He wrenched his arm away from Kendrick as his body responded to the precious scent. He stared into the darkness, trying to focus.

Another scream.

Click-click-click.

A shadow appeared before him, outlined in the faint green from the mold. It was Vanstrom.

"Gar'rth," he said calmly. "Keep moving—we cannot linger here."

"What of the others?"

"Never mind them. There is nothing we can do for them, and in this darkness they will be lost. We must think of ourselves now. It's for the greater good. Go!"

Kendrick tugged his arm again and this time he relented. He felt the man's arm and followed him through the crack.

The stonework tore at his skin and ripped his already ragged clothes. They went up first, and then over and to the right, before emerging into a second chamber. It felt even larger than the first.

When he was through he stood, and here there was light enough for him to see. Far away, a strange roar vibrated through the rock, and the smell of salt was so strong as to deny his nose any other scent. As Vanstrom slipped through behind, Gar'rth took in the details.

They were standing atop a pile of fallen masonry, high above the chamber floor. Dull diagonal beams of daylight sliced from the top right to illuminate the left wall. The light fell on stone arches that supported an ancient and damaged frieze. Winged beings were carved in the stone, and above each pillar Gar'rth recognized the four-pointed star of Saradomin.

"What is this place?" he intoned. Vanstrom, too, was drawn to it. He rubbed his hand across the form of a winged woman who held a great two-handed sword.

Kendrick snorted behind them. Gar'rth turned to see him standing near the crack they had squeezed through, listening for any of his men. There were no sounds anymore.

When he turned, he saw Gar'rth looking to him for an answer.

"This was a temple of sorts," he said. "Many, many years ago. It is a closely guarded secret. Only the most select individuals know of its existence."

"I've never known of it, at least not before today," Vanstrom said. Gar'rth thought he heard a tinge of anger in the man's voice.

"It's a dead place now," Kendrick answered. "Look at the wall. The space between the arches has been blocked, and most of the sculptures have been defaced."

"She was beautiful," Vanstrom said. His hand traced the outline of the warrior woman with a surprising tenderness.

Gar'rth turned his back on the frieze and looked out over the rest of the chamber. He could imagine it as a square, laid out with fountains that now were indescribable shapes. The ground was slick with water and weeds, coated with strange limpets that Gar'rth had never seen before. Decayed wooden barrels and boxes lay abandoned, randomly scattered. About halfway up on all sides, the chamber walls were dark with dampness.

"This equals anything that I have seen on my travels across the river," he said.

"It was cast down and blocked off many centuries ago," Kendrick said angrily. "Whatever good dwelt here has gone, long ago."

Vanstrom's face darkened. Reluctantly he turned away from the frieze and moved to stand next to Kendrick, at the edge of the rubble.

"Let's find what we came for, then, and leave," he said.

Clambering over the rubble, they made their way down the chamber. At the bottom Gar'rth felt the strange vibration once more, stronger now, the roaring closer.

"How will we get out of here?" Vanstrom asked. "The ladder was broken when Ben fell. We might not be able to get back that way."

"Nothing to do about it now," Kendrick said. "Come on."

Gar'rth followed him forward, cutting across the slippery floor. They were ankle-deep in salt water now. Small fishes teased the surface, only to vanish into the miniature forest of weeds whenever they splashed near.

On the other side of the square Kendrick halted. With sudden alarm, Gar'rth noticed that the water was now halfway to his knee.

"The water's rising," he pointed out. "Where is it coming from?"

Vanstrom made a fearful face. Kendrick simply nodded.

"The tide must be coming in," he said. "The sea isn't far away. There is a fissure in the far corner that leads out in that direction. There's a possibility we can use that to escape." He looked doubtful. "But judging from the water line, it won't be long until this chamber is flooded. We have to be out long before then, for the water will bring things with it.

"Come on."

Kendrick ran to the wall's edge and knelt, his hands reaching furiously beneath the surface.

"Help me," he instructed. "We're looking for a ring that's attached to a stone slab. It will take two of us to lift it."

Gar'rth joined in the hunt to the man's left. Vanstrom did likewise. He had only put his hand under the water when he shouted, his bearded face erupting in a grin.

"I have it," he called. His hand surfaced, a black ring held in its grasp. Kendrick joined him and together they pulled a heavy block up a hand's width. Gar'rth put his strength to the edge, and within a few heartbeats the slab was pulled upright.

Kendrick knelt again and reached down, his arm disappearing into the water.

"I have it, Vanstrom!" he said. "I have it."

He stood and pulled from the water a dripping box.

"It's small," Vanstrom said doubtfully.

Kendrick prized the lid open with some difficulty. When it was open, he frowned.

Gar'rth peered inside.

It was a piece of wood, the length of a man's hand. It reminded him of the bark of a silver birch tree, only thicker and with white veins running across its surface.

"W-what is this?" Vanstrom stammered.

Kendrick's face fell. He closed his eyes, his knees shook and his arms went limp. Gar'rth caught the box before he could drop it.

"It is a sick joke," Kendrick groaned. "A joke!"

Gar'rth reached into the box.

Snap!

The moment his finger touched the object it *warped*. He looked in apprehension, and found a wooden dagger of the same pale wood.

"What happened?" Vanstrom asked.

Not knowing what to say, Gar'rth just shut the lid with a snap. Then he faced his companions.

"This might actually work," he said.

19

Gar'rth turned, and found that the waters resisted him. They were up to his thigh now.

"We should get to higher ground," he advised. "Back up the rock pile. We should be out of the water's reach there."

"And then where?" Vanstrom asked. "Is there any point going back into the room we came though? No doubt the others are dead, and we might not be able to climb the ladder now—not after Ben's fall."

"We cannot know that, Vanstrom," Gar'rth replied. "It is the only way we know. We have to try."

The water was chest-high by the time they reached the bottom of the rubble. The incoming tide brought upon its rising waters a fleet's worth of flotsam.

"It is the waste from the city above," Kendrick remarked as they began to climb. "The sea floods many of the dungeons of old. Many things get carried away with the tides." He looked at the water below and bit his lip. "Or carried in." He shivered as he reached the top.

"Now," he said, pursing his lips, "we must see what really

happened in the other room. Gar'rth, you should go first. Your
senses surpass ours."

Gar'rth nodded and stepped up to the crack in the wall. Hardly
daring to breathe, he pushed his way around the tight fold and
listened. Then he inhaled.

The smell of blood was still there, unmistakable as ever. But now
it was tinged with sweat and fear… and the scent of burning oil.

He ducked through. The room was illuminated by a single
lantern that lay on the ground, halfway between the pool and the
alcove. Three bodies lay still. The arm of a fourth man lay severed
at the pool's edge.

Then one of the bodies sat up.

It was Ben Strainge. He breathed slowly, yet Gar'rth heard a
desperation in his wheeze, as though he wished to breathe faster
but was afraid of being heard.

Vanstrom appeared at the werewolf's side.

Suddenly Strainge gasped. Gar'rth looked back and saw a whip-
like object emerge from the pool, swaying left to right as it advanced
across the chamber floor. The snake-thing found the body of the
nearest corpse and coiled around the dead man's ankles. Then it
dragged him backward, beneath the water.

The pool seethed for a moment before falling calm.

Gar'rth opened the small box and withdrew the curious dagger.

Strainge moaned again. He pushed himself into a sitting position
and tried to drag himself toward the alcove. His face contorted in
pain. He had gained only a yard when the snake-thing returned.

Gar'rth watched as the man froze.

The snake-thing swayed for a moment before withdrawing into
the pool again.

"Can you see anyone else?" Vanstrom whispered. "There were
eight of us who came down the ladder."

Gar'rth peered harder toward the other alcove. A white hand

gripped the edge of the stonework. As he watched, a desperate face turned the corner.

"There is one more man," Gar'rth related. "In the alcove. And there's something in the water. Perhaps many things."

Strainge looked to the alcove behind him. Gar'rth heard him moan.

"Help me, Tam," he said in a loud whisper. "I can't move my legs. By the gods, *help me*."

The man named Tam stared in mute horror.

"Please, Tam! Please—"

The snake-thing burst from the water and coiled itself around Strainge's ankle. He screamed as it pulled him toward the pool.

"Tam, you coward! Tam—"

Vanstrom muttered something as Gar'rth leapt out and rushed across the chamber, the mysterious wooden blade in his hand. Strainge screamed again as Gar'rth cut at the thick body of the snake. Then Vanstrom was next to him, pulling Strainge back as Kendrick ran past them to the alcove.

"Cut it, Gar'rth, cut it!" Strainge shouted at him, "or it'll be too late." Gar'rth gritted his teeth and slanted the blade down. The tendril was as thick as his arm. He felt he was cutting it with a child's toy.

The smell of blood was in the air now. He urged the change on, welcoming it.

"Gar'rth?" Strainge said fearfully, putting a hand up to ward him off. In his full werewolf form, Gar'rth did the only thing he could think of.

He bit into the tendril.

Foul blood flooded into his mouth. Behind him the water exploded as something big emerged.

Vanstrom staggered backward.

"Oh..." he whispered. "Gods."

The first tendril went limp in Gar'rth's maw as he bit clean through it. Then he turned to see the face of the beast that stood before them.

It was hunched over on all fours. The size of a bear, it was entirely hairless with thick pink skin that rippled with tensed muscle underneath. Where Gar'rth looked for the face, there was just a neck that folded outward like the petals on a flower, revealing sharp hooks of row upon row of curved teeth. It had no eyes.

From its throat the snake-thing thrashed. Gar'rth saw at once that he had bitten through its prehensile tongue.

Click-click-click.

It stepped forward on four limbs that each tapered off to a dreadful spike, not unlike the legs of a crab. But in all senses, Gar'rth could not have imagined a more unnatural creature.

"A bloodveld," Kendrick said in awe. "Gar'rth, give me the blade. We cannot lose it again."

Gar'rth ignored his cry as the monstrosity advanced. Taking the knife, Gar'rth slashed open the belly of the nearest corpse that lay between them. He *felt* the scent as it hit him immediately. He hoped the bloodveld would feel it, too.

The creature was upon him then and instinctively Gar'rth pulled the dead man up in front of him, using the corpse as a shield. The bloodveld's mouth widened as it jumped up on its front legs.

At the same time, Gar'rth hurled the dead man forward.

The monster's maw raked the body, sliding down right to his waist. The bloodveld dragged itself backward with the corpse's legs protruding from its mouth, vanishing into the pool.

Spinning around, he saw Tam in the alcove, helping Strainge up onto Kendrick's back. Then Kendrick began to climb.

Gar'rth followed then, aware he couldn't hold off another assault from the creature. Vanstrom had just started to climb when Tam screamed.

"It's coming back!"

Gar'rth spun as a black tongue flashed past him. A great force punched him in the chest and he staggered back against the wall. A second tongue raced toward his leg.

It was beaten aside by Tam. His face contorted with unreasoning rage, the white-faced man held the broken rung that had snapped under Ben's weight. As the two tongues raced in again Tam roared and swung it in a wide arc.

Gar'rth stood.

"Get back!" he shouted. "You're getting too close."

The pool frothed as two bloodvelds surfaced and waded out. A third tongue flew between them as Tam successfully beat off another attack.

"Come on, Tam," Gar'rth said. "Come on. We must go!" He slipped the blade into a pocket and reached for the rungs as Tam turned with a mad grin on his face. It was just time enough for the third tongue to coil around his ankle and pull him off balance.

He screamed as a second one whipped around his free arm.

"No!" he shouted. "No not like this not like this not like this…"

Gar'rth froze. His muscles were stone.

We cannot lose the knife, Vanstrom had said. *The opportunity to destroy a great evil—*

"Help me, Gar'rth! For the love of the gods, help me!"

Images of the fallen woman flooded him.

"Gar'rth? *Gar'rth!*"

The third tongue seized Tam's other leg, and like a puppet he was dragged toward the pool's edge.

"Help me!"

"I'm sorry—" Gar'rth mumbled. "I'm sorry."

The third bloodveld surfaced now.

"Curse you, Gar'rth!" Tam screamed. "Curse you and all your kind!" Then he was lifted into the air as the tongues grew taut. He shrieked as his limbs were broken by their strength.

"*Gaaarrrrrrtttthhhhh!*"

A maw snapped shut over his arm. Another one took his leg at the knee. Finally the third took his right foot. They shook their bodies like dogs fighting over the corpse of a rabbit, and Tam's frame was snapped and torn into pieces.

Finally he stopped screaming.

Gar'rth looked away and began to climb, fixing his mind only on the rung before him, one hand over the other. Then he heard voices from above.

He had caught up with Vanstrom. They had reached the missing rungs.

"You'll have to stand on my shoulders, Ken," Vanstrom said. "That way you can climb high enough to grab the next rung up. I'll stand on Gar'rth's shoulders after that."

Gar'rth hardly heard them. All he could hear were the sounds of Tam's horrific death.

I am not a coward, he told himself. *It was for the greater good.* Kara would understand. He was certain of it. *We cannot lose the knife.*

Then Vanstrom was urging him from above. He allowed the man to stand on his shoulders, then he gripped the edges of the ladder, pulling himself up, thankful for the added strength his werewolf form granted.

Curse you, Gar'rth, curse you and all your kind!

Near the top, he paused to resume his human form, mindful of what the survivors might think once he emerged.

Finally he emerged from the ladder into a world that seemed hidden behind a thin veil. He was dimly aware of a tender hand that rested on his right shoulder while an arm snaked around his waist.

"Hello, Soft-Heart."

20

"Vanstrom? Kendrick?" Gar'rth gasped. "Where are they?"

Vanescula smiled mischievously. Her fangs were just visible over her lower lip.

"They are my prisoners, Soft-Heart," she replied. "But they are irrelevant. I am much more interested in you." She leaned close and licked Gar'rth's neck. "You, and your little gift."

He pushed her aside and she let him go. His right hand dipped into the pocket, where his hand closed over the wood blade. He felt its energies thrum through his arm.

"Would you use immortality wisely, Soft-Heart?" she purred. "I wonder."

The opportunity to destroy a great evil, he thought angrily. Suddenly he drew the blade. He grabbed Vanescula by the throat and held the point a finger's width from her eye.

"Do you know what this is?" he asked. "Perhaps *you* are not as immortal as you would have us all believe."

Vanescula didn't speak, but her eyes widened almost imperceptibly as she focused on the object in Gar'rth's hand.

He moved it closer. Her eyes followed it.

"Your friends are my prisoners, Gar'rth," she whispered. "If you strike me with the Blisterwood, then they will die. As will you." She looked to him then, her eyes glaring red. Was it fear that he saw in her, or was this just another game? "Besides, you know what you *really* want.

"You can get close to Tenebra," she continued. "You can deliver the killing blow. And you know what he will do to your friends—to your precious Kara-Meir—if he triumphs."

Her hand moved up to Gar'rth's wrist and gently she pushed the blade aside. Gar'rth let her do it.

"The best place for that object, I think, is in your father's heart." She smiled again. "You, out of all his children, are the most promising, Soft-Heart. If you knew the lives your brothers and sisters have endured, then you would not hesitate to slay him."

"What do you mean?" Gar'rth responded, his brow furrowing.

"Oh, you weren't the first of his experiments." She laughed wickedly. "It took a *long* time for him to work out how to have a mortal child with his werewolf beast. There were many failures."

"What happened to them?" he said, not certain he wanted to hear the answer.

"They died, Soft-Heart. Chained to walls in deep, dark dungeons, never seeing the light, driven insane by their father's—*your* father's torments." She smirked, then backed away. "I have something for you." She reached into her robe and pulled out a book. It was worn, with yellowed pages. "This is your father's diary, Gar'rth. There is much to be learned from it, if you can suffer through his tasteless self-indulgence."

"What of Vanstrom and Kendrick? And Ben?" he asked, taking the book. "What will you do with them?"

"They will return with you to the castle, under my escort. Then you will find out what your father's plans are for the Salve."

Vanescula motioned idly with her hand. "You will then reveal those plans to me." Outside the hovel Gar'rth saw several Vyrewatch glide to the ground, carrying the three Myreque. Strainge was dropped unceremoniously, while Vanstrom and Kendrick were forced onto their knees.

She turned and looked into Gar'rth's soul.

"Then you will kill Tenebra with the Blisterwood."

"And if I…" He gathered himself, and stared defiantly. "What if I don't?"

Vanescula frowned.

"Why wouldn't you, Gar'rth? It's what you want, isn't it?" Her frown turned again into a wicked smile. "Besides, if you tell me what I want to know, then I will give you free passage across the Salve, so you can return to your precious Kara-Meir."

She spun and stepped out into the road, where the Vyrewatch bowed before her. Another gesture from Vanescula, and the prisoners were hauled to their feet.

Vanstrom picked up Strainge, and they prepared to leave. As they did so, Gar'rth thought about her offer.

Free passage over the Salve. He smiled grimly. *I've heard that before.*

21

A shadow fell over Theodore. He was in the castle's armory with Philip, one of the recruits. He looked up to see Lord Ruthven staring down.

"Ah, Sir Theodore," the noble said. "I was told I would find you here, stealing away Varrock's finest young men for service in your knighthood." His eyes fell on Philip, who bowed his head slightly. "Be about your business, boy," the lord commanded. "Sir Theodore and I have matters to discuss."

Theodore gave Philip a nod, and the young man hurried away.

"I am afraid I am to meet with Father Lawrence in his church, Lord Ruthven," Theodore said. "He expects me before lunch."

"What I have to say won't take long," Ruthven replied, "and I can walk some of the way with you. It's about the Kinshra. They are sending an ambassador to Varrock, to take Sulla back."

They left the armory and descended a stairwell.

"That is nothing unexpected, surely?" Theodore said.

Lord Ruthven kept his pace with the knight, speaking quietly.

"We cannot give Sulla up just yet," he explained. "We will only do so once Jerrod is in custody. We cannot leave a beast like that at large."

Theodore stopped near the eastern bailey, now a muster field for bowmen and pikemen.

"So you *would* give him up, then?" he said. "Even after the king gave his word?"

Ruthven returned the knight's challenge with a cold glare.

"Yes," he said. "We will give him up. But only when the werewolf is safely under lock and key." His glare softened a bit. "The stakes are too high for us to honor our commitments to a man such as Sulla," he continued. "If your sensibilities are offended by that, then I am sorry, but such are the times in which we live." He leaned closer still. "You have seen what we face, Sir Theodore. Jerrod will be able to provide valuable intelligence, whether willingly or not. And in the days to come, Misthalin might well have need of the Kinshra.

"We need Falador's support, as well," he added, "and I hope we can rely upon it."

Theodore bowed his head.

"I am not offended by your words, Lord Ruthven, nor the lies you make to a man like Sulla. But I am grateful that I didn't have to make the choices you've made, and look him in the eye."

Ruthven gave a slight shrug.

"There is one more thing," the older man said. "The Kinshra emissary will be none other than Lord Daquarius Rennard."

Theodore stared.

"The lord of the Kinshra himself?" he said, his voice low. "He is foolish, indeed, if he thinks the court of King Roald will be safe to him." Ruthven nodded agreement.

"Perhaps. But he is a clever man, by all accounts. The law of hospitality means that King Roald will dare not harm him, and he intends to meet one of Varrock's representatives outside the city first, where he will seek a guarantee of safe conduct.

"I was hoping that perhaps you would—"

"No, Lord Ruthven," Theodore said, cutting him off. "I cannot go. He is a sworn enemy of my order. I would not be able to—"

"No, Sir Theodore," Ruthven said. "I fear I haven't made myself clear to you." He coughed and cleared his throat. "I want you to ask Kara-Meir if she will go, to speak for the king."

Theodore frowned.

"She is the logical choice," Ruthven continued. "What's more, her presence in the palace has made a number of people... uncomfortable, especially since the incident with the guard. Of course, she will go with an escort, under a flag of truce."

"How is she in any way the logical choice, Lord Ruthven?"

The older man smiled thinly.

"Lord Daquarius will see her presence as a statement of King Roald's determination. He must surely detest her for what she did to his fellow Kinshra knights. Many of his friends likely fell beneath her blade. Yet if she is chosen by King Roald to be his representative, then Daquarius will have no choice but to put aside his hate, if he wishes to come to Varrock."

Ruthven turned his head and frowned.

"If his hate is such that he spurns her and returns home to Ice Mountain, as we expect, then it will confirm he cannot be trusted to support us in the coming war." Suddenly he winked at Theodore. "Such a rejection might work to our benefit, spurring the Knights of Falador to increase their commitment to our cause."

Theodore growled.

"I see what you mean to do," he said. "Varrock is desperate, and your armies prepare for combat. The Kinshra come to parley, but if King Roald accepts them then my own order would be greatly angered, and you would lose the help of a stronger ally. And likewise, he can't simply refuse to see such an envoy, for to do so would be a gross slight to the realm of Asgarnia of which the Kinshra are a part. Even Morytania respects envoys under parley. Varrock can do nothing less." He gritted his teeth. "What annoys me is your belief that Kara will play any role you wish. She isn't naive, nor is she a fool, Lord Ruthven, and she won't be a party to your petty politics!"

The knight turned away, but as he did Ruthven grabbed his arm. Surprised, Theodore saw how angry the older man was. His usually composed face had reddened, and his lips curled in a snarl.

"Petty politics?" he said. "I do not engage in *anything* petty, boy. The future of Misthalin will soon be tested, and I will do what it takes—*whatever* it takes—to make certain our victory and survival." His head jutted forward, coming only a finger's width from Theodore's face.

"If I tell Kara-Meir to ride out to the Kinshra envoy, then she *will* go, do you understand?" Then Ruthven sighed, and let his hand drop. He stepped back and breathed deeply.

"I am sorry, Theodore. I know you have conducted yourself with honor during your time in Varrock, but in my role I don't have the luxury of maintaining such high moral standards. I have lost everything I held dear to the *things* beyond the river." He lowered his head.

"Is it true, then, what they say?" Theodore asked him gently. "About your family? That the Gaunt Herald came to you and offered to heal your wife in exchange for your newborn daughter?"

Ruthven closed his eyes and covered his face with one hand.

"I am sorry, Lord Ruthven. I should not have asked."

"No, Sir Theodore," the lord muttered. "You shouldn't be sorry. But it is all true." He gave a peculiar snort and raised his head to stare Theodore in the eye. "That is why I fight in the war we wage," he said bitterly. "I thought to bargain with evil in my younger years, when I possessed the arrogance of the gods. It made me see the true importance of how life should be lived. Not for gain, nor even pleasure. But for victory over *Him*!"

The old man blinked the tears from his eyes.

"And so you must make a decision, Sir Theodore. I have told you this because I might need you to help convince Kara to go. She should not find herself in any danger.

"Will you help?"

"Perhaps," Theodore said. "Who else will go with her?"

Ruthven smiled.

"I will most likely go. Lord Despaard is gathering the men of the Owls together. Soon they will leave for the Salve to scout the lands beyond the river. I am too old for such an expedition." He snorted again. "Most of my time here is taken up trying to persuade Papelford to help Reldo in his duties. It is a thankless task, and I long to be doing more.

"No, I will likely go with her, and where she will be fire to Lord Daquarius, I will be ice. Together, we will see that his diplomacy fails." With that, he nodded. "I leave you to your decision. Please make it quickly."

The old man left him, and for a moment Theodore stood in silence, thankful again that he didn't have to live such a deceitful life.

Then, remembering his appointment with Father Lawrence, he hastened through the palace, where a growing army drilled and made ready for the coming conflict.

Outside of the palace wall it was little different. The populace was on edge. A feverish excitement buzzed about the merchants in the crowded main square. Men distributed pamphlets, and children watched puppet plays in which the lord of the dead was felled by a knight in white armor.

He fought his way east through the square and then turned north. With a cold chill he realized that the best strategy available to Tenebra would simply be to wait. If nothing threatened from

Morytania for six months or so, then King Roald would be forced
to reduce his army and to send the men back to the fields.

He has had centuries to prepare for this, he knew. *Centuries to our
mere days. What are a few months more?*

Father Lawrence was waiting in front of the church. He was deep
in conversation with two of the yellow-clad city guards who now
stood sentry there, in the shade of the impressive yew.

"Well met, Theodore," the avuncular man said. "I have been
expecting you since your return from Morytania." He clasped the
young knight's hand and shook it firmly. As he did so he leaned
closer and whispered. "The men under Lord Despaard frequently
come here once they end their missions in that land. They find it
important to talk to someone about what they have seen."

Theodore smiled at the rotund priest's enthusiasm.

"I am sorry to disappoint you, father," he said, "but I am not here
to talk about Morytania. Not today."

"Ahh! I think I see." The priest craned his head back and nodded
slyly. "You want to talk about the Lady Anne, then."

"Lady Anne?" he answered in surprise. He hadn't spoken to her
since the night she had ordered him to leave her room. But he had
seen her often enough, watching him from afar.

Father Lawrence grinned at his surprise.

"Come!" he said. "You'll be wanting a drink."

The old man bustled Theodore indoors before he could protest.
The church was empty, for the morning service had finished just
a short time before. Quickly he vanished behind the altar and
emerged holding a bottle and two glasses.

"This is often the best treatment for matters of the heart,
Theodore." He sat on the step and patted the stone at his side. "Now
sit, and tell me your concerns. Of women and their mysteries."

The knight laughed openly.

"Forgive me, father, but it is not about Lady Anne."

The priest's red face shot up.

"Oh," he said, and he sounded disappointed.

"No, it's something else altogether," Theodore began. "You have known me for months now, ever since I came to Varrock." He sighed and sat down. "Always I have tried to do my duty, as best I can."

The priest nodded firmly.

"You have, indeed, perhaps to the exclusion of all else. Here." He filled the glasses, and offered Theodore one of them. "Take this."

The knight declined with a shake of his head.

"But that is my point, father. The Knights of Falador are dedicated to truth, and to peace. But in recent days I have found that trying to live up to these ideals only causes pain, especially in my closest friends." When Father Lawrence said nothing he told the old man of Castimir's trial.

"Cas shook my hand when he left Varrock, so it seems he has at least in part forgiven me, but I am not sure whether he will ever trust me again. Not as before, anyhow." He hung his head and pushed his hands back through his hair. "Did I do wrong, father? In stubbornly refusing to lie?" He shook his head. "Perhaps Castimir was right when he called me a hypocrite? If I was so dedicated to my word—rather than my reputation—surely I would have told him to hand over the books at once, straight after the battle."

Father Lawrence sighed.

"There are no straight answers to your questions, Theodore," he said. "Holy men of all denominations have argued endlessly about this. It all boils down to an unanswerable question: would you value the ethics of consequences over those of means?" He took a sip from his glass.

"You take your orders from Saradomin, my friend," he explained. "Adherence to your word and your duty is by divine command, a command that cannot ever be wrong." The old man sighed. "Yet so does our bold inquisitor. Raispher also labors under such an impression. If he interprets something as his god-given duty, he will burn the innocent, consequences be damned."

"What?" Theodore stiffened. "He isn't doing *that*, is he? It would tear Varrock apart."

Father Lawrence took another quaff.

"Not yet," he admitted, grinning, "though he has been seen with his chosen orderlies, gathering firewood." He took Theodore's full glass and held it up to the light.

"We are all the same, in a way," he commented. "You, a knight of the church. Me, a simple priest, and Raispher, the zealous inquisitor. We must all balance means and consequence. Even King Roald, and for him the task is much, much more difficult."

"How so?" Theodore asked, thinking of his conversation with Lord Ruthven. "Doesn't the king rule by Saradomin's command, as do I?"

"He would have you believe that." The priest took a taste from Theodore's glass, and nodded in approval. "That he is a great man, led by divine insights. But in truth, there are no great men. There are just men, good or bad. And a man who pretends to be great— such as a king—will *always* be torn between the means and the ends." He drained Theodore's glass in one great gulp, paused, and then continued.

"Do you know the difference between a good king and a bad one, Theodore?"

The knight thought for a moment, and then shook his head.

"The difference between a good king and a bad one is that the good one regrets his power, for he will have to use it to make life-breaking decisions." Father Lawrence stared him in the face. "But the bad king, Theodore," he whispered. "The bad king will revel in his power, using it simply because he can."

The priest looked up to the stained-glass windows. The midday sun gave them a suitably holy glow.

"And I can tell you, Theodore, that King Roald has his regrets."

They sat in silence for a while, enjoying the colors that flooded the church.

Yet I am no closer to an answer, Theodore thought. *If a king may have doubts, how can I hope to know what is right and what is wrong?*

"Certainly I never thought of it in that way before, father." He lowered his head. "But what of Castimir? He was my best friend, and he is certain that I let him down."

A serious expression came to Father Lawrence's face.

"Castimir acted with deceit when he took the books," the priest said, "and he expected you to do the same, simply to cover up his own folly."

"But I let him keep them, after the siege," Theodore countered. "I didn't even question him. Was I so neglectful of my duty then that I lost hold of the truth?"

Father Lawrence shook his head and poured himself another glass.

"Firstly, Theodore, you are a man. And as I have said, men will always be torn." He took a sip. "Secondly, it is impossible to have a set of rules that apply to all circumstances. Take Castimir, for example, after the Siege of Falador." He rested a hand on the knight's shoulder. "You and he had fought and killed, side-by-side. You shared danger and braved death."

Theodore found himself nodding, for it was all true.

"And after the war, you both saw the injured and the dying in a city that had escaped death by the narrowest margin. You saw new widows and orphans, surrounded by soldiers dying from their injuries, and others who went mad from the pain of their wounds."

"Yes," Theodore whispered, recalling the horror. "That is all true," he said softly, a lump in his throat.

"And in all that misery, Theodore, when clean water was more precious than gold, when it was simply enough to have survived, when others needed your help, and the bodies needed burning, how could you possibly be expected to think twice about a few old books, written in a language no one understands?"

He squeezed with his hand.

"Those were your duties then, Theodore. You were not tasked to be Castimir's watchman." He shook his head. "No, my brave knight, ethics are relative. They must be, or else we will go mad."

Theodore looked at him, and to his surprise, the priest was smiling again.

"Based on my own experience, I would advise you to form a compromise," he said. "When a dying man confesses his sins, for me to tell his wife will only further her misery. It serves no good purpose." He drained the glass, and stood, reaching out a hand to help Theodore to his feet.

"Take enjoyment in the small things, and always try to act with a good motive, when you need to act at all."

22

"You sent for me ma'am?"

Kara watched Lucretia for a moment without speaking, attempting to gauge her mood. But the elderly maid gave no hints.

Has Caroline spoken to her? she wondered.

"I did, Lucretia," she said warmly. "I would like to thank you for taking Pia and Jack under your wing. The king's palace needs servants and errand boys, especially in days like these, and giving them both work was an excellent idea."

Lucretia nodded.

"Work is the key to discipline, ma'am," she remarked.

"And how do they fare?"

"They both have a lot to learn, but they are both willing. From what I gather of their experience beyond the river, it has encouraged them to accept their new situation."

Kara smiled.

"That is good news." She felt her palms grow sweaty as an awkward silence fell. "And the Kandarin ambassador, Sir Cecil—how has he behaved toward them?"

"He ignores them, as a man of his station should. I am aware of his request for their extradition, and of your offer to pay King Lathas on their behalf." A hint of a smile flickered across her severe features. "It has stalled him, for now." Kara clenched her fists and Lucretia's eyes narrowed.

"I beg your pardon, ma'am, but you didn't call for me to talk of your wards. I would venture to say that what you really seek is knowledge of my mistress—is that not so?"

Kara felt herself losing the initiative. She pursed her lips.

"You are bold for a maid, Lucretia," she said. "And perceptive." The old woman smiled sourly.

"When you reach my age, Kara-Meir, nothing surprises you anymore. There are few things I haven't seen. All I care is that my lady is happy, and that her honor remains unmarred." Her voice rose. "She most certainly was *not* happy when she returned to her room, the night you killed the guardsman. And whatever passed between you has caused a rift between her and Lord William, as well.

"One that has caused her no small misery," she added curtly.

Kara smiled, and the maid seemed startled.

"I respect everything you've said, Lucretia," Kara said. "And you should know that I wish no harm upon the Lady Caroline, for she aided me when I first came to Varrock. But I am concerned for her." She paused to let Lucretia speak, but the maid said nothing. "It is Lord William who concerns me," she added.

Lucretia remained silent.

"He is not a Saradominist," Kara explained. "And in the days to come, anyone who isn't will likely be regarded as an enemy of the king. Especially with Raispher and his Inquisition." She shook her head dismissively. "What can you tell me of William's family?"

"I have known him since he was a boy," Lucretia said, her expression unreadable. "You won't have cause to worry on his behalf. He is an honorable man. Of that I am certain, beyond the shadow of a doubt."

"And his family? Specifically his cousin. Are they well respected?"

Lucretia thought for a moment.

"His cousin… that would be Rudolph." She frowned and her face soured. "He was born outside of wedlock, and because of that he won't be allowed to inherit the estates of his father. Those will go to his younger brother, who was born within marriage." Kara nodded.

"I see. No doubt Rudolph was angered by the unfortunate circumstances of his birth. But tell me, what kind of man was he?"

Lucretia froze, and Kara cursed herself silently.

"*Was* he, ma'am?" the maid said. Kara bit her lip.

"He is dead, Lucretia," she said. "I was forced to kill him. He was one of the Zamorak insurgents who attacked the refugees from Morytania. He was going to kill Pia and Jack."

The maid's eyes widened, but she held her tongue.

Perhaps you haven't seen as much as you like to think, Kara thought smugly. But she didn't say so. Instead, she stepped forward and placed her hand on the maid's bony shoulder.

"Now you understand why I am concerned about Lord William, Lucretia," she said as gently as she could. "And of what harm this association could do to your mistress."

The maid nodded.

"I will tell you all I can recall of his family, ma'am." She looked doubtful, but Kara heard new respect in her voice.

Ebenezer sat in the corner of the room and sipped his wine. Doric, watching him from a stool at the table, remained still, smoking in silence.

"The arrogant… the blasted… the *imbecile!*" the alchemist blustered.

Doric nodded.

"Probably. But you saw what it did to him." The dwarf took his pipe out of his mouth and blew smoke into the air.

"Papelford will be the doom of us all," Ebenezer muttered. "Reldo is swamped with the volumes that his predecessor withheld from him." He took another swig of his drink, washing it around his mouth before he swallowed. "It's a whole new library!" He swore, and his hand shook violently.

He was so tired. More so, it seemed, than after his wounding at the hands of the Wyrd.

"Papelford *has* to help us, Doric," he said. "We don't have time to search through these new tomes. Blast it all!" He put his glass down on the windowsill and wrung his hands together, bleaching them white. "He has to share with us what he knows."

His blood pounded in his forehead. He felt dizzy.

"I will ask the king," he said decisively. "I will get the king to *order* him to help us. He won't... he won't refuse us then—"

His heart hammered in his chest. He felt pain shoot up his throat and settle like a yoke around his shoulders.

He tried to breathe.

"Doric..."

The dwarf leapt off his stool and ran to his side.

"Ebenezer!"

The alchemist's world went dark and his vision failed. He felt Doric's hands tearing at his shirt collar and recalled how he had thought that very morning that it was tighter than usual.

He felt air flood into his bursting lungs, but the dizziness remained. His blood throbbed inside his skull, but the pounding was the only thing he could hear.

"D-Doric..."

Past the dwarf's shoulder, the door opened and Sally entered the room. Her look of confusion was replaced by one of horror.

Not her, he thought. *Don't let her see me like this, not after all the suffering she has gone through with Albertus.* Ebenezer watched her intently as she shut the door and ran forward. As she passed the table she took a goblet of water.

"Sally…" he wheezed. She and Doric exchanged hurried words, then the goblet was pressed to his lips and cool water calmed the searing in his throat. The pressure around his shoulders faded, and he breathed easier than before.

"You should rest," Doric advised, and Ebenezer could hear him now. The dwarf pressed his shoulder tightly. "You have been working too hard with Reldo and Ellamaria. There are others who can do that."

The dizziness vanished and the throbbing in his head calmed. He nodded and for the first time noticed that Sally was crying. The gray-haired woman was clothed in black, her round face blotched from her tears.

"I am sorry, Sally," he said softly.

But the woman tried to smile.

"Fiddlesticks, Ebenezer!" she gasped over her sobs. "I can't lose you, not now." She put the goblet down and held his hand tightly. "I always hoped that you and Albertus and I would sit around the fire in our later years, to talk of all the things you'd seen in your travels." She wiped away a tear. "Now Albertus is gone—even his body was stolen by those wretched thieves. Only you and I remain of the old crowd."

He managed a smile.

"The old crowd?" he whispered. "Yes. They are all gone now, aren't they? Your husband, Erasmus—he was a good man, and Isaac, and so many others. All gone now." He sighed.

"We should get you to your room," Doric urged. "The others will be here soon for lunch, and you won't want to cause them any undue anxiety. I'll return and tell them you were just tired. Come," he said. The dwarf took Ebenezer's hand and hauled him gently to his feet. "Lean on me, alchemist."

They moved out of the lunch room and up the great staircase. To Ebenezer's aching body, every step seemed twice as high as he recalled, with twice as many stairs as before. By the top the dizziness and throbbing in his skull had returned.

Soon he was in his bed, and Doric left. Sally remained, and reminisced about the years they had known each other.

"I was always envious of my sister," she confessed, "before I married Erasmus, of course." She laughed. "How lucky Eloise was to snag you! I often thought—after Erasmus died, and then Eloise—that we… well, never mind. It was all so long ago. And of course, there was Albertus."

Her voice fell off, and when she spoke again it was grimmer.

"It makes me so angry," she said. "Why would anyone go to the trouble of burning and stealing corpses after they had already been butchered? Those animals need to be caught, and punished!"

Ebenezer smiled at her righteous anger.

"Why burn the bodies?" he said aloud. "These people want to cause fear, Sally. They foment panic. I find it stranger that they burned the bodies at all, rather than mutilate them. The latter would have caused even more outrage."

Sally sighed.

"It must have been a magical fire," she said wearily. "To have burned the bodies beyond recognition. Such disrespect."

The door opened and Ebenezer saw Doric peer around its edge. The dwarf gave a grin so joyful that Ebenezer might have been a freshly discovered seam of gold ore.

"How do you feel?" he asked, closing the door quietly and walking over to the alchemist's bed.

"I am cold, Doric. But I am comfortable now, thank you." His face darkened. "You haven't told the others, have you? I wouldn't want them to worry on my account, not in such an hour as this."

The dwarf nodded.

"All I told them was that you were tired after arguing with Papelford." Doric winked. "It's the truth, after all." He pulled up a chair, turning it so he was facing Sally as well. Then he continued.

"There have been developments," he said. "Lord Ruthven has asked Kara to leave Varrock and go with him to parley with the Kinshra. At first she thought the idea was ludicrous, but then she agreed to it."

"Why?" Ebenezer asked. "Surely there are better uses for her skills, what with Gar'rth and…" He looked to Sally, and hesitated. "… and the Black Prince planning his return."

The dwarf followed his gaze and nodded.

"I think Kara agreed so readily because she feels uneasy in the castle now, since she slew the assassin." He lowered his voice. "She doesn't know who to trust."

Doric pulled out his pipe and tamped a pinch of tobacco into the end. Ebenezer looked longingly as the dwarf lit it and inhaled with a resounding sigh.

Sally saw his craving look.

"Not for you, old man," she chided. "Just water. And bread, with butter if you are lucky—and only if you behave!"

Ebenezer scowled in mock indignation.

"I would be better off as a prisoner of Drakan," he grumbled. Then he turned to Doric with a questioning stare. "Are there other developments?"

"Nothing so dramatic," the dwarf said. "There is still a rift between our young friends, more so now that Arisha and Castimir have left."

"It was a mistake for Kara to lie to the king about her relationship with Gar'rth," Ebenezer said. "It gained her no advantage, and has only caused hurt." Doric nodded.

"I think she knows it, but too late. And now Theodore won't

believe her," he said. "It's causing the squire no end of trouble." He chewed on his pipe.

"But what of Lady Anne?" Ebenezer asked. "She was distraught when we first feared the embassy was dead. It was quite obvious she has strong feelings for Theodore."

"And he does for her, I think." The dwarf inhaled as Ebenezer laid his head back on the pillow.

Abruptly, Sally stood.

"Well, I know one thing I can do," she said. "I will visit Reldo, to help with his investigations." She smiled wanly. "Someone has to, or he'll collapse from exhaustion as well."

"Ask him about the bodies, Sally," Ebenezer urged. "It's simply not natural, after all this time."

Sally nodded and left the room.

"You refer to the Wyrd's victims, don't you?" the dwarf asked, and the alchemist nodded. "Are they... are they really as fresh as the day they were slain?" His face wrinkled in disgust. "Have they not even *begun* to decay?"

Ebenezer gave a macabre grin, for in truth, the mystery excited him.

"Not in the slightest, Doric. They are all there—even Lady Elizabeth, the king's betrothed. She was the first to be killed. Since then there must be a hundred others, all locked in the crypt below the palace."

Doric shivered.

"It is the power of Morytania, Ebenezer. It runs contrary to nature." He looked the alchemist in the eye. "I am glad they are locked in the crypt. But tell me, who has the key?"

Ebenezer smiled and pointed toward his jacket, hanging over the back of a chair.

"I took it off Papelford the same day he was dismissed."

23

The boy nodded to Castimir as he entered the great hall, then pushed his way through the patrons and stepped toward him.

Castimir took a sip from his ale, and waited.

"Hunding reports that two travelers from Varrock have arrived." The boy's eyes widened. "They have asked after you and Arisha. Hunding says they carry a message from the king."

"Have you told Arisha?" Castimir asked. The boy nodded.

"She is with her mother, Haba. Litara has gone to inform her. I dare not interrupt a meeting between two priestesses."

The disgraced wizard stood quickly, abandoning his ale and half-eaten steak. His urgency did not go unnoticed by the nearest tribesman, a tattooed hulk who had decided to act as Castimir's personal bodyguard.

"Wait, outlander," he said, his voice like echoing thunder. "You must not be rash. The priestess has asked that I look after you. I must honor her request." His eyes narrowed. "Here—put this on." The man removed his cloak and handed it over. It was heavy, and far too big for him.

But he took it and slid into it without daring to complain.

"What are you thinking, Haakon?" the boy asked.

The hulk grinned. He ruffled the boy's head.

"Let us see what manner of men these are, before we act." He pulled a heavy, two-handed sword from the shadows under the table and moved toward the door. "Come."

Castimir pulled the hood over his head. He felt for the two knives he wore upon his belt and adjusted the studded-leather armor that guarded his body. He still ached from their ride.

Outside the great hall the world had grown dark. They had arrived before dawn that morning, at the end of a two-day stretch, and it had been Arisha's idea to watch for any sign of pursuit. She had briefed her kinsmen to help hide their presence, then they had taken the day to re-supply in preparation for the longer and far more uncertain journey.

Now, as the low clouds threatened rain and the rumble of far-off thunder could be heard, he followed Haakon past the wooden huts of the settlement known as Gunnarsgrunn. They headed for the clearing that occupied the south of the settlement, where visitors would arrive.

The boy hissed suddenly in warning, and Castimir followed his gaze. Two cloaked figures stood by their horses, taking warmth from a torch that burned in its sconce. He stepped back into the shadows and watched them carefully, unwilling to take the chance that they might know him.

The breeze quickened. Castimir detected the freshening smell of rain on the approaching storm.

One of the travelers removed their hood. It was a man with a black beard and scarred face. Castimir could not recall seeing him before.

"Outlanders," a woman's voice called to the newcomers, her words carrying over the chill winds. "This way. Come." She approached them, carrying a torch in her hand. She raised the burning brand and Castimir saw the attractive face of Litara. The blonde-haired woman gestured impatiently. "The priestess is eager for word from Varrock. *Come.*"

Castimir was about to follow when he felt Haakon's hand set firmly against his chest. He couldn't have moved, even if he had wanted to.

"Not yet, outlander. Not yet. We must be sure." He shook his head.

The two figures caught up with Litara and accompanied her along a narrow street. Haakon dropped his hand and followed, walking swiftly.

When they vanished around a corner, Castimir broke into a run. Instinctively his right hand thrust its way into one of his satchel's side pockets, pulling out a set of rune stones he had carefully put there before leaving Varrock.

But dare I use my magic here? he wondered. *The tribesmen distrust magic, and have no love for wizards—even fallen ones.* Nonetheless, if Arisha was threatened, he knew there would be no choice.

He turned the corner as the skies opened. Droplets the size of small stones slanted into his face. When he blinked away the water he saw the three shapes vanish into a hut.

Haakon ran past him, and as he did so Castimir heard a cry.

The door burst open and one of the messengers leapt out. Castimir hadn't seen the person's features until now. It was a woman. She looked up just in time to see Haakon power into her, his clenched fist flying.

Crunch.

She flipped over, propelled by the force of the warrior's blow. In her hand, Castimir noticed a curved black dagger, similar in design to the one the assassin had carried in Arisha's room.

"Arisha!" he shouted, sprinting to the hut's swinging door.

Inside, the scarred man struggled vainly, restrained by Litara and two broad-shouldered men. Arisha huddled nearby, clutching her shoulder and gasping. Her furious eyes bore into the man.

"What were you thinking?" Castimir choked. "He could have killed you!" He ran to her side and pushed her hand away. Blood coated her blue robe. She gasped again. She gritted her teeth and snarled.

"I… h-had to know," she gasped. "Had to find out why… why they want me dead."

The stain continued to spread. Castimir felt sick. He had seen death many times in the months of riding at Kara-Meir's side. But this, seeing someone he loved—

I can lose my place as a wizard, he thought furiously. *I can lose anything in the world—but not her.*

"C-Castimir!"

Arisha gasped, then her eyes rolled up into her head, and closed.

"*Arisha?*" he said. Still she breathed, but irregularly.

A rough hand pushed him aside. Litara bent forward with a knife. She cut the fabric of Arisha's robes in a hurried but steady manner. To Castimir it seemed dream-like. He was only vaguely aware as Haakon and the other two men dragged the assassin out into the rain, their voices all but lost in the storm.

The cries that followed were much easier to hear.

When the wound was exposed, Castimir paled. The assassin had tried to slash her throat, but instead had cut her just below the collarbone. It was a deep wound.

He saw the uncertainty in Litara's face, but before he could speak he became aware of another presence in the room. A dark-haired woman stood over them.

"Bring her," the woman said firmly. "Bring my daughter to my home." She looked at Castimir for the briefest moment, through blue eyes that were exactly like her daughter's.

Castimir moved to help Litara, but her mother's hand fell on his shoulder.

"Not you, outlander," she commanded. "You have done enough." Then, without another word, she left.

Haakon returned, lifting the injured woman in his arms.

"She is not dead yet, outlander," he said. "Go. Wait in the long hall."

Castimir knew there was no point in arguing. Deflated, and feeling as unwelcome as ever he had been, he trudged back through the rain, oblivious of the cold sting that lashed his face.

For an hour or more he sat by himself in the great hall of the tribes. The open fires could not warm him, and no drink in the world could lighten his mood.

The attitude in the hall itself had grown tense. The revelry for which it was famed quickly dissipated as word of the attack got round. Castimir heard it, whispered from mouth to ear, passing like a contagion among the men and women. And like a contagion, it left all who experienced it silent and somber.

He felt the glare of Arisha's people fall on him many times, and remembered with a pang of sorrow how it was in this same room that he had seen her for the very first time. That was the same night he met Kara and Doric, as well. A night of meetings and friendship, the prelude to an adventure that had made him famous.

An anonymous man refilled his drink. Castimir looked up to thank him, but the server had gone as swiftly as he came, moving to others in the hall.

They are such a contrary people, he reflected. *So unlike Aubury, Roald and the knights. More honorable than all of them,* he decided. *And yet more fickle. Dangerous, too.*

His eye fell on a young boy, only waist-high, whose elder kin were directing him on how to start a fire with a longbow. The boy knelt with his bare foot pressed hard onto a wooden board, notched along one edge. In the largest notch he placed a wooden spindle that was entwined in the outside edge of his bowstring.

Very quickly, and to the encouragement of his kin, the boy pushed the bow forward and then pulled it back, turning the spindle with the string in the board's notch at his feet. For a long moment he did this, gritting his teeth, until a pale wisp of smoke drifted up from the board. The boy cried out in delight.

Castimir was so caught up in the scene that he only noticed Haakon when the hulk sat down next to him.

"She will live," the barbarian said before he could ask. Castimir gasped in relief.

"Can I see her?" he asked. Haakon shook his head.

"Her mother thinks it unwise. She is a gifted healer. She has made a poultice from rotting bread."

Castimir's face revealed his disgust.

"But you must do something," the barbarian said. "The two captives—they must tell us what they know. Arisha's mother expects you to question them." The huge man's hand wrapped itself around Castimir's wrist. "As her man, you must protect her. You must show the priestess Haba that you can be strong for her daughter."

He felt his insides grow cold.

"You need to do this, boy," Haakon advised. "We know you used to be a wizard." His eyes hardened. "But you have been expelled by the Tower. You have embraced our ways—the ways of nature over runes—and because of that your love for Arisha is tolerated. Still, some have their doubts." His grip tightened. "You can end those, this night, by seeking justice."

"I thought the people of the tribes never executed their own," Castimir said quietly.

Haakon frowned.

"We respect life," he replied. "The death sentence is reserved for the most serious of crimes. But these assassins are different. They are outlanders who abused our hospitality to attempt to murder a priestess." His eyes grew bright. "There can be no mercy for such cowards."

Castimir gritted his teeth and nodded.

The rain was still pouring as Haakon led the way. Lightning flashed overhead and yet Castimir didn't even blink.

I came so close to losing her. Now I must be strong.

They passed through a gap in the southern fence that led to an open quarry. Piles of black coal and red clay lay in neat mounds, and a sweet burning scent, strangely familiar, turned his stomach. The barbarian stopped, and Castimir saw the two assassins. They were face down, their limbs tied. Several men stood around them in a wide circle, and they all looked at him with undisguised expectation. Suddenly self-conscious, he turned away to peer at a coal pile. A lean dog stood there, drawn by the smell.

Then he knew what it was. He had experienced it before, sometimes caused by his own magic. It was the smell of burning flesh.

"We have already started," Haakon explained as he took a steaming iron rod from the coals of a protected fire. It glowed bright red. "We need to know who sent them, and it is your duty to loosen their tongues." He held the iron out, and waited. "Haba expects it.

"So does Arisha."

Castimir nodded. He remembered Arisha, and the terrible wound.

I need to be strong.

He heard the dog growl from the summit of coal, then another, and another, as more joined it. The pack was moving in for a feast.

Castimir took the hot iron, and approached the nearest prisoner.

Arisha was sitting up in her bed. A bearskin blanket covered her legs. Her usually pale skin was yellowed, shining with perspiration. When Castimir peered at her closely, he saw with concern that her eyes were feverishly bright.

"You did what you had to," Arisha murmured. Her hand reached out to his and took it in a surprisingly firm grasp. "Not for me, Castimir, and not for us, either, but for everyone. Whoever wants me dead must fear me beyond the rest of you. And there's only one reason I can think of for that.

"It must be the runes," she whispered. "It must be the idea that I can retrieve the essence vital to the Salve." Castimir nodded his agreement.

Suddenly she looked into his eyes with alarm.

"No one outside of the king's private council knew of our mission," she hissed. "Someone there must have orchestrated this. Someone in Varrock."

He nodded again, but said nothing.

"Talk to me," she said after several heartbeats. "Please, say something."

"Talk to you?" he answered. "Tonight I have done something of which I never thought myself capable, Arisha." Tears sprang to his eyes. "I *hurt* them—both of them. Yet they gave away *nothing*—they said nothing about the person who sent them." He wrenched his hand away from her and balled it into a fist.

The smell of the burning flesh followed him. He gagged.

"I have done something evil, Arisha," he said. "I carried on hurting them even when I was sure they didn't know. And a part of me actually *enjoyed* it, when I thought of what they had done to you."

He fell silent as Arisha stroked his hand.

"We will leave," she said, "as soon as possible." He shook his head.

"You can't," he insisted. "You aren't nearly well enough."

"I'm not hurt as badly as I look, Cas," she answered. "And it is more important than ever that we move as quickly as we are able. When these two don't report back, then whoever sent them will send more."

He knew she was right.

"Where?" he asked.

"I don't know yet," she confessed. "My mother refused to tell me. Even King Roald's warrant did not sway her. But I will try to speak to her again tomorrow."

The door opened suddenly, causing him to jump up in alarm. There stood Haba, holding a bag. She stared at him coldly.

"Mother?" Arisha said.

The priestess stepped in. She was taller than Castimir, and he felt awe. Respectfully he bowed on one knee, and then stood.

"My daughter has told me of her travels beyond the holy river," she said. "You and she have walked among demons and all manner of creatures abhorrent to nature. Now those demons threaten our world." The priestess looked at her daughter, and her eyes softened. "I cannot tell you where to seek the essence you so desperately need," she said bluntly. "To do so would be sacrilege of the highest order, and would bring death to the oath breaker. Our wars against the runes were holy crusades."

She stepped forward and her voice dropped to an urgent whisper.

"But there lives a man by the name of Kuhn." Arisha gasped, and a look of disgust passed over her face. "Kuhn is an exile. He was once of our tribe." Haba turned toward Castimir. "He cannot return, for he is a murderer. Yet he lives now in Edgeville. He has the information you need, but he is a dangerous man."

Castimir smiled. Edgeville was little over a day's ride from

Gunnarsgrunn. His smile vanished, however, when he saw Haba frown.

"From there you will need to journey into The Wilderness," Haba told them. "You will need this." She handed Castimir the bag. He loosened the string and peered inside. There he found an ivory horn.

"It is the horn of a unicorn," Haba explained. "Take it with you, for you will need it to gain the trust of those who dwell upon the Mountain of Fire."

"The Mountain of Fire? I have heard of it," Arisha said, "but I don't know where it is."

"You will," her mother said. Castimir just stared.

"Tell me, Haba," he said, a bit startled at the sound of his own voice. "Why have you changed your mind? Why are you helping us?"

Haba smiled, and again Castimir thought how like Arisha she looked.

"Why would I help a fallen wizard locate the essence?" She locked him with her gaze. "Our wars may have ended generations ago, but the distrust remains." She stared angrily at Arisha's shoulder. "But when your enemies tried to murder my daughter in my own home, I knew that your actions had angered someone—a person of no small influence. By trying to kill you, they proved that your story has merit.

"Castimir, you have proved yourself capable of making difficult choices, and of doing what is necessary. Therefore you go with my blessing."

24

They left Gunnarsgrunn at first light, and headed swiftly north. The ground was soft after the rain, and the trees gave off a sweet scent of pine and resin.

"Theodore should get my message within the next two days," Castimir said. They had decided it was prudent to warn their friends of their suspicions. "Then he and Kara will have to decide what to do in Varrock."

They rode in silence for a long while, enjoying the sunshine that had followed the storm. Arisha's color was still off, and Castimir watched her carefully, never straying far from her side.

"You have never been to Edgeville before, have you?" she asked when they stopped for lunch and to let the horses graze. Castimir's yak stood patiently nearby.

"No," he answered. "Is it as bad as they say?"

Arisha smiled. Her face was still sallow, and every time she moved her left arm, she clenched her jaw in pain. Her mother had applied a moldy compound to the wound and wrapped it in a fresh bandage before they had left. It was something Castimir found revolting.

"It is worse than they say," she replied after a moment. "You've heard of Solus Dellagar, the murder mage?"

Castimir snorted in disdain.

"And the Edgeville Incident? Who hasn't?"

Arisha managed a slight smile.

"There are different stories, but remember, when it happened, I was living in Gunnarsgrunn, only a day's ride away. We *saw* it happen, or at least part of it. For several nights the sky raged with all manner of colorful specters. Some swore the end of the world had come, while others said that a dragon had swept down from The Wilderness." She sighed and eased her left arm into a better position. "Nonetheless, after the first night my people sent scouts to discover the truth."

Castimir's heart quickened.

"Your people actually saw what happened?" he said. "There have been so many stories told, it seems as if the truth is impossible to learn." He smiled suddenly. "Four years ago or so, I was traveling with a master wizard, acting as his apprentice. He was a lazy fellow, though kind-hearted." Castimir frowned as he checked his memory. "We were in Draynor, I think, when news first reached us of the atrocity. By then word had traveled far, and we had no doubt that it was inflated." He sighed. "Almost immediately, people began to act differently. They realized what power a great wizard could command, and they became less friendly after that."

He wondered if Solus Dellagar surpassed even Sedridor in power. According to some of the stories, it had required an army to bring him down.

"They say he killed at least eight hundred people."

Arisha nodded.

"Perhaps he did," she said. "When our scouts returned, they told of a pitched battle, with the Knights of Falador and the Kinshra fighting side-by-side to destroy him. Whatever the truth, the town of Edgeville was never again the same." She sighed. "It was all but deserted, becoming a haven for all sorts of lawless men who forayed into The Wilderness.

"It was still a lawless place," she added, "when I was there six months ago, after fleeing from the monastery with the monks. The king assigned a governor to change that, but he couldn't govern a classroom full of children. He's supported by a garrison of King Roald's men, none of whom could be trusted to serve anywhere else." She rolled her eyes. "Most of them are drunkards."

"This man, Kuhn—your mother warned us that he's dangerous." Castimir took a bite of the meatloaf that the tribes had prepared for them the previous day. "What'd he do?" he said through a mouthful.

"He murdered a man in a fight over a woman," Arisha replied. She winced, and avoided his curious stare.

"What sort of woman?" he asked.

Arisha clenched her fist.

"It was my mother, Cas." She lifted her eyes to him and Castimir saw how upset she was. "The man he killed was my father. It was a stupid drunken argument that grew out of control. Apparently Kuhn struck him and he fell, hitting his head on stone. He died two days later."

Arisha exhaled sharply. She bent her arm into a different position and winced again.

"I'm sorry," Castimir said. "I didn't know."

"I would have told you anyhow," she confessed. "You would have needed to know before we met him."

A bird flew overhead, crossing the sun.

"Come," she said. "We should be getting on. Who knows what people might be following in our tracks." She glanced back, then looked ahead. "When we get to Edgeville, we shouldn't use our real names."

• • •

It was growing dark when they approached the town. There had been no sign of any pursuit, yet it was what lay in front of them that worried Castimir now.

The first he saw of Edgeville was a series of ruined buildings— hollow gray stone structures whose interiors had rotted away to nothing. Behind rows of such dereliction, an old church with a missing roof stood in a perilous state, its windows broken and its tower partially collapsed.

Arisha offered to go first, but it was clear to Castimir that it would not be wise. Instead, he led the way forward, guiding his horse and yak. They passed between broken walls and areas where glass shards covered the ground. Often, the wind was funneled through the ruins, chilling where it touched bare skin and moaning a ghostly cant in his ear.

The dead souls of Solus's victims? he wondered with a shiver. *Perhaps seeking vengeance on any magic-user who passes near their graves.*

Once they had passed through the initial ruins he caught sight of people. There was a large square that served as a marketplace, its stalls closed up for the night. Still, several small crowds stood outside, for the air was hot. Of King Roald's garrison, the only sign was a sleeping drunk, his yellow tunic stained with substances Castimir wasn't keen to investigate.

When they crossed the square, some of the onlookers grew silent and regarded them with obvious suspicion. Others were openly hostile.

"Haven't seen you here before," someone said as they drew near. "Those are fine-looking beasts, though. You'll need someone to keep an eye on them."

A man staggered forward. He reeked of alcohol and spoke

through a mouth that didn't contain a single tooth.

"I'll do it, sir," he said. "For a gold piece, sir." He held out his hands in the manner of a beggar.

Castimir was saved the trouble of answering when a young woman stepped out from among the shadows and tripped the beggar. He fell on his back, eliciting peals of laughter as the raven-haired woman bowed.

"Is that any way to treat a veteran of the war?" the drunk shouted angrily. "We drove the enemy before the walls of Falador, and crushed them between us! I was a knight back then—a knight!"

Castimir's attention was roused.

Perhaps he's heard of me, or of my friends?

"You fought in the Siege of Falador?" he asked.

"Aye, young man. I did. I came south under Lord Sulla's banner, and watched as he turned certain victory into absolute defeat." He stood and blinked away his tears.

Castimir breathed deeply.

"And if ever I see him again," the drunk added, gripping an invisible dagger with his hand, "I'll put out his other eye, and cut off his—"

"Shut up, old man," the raven-haired woman said. She turned her dark eyes onto Castimir, and he felt his face redden. Her dress was lower and tighter than any he had seen before—indecently so. "You'll be wanting somewhere to stay for the night," she said. Castimir nodded, and she continued. "I know just the place. Your animals will be safe there as well."

Castimir glanced at Arisha, who nodded discreetly. They followed the girl to a large gray stone building that stood in better shape than any other in the immediate vicinity.

"Are you members of the Forlorn Souls?" the girl asked as she guided them around the side, to where a small courtyard had been turned into a stable. A watchman let them pass without question.

"The Forlorn Souls?" Castimir repeated.

"The mercenaries," the girl clarified. "It's what they call themselves. It's like their guild, I guess. Rumor has it that the king has sent them a message, for he has need of their services."

"Are you a member of their guild?" Castimir asked.

"No, sir, not me." She smiled. "I'm from a different guild—"

Arisha coughed from behind. Castimir turned and caught her good-natured scowl. The girl saw it too. She curtseyed very briefly.

"Pardon, ma'am. I wasn't aware—"

"We'll want a room, if any are available," Arisha said without malice. "And stabling for our animals. It will be worth your while. Tell me, what is your name?"

The girl smiled up.

"They call me Loquacious Annie, ma'am."

Arisha laughed.

"That's very good, Annie. Tell me, do you know a man called Kuhn? He's from Gunnarsgrunn. A barbarian."

The girl's face darkened. She ran her hand through her hair and looked to one side. When she spoke, her voice was tense.

"Yes, ma'am, I do," she said. "He's not as nice as the others. He's not a kind man."

Arisha nodded.

"I know, Annie. But I need to see him. If you arrange a meeting, I will pay you handsomely."

Annie looked doubtful.

"You won't… you won't *hurt* him, will you?"

"We're not murderers, Annie," Castimir said. "I promise you, neither of us shall hurt him unless it's in our defense."

Annie laughed.

"Oh, no, sir, I don't care about Kuhn, but he's a member of the Souls, you see. If anything happens to one of them, then the others like to even the score. If they found out I'd been involved…"

She brought her clenched fist down onto her palm, to illustrate the point.

"Go, Annie," Arisha told her. "Find the landlord, and then find Kuhn." When she had gone, Arisha turned her glare to Castimir. He felt himself wither under its power.

"I didn't know she was a…" he muttered. "Really."

Arisha smiled, breaking her spell.

"Men," she sighed. "You're all alike."

Within an hour, they were seated at a table on the second floor. The bones of a roasted chicken lay piled upon their plates.

Outside, through the window of their private dining room, the marketplace was just visible. It was late now and the square outside was near deserted.

Castimir watched Arisha intently, hoping she wouldn't notice. Her breathing was slow and her skin had not shaken off its pallor. Since taking their room she had changed and washed and rebandaged her wound. It seemed she knew what she was doing, yet he was sure he wouldn't be able to sleep that night.

Her injury terrified him. So much could go wrong with it, especially when traveling. And in such a place as The Wilderness…

A fist battered on the door, startling both of them. Castimir stood, but before he could move it swung inward and a large man stalked in. He looked as if he was made from wood. His face was brown and weathered. A white mustache merged with a beard that was cut short. Leather armor covered his body, leaving his arms exposed.

A knife was thrust into each boot, while a hatchet at his belt hung by his sword scabbard. He folded his arms as his deep eyes set on Castimir.

"I am Kuhn," he growled. "Who are you to—"

He stopped when he saw Arisha. His arms opened and his fists clenched.

"*You*," he growled. "I recognize you. What do *you* want?" He advanced upon her. "Is it your mother?

"Is she dead yet?"

Anger made Castimir bold.

"Hold your tongue, murderer." His hand delved into the side pocket on his satchel. He had come prepared. "Don't dare speak with such disrespect to a priestess of your people."

Kuhn turned on Castimir. Arisha stood quickly, hiding her weakness.

"Who are you?" the barbarian demanded. The man's hands darted forward and grabbed Castimir by the collar. Feet kicked empty air as Kuhn lifted him off the floor without the slightest effort.

"I *am* a murderer," he spat into Castimir's face. "You're right about that. So one more ain't going to matter, is it?"

"Stop, Kuhn!" Arisha said firmly. "We need your help. We come at the behest of King Roald himself. We even have the king's warrant."

Kuhn frowned. Still he didn't lower Castimir.

"Think, Kuhn," Arisha urged, moving around the table. "Help us, and I could even get you a pardon, forgiving any crimes that you have committed against Misthalin's laws."

The barbarian gave a sneering grin.

"I doubt that," he replied. "I doubt that a *lot*."

"If you were wanted that much, then the Forlorn Souls would have taken you already," Castimir wheezed. "They cannot operate without Varrock's consent, and they won't harbor murderers."

Kuhn ignored him. His eyes remained fastened on Arisha.

"Our need is great, Kuhn," she said. "I need you to lead us into The Wilderness—to the place only you can show us. I need you to take us to the Mountain of Fire."

Castimir was dropped to the floor. Kuhn turned fully on Arisha.

"This is some sort of test, isn't it?" he said warily. "You are a priestess of the tribes. There is no way you would want to go there."

Arisha nodded.

"But I must," she said. "Not for the sake of our people, Kuhn, but for the sake of the kingdom."

Kuhn peered down at Castimir and gave a contemptuous snort.

"I care nothing for 'our people,' for they sent me away to die," he said. "I have little concern for the kingdom, but I do love gold—and the power it brings over these weak outlanders. The pardon of Roald would be useful, too."

"I can promise you both," Arisha lied.

"Good," he answered. "Then I will believe you—for now—and guide you there. But you must be prepared for what you will find. It is a sacred place, erected in memory of the crusader wars we fought against the wizards, and those who would use runes for their own gain.

"It is still guarded."

Arisha frowned.

"By whom?" she asked. "The crusades ended generations ago."

Kuhn crossed his arms, and wore a leering smile that seemed designed to offend.

"It is watched by those who have given their flesh to their unending duty, by the Untainted. Poor, brave, deluded fools."

"The Untainted?" Arisha gasped. "But they are myths—"

"No, they live," he said, cutting her off. "In their own peculiar way, I suppose. And they watch. They guard the spoils of the crusades."

Arisha bowed her head.

"What are the Untainted?" Castimir asked.

"I had always believed them to be legend," Arisha said, "for their lives span many decades." She closed her eyes and grimaced. "But the price they pay for such longevity, if the rest of the legends are true..."

"They are," Kuhn said. "Mostly, I think."

Arisha gave a fearful sigh. Then she looked Castimir in the eye.

"They are lepers, Cas—lepers who live with pain for years beyond measure. They were once great warriors, and to live a life of daily agony that spans generations is a test. They believe that only at the end of such a trial can they earn the right to sit in honor before Guthix."

"Do you still wish to go?" Kuhn asked.

Arisha nodded.

"We have no choice. None at all."

25

"It's *her* blood mark, isn't it?" Tenebra seethed. "The witch has interfered again."

Gar'rth braced himself for his father's anger, suddenly conscious of the Blisterwood weapon he had hidden inside his coat.

But nothing happened.

Vanstrom kneeled silently in the shadows, alongside Kendrick and Strainge, who sat with ruined legs. All around them, in the darkness at the edge of the pool, Gar'rth could see distorted figures. Dozens of them.

Zombies, he realized with a chill. *Tenebra's own creations.*

"Still," the vampire lord said, composing himself, "it is not unexpected. Not in the slightest. Perhaps she has grown tired of her playthings, and seeks new amusements." His wild eyes gripped Gar'rth. "Perhaps she hopes that in shielding you from my powers, she will goad me into destroying you myself, now that your value is so much less to me than it was before."

"I think not, Father," Gar'rth said. "I know that there are others whom you bred. My siblings. I know that creating me was no easy task." He held the vampire's stare. "And without me, you have no suitable heir to the throne of Misthalin." He stepped forward, emboldened by his own words. "And *that* is what you crave, isn't it, Father? I know it is, for Vanescula gave me your diary. I am the keystone of your plan."

Tenebra nodded silently. He raised an eyebrow and Gar'rth thought there was the glimmer of a smile on his marble face.

"You have worthwhile qualities, son," he muttered. "Righteous anger. Hatred. Physical strength and skill. All are necessary in a king." Tenebra leered suddenly. "But you are compassionate. There can be no room for that. Not in a king. Not in a man whose job is to rule an empire.

"Take Kara-Meir, for example."

Gar'rth tried to disguise the anger his father's words inspired. Yet he was certain he failed.

"I have already told you what I will do with her and your friends, once our victory is complete," Tenebra continued. "But there is no need for such threats—your future is already written." His smile grew to hideous proportions. "I have seen her dreams. Dreams of Theodore."

Gar'rth's stomach knotted. Bile rose in his throat.

"You lie!" he gritted. His hands balled in rage.

"She will abandon you," Tenebra continued. "It is inevitable. You will be hated and cursed by them—by those alongside whom you once fought.

"I have seen it, my son," he said. "Kara-Meir *hates* you, and everything you represent."

Tenebra turned his gaze aside.

In that instant, Gar'rth acted. He drew the Blisterwood and lunged forward, aiming to cut his father across the throat.

Vanstrom cried out as he covered the distance in the blink of an eye. Tenebra turned, and Gar'rth rejoiced at his father's astonishment as the weapon scythed toward his throat.

"No, Gar'rth!" Vanstrom leapt up with a speed Gar'rth had never encountered in the living. The man's hands wrapped around his wrist, and his grip was unnaturally strong. He sank to his left knee and pivoted, forcing Gar'rth to the floor of the chamber.

"What have you done, Vanstrom?" Strainge demanded. The man didn't reply. He twisted Gar'rth's wrist until the Blisterwood dropped. Then he scuffed the weapon behind him, toward Tenebra.

"V-Vanstrom?" Gar'rth wheezed. "Why?" Over the man's shoulder, Tenebra loomed, watching intently.

"Why?" Vanstrom repeated, his eyes blazing. From their depths a vicious red tint crushed Gar'rth's hope. "Why?" he asked again, laughing. His face rippled, boiling from beneath, his flesh melting down the sides of his cheeks and across his jaw. His beard fell loose as the flesh dripped across his ragged shirtfront.

"No, oh gods, no!" Kendrick whispered.

Finally the thing called Vanstrom Klause stood upright. The scaled visage that hissed through the wreckage of a face widened in a satisfying smile.

"You're one of them!" Kendrick moaned. "One of the Vyrewatch."

"But y-you had a scent!" Gar'rth said. "How?"

"I have no true scent," the creature corrected. "But this…" He waved his still-human hand in front of his face. "This *thing* that I wore, this travesty of life, this blasphemy, was enough to fool you." It looked at Strainge and the weeping Kendrick, and smiled in delight. "For years I have run with the Myreque. Learning their ways, delighting in the deaths of those who struggle for a 'better' world." It turned back to Gar'rth, and he felt the red eyes fasten upon him.

"Did you feel it too, I wonder? The power and the lust for blood when you let Tam die?" The thing's tongue licked its lips. "And what a death he endured! Cursing your name as you left him to the bloodvelds. I heard everything."

Kendrick gaped in disbelief.

"Gar'rth?" he said weakly. "Tell us it wasn't so." He crouched next to Ben Strainge, and both looked at him with horror.

"It wasn't like that," Gar'rth muttered. "It wasn't." His breath came in deep gasps. Panic was rising. "I h-had to keep the Blisterwood safe, didn't I? That was what… we risked everything for it."

"Ah, the Blisterwood." Tenebra knelt. He held out a black cloth and wrapped the weapon in it carefully before hiding it in his robes. "The one weapon that can destroy us. The Myreque's only hope to inflict a serious fatality among the vampire hierarchy." He stood and advanced over the two cowering men. "Now it is mine."

Then he turned back to his son.

"You see, Gar'rth, how impotent your efforts have been? From the very start you have been performing to my plans. Vanescula tried to turn you against me, and Vanstrom guided you to the Myreque. You helped them recover a weapon I need to exact my revenge." His red eyes sparkled in the dull light.

Mirroring his father's triumph, the other creatures advanced to within the limits of Gar'rth's vision. Grinning faces of the undead regarded him victoriously. Their bloodlust made them drool.

"But he—he helped them escape!" Gar'rth said. "Vanstrom helped Kara and the others cross the river."

Tenebra nodded.

"Indeed, just as I asked of him. Have you forgotten the last remaining key? I needed another servant in Varrock, a powerful one. Thanks to Vanstrom, that servant is in place, awaiting my command."

Vanstrom hissed a laugh.

"Your friends," it said. "Like young Pia. So *fresh*. I was so looking forward to consuming her. But she isn't innocent, Gar'rth. She is a murderer, too. I have seen it. I have shared in the blood we spilt together in our final hours on Hope Rock."

Gar'rth growled.

"And now, my son, you have reached the end of your road." Tenebra stood over him. "It is time to put aside your folly and join my cause." His father looked to Kendrick and Strainge. "Show me your dedication. Kill them both, my son."

"No," Gar'rth whispered. "No…" He turned aside, unable to endure the looks the two men gave him.

"Do it," Tenebra said. "Embrace Zamorak, and be free. Do it, and join me!"

Gar'rth felt Tenebra's mood change, for it was reflected in the creatures that stood around the pool. They transformed from drooling beasts to fearful shadows.

"If you won't kill them, then I will," Tenebra told him. "And once that is done, I will lock you away, in a dark prison where you will not be fed. But you won't be alone, for I shall cage a human child with you. And when hunger overcomes you, you will eat. You will eat or you will die."

Gar'rth cringed. He cursed the world. He cursed Kara for leaving him, cursed her for not killing him when she had the chance.

"What is it to be, my son? The lives of two fighting men, or the blood of an innocent?"

"I will not do it!" Gar'rth roared suddenly, rising to his feet. "I refuse!"

Tenebra remained still for a long moment.

The Vyrewatch licked its lips and hissed.

"So be it," Tenebra answered. He turned and grabbed Kendrick by the throat. The man screamed as he was lifted into the air. Gar'rth closed his eyes as the cry was cut short, replaced by the sound of tearing flesh.

"Kendrick!" Ben Strainge shouted. "Gar'rth! Gar'rth, help—"

His cry, too, was silenced, replaced by a gurgling that lasted only a moment.

When Gar'rth opened his eyes, the bodies of the two men lay at Tenebra's feet. His father watched him as if from afar, his eyes glazed. Around the sides of the chamber the creatures he had created writhed and wriggled in an ecstasy, sharing in their master's abandon.

"They experience what I feel," Tenebra explained. "They feel what I feel, and they would march to certain destruction in my service, as no human soldier ever could. They would serve you as well, Gar'rth, once you give yourself to Zamorak."

Strainge's dead eyes were still open. They gazed accusingly at him.

Coward, they screamed silently. *Coward, and traitor.*

"I w-won't do it," Gar'rth said. "I won't—"

Ben Strainge blinked. The dead man tried to stand on his shattered legs, only to fall. Kendrick, too, was moving—his head bent at an obscene angle. Tenebra smiled.

"Enemies in life, they will serve me now, my son. They will crawl on their bellies to obey my commands. And they are not the only ones."

Tenebra waved his hand. Instantly Gar'rth was hurled backward. *Crunch.*

Whether the sound was his breaking bones or the crumbling of stone, he didn't know. Pain burst through his body and he lay in a heap upon the ground.

"As Vanescula revealed, you are not the first of my children," Tenebra explained. "I have bred dozens over the centuries. *Hundreds.* All—save you—are abominations. It is a drawback of my vampirism." Tenebra moved to stand over him. His blazing eyes narrowed. "And many of them still live, in a sense. Your siblings will help us in our war." He pointed at Gar'rth accusingly. "As *you* will help when you have embraced Zamorak."

The undead surged above him.

"You can keep my diary." Tenebra's voice echoed over his struggles. "It will show you how far a great man can fall, Gar'rth. It will make your own fall easier to accept.

"Take him!" he commanded.

Gar'rth was lifted over their heads and carried from the room. Clutching hands rifled his pockets and tore free his belt, ripping the wolfsbane dagger from him. His boots were pulled off, too. He was hauled first through the library and then down unending passages of black rock before finally finding himself on a cold floor in a room without light.

And there, was the most horrifying image of all.

A young girl, sitting huddled in the darkest corner.

Silent and waiting and very, very scared.

Gar'rth felt his hunger grow.

26

Her hands were raw. Her wrists ached and her shoulders burned from the exertion. And her back! She had rarely felt such pain.

Pia dropped the scrubber into the bucket of hot water at her side and looked back over her shoulder toward the main hall below. Each step of the great staircase she had cleaned. She felt as if she had never worked so hard.

Still, she thought with a smile, *the old shrew won't be able to criticize me now.*

She stood with a grimace. Part of her wished that Kara could see how eagerly she was working, to prove how thankful she was of simply being alive. But Kara had journeyed north with Lord Ruthven and a small escort to parley with the Kinshra. Pia didn't even try to understand the politics of it.

As she took a deep breath, her slender hands on her hips, a troop of grim-faced soldiers passed below her.

Please don't let them climb the stairs. She heard snatches of their conversation as they tramped over the flagstones.

"We need to be ready to move out in a few days," one said.

"Aye," the fellow next to him replied. "To make sure the dead stay dead. Just glad the wizards are on our side."

Their conversation was lost as they vanished through the doorway.

The bells of Father Lawrence's Saradominist church signaled the fifth hour of the afternoon. She had finished earlier than she had expected.

That meant she would have time for Jack before her meeting with Lucretia.

She took the bucket and made her way carefully down the stairs, then into one of the many passageways that led away from the main hall. As she passed rooms and junctions she heard snippets of still more conversations. Each of them was tense and nervous.

"The prophecy will come true, I tell you. One king for the living and the dead!"

"The army eats more in a single day than the entire palace eats in a month. Where is it all going to come from?"

Once, she heard a familiar voice.

"Saradomin will prove his strength in the battle to come, and his enemies will burn!" It was Raispher. Quickly she ducked into an alcove and pretended she was washing the bust of a long-dead monarch. The scent of incense made her wrinkle her nose as the priest and his entourage passed by.

She breathed a sigh of relief.

What would you say if you knew how I was raised? she wondered. *There was no place for Saradomin in Kandarin's thieves' guild.* Not for the first time, she thanked her fortune that she was only seen as a servant girl.

It wasn't just Raispher who worried her, however. Recently she had noticed how the palace soldiers would glance at her. A quick stare when they thought she wasn't looking, or an open grin from some of their bolder fellows. It made her nervous, and in the maze-like palace she was uncomfortable walking alone.

Pia took her bucket and walked out into the afternoon sunlight. The eastern bailey was filled with tents as King Roald's army mustered and trained. She caught sight of Sir Theodore and his chosen men, each now respected enough to train the newer recruits of Misthalin's army. It had kept the knight busy, Pia knew, and from the gossip she had heard he was well regarded by his peers.

She emptied her bucket down the nearest drain and then made her way toward the kitchens to find her brother. Inside the uncomfortably hot room, she found Sally standing over Jack.

"You're as daft as a kebbit, Jack!" Sally crowed in good-humored despair. "You *know* Ebenezer likes butter on his bread." She handed the boy a porcelain butter dish. "Now come on. We will take these to King Botolph's Tower."

The old woman turned and caught sight of Pia as she deposited her bucket and damp scrubber. She flashed a comforting smile. The way she mothered everyone around her made Pia wonder what her own mother would have been like, had they had more time together.

"You should come too, Pia. There are a lot of strange people in the palace these days. It's safest in the anteroom where Felicity is being guarded. You are known there." Her eyes lit up. "And you can carry this." She took a cake from a nearby table and handed it to Pia. "It's Reldo's favorite. He will need it when he comes to see Ebenezer tonight, for he's spending far too much time among Papelford's books.

"Now, forthwith!"

The three made their way up to the second floor. Much of that area was given over to the galleries. The artwork always impressed Pia. Great men, all long dead, sat upon their chargers amid scenes of warfare, while sculpted busts gazed forever forward, never blinking.

"Oh," Sally said, coming to a sudden stop. "I am sorry, ma'am. I didn't notice you there."

Pia craned her neck to see. Lady Anne stood at an eastern window, her face lit by the afternoon sun. She gave them an oddly timid smile, like a person caught doing something she shouldn't.

"That's quite all right, Sally. I was just… admiring the view of Varrock's army." She turned to them and regained her composure. "Tell me, how is Felicity?"

"The babe sleeps well, ma'am."

Lady Anne smiled and gave a quick nod before turning back to the window. When she didn't say anything more, Sally gave a brief curtsey and hurried past. Jack and Pia followed.

The servants speak ill of her, Pia mused. *And when the men speak of her they do so… disrespectfully.* She frowned angrily and gave a last look at Lady Anne, standing alone by the window. To Pia she seemed very sad.

She's said to be one of the most beautiful women in the kingdom, Pia thought. *It seems unfair that people should think so little of her.*

As they left the gallery Jack spoke.

"Isn't that the Lady Anne who Sir Theodore—"

"Jack," Pia said sharply. "Hold your tongue."

Jack frowned, and Sally laughed.

"But that's what they say, isn't it, Pia?" he protested. "You've heard them, too. I know you have."

"The servants say lots of things, Jack," she replied. "That doesn't mean we should repeat them."

"They say Lady Anne is ill," he muttered. "They say she is sick with love for Sir Theodore." He wrinkled his face up in thought. "Can you really be sick with love, Pia?"

Sally chortled merrily to herself.

"No," Pia said stiffly. "Only stupid."

The passage led onto the landing above the great staircase. They followed Sally and entered a long corridor, which led to a large, windowless anteroom. At the opposite end was a shadowed spiral staircase that led up to King Botolph's Tower, where Felicity was guarded. It had been chosen for the simple reason that no one could get past the anteroom without being seen by the men who waited there.

Six guards stood on watch, two on either door and two more by the chimney near the tower's stairs.

It's like a prison, this room, she thought. *We could be deep underground.* She cast a look over the long table around which a dozen men sat.

Gideon Gleeman was there. His long face was expressionless. She offered him a smile, and he gave her a brief nod.

The poor man is lost, she thought. *Others have said it, too, both servants and nobles alike. Since his return from Morytania, Gideon seems barely human. There is no joy in his eyes.*

Karnac was there, at Gideon's side, and he was speaking. The jester held a quill in his right hand and was writing in a book. Pia had seen them like this before. Karnac was recalling all he could of his homeland, in the hope that some useful information might be gleaned from his stories.

The gnome called Master Peregrim was also present. He was fatter than he had been when they had found him on Hope Rock, and he was busy forcing a pear into his mouth. He tossed Pia a sly wink as he bit down, the juice flowing over his chin.

"You wait here," Sally instructed them. "Leave the cake on the table for Reldo. And the butter for Ebenezer, when he comes back down from the tower." She gave them a last smile before climbing the spiral stairs.

Pia sat with Jack on a bench, out of the way. Her brother began to play with one of the shards he'd brought back with him from the land of the dead.

"I've been thinking, Pia," he said quietly. "Perhaps I should learn how to use them. I mean, you saw what the spirit lady did to the werewolf. I could be useful in the troubles to come."

Pia smiled and ruffled his hair.

"Leave the fighting to others, Jack," she said. "We always did in Ardougne."

"Hmmm." That meant he was unhappy with her answer. "Perhaps I'll speak with one of the wizards," he added.

The thought of fighting made Pia shiver. She had tried so hard to forget what she and Vanstrom had done when Hereward had tried to stop them.

I could wash all the stairs in all the cities of the world, and still not wash his blood off my hands, she realized. *Poor Vanstrom, too.* She felt the tears come to her eyes, and she bent her head forward so her hair would prevent anyone from seeing her misery.

For perhaps an hour they sat there, listening to Karnac's droning voice. Suddenly the grandfather clock near the stairwell chimed the hour. Startled, Pia jumped up.

"I have to go," she told Jack abruptly. "Lucretia wanted to meet me before the hour was up. I'm late!" She stood and patted her brother on the shoulder, then turned toward the door.

The old shrew won't be happy, she fumed. *And I tried so hard to clean the stairs—to make her proud of me.* Pia cursed as she ran, but when she got to the foot of the great staircase, there was no sign of the woman. It was unlike her not to have waited.

She never misses an opportunity to criticize.

Long moments passed. The daylight outside faded and evening began. People came and went. Armed men stomped through the hall and anonymous noblemen went about their private business. Of Lucretia however, there was no sign.

Finally Pia knew she had to ask someone. Lord William entered the hall from a discreet doorway, peering around first, looking as if he was afraid he might be seen. Spotting Pia, he gave her a friendly nod, and then stepped out.

He is Kara's friend, and Sir Theodore's, too, she remembered. *He will help me.* She stepped forward as he neared.

"Excuse me, your lordship." She attempted a curtsey that nearly made her fall. The young nobleman's eyes fired with amusement.

He's only a few years older than me, Pia noted.

"You're Pia, aren't you?" he said, perhaps to put her at ease. "Kara-Meir's servant."

"Y-yes, sir," she said. "But I was wondering if you could help me. I am to meet Lucretia here, but she's an hour late. It's unlike her, sir."

Lord William nodded. His gloved hand stroked his manicured beard. His eyes never left her face, and she felt herself blush.

"That is unlike her," he said quietly. "Most unlike her. She is maid to Lady Caroline, you know."

Pia swallowed and nodded. Lord William glared intently. Something in his eyes made her afraid. She lowered her head to avoid his gaze.

He stepped closer, close enough that she could smell the soap that he used. Lord William was well known for his cleanliness.

"P-please, sir," Pia whispered, moving her hands behind her back where she curled them into fists. She heard him step back. After a moment she looked up.

The nobleman regarded her coolly.

"I haven't seen her," he said. "And there are a lot of new faces in the palace now. You really shouldn't be wandering alone. Not with an army encamped within our walls. Duke Horacio will be here tomorrow, with a thousand archers from the southern dales. Take care then, for many of them are men who have been pressed into service from their homes. Unhappy men." With that, he turned aside and headed up the great staircase. Pia sighed thankfully.

He was right, of course, but she still had to find Lucretia. Quickly, she left the main hall, a fear growing in the pit of her stomach. She searched until the sun went down. Nobody she asked had seen the woman for several hours. Finally, she even tried to retrace Lucretia's last steps, to see if she had perhaps fainted or fallen.

She remembered a small room to the north of the palace, where her teacher dried her mistress's clothes, for the room was situated between two chimneys and the heat from the fires often radiated through the stone.

The room was dark. Stepping inside, Pia felt the heat first, and then a silk garment that brushed against her face. She pushed it aside irritably, trying to get her eyes used to the gloom.

She gave it several heartbeats, and just as she satisfied herself that there was no body at her feet, she heard a voice. It was coming from the chimney to the left of her, where there was no fire.

"So the barbarian witch and her wizard have escaped us again," a bitter voice wheezed. Though muffled, it seemed vaguely familiar. "Are you certain of it?"

"Neither of our assassins has returned from Gunnarsgrunn," a younger voice replied. "We should assume that they have been killed."

Pia froze. There was a small gap in the rock at the rear of the chimney, wide enough that she could see through. The room beyond was dimly lit. A hooded man moved across her narrow view, too quickly for her to catch any details.

"Is there any danger to us?" the wheezing voice asked.

"None," came the answer. "They know nothing of our plans."

"Very well. Then we must return to the matter at hand."

"We have never hit anything as large as this," the younger man said. Pia heard a blade scrape from its scabbard, and the clunk of metal-rimmed boots as they landed on the flagstones. "If we succeed, Varrock will have nothing to see it through the winter. The people will starve, and panic will ensue."

The older man chuckled faintly.

"Yes it will. Come next spring, the people will have suffered so much that their allegiance will be given easily."

"And what of you?"

"I will grow strong again. That was his promise to me. No more biting agonies, no more pains keeping an old man awake at night. No, my elevation is at hand."

"Then in Zamorak's name, it shall be so," the warrior said. "The men are gathered. We shall do it tonight."

Pia recoiled in shock. When she looked again, a moment later, the room was dark.

"Soon?" she asked herself. "How *soon* is that?" Fear gripped her. Who could she tell?

Who would believe her?

27

Theodore raised his hand. Behind him, the twenty armed recruits came to a stop, the iron shoes of their steeds clattering on the road. He heard Doric groan as the dwarf tottered in the saddle behind him.

"Are you sure about this, sir?" Philip asked at his side. Theodore peered at the men behind him. He let no uncertainty show in his expression.

"It is the right thing to do," he said quietly. But Philip persisted.

"I still don't know why you didn't have Hamel call out the guard, sir. If we face a real fight, then surely we would have been better to bring them, as well?" There was a slight quaver in his voice. None of his men had ever seen true combat before, beyond fighting in the lists, or in the melee at the Midsummer Festival.

He bit his lip in doubt and peered into the gloom that lay ahead of them, down the wide street. Several alleyways led into it, and at the end the king's granary stood behind a low wall. Several Varrock guards, clad in yellow tunics that covered their mail, waited by the low gate and more stood upon a wooden walkway that crept up the side of the stone building. The men at the top were armed with bows.

"Sir?" Philip said, prompting Theodore to answer his question.

"If we mobilize the guard, word might reach the insurgents," he explained. "We need to get them tonight. All of them."

In truth, I dare not involve the guard, he thought. *Someone in the palace is acting against us. Castimir's letter makes that near certain, and what Pia overheard has confirmed it.*

His back ached dully. The old war wound had never gone away.

"Squire!" Doric hissed, pointing. A lone rider rode out of one of the adjoining alleys and up to the granary's gate. A knight in blue-tinted armor.

Instinct flared inside him. He recalled Pia's account of the attack on the refugees.

A knight and a wizard.

He drew his sword.

"Come on!" he cried, kicking his spurs against the horse's flank. It was no horse of Falador he was riding, for his own mare remained at Paterdomus. But the Varrock-trained steed jumped forward with a pleasing eagerness.

His men followed. Philip screamed a challenge and those behind took up his yell. He heard Edmond laugh manically as the sounds of their hooves, clattering on the cobblestones, echoed off nearby walls.

He felt Doric tighten his grip and heard him curse an unknown blasphemy in his own tongue.

The knight at the gate drew his sword. An arrow felled the nearest guard as his fellows raised the alarm.

"Sir!" Philip shouted. Theodore glanced to his left and saw a red-cloaked man at the end of the nearest alley. The figure gestured with his hands.

"Magic!" Doric yelled. The knight veered his horse to one side, away from the incoming spell. Behind him several men cried out. He heard at least two fall from the saddle as the horses reared up. Then he felt it too. A wall of air punched him, hard enough to stagger him slightly.

If I had been at the center of the strike, then it would have unhorsed me for certain. He gestured with his sword in the direction of the wizard, and the last half-dozen of his riders veered off to confront him.

Crack!

Something hit his chest with enough force to bruise his flesh even beneath his armor. He reined his steed to a halt, growled angrily, and found an arrow embedded in his breastplate. He wrenched it out and looked for the source. Above him, on the rooftop to his right, several archers appeared. Some exchanged fire with the archers of the city guard. Two others loosed their arrows behind Theodore, toward his men.

Philip pointed right, to a street in the direction opposite the wizard. A body of armed men ran from the junction. Several made toward the granary. Others—some carrying pikes—glanced hesitatingly at Theodore's group.

Theodore cursed. He hadn't expected such an organized assault. He looked to the granary and saw that the gate was now open. Only two guards remained to face the knight in blue.

"Edmond!" Theodore shouted, and he gestured right, to the junction. "Take five men. Keep those irregulars from getting to the granary!" Then he pointed his sword forward. "Philip, you and three more engage the knight."

As his men departed Theodore saw that four had already fallen to the wizard's attack. One lay under his horse, unmoving. The other three staggered to their feet.

"Two of you, help him," Theodore ordered, gesturing to the man under the horse. Then he pointed to the last man. "You, watch their backs."

"Theodore!" Doric shouted. "The knight at the gate!"

Theodore's curse died in his throat as he comprehended the

situation. Of his four recruits, who he had tasked to engage the mysterious knight at the granary entrance, two had already been knocked from their saddles. He watched in amazement as Philip joined them, succumbing to a vicious backhanded blow from his foe's sword hilt.

The last of his four recruits landed a solid strike against the knight's helm, a blow that should have unhorsed any normal armored warrior. Instead, the man simply yelled in anger and turned his full attention to his last remaining enemy.

Theodore knew his recruit didn't stand a chance, unaided.

"Rune-metaled armor," the dwarf gasped. "Be careful, squire. It's far harder than Kara's adamant, and you've seen what that can do."

Theodore nodded. To his right, Edmond and his five men charged and hacked among the irregular troop. Some of the enemy had broken, but others surged past them toward the gate. To his left, the six recruits who had veered off to confront the wizard were battling another dozen of the insurgents who had poured out of the alley.

That left only himself and Darnley, his final mounted recruit.

"Sir?" Darnley asked uncertainly.

"The gate," Theodore instructed. "We must take down that knight."

The two horses charged forward. An arrow flicked across his vision before clattering upon the cobbles to his left.

The knight first, he thought. *Secure the granary.*

The rune-knight parried the attack of Theodore's remaining recruit, ensuring the novice raised his arm high. With a cold fury Theodore knew what would happen next. The knight thrust the tip of his sword into the exposed armpit of Theodore's mounted recruit. The young man fell silently from his horse, leaving no one else to confront their strange foe. Theodore felt his fear grow. It was a fear not even his anger could subdue.

As he raised his sword, the knight cantered backward, behind the low wall. Theodore and Darnley rode through, unable to turn sharply enough to engage him.

"Theodore!" Doric's words were fear-filled. "He's got powder!"

The dwarf leapt from the horse as Theodore turned. The knight held a black canister in his hand, a finger-length fuse hanging from its top.

Burning arrows flew overhead from the rooftop in a concentrated group. They weren't aimed at Theodore or his companions. Rather, they peppered the wooden double-door that led into the granary's circular stone tower.

Theodore moved his horse deliberately between the blue knight and the burning arrows.

"You'll have to go through me to ignite the powder," he said.

The knight just growled. Then he fastened the black canister to his belt and readied his sword.

"Who are you?" Theodore shouted. "Do you have honor enough to offer me your name before we fight? I am Sir Theodore Kassel, Knight of Falador and—"

"I know who you are." Theodore felt his fear grow at the sound of the ice-cold voice.

"Then you know that I have killed many knights," he replied angrily.

"I do, and better than you could suspect."

"Who *are* you?" Theodore demanded.

The mysterious knight raised his hand to his visor. Carefully, still holding his sword, he lifted it.

The scent of death drifted forth. The scent of decayed flesh.

"S-sir?" Darnley stammered.

"That's impossible," Theodore breathed stiffly. "You're already dead."

"Yes," the decaying face mouthed.

"Squire?" Doric breathed. "You know this abomination?" He moved closer to their opponent.

"It's the Black Boar, Doric. The man I killed in the melee the day of the Midsummer Festival." He raised his voice. "How have you done this, Lord Hyett? How have you come back?"

"The Gaunt Herald found me," the specter replied. "In my final moments he came through shadow and earth and demanded an oath to serve him. I gave it freely, and he showed me what will be. Varrock will fall. A king of the dead shall rule over a kingdom of the living, as the prophecy foretells.

"But it is no place you will ever see."

The visor shut. The creature straightened his arm and his horse charged forward.

"For Saradomin!" Darnley shouted with full voice. The youth rode forward. Spurring his own steed into motion, Theodore did the same.

As the three horses grew nearer, Theodore caught the flash of one of the dwarf's two hand axes spinning into the knee of Lord Hyett's animal. The horse faltered.

Darnley reached their enemy first. The youth's blade was aimed intelligently, its edge crashing against Lord Hyett's visor in a blow that would have unhorsed any normal man. But the Black Boar had been a powerful warrior in life. Theodore could only guess at what the Gaunt Herald's magic had cursed him with in death.

Hyett shook off Darnley's blow as Theodore thrust his own sword forward. He aimed deliberately for the metal canister that the Boar had hooked on his belt. It tore away as Theodore's tip cut its strap, and fell free.

The Black Boar took advantage of the opening. Hyett smashed his sword hilt into Theodore's visor with an echoing clang that deafened him. He felt his body go faint as he fell from the saddle.

Doric shouted something as he landed. Darnley invoked

Saradomin's name again.

"Theodore!" Doric shouted, next to him. "The insurgents have made it in. We're outnumbered."

His head swam and his ears still rang. He opened his visor and looked. Doric stood above two dead insurgents, his axe slick with blood. Nearby lay a third who was dying horribly.

He looked to Darnley, who was weakening as the combat progressed. The Black Boar shook off his blows with mocking laughter, for his rune-crafted armor seemed impervious to cold steel. At the gate, several more insurgents charged in on foot, knives glinting under the light of their torches.

Behind them, two of Theodore's recruits gave chase on horseback. The first swept his blade down, taking the nearest insurgent in the back, severing his shoulder as he rode by. The man fell with a shriek.

The insurgents ran around the side of the granary tower, with the two recruits in close pursuit.

Theodore gritted his teeth, stood, and took the reins of his waiting horse.

"Wait, squire," Doric urged. "We can't beat that rune armor. Not with our weapons." The dwarf winked up at him. "But we can with this." He pulled aside the leather jacket he wore over his mail, revealing the Boar's canister, stuffed into a pocket. "I took it after your knight distracted him."

"We will need to get close," Theodore said. "Darnley can't keep it up for long."

The recruit had taken to cantering back after every exchange. The Boar roared angrily and took the bait each time. It seemed the horses were circling each other, and the Boar's steed moved awkwardly, its foreleg stiff.

"Darnley's keeping his distance," Doric observed, "buying us time." Then the dwarf unclipped his belt. He coiled the leather around the canister and drew it tight. "We will only have a few seconds, once the fuse is lit," he added. "It might be best to tie it to Hyett's saddle, somewhere behind him where he can't reach."

Theodore nodded as he mounted his horse.

"With his visor down, he'll be unlikely to see it," he said.

Doric ran to the burning door and extracted one of the arrows. Fire crept along its length.

"I'll help Darnley with the distraction," the dwarf said, handing the arrow over.

Theodore took the belt and lit the canister's fuse from the burning arrow. It hissed to life with alarming speed. Then he turned his horse to approach the Boar from behind.

Darnley saw what he was up to. He redoubled his attack, taking greater risks and keeping the Boar busy. At the same time, Doric ran in, holding his axe in both hands and swinging it toward the horse's face.

Theodore charged alongside Hyett and bent down, his heartbeat counting the moments. He hooked Doric's belt behind the strap of Hyett's saddle.

"What?" Hyett's ice-cold voice sounded as he noticed Theodore's presence. Doric shouted a warning and Darnley cried out. Somewhere metal crashed against rune.

Theodore slipped sideways from his saddle as his horse neighed, then slumped forward suddenly, lifeless. He cursed as he fell. The strap remained undone.

And the fuse had near burned out.

"Squire?" Doric shouted.

"Get clear!" he answered.

"What have you done?" Lord Hyett screamed down at him. His horse reared up on its hind legs. Darnley appeared behind it, and embedded his sword tip in the animal's rump.

It leapt forward with a neigh and bolted toward the gate.

Theodore's eyes were set on the canister. It bounced on the horse's flank and the leather strap lost its tension. At the same time, the fuse burned into the canister.

"Doric?" he shouted. "Darnley!"

His words were obliterated in the explosion that followed. Hyett's horse was engulfed in a blaze of fire, followed instantly by white smoke. Darnley fell from his horse, the beast collapsing sideways as a concussion of heat roared over them. Doric lay on the ground, curled in a ball.

When he finally mustered the strength, Theodore stood and tried to speak. His throat was dry and his face stung. The sound of the world was muted, for nothing could compete with the echoing roar that rolled across the city.

He saw Doric stand. The dwarf was white with dust. Together they gazed into the smoke. Seconds went by before the wind dissipated it.

The granary wall had collapsed. The force of the blast had damaged a nearby building, as well. In the small area beyond, where the roads met, there was no sign of Lord Hyett or his horse.

Doric gave a great grin.

"I reckon he's staying dead this time, squire."

Theodore couldn't stop his own grin of relief.

Nearby, Darnley stood.

"What was that?" he asked, awe in his voice. "Was it magic?"

Theodore shook his head.

"Just black powder," he answered. "A dwarf invention originally, although the Kinshra used it in their artillery against Falador. There are people who have experimented with it in Varrock since then, but I don't know how the insurgents would have come by it."

"Well, let's hope they don't have any more," Darnley whispered. He grinned and bowed to Theodore. "Sir," he added with respect.

Theodore nodded. "Call the men into the granary, Darnley. The fires must be extinguished. The Varrock guard will be near now. Even they couldn't have failed to notice the explosion."

The young man nodded and ran toward the gate. From behind the granary tower the two recruits who had pursued the insurgents appeared. Theodore pointed, and they followed Darnley.

Then he saw the dark look Doric gave him.

"We left some of Albertus's powder in Morytania," the dwarf whispered. "Gar'rth knew of it. Could he have sent it to the insurgents?"

"If he has, then he has abandoned us, Doric," Theodore answered grimly.

28

Silence passed for a moment as Theodore wrestled with his dark thoughts.

Darnley returned. His visor was open and his face was torn in rage.

"It's the men who rode after the wizard, sir," he gasped. "They were knocked from their horses, and had their throats cut. Five of them at least."

Theodore's stomach tightened.

"But there were six," he said. "Where is the last man?"

"There was no sign of him," Darnley answered.

Horses appeared at the shattered entrance. Theodore looked up to see Edmond, his visor pulled back.

"None of us fell, Sir Theodore," the man said. "We scattered the attackers with a charge. Six of us went, and six of us came back. The archers fled from the rooftops when they were in danger of being cut off."

Darnley gave a cry and pointed to the shattered wall. From underneath a pile of stone, a figure moved. Theodore hastened forward to clear the rubble away. They found Philip, and the three others who had rushed to confront Lord Hyett at the gate. Philip stood and immediately helped another half-buried man from the rubble to his feet. The remaining two men were dead.

"The cost has been high," Theodore said.

"Aye," Doric replied. "But the cost of failure would have been worse."

The sound of a horse reached their ears through the gathering fog. A single rider emerged, wearing the armor of Theodore's recruits.

"Sir Theodore?" The newcomer slid his visor up as Theodore stepped forward.

"It's me, sir—Robert. I followed the wizard after he unhorsed the others with his magic. We might be able to catch him yet."

Theodore's heart leapt.

"We must get him! He must pay for what he did to our friends." He moved toward the nearest horse, only to have Doric's hand seize his wrist.

"The granary, squire," the dwarf said. "That was what we came here for. Let Varrock round up the others."

Theodore gritted his teeth.

"Not after what they did, Doric."

"And what if they come back?" the dwarf countered. "The granary door is burned to a cinder now, and it's a miracle the grain hasn't gone up like the black powder. We need to put out the fires, or all we have sacrificed will have been in vain."

He's right! Theodore cursed inwardly. But before he could speak, an echoing thunder approached—the sound of many horses and men, racing down the cobbled streets. Through the remnants of the smoke, a host of men appeared. At their head rode Captain Rovin, with Hamel at his side. Among the throng, Theodore saw Lord William.

"Philip, explain to Captain Rovin what has happened here. Darnley and Edmond, come with me, along with you, Doric. We have a wizard to hunt." The knight took a horse from the nearest of his men and lifted Doric before him.

Lord William rode near. Theodore ignored him, and followed Robert's lead.

"You don't trust him at all, do you?" Doric whispered as they gathered pace.

"After what Kara told us before she left? No. Do you?" Silence told him all he needed to know.

They followed Robert along several narrow side streets. From all around sounds echoed—of men chasing down cobbled pavements, of dogs barking, and the occasional scream. When they paused, Theodore saw that William had followed.

"Captain Rovin has given orders for anyone abroad to be detained," the nobleman explained. "When we left the palace, he sent two groups down the east and west roads to try and round up any who might try to flee."

Theodore didn't reply.

"Theodore?" William prompted.

"Don't worry yourself, lad," Doric replied on his behalf. "It's like this at times, after a battle. All he can think about is this wizard who had his boys butchered."

"I'm very sorry," William whispered.

Theodore felt his anger rise. Concentrating, he remained silent. *Are you really sorry, William?* he thought. *As a worshiper of Zamorak, you have lied to me by pretending to be my friend. In such days as these, I cannot afford such weakness again.*

Robert signaled from up ahead, and they caught up with him, emerging onto a main roadway.

"I followed them out here, sir," he said. "I think they knew they were defeated, and so they split up. Some ran north, others south, some straight on."

A scream sounded from nearby. A woman ran out onto the road, two men in yellow tunics chasing. She was brought to the ground a hundred yards from where they waited and restrained by both men.

"Stop!" Lord William called, riding toward them. "What do you think you are doing?"

One of the men pulled the woman's head back by her hair and readied his knife. Then he cut her throat.

"Theodore!" Doric gasped.

"I told you to stop!" William raged. "I *commanded* it!"

The accomplice stood. He bowed as Theodore rode up alongside William.

"She was a Zamorak worshiper, my lord." He looked to his friend, the man holding the bloody knife, and then back to William. His face paled slightly. "W-we have orders, your lordships. Orders from His Grace Raispher and the Inquisition. We are to do a house-to-house search of this area. Any who we find with religious contraband, and those who resist us we… we have been instructed to kill."

"Sir?" Edmond said. Theodore noticed how he had drawn his sword. Darnley, next to him, had done the same. Doric dismounted.

"Take them into custody," Theodore ordered. "Kill them if they resist."

"We act on orders of his grace!" one of the men shouted as Edmond produced a coil of rope from his saddlebag. "Y-you have no right to do this. No right at all!"

"I have a right," William seethed. "As a lord of the realm, I am tasked with keeping order. I do so now."

Edmond dismounted and Doric forced the men to their knees. One of them spat.

"You are known to us, Lord de Adlard. You are known to his

grace, as well. The Inquisition will be coming for you, coming for you soon—" A rope was used to gag him and another bound his hands behind his back.

"Is he telling the truth, Lord William?" Theodore asked frostily. On the night breeze, the smell of burning reached them from the south. It was followed by a series of cries, and the sound of steel clashing against steel.

William looked him in the eye. For some reason Theodore found it unnerving.

"I fear so," he said. "Raispher is a fool. He will use any excuse he can to further the cause of Saradomin, and he will use any means to do it." He looked to the body of the woman, and paled. "No matter what the cost.

"Let us depart. There will be blood this night. I know it."

Theodore felt certain William was right. It made him ill to be associated with such a man as Raispher was proving to be.

He scanned the area, and saw that a troop of men were hurrying south. Theodore recognized the banner of King Roald's herald.

"Sir Theodore." The messenger nodded in respect. "Word of tonight's deeds has reached the king's ear. He requires your presence at once, so he can hear your account. Your men have already been instructed to return from the granary, and will await you in the stables."

The knight nodded. He was exhausted.

And the wizard has escaped us, he thought angrily.

When they dismounted in the palace stables, William put his hand on Theodore's shoulder.

"We need to talk, Theodore," he said discreetly. "There is a gulf between us, a gulf that has no reason to be there."

"Very well, William," he said. "But we must be quick, for I am to see the king. Come!" As they walked out of the stable, three men advanced to meet them. Two wore white robes over their chain mail. Their leader was dressed in the white robes of a priest of Saradomin. His pale and puffed-up face regarded them coldly.

"They don't look friendly," Doric said from nearby. The dwarf's words summoned the attention of Theodore's men. Edmond looked on impassively. Darnley gripped his sword while Philip sneered.

"It's the Inquisition," he noted. The three men stopped before them.

"Lord William de Adlard?" the leader said.

"Yes." William's face was pale. His breath came in short gasps.

"I have a warrant from His Grace Raispher." He tapped his open palm with a bound scroll. "For your arrest and interrogation."

William didn't say anything. Doric growled.

"On what charge?" the dwarf demanded.

"Of heresy, of course. Of worshiping *Him*."

Silence fell.

"Do you deny it?" the speaker said.

William nodded.

"I am no enemy of Varrock. I swear it."

"As would anyone suspected of involvement in the insurgency."

"I have no involvement there!" William cried.

The speaker smiled.

"Lord William, please do not engage in theatrics. The hour is late. We have searched your rooms in the palace and have found books relating to the chaos Bishop Lungrim. Your cousin Rudolph was slain by Kara-Meir for his attack on the refugees, and in the last hour your uncle was killed by the palace guard. He used magic trying to stop them, and it was quite obvious that he was one of the leaders of this insurgency."

Theodore's stomach went tight.

"William?" he said. "Is this true?"

William gagged, and put his hand over his mouth.

"My… my uncle?" He shook his head. "But I haven't seen him in *months*. I-I haven't… I don't have anything to do with this."

One of the men stepped forward and grabbed William's wrist.

"Theodore!" the young lord said. "Theodore, *please!*"

"He's a knight of Saradomin, Lord de Adlard," the speaker laughed cruelly. "He won't lift a finger to help you. Not when your uncle was involved in the deaths of his men."

"Theodore! This has *nothing* to do with me! I swear it. Theodore, you *know* me!"

Theodore exchanged a look with Doric. The dwarf gritted his teeth and nodded.

"Wait," the knight said firmly. The speaker hesitated. The man who had grabbed William's wrist let it drop. Theodore counted five heartbeats before speaking again. Perhaps sensing his change in mood, Philip and Edmond stepped from behind him, while Darnley drew his sword. Three more of his men did likewise.

"What is your name?" Theodore asked the speaker.

"Me?" He spoke as though only a fool would ask such a question. "My name is Lord Mews. I am secretary to his grace."

"I've never seen you at court before," Theodore said. "I've been here for six months."

Lord Mews clapped his palm against his chest and smiled condescendingly.

"One doesn't like to advertise oneself, Sir Theodore. But I must say, I've seen you quite a *bit* around the court."

"That doesn't change anything," Theodore said grimly. "I don't know you."

"B-but I'm Lord Mews!" the man whined. "I have a warrant here, for Lord de Adlard." Theodore grabbed the scroll from his grasp and tore it open.

"Y-you are obliged to hand him over, Sir Theodore."

I couldn't help Castimir when he needed me, Theodore thought. *And this city is tearing itself apart.* He looked over the scroll and into Mews's watery eyes.

"Have you ever killed anyone, Lord Mews?"

"Me? Goodness no, I've never—"

"I have." Theodore stepped forward, his head halting a hand's breadth before the peer's doughy face. "Many times. I killed a man tonight, in fact. Though one I'd already killed before, so I'm not sure if that counts."

"Y-you jest, Sir Theodore."

"No, I do not. I've killed and fought for what I believe in. I've seen strong men ruin their bodies for the convictions they hold. Have you?"

Mews said nothing.

"No. I didn't think so. Men like you... men like you..." He felt his rage building.

Theodore lashed out. His fist caught Lord Mews in the stomach.

"*Hrrrr—*" As the man doubled over, Theodore pushed his arm behind his back and grabbed him by the collar. Mews's two men reached for their swords, only to stop as Darnley and the others surrounded them.

"Men like you," Theodore said, "need to know humility." He forced the old man's face into the nearest trough of water. He made certain his head was totally submerged before he pulled it out.

"Y-you're insane!" Mews gurgled as he gasped for air.

"Of course I am," Theodore snapped. "I've fought in hopeless battles and been a prisoner in Castle Drakan. Those aren't things sane men do." He dunked Mews again, and held him for a longer time. He pulled him out and thrust him to the ground, where mud and water covered his white tunic.

"Raispher will hear of this," Mews gritted. "We'll be back. We'll be back with the guard, and a *king's* warrant this time."

"Then we'll be waiting for you," Theodore said. "As a Knight of Falador I have some jurisdiction in ecclesiastical matters. I probably rank higher than you do. So I'll keep this." He picked the scroll off the ground where it lay. As Mews struggled to his feet, Theodore's boot found the man's backside. The blow sent him sprawling.

It was only when they were gone, casting terrified looks over their shoulders, that Theodore and Doric took William aside.

"Thank you," the young lord said tearfully. "I mean that. Thank you."

Theodore exhaled.

"I want the truth, William," he said. "I *demand* it. Kara told me you were no believer. She told me that you worship *Him*." William nodded.

"It's true, Theodore," he admitted. "It's all true. I do worship Him. But it is not in the way you believe. I had the books on Bishop Lungrim because I was talking with Sulla when he was here. I thought it best to learn as much as I could about him. And as for my cousin and uncle..." William smiled grimly. "I've had no contact with them for many months. They are not a part of my family that I am proud of." He wiped away his tears.

"I once asked you if a man could ever be cursed, Theodore. Do you remember?" Theodore winced. He did remember. He had accused William of being a coward. It had been an ugly scene.

"I do, William. It was when we first thought Kara was in Varrock."

"That's right." He nodded. "But I *am* cursed, Theodore. All my life I have wished to be brave, and to be strong and honorable, like you. But I can never be those things. Never." He sobbed, and wiped the tears away on his sleeve.

"I was born different, Theodore. My parents discovered this when I was an infant, so long ago I can't remember the day.

RUNESCAPE

Apparently I fell from a horse." He laughed. "My father had grand ambitions for me. His father had been a chancellor, and further back there was a general or two." William shook his head. "But when I fell from the horse, I injured myself." He sighed. "I bled, and I did not stop bleeding."

Doric's eyes narrowed.

"What do you mean?" he asked.

"My blood doesn't clot, Doric. If I am injured, even in the slightest way, then I will likely bleed to death." He looked Theodore in the eye. "That is why I am cursed, Theodore."

"Then how did you survive the fall?" the knight asked.

William laughed without humor.

"I was saved by a priest. By a priest of Zamorak. He invoked the god's blessing on me, and my wounds healed. But there was a price—my parents were instructed to school me in His ways. Of course, it ended any martial career my father wished for me. To him, I was a disappointment from that day on."

Theodore bowed his head. He didn't know what to think.

"On his deathbed, he never even called for me, Theodore. I think I must have represented a failure that he couldn't face at the end." He peered into the knight's eyes. "Can you imagine how that makes me feel?"

Theodore reached out and put his hand on William's shoulder.

"But I have never, *never* lied to you, Theodore," he continued. "I am a good man, an honorable one. But I am a worshiper of Zamorak."

"Then what is your involvement with the insurgents?" Doric asked. "A man as well placed as you surely would be of use to them."

William smiled.

"That's the funny thing, isn't it? The leader of the church in Varrock, of *my* church, has only ever asked me for court gossip and the like. It's never been anything important. Once a month I go there to take possession of a potion that will stop the bleeding, should I cut myself. I was there recently, and I haven't been asked anything about the insurgency." William sighed and fiddled with his silver brooch. "I don't think the local church has anything to do with it, in fact. This must be an assault by others from outside Varrock—others who are far more powerful than those in my congregation."

"Such as those who could bring back the dead," Doric whispered. "With help from the Gaunt Herald."

"And the Black Prince." Theodore nodded. "He's probably been building this group up for years."

William's face showed his curiosity.

"You should go, William," Theodore advised quickly. "Mews will be back for you, with more men this time." William nodded and took off his glove. He held his hand out to Theodore, who took it gravely.

"I realize that I *have* lied to you, Theodore," he said, smiling suddenly. "I deceived you when I led you to Lady Anne in the galleries. But it was just that once."

Theodore found himself smiling.

"That is a deceit for which I am glad, William. She and I have reconciled our differences and..." He felt himself blush. "Never mind."

William took Doric's hand before straightening his clothing.

"You might be able to get to Falador, if Mews doesn't attempt to close the border," Theodore said. "But I suspect he will send a pigeon to every sentry, and likely before the sun is up."

"Or perhaps south to the dales of Lumbridge," Doric said. "Or your estates."

William smiled.

"That's the first place they would go, I think. Besides, I have an idea of my own, but I thank you both for your help. And please, always, remember this: I am your friend." He turned and hurried toward the palace, his dark cloak quickly concealing him in the shadows.

"Well, squire," Doric said quietly. "I hope you know what you've done. If not, we'll burn for it." He grunted. "And dwarfs don't burn well."

Theodore laughed. His men stood patiently outside the stables, watching him.

"They won't burn a hero of Varrock," Theodore said grimly. "And now I have an audience with the king, during which I fully intend to mention Lord Mews and his two murderous underlings."

29

"I've been kept here for days!" Sulla raged. "How much longer are we going to wait?"

He growled in the darkened room. Even at midday the windows remained shuttered, as they had been since his arrival. He knew they were on the second floor of a room overlooking a busy street, for at all hours the sounds of Varrock rose from the cobbles. Except for last night, Sulla recalled. There had been a different sound then. A familiar one. The sound of black powder exploding, followed by the cries of a city in violence.

It had unnerved him.

"I asked you a question!" Sulla hissed, but the man in black just sat, and watched.

As he always does, Sulla thought. *My keeper!*

Simon smiled maliciously.

"Today," he told Sulla. "You will go to Jerrod today." He paused, then continued. "Lord Ruthven would like to have been here, as would Lord Despaard, but both are… otherwise engaged." He spun the two-bladed knife in his right hand. "Still, we need Jerrod now. We need to discover what he knows about the enemy."

Sulla snarled.

"Then we've delayed long enough already," he spat. "Jerrod might have lost his nerve and fled."

"That wouldn't surprise me in the slightest," Simon agreed. "Werewolves are cowards at heart. How you can trust him is beyond me." He grinned mockingly. "But we aren't taking any chances with you, either." He sheathed his dagger in one easy move. "Personally I don't think you would be stupid enough to run. I mean, where would you go? The Kinshra are said to have spies everywhere."

Sulla laughed.

More than you know, Simon, he thought.

"They do," he agreed. "Even in Varrock." He looked sidelong at the guard, mindful of his expression. "Probably even in the court itself, in the palace. Maybe those two young ladies who entertained me so inadequately."

Simon stood and smiled grimly.

"Anne and Caroline?" He shook his head. "I doubt they have interests other than who they plan to marry."

A footstep on the stairs made Sulla turn his head. A thick-set man appeared who ignored him entirely. He reminded Sulla of a blacksmith.

"It's time," he told Simon. "The men are in place."

"Very well." Simon rose. "Come, Sulla." He made it sound like the sort of command he would give a dog.

Sulla walked between them, down the stairs. At the bottom waited two more men, one dressed as a beggar, the other a priest.

"There are others, too, Sulla," Simon explained. "Trust me, you won't be able to run. And I'll be with you every step of the way."

The door was opened and Sulla shut his eyes against the light. When he opened them, the priest and the beggar had gone.

"You follow," Simon ordered the blacksmith as Sulla was

pushed out into the hectic street. "Well, Sulla, where do we start?"

"Take me to the Blue Moon Inn," he ordered. "We will start there, but it won't be quick. Jerrod is cautious."

"That's fine, Sulla. So am I." Simon stepped ahead of him and led the way.

The city of Varrock was in a state of disarray, Sulla quickly realized. Guards stood in groups on nearly every corner. An army of bowmen marched in a long column, following in the trail of a bearded man who rode under a blue banner with a white arrow tip across its center.

"Duke Horacio from Lumbridge and the dales," Simon observed. "He's brought a thousand men with him from the south. Very soon, King Roald's army will be ready."

To Sulla the soldiers seemed weary and exhausted. He recognized them as conscripted men, suffering under the merciless sun that burned their faces and baited their tempers.

"They will break," he told Simon. "They are farmers and husbands, not warriors."

Simon smirked.

"We have warriors too, Sulla. The Kinshra are sending an embassy to Varrock. Some say it is to aid in the coming battle. And the Knights of Falador may ride to our aid, as well."

Sulla's eyes narrowed.

If the Kinshra are offering their aid, then surely they will expect something in return, he realized. But he remained silent until the last of the column had marched past.

They then turned south and west. Here the city was poorer, and Sulla saw the signs left by the activity of the previous night. Guards were more plentiful, citizens rushed on their way, and once, after turning a corner, Sulla gasped.

Two men were hanging from a small scaffold.

"I didn't know King Roald was so ruthless," he said. Simon shrugged.

"Normally he isn't. But these are not normal times. These two were hanged for murdering a woman."

"But they are dressed as guards," Sulla remarked.

"Yes. But last night unrest seized the city. With the guard came men of Raispher's Inquisition. And some went too far. Many of the inhabitants here are Zamorak sympathizers, who fought back in the belief they were about to be slaughtered. Dozens were killed in the riots.

"Sir Theodore urged King Roald to show the city that justice was done. It seems a wise choice."

"He's a fool to challenge the authority of the Inquisition," Sulla said.

Simon shrugged again.

"Perhaps he is. King Roald brought it back to keep the nobility in line during the crisis, for there are secret heretics in court, as there have always been. I don't think he expected that it would spill out into the streets."

"Secret heretics? Like my young friend, Lord William." His guess drew a surprised look from Simon.

"He has vanished," the man acknowledged. "His uncle and cousin were a part of the insurgency. Both are dead now. Somehow he escaped before the Inquisition could apprehend him." Simon stopped and pointed to a gray stone building farther along the road. "That's your inn, Sulla. Let's get to work."

"You are wasting our time, Sulla," Simon gritted some hours later. "Take me to Jerrod. *Now.*"

The two men stood at a junction, with their backs to a crooked alley. Simon toyed with the hilt of his knife under his cloak. Sulla wondered whether he did that when he was nervous, or angry.

He gave Simon a taunting smile.

"I told you Jerrod was cautious. He will find us when he is satisfied of his safety."

"We've wandered street after street for hours," the man replied. "And nothing happened at the Blue Moon Inn. You're playing games, Sulla." He shook his head and grunted. "I've half a mind to take you back to the palace and leave you to starve in a dungeon."

Sulla tutted.

"That wouldn't do you any good," he said. "I would suffer, truly, but Jerrod would be at large to terrorize your city. Then there are the documents—ones that could give your nation an advantage over others. Those are worth a fortune on the open market." He watched Simon's face expectantly. "A *large* fortune. Enough for a dozen men to live a hundred years in luxury."

Simon smirked.

"If you mean to bribe me, you've come to the wrong man, Sulla. None of my order seek wealth or power. We've all lost someone special to horrors such as Jerrod. Vengeance and vigilance are what we live for now." His hand shifted under his cloak. "You have sold out your allegiance to humankind by allying yourself with such a beast. You are scum."

"Thank you, Simon. It's good to know where we stand."

They remained in silence for some minutes. Simon growled and his impatience was obvious. Carefully and discreetly, Sulla examined his surroundings.

I gave the right signal at the inn, he recalled. *Someone will have reported back to Jerrod. He will know what to do, and when to do it.*

The chimes of a church bell clamored the sixth hour. Sulla looked expectantly at the three roads that met at the junction. He recognized the priest and the beggar, as well as the blacksmith, each standing back and waiting. They would be as impatient as Simon, he knew.

And Jerrod will have them all now, he thought with a smile. *Whatever disguise they might use to cover their roles, they cannot hide their scents. Not after hours of walking.*

Still, the yellow-cloaked city guards were present in considerable numbers. He hadn't reckoned on that in his plan.

"Well, Sulla?" Simon asked. Irritation sharpened his words. Sulla shrugged.

"Perhaps it's the guards?" he ventured. "The insurrection has brought them out onto the streets. Jerrod might be nervous about appearing." He gazed at Simon coldly. "Perhaps he thinks you mean to butcher him."

Simon grunted.

"If we had my way we would."

Clack-clack-clack.

A hay cart drew toward them from the east. Sulla breathed in relief. The fresh red paint stood out in a bright dot on its side. He turned toward the crooked alley, careful not to do so too swiftly.

A hooded man appeared. Sulla saw him drop his left hand from long, flowing sleeves and spread his fingers. Two of them were stumps.

The cart was close now.

Clack-clack-clack.

"Sulla?" Simon asked curiously. "Is that... is that *him*?"

"Come, Simon," Sulla instructed. Then, he spoke louder, to be heard over the oncoming cart. "I will go to him. Keep your men back."

"We go together, Sulla," Simon said firmly. He turned to his men, and then swore. "Gods!"

The cart veered off the road and headed straight toward them. Sulla, prepared, ran into the alley.

But Simon was quick. He followed on Sulla's heels as the cart crashed against the wall, its wreckage blocking the entrance. The driver shouted, leaned down, and cut the horse loose.

"Sulla!" Simon's voice was left in his ears as he ran. He glanced back over his right shoulder to see the cart erupt into a blazing fire. Beyond, men screamed.

They won't be able to get by that for a good few moments, Sulla thought gleefully.

"Sulla!"

Simon ran after him. Sulla could hear him gaining. But Jerrod was waiting. The werewolf opened a door in the wall where he stood.

"This way, Sulla," he instructed. Sulla dove in, slipping down three stone steps to find himself in a courtyard that was open to the sky. Behind him Jerrod locked the door with a single bolt.

"He'll climb over," Sulla said. "And he's got one of the two-bladed daggers you hate."

A look of fear passed over Jerrod's face.

The door rattled violently as Simon barreled into it.

"Sulla!" he roared. "I'll have you and your creature, Sulla. I'll gut you both!"

"Come." Jerrod pointed across the small courtyard to another open door. A poverty-stricken family stood huddled nearby, watching.

The werewolf guided him up a flight of creaking steps. Thin faces and the uninterested eyes of those who had long since ceased to hope followed them as they climbed higher.

"Sulla!" Simon's voice roared up from the bottom of the stairs. Then, "A hundred gold for the two fugitives! Do you hear? Do you understand?"

It was as if a spell had suddenly been cast. A wiry man barred Jerrod's way. But the werewolf didn't even slow. His right hand lashed out, hirsute now, and long claws raked the man's face. He screamed and fell back as they ran by.

Jerrod let his hood fall. His werewolf face growled at the beggars and his red eyes promised death. Their will dissolved. Not for the wealth of kings would these people dare interfere. Sulla gave a satisfied smile as he watched them push one another aside in order to avoid the oncoming monster. He laughed openly when a woman kicked aside an infant just to press herself into a doorway.

It's been long since I have rejoiced in such fear, he thought.

They reached the top of the stairs. Simon shouted again from below, but there was frustration in his voice. Jerrod opened the last door and ran out onto the flat roof. Sulla winced in the sunlight.

"Over here, Sulla," a female voice cried from a distance. He shaded his eyes with a forearm.

"Turine?"

A black-robed woman in her mid-thirties stared across from a neighboring rooftop. A ladder bridged the gap between, with wooden planks lying over its rungs. Turine flashed a wicked smile and waved him on as the wind took her raven hair.

"Don't be frightened, Sulla," she teased. "I gave you my loyalty when you spared my life, and I do not take my oaths lightly." Her eyes narrowed as she regarded Jerrod. "Especially not when they are backed up by your friend.

"And your money, of course."

Sulla didn't respond. He tested the boards with his foot. They creaked and bent, but the wood seemed solid enough. The alley below seemed far away.

Quickly he ran across, eager not to show his fear. When he turned again, he saw Jerrod follow. The rooftop door burst open and Simon emerged, his two-bladed dagger held out.

"Sulla!"

Turine gasped and turned her head away. She slid the hood up to cover her face.

"It's too late for that, girl," Simon said. "I *know* you, and you will hang for what you've done. Helping enemies of the king is unpardonable."

Jerrod growled menacingly.

Simon grinned then. He gestured with his weapon, and advanced onto the ladder.

"I know what this does to your kind, creature," he said. "I know how weak it will make you." With his free hand, Simon drew a short sword. "I want those documents of yours, Sulla. Despite everything, I want you alive." He stepped onto the ladder. "I was even asked to spare Jerrod, for the deal we offered him is a true one."

Turine backed away across the roof. Jerrod—his red eyes held by the dagger—cowered nearby.

"Step back, Sulla," Simon ordered. He was halfway across now.

Sulla turned to the sorceress.

"You will hang if he lives, Turine," he muttered quietly. "Neither Jerrod nor I can best him."

"That's one of Despaard's men!" she said. Sulla smirked.

"I see," he said. "So he'll hang you twice, will he?"

Turine's gaze faltered. She dipped a hand into her robe.

"I said stand back, Sulla!" Simon shouted.

Then Turine gestured with her hands.

"What are you doing?" Simon cried. "Don't be a fool. I'm a king's man!"

Whoosh.

A blast of air made Sulla stagger. He fell to his knees to save himself from being pushed any nearer the edge. He saw Simon turn to jump, but before his feet left the board, wind slammed into his back. The force of it propelled him into empty space. He dropped both weapons as he thrust his hands forward, to seize the edge of the opposite rooftop.

His face hit the wall with a crack. He gave a cry and slid down, holding the edge by his fingertips alone. He tried to pull himself up, and his feet scrambled against the wall. Each time he rose slightly, he slipped back with a cry of rage.

"I doubt that you're strong enough," Sulla called. "Turine probably broke a few of your bones with her magic wind." He felt himself grinning. "Best just to let go, Simon. End the agony."

"Sulla…" Simon gasped, turning his head sideways. Blood covered his face.

Jerrod growled in delight.

At his side the mage covered her mouth in her hand. Her face was pale and she swayed like she was drunk.

"I-I've never…" she muttered. "I've never murdered anyone."

Simon's right hand slid from the edge.

"No!" he cried. His left hand followed an instant later. He screamed as he fell. His body scraped the wall on the way down, twisting him.

Crack! He landed face down on the hard stone of the alley.

Sulla jeered. Then he spat at the unmoving man.

"I can smell it," Jerrod said with relish. A moment later, a crimson pool surrounded the fallen man. Two guards ran to the body, and pointed up.

Sulla stepped away from the edge and looked at the mage. Turine was pale, her eyes filled with tears.

"What now for our escape?" Sulla asked. She didn't answer. Her vacant stare annoyed him.

"If you don't answer, Simon will have his murderess for company," Sulla growled. "*What now?*"

Her eyes focused on him.

"There are two yellow cloaks for you to put on," she said, her voice little more than a whisper. "We will cross another rooftop and then descend into a courtyard where horses wait. We will ride out as members of the Varrock guard. Mergil and the Mad Axe are waiting for us. *Gods!*"

She covered her eyes and swayed again.

"He would have killed you, Turine," Sulla said. "And he wasn't a very likeable chap in any case. Now, lead on."

30

The land was as barren as Gielinor's moon.

Castimir stared north from his horse, and shielded his eyes from the sun. Before him, stretching into the distance, was a range of low hills without a single living tree. The grass was yellow and thin, and Kuhn had warned them to feed their horses with hay they had brought from Edgeville.

Behind him, his yak dipped its head and sniffed. Castimir watched it with mild interest, wondering whether he should prevent it from eating the ill grass after it had abandoned him in Morytania.

Kuhn rode alongside Arisha. Castimir lifted his head and gazed hard at the barbarian.

"You are a strong woman, priestess," Kuhn remarked. "Perhaps stronger than your mother, even." The murderer's eyes flicked to Castimir.

Arisha nodded once, but said nothing.

Kuhn growled before turning his attention back to the north.

"The Mountain of Fire is a day's journey from here," he explained.

"And what reception can we expect, Master Kuhn?" Castimir asked without sarcasm.

"The Untainted sometimes trade with outsiders," he said. "They share the peoples' rules of hospitality, for the most part. If you lie to them or abuse their trust, however, then they will slay you for it."

Castimir caught Arisha's worried look.

We might very well have to steal from them, he thought. *But after all I have suffered, and the suffering I have brought on others, I am ready.* Despite the sun, however, he shivered.

Before he could utter a word, the barbarian rode forward with a single command.

"Come!"

The land grew wilder with every mile, and it wasn't long until the earth lost its grass altogether and became fractured rock, parched and lifeless.

With every opportunity Kuhn took the higher ground to observe what was ahead. In the afternoon, he returned from the summit of a hillock to report the presence of riders, some way off.

"Should we run?" Arisha asked.

Kuhn shook his head. "I think they were making for the graveyard ruins," he told them. "Those lie to the east—a meeting place of sorts, for those who travel here. No one I've ever met knows their true nature, for legends are as common as flies where this realm is concerned. Some say a great empire once existed here, stretching from Edgeville out across the whole north. But that was in the time of the God Wars, and much that lived then is gone." He muttered to himself and looked nervously around. "Though perhaps not gone enough," he added quietly.

They rode onward uneasily as the light began to fade. With each moment Kuhn's mood grew worse.

"Come, outlander—we must make haste before true darkness

falls. It would not be good to be out here come nightfall. Not good at all."

Arisha, riding slightly ahead, put her hand up abruptly.

"Silence!" she hissed. "Do you hear that? Horses!"

Kuhn swore, and Castimir heard them now, an advancing thunder from the west. He was about to speak when the first horseman crested the summit of a small hill to his left.

"Hold!" the rider shouted as he galloped toward them. Behind him came others, at least a dozen mounted knights in black armor. They rode under a red banner—one that Castimir recognized with a feeling of dread.

The Kinshra! he thought, reaching for his runes. *If they are men of Sulla's nature, then we will be enslaved or slain.*

"Barbarians, and one other," the rider cried over his shoulder. "Probably a mercenary out of Misthalin, sire." The black-armored men circled around them, their lances lowered. Castimir looked to Arisha and saw her shake her head discreetly.

"Your names," the rider demanded. "Now."

"Your banner is known to us," Arisha said steadily. "I am a priestess of the tribes, but this day we ride under a warrant from King Roald himself. You would be advised not to cause us trouble."

One man rode forward, his visor lowered.

"I am Lord Daquarius," he said. Castimir nearly sighed with relief. "And I am making my way to Varrock to parley with King Roald. We have had many reports of strange goings-on regarding the intentions of Morytania. I have no intention of impeding any who ride on his majesty's business, but you will need to prove it."

The lord of the Kinshra lifted his visor and stared at them each in turn. His face was dark-skinned and handsome, and he was far younger than Castimir had expected.

When he drew near Castimir, the wizard reached into his satchel. Several of the horsemen raised their lance points.

"I have the warrant," he explained. "From King Roald. He demands that any man help us if we are in need." He held up the parchment and Lord Daquarius took it with deliberate slowness. After a moment's reading, he nodded.

"It looks true enough," he said. "But who are you three? And what is your business out here?"

"My name is Haba, sire," Arisha said quickly. "This man is Kuhn, of my tribe, and this," she nodded to Castimir, "is Cas. He is a mercenary, and has been pressed into Varrock's service in Misthalin's time of need."

Daquarius nodded gravely. He handed the warrant back to Castimir and smiled.

"My sight isn't what it should be—perhaps it is the light—but I noticed Lord Raven's name on the warrant. It has been long, indeed, since I have seen him. Tell me, Cas, how is he?"

Castimir frowned.

"There is no Lord Raven I know in Varrock, sire. I think, perhaps, you mistake the signature for Lord Ruthven?"

Daquarius's smile broadened.

"Indeed I do," he said amicably. "Tell me some news of Varrock, so we better understand what lies ahead of us."

Castimir grinned.

"The news that would most interest you would be that of Sulla, sire. He is being kept under lock and key, at least for now. But his werewolf ally, Jerrod, is still abroad in the city." Daquarius nodded.

"Very good," he said. "Truly, you do know Varrock and its principals. But the hour grows late, and things darker than anything we can imagine will soon stir. Will you ride with us for a little way, and spend the night at our encampment? You will be my guests, protected under the law of hospitality."

Arisha bowed in the saddle.

"That is kind of you, sire. Truly, your reputation is deserved. But we make for the Mountain of Fire tonight. It is not far away."

Daquarius frowned.

"I have never heard of such a place."

Kuhn growled.

"That is what the people call it," he said. "You will probably know it as the Isle of the Lepers." A sudden chatter of disbelief ran around the circle of knights. Some backed their horses away as Daquarius looked on in undisguised amazement.

"But why?" he asked stiffly. "Why would you go there?"

"We ride in the service of King Roald, sire," Arisha reminded him. "And if we make haste, we will arrive before nightfall."

Daquarius nodded.

"Very well, then. May Zamorak have mercy on your souls." He closed his visor and gestured to his men. "Farewell! We shall pass news of your journey to those in Varrock." The knights broke the circle as their leader led them east.

"That went well," Castimir said when they were gone. "I thought we were done for when they came over the hill."

"Aye," Kuhn muttered. "The Kinshra have been known to butcher or enslave travelers. But this new lord, Daquarius, he's known for his loyalty to his men. He is a more adept leader than Sulla ever was."

"You mean he's not a mad dog," Castimir said wryly. Yet for all that, he felt as if he would have trusted the Kinshra lord, if he had given his word.

"Come on," Arisha called to them. "We haven't long until darkness, and we must reach the mountain tonight."

Darkness fell over The Wilderness quicker than Castimir expected. And with it came the sounds. He was no stranger to travel, having journeyed across White Wolf Mountain with the first travelers to brave the spring melt. And he had close experience with the wolves that gave the mountain its name. He had heard them in the dead of night, when he was far from help and waist-deep in the snow.

But he had never heard anything like what he heard now. Far-off cries chilled his very soul, carried to him on a wind that seemed to have a voice of its own. It whispered obscenities and taunts, and mocked all his hopes. It made him wonder if he were going mad.

"Does anyone else hear that?" he asked. "The voices?"

"On the wind?" Kuhn asked. Castimir nodded. "It happens sometimes," the outlaw explained. "But once you've heard them the first time, they lose their power. Farther north, however, after days of travel, the winds are not so impotent."

Castimir turned to Arisha, who nodded.

"It's true, Cas," she said. "When Kara and I traveled in The Wilderness with Gar'rth, we heard them, too. But only for the first few hours, and always at night." She sighed and looked north. Yellow mirages seemed to brighten up the land ahead. "The voices cannot harm you, but there are many things out here that can." She pointed to the yellow glow ahead. "What is that, Kuhn?"

The barbarian smiled.

"That is your mountain, priestess. That is the lava that surrounds the sacred isle. Come, we are close now." He spurred his horse on, wearing a triumphant grin. The man's enthusiasm was contagious, for even Castimir's yak started forward with haste.

It wasn't long before they found themselves at the edge of a broiling lava flow.

"This is it, priestess," Kuhn said. "This is your Mountain of Fire." He nodded across the flow. Several figures covered entirely in ragged swathes watched them from the opposite bank. Beyond them—where the island rose in a steep but by no means mountainous slope—lay a warren of homes carved from rock.

Castimir stared in awe. Upon one of the lower terraces were several immense humanoids clothed only in loincloths. Some were yoked, in the manner of oxen. Others were shackled about the necks and ankles.

"Hill giants," Kuhn observed. "The Untainted use them for their labors."

"How many of the Untainted are there?" Castimir asked. From his position, he could see about a dozen.

"I doubt more than a hundred, now," Kuhn replied. "I have traded with them in the past, for there are few people who come here willingly. The legends of the leprosy keep people away—even those who might gather to plunder a settlement."

Castimir felt a moment's panic.

"This leprosy," he mused aloud. "Is it... can we catch it?"

Arisha sighed.

"They are not true lepers, Castimir. They were my peoples' greatest warriors in the time of the crusades. They took an oath to guard the runes they seized from the Wizards' Tower, an oath that would keep them alive." Her voice grew hard and shallow. "But legends have it that death would never cease trying to possess them, grinding down their spirit, infecting them with more agony than any man has endured, all in the hope that they might take their own lives. Some have."

"It's an ironic name they took for themselves, isn't it?" Castimir commented.

Kuhn turned on him.

"They call themselves that to *celebrate* their pain. To them, a life without pain, without trial, *that* is a tainted life." He growled. "Through their suffering they become closer to Guthix." He snorted. "Or that is what they believe."

He looked at Arisha carefully. "But now that we are here, priestess, what do you intend to do?"

Arisha took the bag her mother had given her. She loosened the string and took out the horn.

"They will recognize this, I think," she said as she lifted it. "It will gain their attention, and perhaps their trust."

"Gain their trust?" Kuhn repeated. "For what?"

Arisha hesitated before putting the horn to her lips.

"So that I can convince them to give us the essence we need to save the River Salve, Kuhn," she said solemnly. "The fate of the holy river depends upon our success. And with it, all the nations of men." She turned and held his gaze steadily. "Have no doubt, that is what is at stake here. That is why King Roald himself has given us his warrant, to compel aid from anyone we need. And that is why, Kuhn, the rewards for our success will be so vast. Rewards you will share in, should we be successful."

Kuhn grinned wolfishly.

"Then let's not let a few old lepers get in our way, hey?"

Arisha breathed in and put the horn to her lips. Then she blew.

HO-ROOO!

Castimir listened as the sound rose—then faded—across the blistering lava moat. He saw the swathed figures become suddenly animated. One ran back toward the terraces, while others waved their hands and pointed to a rocky prominence on the near side of the bank.

One of the Untainted ran to a structure that sat upon a great wheel. Gears connected a wooden walkway to a solid beam the size of a tree trunk that formed part of a capstan, where two shackled hill giants waited. The man produced a whip from his belt and lashed out at the half-naked creatures. Immediately they put their brute strength to work. As they pushed the beam the capstan turned. The gears rotated against the wheel, and the walkway angled across.

Soon it rested on the rocky outcropping, forming a bridge over the lava moat.

Kuhn went first. He rode straight across. Castimir hesitated, and glanced nervously at the lava.

"Quickly, Cas, follow him," Arisha urged. "I want to make sure he doesn't say anything unfortunate to our hosts." Her logic slew his fear. He dragged the lead and for once the yak followed him without complaint.

The heat from below was intense. He was glad he only had to endure it for a few heartbeats, or else, he thought, he might faint. He caught up with Kuhn before the outlaw had finished his greeting.

"This man is Cas, Master Einarr," Kuhn told the nearest of the Untainted. "He serves the priestess."

Arisha joined them, and the hill giants were lashed once more. As the walkway veered back to the bank, the man called Einarr advanced toward Arisha and stared at her minutely. He didn't bother to give Castimir even a passing glance.

Einarr sniffed through the robes. Only a gap for his eyes and mouth existed, but in the glowing red shadows of the night, it was impossible for Castimir to see where the gray rags ended and the skin began. His eyes were two black ovals that reminded him of Gar'rth.

"So, priestess," he said in a rasp. "You come with the horn of our people. You have been sent here for some great purpose, have you not?"

Arisha dismounted and bowed her head.

"I have, Master Einarr. It is a matter of the utmost importance."

31

"We cannot permit anyone to take the essence," Einarr said, seething. "Even to ask for it, priestess, is against our ways.

"It would take the word of the chieftain of the tribes, of a *chieftain-general* even, and there hasn't been one of those since the crusades." He growled savagely. "Have you in Gunnarsgrunn forgotten the crusade that *we* fought in?" He pointed to Castimir and his outstretched finger shook. "Have you become so sullied by outlanders that you ignore *our* sacrifices?"

Arisha's face fell.

"No, Master Einarr, but the need is great—"

"You come here and tell us of undead creatures mustering at the Salve. Of a vampire who wishes to take the king of Misthalin's place." His outstretched hand clenched and he beat his chest. "I say these are *lies!*"

"Please, Master Einarr, you know they are not," Arisha said, her voice rising. "I have *seen* these things. I have been given the horn of the unicorn by our people, to prove my word. And I will swear an oath on Guthix, *any* oath, to prove it so."

Einarr remained silent for a long moment, and the Untainted glanced anxiously at one another. Some nodded, others mumbled, but all waited on Einarr's word.

"Any oath?" he said slowly.

Arisha nodded boldly.

"Any oath," she confirmed.

Einarr stroked his swathed face in thought. Then he shook his head.

"It would make no difference," he rasped. "There is nothing you could say that would have us break our oaths."

Arisha stared angrily, and drew breath to speak. Einarr just shook his head.

"There is no more to be said. You will stay here with us tonight, but tomorrow you will leave." He gestured to a man who stood to his right. "Thorfinn will make certain you are provided for, and that your beasts are fed and bedded."

The man Thorfinn stepped forward. He bowed to Arisha. Like all the Untainted, he was covered in rags that reminded Castimir of the stories he had read of the desert dwellers and their mummies.

"Come," Thorfinn said. "Lead your animals this way." When Castimir pulled his yak forward and led his two animals up the gradient toward the terraces, the Untainted gave a gravelly laugh.

"It has been many, many years since I have seen such a beast. They are common in the far north, in the land of my birth, but to see one here is a new experience. Where did you come by it, outlander?"

"I purchased him off a Fremennik trader after my mule was killed crossing White Wolf Mountain," he explained. "But he's an altogether unfriendly beast. He's cowardly, for one thing, and obstinate." He paused to grin at Thorfinn. "Generally, he's a pain in the—"

Arisha stumbled ahead of him. With a high-pitched sigh she fell to her knees, and then slumped on one side.

"Arisha!" Castimir shouted, running to her. Her face was pale and her breath came in weak gasps. With a grimace she reached for her shoulder where the assassin's knife had pierced.

"She was wounded just two nights ago," Castimir explained. "It must have been worse than I thought."

"Why didn't you tell me this, outlander?" Kuhn fumed as he gazed down upon her. "Get out of my way!" He pushed the wizard aside and picked Arisha up. She looked like a child in his arms.

Without a word, Thorfinn guided them up to the middle terrace and into a chamber carved into the ground. Castimir tied their animals, and followed them into the darkened antechamber. Three doors led off the circular room.

"Where?" Kuhn grunted.

"The right door," Thorfinn advised. "There is a bed inside. She can rest there."

Kuhn carried Arisha through. Thorfinn took a torch from the wall and lit it.

"I will go for a healer," he said as he set the torch in a sconce. Then he left.

When his footsteps had faded, Arisha sat up suddenly.

"You shouldn't move!" Kuhn commanded. She gave him a grim smile.

"My wound isn't *that* bad, Kuhn," she said.

"Let me see it," Kuhn requested. He pushed her back down with his huge hand. Seeing that he wasn't going to be swayed, she did as he said with a sigh, untying her top and sliding the robe down her arm.

Castimir gasped in horror. The skin around her wound had darkened, and her veins stood out in a bright and unnatural color.

"The wound is tainted," Kuhn observed. He leaned forward and sniffed it carefully. Then he drew back. "The mold you've used has slowed it, but not stopped it. Now it's in your blood. Still, it's not too late.

"Not yet."

"Good," she said. Castimir looked down at her in amazement. She saw his face and nodded. "We need to buy time while we are here, Cas," she explained. "It's clear that Einarr will never give us the essence, so we will have to steal it."

Kuhn grunted.

"Steal it?" he said. "Even if we did, we couldn't escape. In a few days you'll be too weak even to stand."

Arisha blinked at Castimir. He noticed how her eyes shone.

"Then you must leave me, if necessary," she said, her voice matter-of-fact. "The price of failure is too great to pay."

"Don't be foolish," Castimir said. He reached out for her hand and she took it tightly. It was hot, and her skin was wet with sweat.

"You know it's true, Cas. You've seen the same things as I." She sighed, and closed her eyes. "You know it's true." After a moment, she continued.

"Tonight, while I lie here, you must find out where the essence is. If you can take it, then do so. But you must do it without them knowing."

Kuhn nodded.

"I might be able to do it. I know how they think, and as I've traded with them before they will most likely ask me to procure some goods for them. During the negotiations, I might be able to find out where it's kept." He crossed his arms and gazed at Arisha coldly. "But how much will we need?"

A look of uncertainty crossed Arisha's face.

"The legends say that the old kings of Varrock used to make an offering of essence upon their coronation," Castimir said. "If we assume that the legends are accurate, then it might be as much as one man could realistically carry."

"We don't know, Kuhn," Arisha whispered. "That's the truth of it."

Footsteps sounded. Thorfinn and Einarr appeared with another of the Untainted.

"Check the priestess, Magnus," Einarr commanded the newcomer. "See if you can do anything for her." Then he and Thorfinn departed.

Castimir stood aside and watched Magnus examine her for what seemed like an eternity. Throughout, Magnus pinched Arisha's skin around the wound and sniffed it, as Kuhn had done. He turned to Castimir, his black eyes shining through the two slits in his swathed face. "Do you have the weapon that did this?"

"No," Castimir answered. "Why?"

Magnus glowered.

"She has been poisoned. The blade that cut her must have been coated in something." He turned back to Arisha and pulled the rags from about his right hand. Castimir was about to question him further, but put his hand over his mouth when he saw the limb.

Magnus's hand was gray, but its stone hue was blistered with horrific purple sores surrounded by yellow septic rings. As Magnus turned his wrist, it caught the torchlight and Castimir knew the sores were weeping.

The healer put his wrecked hand on Arisha's forehead and held it there for a moment.

"She will become fevered soon," he told them. "The poison has had time to work its evil in her body, and unless I can find out what it was…" Magnus fell silent.

"There must be something you can do?" Castimir said. Magnus turned to him and spoke through gritted teeth.

"I will try, outlander. I will try."

Kuhn shook his head bitterly. Casting an angry look at Castimir, he left the chamber.

• • •

Castimir watched as Magnus worked. Bowls of hot water were brought in, and Arisha's wound was washed. Occasionally she would cry out or gasp from the pain, and Castimir would cringe.

I cannot lose her, he thought for the hundredth time. *Not after all we've been through.* And yet no spell he could cast could change her fate in any way.

He felt a hand on his shoulder in the dark of the chamber. He gasped in surprise. Kuhn had returned, alone.

"You should go, outlander. This is not the place of a man, not where sickness dwells."

Castimir ignored him. Kuhn's grip tightened. He gazed knowingly at Castimir and tipped his head to one side. Then he looked quickly at Magnus, who seemed oblivious to their conversation.

"You *must* go," Kuhn whispered. "I need your assistance."

He tapped a bulging satchel that ran across his shoulder. With another look to Magnus's back he opened its flap by the slightest margin. Inside Castimir saw what looked to be gray plates lying on their side, stacked in a row. He frowned as Kuhn fastened it again.

Castimir went cold.

"Is that—"

Kuhn nodded briskly, and they stepped into the next room. No one was there.

"There is more," the barbarian said. He took Castimir by the arm and leaned close. "Much more. They keep it in a mineshaft on the upper terrace. The shaft needs repair, and Thorfinn led me there to show me what they needed. He proposed that I would return with the necessary provisions and that they—as they always do—would pay me in the gold they mine from below.

"I don't think he ever imagined that when we parted, I would double back," he said. "Truly, their time in isolation has caused them to forget many of the evils of man." A hint of regret flickered across his features. It quickly disappeared.

"Now, boy, it is your turn," he continued. "There is no way to know if what I've taken will be enough. And we cannot afford to be wrong." He yanked a foul-smelling robe from his bag, followed by a long bandage. "Wear this," he said. "You will be able to slip into the mine without arousing any suspicion."

Castimir took the robe and shuddered.

"Where did you get it?" he asked. Kuhn just smiled.

"Now go," he said. "We haven't much time before Thorfinn wakes, and he may discover what I have done. Wrap the bandage over your head."

Reluctantly Castimir removed his satchel and donned the robe over his studded-leather. With a grimace he wrapped the bandage around his face, nearly gagging from the rank odor of human decay. Kuhn moved behind him and made an adjustment.

"That'll do," he said, amusement in his voice. "Now, off you go."

"Pass up my satchel," Castimir said. Kuhn did as asked, looking puzzled as the rune stones clinked together.

"It's heavy!" he said. "You will need to empty it, else you won't be able to fit anything inside."

"Get another from my yak, then," the wizard replied. He swung the satchel over his shoulder, and then waited. Kuhn growled.

"Very well," he said. "But none of the Untainted use such bags as yours. It is much too fine. You will stand out."

"We'll have to risk it," Cas replied. "There's no time to find others. Besides, most of them will be asleep, won't they?" Kuhn made a face, but disappeared out into the night. He returned a moment later, holding a shoulder bag.

"That will do," Castimir said as he took it. He draped it across his chest, resting it on the hip across from the bag that held his runes. "Now, where do I go?"

Kuhn led him out and pointed north toward the third terrace above them.

"At the center of the terrace," he said quietly. "Do you see it?" Castimir let his eyes adjust. The night was clear and the moon added to the luminescence from the lava below. A row of caverns, very similar to the one from which they had just emerged, stood at the far end of the terrace. Torches burned at irregular intervals. In the middle gaped an opening that was bigger than any other.

Castimir pointed up to it.

"That one?"

Kuhn nodded.

"It is where they keep most of their communal supplies. A hundred yards in there is a chamber on the right. That is where you will find the essence. Lots of it. Take as much as you can." Kuhn pushed him in the back. "Go now. I will see to Arisha, and prepare to cross the bridge."

Quickly, though careful not to draw attention, Castimir hiked up the road to the third terrace and made straight for the mine. With each step he turned his head to watch for others. Midnight had passed two hours before, he reasoned. If the Untainted slept like normal men, then most of them would be doing so. And of the hill giants, there was no sign.

A cry came from his left. He turned instantly, fear cutting at his belly as though it were a knife. A single figure stood under a nearby torch. He raised his hand in greeting.

Castimir returned the greeting in a similar manner, but he didn't dare stop.

This is foolish beyond belief, he thought. *Kuhn has led us into disaster. Why did he have to act so soon? He had to prove himself to be the bigger man...*

He gritted his teeth in anger as he approached the mineshaft and looked inside. It fell steeply down into darkness, for there were only a few torches that lit the entrance. On the left of the passageway, vanishing into the gloom, stood a train of wheeled open-top carts.

Curiosity got the better of him. Castimir approached the first.

The cart was laden with brown ore. He reached out and picked up a lump of the unrefined mineral, wondering what it was. Gold flecks caught the torchlight as he held it up. He smiled grimly, wondering how much the ore would be worth, once it was smelted.

As he put the mineral down, he gave a strangled gasp.

Beneath the rocks, at the very bottom of the cart, was a body. It was one of the Untainted, Castimir saw immediately, for his skin was stone-gray all over. Sores and blisters covered much of the corpse. He nudged the body and the man's dead limbs fell softly aside.

It wasn't yet stiff.

There was a wound in his back, bleeding profusely. Something— probably a knife—had been thrust into the base of his neck. Several other cuts had mutilated his back.

Thorfinn? The features were difficult to distinguish, but it looked like their host. *Did he find out what Kuhn was up to?*

His skin chilled.

But Kuhn said Thorfinn would soon wake, he recalled. *He's lied to me! But why?* A heart-freezing doubt sickened him, as he remembered how the barbarian had looked at Arisha. *Gods!*

Taking a burning torch from the nearest sconce, he moved quickly to the chamber Kuhn had described. He entered through a short passageway carved into the rock and emerged in a large room, too big for his small torch to fully illuminate.

Stone urns stood in serried ranks before him. He took the lid off the nearest and peered inside.

Essence! He exhaled in surprise, and then held the torch higher. There were *dozens* of the urns.

"If Aubury were here with me now," he whispered in awe, "this would surely be the greatest discovery any of the Tower has made in a generation." He shook the pride from his head and forced himself to concentrate on the present. Moving the torch back down, he peered once more into the urn.

The gray stone plates stacked one atop the other inside. He reached in and withdrew as many as his free hand could grasp. Each was similar in size to a large dinner plate.

"How many do we need?" he asked himself. "How many to cleanse a holy river?" He lifted the rounded objects into his shoulder bag. Twice more he reached in, and by the time he was done fifteen of the plain gray tablets filled his satchel. Their weight caused his shoulder to ache.

"It'll have to do," he whispered. "I can't carry more."

Castimir hefted it over his shoulder, wondering how he could possibly hide it beneath Thorfinn's rags. Grimly, he knew he couldn't.

I'll just have to chance it, he decided. *May Saradomin watch over me.*

He ran from the chamber, his heart hammering, his breath coming in excited gasps. The main passageway was deserted. Castimir grinned suddenly, hope rising inside of him.

But as he exited the mineshaft, his hope died.

The terraces below were crawling with armed men. The bridge had been turned across the lava moat, a stark line against the orange flame. There was just enough light for him to see at least three horses crossing, followed by a shambling creature.

His yak.

"Kuhn," he whispered in anger. "Kuhn, you traitorous son—"

ARROOOO…

The horn's sound drowned out his curse. He examined the terraces below and found its source. A group of men were saddling a score of horses in the light of a dozen torches.

Without thinking he ran down the path, making for the party. As he neared, he slowed to a fast walk and reached into his first satchel. Breathing heavily, he carefully picked a handful of runes, mindful of being seen.

I just have to make it across the bridge, he thought. *That's all I have to do.* He didn't dare contemplate being alone in The Wilderness. *One thing at a time...* But when he reached the horses he realized that the choice was no longer his to make.

"Svein will lead you!" Einarr said. He stood before the horses and those who readied them. "Try to bring them back alive. The priestess is the instigator—no warrior would defy her commands. But she must be taken alive, for the chieftain of the north must sit in judgment of her crime."

"Yet she came with the horn of our people," a voice protested. It was a massive individual who carried a war hammer in his hand. "How can that be?" He pointed the hammer toward Einarr. "Has Gunnarsgrunn forgotten our sacrifice?"

Other voices murmured in agreement. Castimir took the reins of a horse and stood next to it, ready to mount. No one protested.

"No, Holdbodi," Einarr said, though doubt crept into his voice. "They wouldn't do that to us."

"But Magnus told us what he saw in Kuhn's bag, Master Einarr," Holdbodi growled. "He saw the holy essence. Kuhn has stolen it! And now they are fled." Holdbodi turned toward Castimir. He could feel the man's stare upon him. He clenched the runes in his right fist, and prepared to strike.

But Holdbodi turned back to Einarr.

"They cannot be allowed to escape," he said. "And then we must send an emissary to Gunnarsgrunn, to discover the truth."

"Aye!" Most of the Untainted cheered, raising their fists into the air. Castimir followed suit, being careful to ensure that his clenched fist was hidden in the rags.

"Aye!" he cried in a deep voice.

Einarr waved his hands for calm.

"Very well," he said slowly. "An emissary shall be sent at dawn. But the thieves must be taken as soon as possible. Go now, Svein Lightning Arrow, and you, Holdbodi the Hammer. Lead these men, find the guilty, and bring them back—the rest of us shall follow at dawn."

Castimir's insides chilled at Einarr's words.

Those names are infamous in the annals of the Tower, he recalled. *For both were mage-slayers of legend.* He breathed in deeply, and mounted his horse as others around him did likewise.

Moments later, they thundered into the night.

32

Twenty-four men galloped across the bridge. This time Castimir hardly noticed the wall of heat.

Svein and Holdbodi led, at times slowing to follow the tracks that Kuhn had made in his flight. Frequently they would dismount and examine the ground under the light of their torches. They had ridden for two hours when Svein pointed to the east, then to the south.

The horses have gone east, but my yak has turned south, Castimir noted with some confusion. After a brief discussion the group followed the eastern trail.

Twenty-three of them, the wizard thought cautiously. *That's too many for me.*

Dawn broke, and every muscle burned. Fatigue pressed him to sleep, but he knew he could not.

Over the eastern horizon the sun illuminated an irregular skyline. At the highest point stood a jagged ruin, with ancient walls and tottering pillars. As they drew near, he saw the sunlight reflect off raised lances.

The Kinshra, he realized with a sudden hope. *Kuhn has made straight for them.*

Daquarius is our only hope.

Holdbodi signaled a halt as a dozen Kinshra knights formed a line in the shadow of the wall. At the front, waiting on his horse, was Lord Daquarius himself, his visor raised.

Svein and Holdbodi rode forward.

Daquarius did, too. They met midway between the groups, too far away for Castimir to hear anything. But he could see that the discussion was heated. Svein gestured and shouted. Daquarius shook his head. Then Kuhn emerged, walking out behind the Kinshra horsemen.

Holdbodi turned and spat, then rode back. A moment later Svein followed. Alone, Daquarius returned to the high ground of the ruins.

Within moments twelve black knights trotted forward, gaining speed as they advanced.

They are organized and trained, Castimir thought. *But the Untainted have lived with war and pain for three generations or more.* He feared for the men of the Kinshra.

Svein let fly his first arrow with uncanny precision. In the rising dust a horse pitched forward, the rider tumbling over its head. Even before he hit the ground a second arrow struck home, and another steed collapsed. Two more arrows, and two more horses died.

Gaps appeared between the Kinshra riders.

Holdbodi raised his hammer and roared.

The Untainted surged forward, Castimir's horse taking him with them. The two forces collided with shouts and screams and the crash of metal. A lance skewered one of the Untainted and lifted him from the saddle, but still the dying man dragged himself along the pole, decapitating his killer with the edge of his blade.

Svein remained separate and picked his targets carefully. Each time an arrow flew a Kinshra horse fell. Above it all, Holdbodi's hammer rose and fell, crushing heads and breaking bodies.

As quickly as it had begun, the one-sided fight ended.

Castimir felt his rage grow. He pulled away from the melee and dug into his satchel.

A second line of knights formed on the rise. Svein threw back his head and roared.

"Cowards!" he shouted. "Come down and die with your friends!"

The Kinshra remained immobile.

Castimir concentrated, then urged his horse forward toward the archer. Svein turned and stared, first in anger, then in confusion.

A stream of fire raced from the wizard's right hand to engulf both rider and horse. Man and animal screamed together as Castimir's own steed bucked in surprise. He fought for control of his animal, guiding it toward the Kinshra line. Behind him he heard Holdbodi shout in anger.

Horses galloped in pursuit. Ragged men cursed him incoherently.

"Come on!" he screamed to the horse as it bucked madly. Ahead of him, a lone rider rode out from behind the Kinshra line. He was dressed in a black robe.

A wizard's robes, Castimir realized.

The lone figure gestured and fire engulfed the air between Castimir and his pursuers.

Screams sounded behind him. With a hideous laugh the Kinshra wizard threw waves of flame into the core of the Untainted, seeming to delight in their fear. At the same time, the Kinshra knights lowered their lances, and charged.

The sounds of pursuit disappeared. Castimir's horse finally calmed, and he turned.

Holdbodi raised his hammer and pointed west. Those of the Untainted who weren't burning galloped away.

Still the cackling wizard picked off his enemies, one after the other.

Daquarius rode toward him, his weapon at the ready, and suddenly Castimir knew why. He reached for his hood and pulled it aside, then waved quickly in a somewhat panicked greeting. The Kinshra leader reined in his steed. He turned, then, toward his wizard.

"Enough, Hazlard," he bellowed. "Enough!"

Reluctantly the wizard relented and rode back to the safety of the Kinshra line.

"See if there are any survivors," Daquarius ordered his knights. Then he rode toward Castimir.

"I know who you are, wizard of Saradomin," he said grimly. "You are Castimir." His eyes glared. "*The* Castimir, who fought my order at the Siege of Falador, and slew many of my men." He raised his sword. "Normally I would kill you now."

"How do you know?" Castimir muttered.

Daquarius smiled without humor.

"Your name was on King Roald's warrant. Yours and Arisha's." He leaned forward and spoke coldly. "I will not forget the harm you have done to my order, mage, but I respect the wishes of Misthalin's ruler, and now I know the reason for your venture.

"Kuhn has explained it, and the priestess has confirmed his words." He sheathed his sword. "I will escort you to Paterdomus. Then King Roald will have no alternative but to greet me as he should, and the interminable games of politics will end." He spat into the dust.

"As of this moment, wizard, the king has no more valuable ally than me. For if I wanted the essence, then I could simply slit your throats, and take it myself."

Castimir nodded.

"One thing more… *Cas,*" he hissed. "The name of Castimir is well known among my men. Don't let them know that it belongs to you, for they might not possess my restraint. The same must hold for Arisha. She is now Haba.

"Do you understand, *Cas*?"

He nodded again, and licked his dry lips.

"Thank you, Lord Daquarius," he said, struggling to keep his voice steady. "You are as honorable as your reputation."

The Kinshra leader simply turned his head and looked coldly away.

"My lord," one of his knights called. "There is a survivor!"

It was Svein. His rags were burned away, his skin charred. He lay prostrate on the ground, his melted flesh leaking in a pool that surrounded him.

"Let me burn him, sire!" Hazlard hissed.

"Stay your hand, wizard," Daquarius commanded, dismounting. A visible look of distaste crept over his face as he regarded the mage.

Svein looked up. He saw Castimir and gritted his teeth in agony.

"So y-you are a w-wizard then," he labored as Castimir dismounted. "Th-the witch who betrayed our people has committed the b-basest sacrilege. Sh-she will be h-hunted. Hunted f-forever."

A small group gathered around. Kuhn was among them. Castimir saw him and they exchanged a long look.

"A-and you, Kuhn," the Untainted said hoarsely. "R-redeem y-yourself." His head fell with a sickening crunch. "Y-you know how, Kuhn... y-you know how."

The barbarian just turned his back to the dying man.

"We should leave here, immediately," he advised. "The Untainted will be back soon."

Castimir nodded.

"And Einarr with them," he agreed. "This party was meant to find you and slow your escape. The others will follow quickly."

"How many?" Daquarius asked.

"Nearly a hundred more," Castimir said. Daquarius cursed.

Svein laughed, the sound quickly turning to a choking cough.

"Th-they will f-follow her to the ends of the w-world," he said. "It is their sacred duty."

"Why her?" Castimir roared angrily. "Why not me? Why not *Kuhn*?"

"Because she is the one who has betrayed the people," he said. "We sought to save her life, and she betrayed us. She is the one who must be judged."

"They will have to go through me first," Castimir said.

Kuhn nodded.

"Aye," he agreed. "And they will."

They mounted quickly.

"We ride north!" Daquarius commanded.

"North?" Castimir echoed. "But Paterdomus is east!"

"The Untainted will not relent," Daquarius explained as the rest of the Kinshra rode from the ruins. "And they will have the benefit of speed, so we must use guile."

Arisha joined them, and Castimir understood. She sat on her horse, her face waxen and coated in sweat. Her veins stood out in her neck, as if a glowing blue and purple liquid burned within them. Her cracked lips parted in a weak smile.

"Kuhn told me that y-you were dead," she said. "I had lost hope…" She looked around, and found the barbarian. Her eyes burned with rage.

Castimir followed her gaze. The barbarian looked back at him with an evil stare.

There will be a reckoning, Kuhn, he promised. *I know what you want, but she is mine.*

33

Gnawing hunger. Freezing darkness.

The whimper of a young girl.

Occasional light from the shaft above. Light by which to read snatches of his father's diary. Water poured down that same shaft, to clean the filth from the prison. It was icy, and caused the girl to scream.

How many days had gone by he couldn't know. Often he talked, though the girl never replied. He believed her to be a mute.

Still he talked. He talked to Kara, with Castimir and Theodore, and every hour he would thank Ebenezer for some remembered kindness.

He named the girl Anya. She was ten, the daughter of the miller. She had two older brothers and kept a small puppy that she had rescued from drowning in the village well. Sometimes the village was within sight of the high white walls of Falador. Sometimes it was elsewhere, in an imagined and impossible world of permanent summer where there was no evil.

Where there was no hunger.

The hunger was relentless. His stomach ached beyond pain. He had bitten his arm and drunk his own blood to appease the emptiness, yet the sight of it, of its unnatural blackness, was a chilling reminder of what he was.

A werewolf. A killer and a predator.

Several times he tried to force the door to his prison. Fearful of using his full strength, afraid of what the change would mean for the girl, he refrained from taking his werewolf form.

Instead, he raged against the immovable door. His hands were bloody and raw, yet the pain was nothing compared to the hunger.

"Tenebra!" he shouted through the grate. "I'll do it—swear fealty to *Him*. I'll take a life, but not this way! Please... *Tenebra!*"

"Father..."

There was never any answer.

One day Anya was at his side, hugging him, and he imagined her words of comfort. *Hush, Gar'rth, hush. Did I tell you about the time my puppy chased a cat up a tree?*

He gritted his teeth and shuddered from the hunger.

"Mad... I'm going mad..."

"You are not mad, Gar'rth." It was Theodore as he had last seen him. "There are few better men than you," the knight said before vanishing in the darkness of the prison. High praise from a man such as he.

Gar'rth shuffled back to the beam of light that came from the shaft above. To take his mind off Anya and the pain, he opened his father's diary. As he read he envisioned a man only a few years older than himself. A man who had earned the respect of all who met him, a man whose word was binding and fair, who inspired hope in anyone who heard his name.

Soldier, general, statesman, philosopher. The finest son Misthalin had produced in all its history. Tenebra.

The monster who had left him here to eat a girl.

Tenebra, the captured prince of Varrock who a thousand years ago had endured nearly two decades of torture at Vanescula's own hand. A man who had tried to take his own life, only to have her bring him back from the very edge of death.

Tenebra.

Hero.

Monster.

Another vision appeared before him. Tam. The man he had left to die.

"You could hang yourself, Gar'rth," he suggested bitterly. "Tenebra left you in your princely robes. Make a noose from your shirt or your jacket. Go on. *Coward.*"

Something bounced down the shaft and hit him on the shoulder.

It was a crust of bread. As was their custom now, he split it between Anya and himself. He hated bread. It bloated his stomach and often made him sick. But he had to have something to combat the pain.

Anya ate quickly. The small amount of food entering her famished stomach caused her to grimace in pain. But she didn't finish, for she tore her bread apart and offered Gar'rth half.

Such kindness, he thought through the agony. *For one so young. So innocent.*

He raged in despair and wished he still had his wolfsbane dagger. With that, he might have been able to end the pain and save Anya's life. But Tenebra's creatures had torn his belt from him as they had carried him to the prison. Every single pocket had been rifled. Even his boots had been taken.

Boots.

Leather.

Food.

The only thing he had been allowed to keep was the diary. He decided that, when the water came next, he would tear a few of the

ancient pages free and soak them. That would make them easier
to swallow.

He looked to Anya, wondering if she would wish to do the same.
But she was asleep.

It was often this way. After she ate she would sleep. Her breath
was shallow.

She will die soon, anyway, Gar'rth thought. *And if I don't take her
life, then Tenebra will.* He pulled his knees to his chest and wept
in despair.

"Why didn't you kill me, Kara? Or you, Theodore? Why let a
monster like me live? Why?"

A rush of air billowed from the shaft above him.

"Anya," he called, bracing himself. "Anya, get up. The water's
coming."

The girl didn't move.

"Anya! Get up, Anya! The water's coming!"

He moved to her side and lifted her in his arms to hold her
against his body. Her head lolled on his shoulder. Her breath was
so very shallow.

"Anya?" He shook her roughly. "Anya… please don't leave
me here… I want to hear of the mill and the puppy and your
brothers…"

"*Anya!*" he screamed.

WHOOSH.

The water poured in, drenching them. He raised his open mouth
and drank and drank and drank.

Still Anya didn't wake.

"Drink, Anya," he gasped. "Please."

When she didn't respond, he carried her out of the cascade and
sat her in the knee-high water. It would drain away within just a
few heartbeats.

Quickly he opened the diary and grabbed the first few pages. He pulled, but somehow the paper resisted.

"What?" he cursed angrily, and then tried to tear it with all of his strength.

Nothing. The pages remained intact.

"H-how is this possible? How?" he lowered his head. The book fell from his hands and splashed in the water, now no higher than Gar'rth's toe.

She won't live for long, he thought. *The hunger and the cold will shrivel her, and she will die here.*

A savage and angry hope flared inside of him.

If she dies, then I can't kill her, he reasoned. *But Tenebra might think I have, if I consume her after—*

Yes...

As quickly as he thought it, Gar'rth was horrified. He moved to her side and held her. Her skin was frozen. He felt her heartbeat, faint and irregular.

He clutched Anya tightly against him and closed his eyes. His teeth chattered uncontrollably.

"Oh dear, Soft-Heart. This is no way for a prince to live."

Gar'rth opened his eyes. Vanescula stood before him, smiling.

He bared his teeth in a growl.

"Oh, tut-tut, Soft-Heart." She sucked her lips in mock disapproval. "You are cold. Come." She held out her long, sensuous arm. "Come to me. I will warm you."

"L-leave me," he responded. "Leave *us*. There is nothing here for your evil schemes."

Vanescula scowled.

"Evil?" she said, scolding him. "There is no such thing as good or evil, Gar'rth. There is only perspective." She stepped forward with a speed he hadn't expected, pushing Anya aside and lifting him by the neck without the slightest strain.

"Get away from me!" he growled. He drew his hand back to claw her face, but she batted it aside with a single effortless flick of her hand.

His remaining strength left him. He fell forward. Vanescula caught him and placed his head on her shoulder. Her right hand stroked his hair.

"Hush, poor Soft-Heart, hush," she whispered in his ear. "Very soon your trials shall be ended. And I still owe you at least one favor, I think, for the service you did me."

She stepped back slightly and Gar'rth stared through blurred eyes into her perfect pale face.

"What service?" he asked warily.

Vanescula smiled mischievously. Her pointed teeth dipped over her lower lip.

"You *frightened* me, Soft-Heart!" Her eyes blazed passionately. "I haven't known fear for decades—not true fear. When you held the Blisterwood to my throat, for a moment I thought you were actually going to do it! The sensation was delicious, and I wish to repay you."

"Then you will help me?" he asked. "You will help Anya?"

Vanescula frowned, as though he had told a joke she didn't quite understand.

"You must help her, Vanescula. She is so young—"

"Silence, Soft-Heart!" Her cold hand cupped his cheek, ever so delicately. "You know nothing of her—'Anya' is a fabrication. You gave your food a name and a personality to stop yourself from taking its life."

"No—it's not true."

A strange look of sympathy passed over her alabaster face.

"She will be dead soon, Soft-Heart. There is nothing you can do for the scrap. But we still live—" Vanescula cocked her head,

"—in a way, anyhow."

She pushed Gar'rth back to the cold tiled floor, sat astride him, and leaned forward to whisper in his ear.

"Don't resist, Gar'rth," she said. "You *can't* resist. You are as weak as a newborn and hopelessly confused.

"Anya is dead, Gar'rth," she continued. "Dead."

He felt Vanescula's lips upon his neck. He shivered when her tongue licked his jaw. Then he was lost. Lost in infinite pleasure accompanied always by fear. Always Vanescula whispered to him, and before he slept, her final, haunting words.

"You will kill him for me, Soft-Heart. Promise me you will kill him for me."

"I promise…"

"Good boy," she purred. "Very good. Sleep now, for soon we shall eat."

He awoke, alone, feeling revived. A delicious smell stirred him. He stretched and sat up.

And stared straight into Anya's dead eyes.

"No! No! *No!*"

Her throat was torn open. Her blood stained his torso and his arms. His face was sticky with the remains of the feast.

"Noooo!" He howled the word and knelt over the corpse. "Anya! Anya, *please*. I didn't…"

Then comprehension dawned on him.

"Vanescula!" he cried. "Witch!"

He leaned over the body and closed its eyes with the flat of his bloodied hand. It left an accusing red stain over her young face. A stain he could never wash away.

"I'm damned now," he told himself. "Like the others." He hugged her body. The door swung open. Tenebra was there.

"You!" Gar'rth snarled, and he stood. "You did this!"

He leapt at his father and willed the change.

Tenebra's hands shot up, stopping Gar'rth's jaws just short of his throat.

"Yes," Tenebra said with undisguised glee. "This is the son I have been seeking. That is the anger you will need!" He strained as he pushed back Gar'rth's tearing claws. "You feel the power of Zamorak inside you—I can see it." Tenebra gritted his teeth and shoved. Gar'rth shot sideways along the corridor, rolling before he came to a stop. Leaping up, he charged again.

"Zamorak is chaos," Tenebra continued as Gar'rth closed. "He is freedom to do what you need to do. Zamorak is the strength to act." Tenebra laughed as Gar'rth leapt, then transformed into a misty column through which his son flew. As Gar'rth struck the floor, his father materialized.

"Enough, Gar'rth, for we have much to do."

Gar'rth ignored the words. He turned, growling, but his growl faltered and his aggression died when he saw what his father held.

Tenebra brandished a wolfsbane dagger.

"You hate me now," he said calmly. "I understand that. It would be absurd if you didn't. But I have set you free." He peered intently. "One day you will understand.

"Now, come!"

Tenebra walked quickly. Gar'rth followed at a distance. When they entered a stairwell, Tenebra spoke again.

"I will teach you, Gar'rth. I will teach you magic that is beyond any human wizard. Your strength and speed will make you powerful beyond the measure of any mortal warrior." He stopped, and looked down. "One day, having learned from my experience, you will be among the greatest of kings. We can recast the human race, my son. We can reorder the world."

"Your experience?" Gar'rth spat. "Your diary reveals that you were once the best of men. You have fallen far, Father. Don't try to justify your evil."

"Evil? There is no such thing. The follies of all men are too apparent to ignore when seen through such eyes as mine. Evil would mean not using my power to correct the wrongs of this world. Indifference. *That* is evil, Gar'rth."

"Vanescula told me something similar," Gar'rth remarked bitterly. "I didn't believe her, either."

Tenebra smiled.

"Ah, yes, the princess," he said. "We are going to see her now, Gar'rth. Together. We must pay our respects to her before we begin upon our great journey." He turned, and continued upward.

Gar'rth followed his father closely now. He could feel the power of Anya's blood pumping in his veins. He had tasted human blood before, but never the blood of an innocent.

I hate what I have done, he pondered in puzzlement. *Yet for others of my race, there is no regret, once they are blooded. Only joy.*

They emerged into the twilight of evening on the highest parapet of Castle Drakan. To the north Gar'rth could make out endless swamps. To the east stood a second great city—just beyond the walls of the castle, visible only from this height. He assumed it was Darkmeyer. To the south, the ghettoes of Meiyerditch carried as far as he could see.

While to the west, another sight awaited him.

Vanescula. She sat upon the edge of the wall, waiting. Her smile grew as they neared. Gar'rth growled at the sight of her.

"So Tenebra, I have kept my promise to you." She looked at Gar'rth with her red eyes. "I gave you your son—the one you wanted. Now that his Soft-Heart is dead thanks to my… charms, will you honor your promise to me?" She slid off the wall and walked toward Tenebra. "Tell me how you are going to cross the River Salve!"

Tenebra nodded.

"That was, indeed, our arrangement," he said. He passed her without a glance and walked to a small balcony. Vanescula growled and followed him.

"Well?" she said.

"You have told the Vyrewatch and Malak not to interfere?"

"As we agreed," she answered with a mock bow.

"Good. Then I shall tell you what you wish to know." Tenebra turned and beckoned to her with a smile. "Come, Vanescula, princess of the night, come and let me whisper it in your ear, as we whispered all sorts of things in centuries long gone."

She sneered, but still she stepped toward him, and into his embrace.

"It could have been *us*, Vanescula. Together. You gave me the gift in order to rule Misthalin when the time came," he said. "At first I was a plaything for you, then a pawn in a long game. And now..."

Vanescula gasped painfully. Her eyes widened and her mouth flew open.

"Now I will invoke the prophecy," Tenebra said. "The blood of innocents will remove the barrier."

Vanescula stepped back, her hands clutched around her stomach. The Blisterwood blade protruded from her body.

"There can be no doubt," Tenebra continued, "that I have surpassed you, my creator." Vanescula reached out to Gar'rth. The face he had once thought beautiful cracked open in agony.

"Please, Soft-Heart," she said. "Remember your promise." But Tenebra seized her by the shoulder and pulled her backward. He removed the Blisterwood from her stomach. She gasped in pain and fell to her knees. Then she looked up.

"I don't want to die..."

Tenebra smiled.

"You've been dead long enough already, cursed witch; and that's not dead enough." He stabbed her again. Vanescula screamed as the blade pierced her breast. Gar'rth watched, mesmerized, as his father twisted the blade savagely and lifted her to her feet.

"But I want you to know pain," he told her, his face twisted with hate. "I want you to know *fear!*" Then he gave her a push.

Vanescula tripped back over the balustrade, cried out, and vanished from view. Gar'rth ran to the edge and stared down. Black wings sprouted from her shoulders as she spiraled down, writhing in agony. She hit the rooftop of a tower far below, landing with a horrific *crunch* that seemed to shatter her left wing.

Then, with a final scream, she fell again from the edge and beyond Gar'rth's sight.

He turned to find his father regarding him calmly. Reaching into the folds of his cloak, Tenebra withdrew the seal of King Roald— the one that the embassy had brought with them.

"Now, son, we have much to do," he said. "Tonight, I will send my messenger to King Roald, and we will march west. To Paterdomus, and then Varrock." His red eyes blazed as he thrust the seal toward Gar'rth, who took it awkwardly.

"Tonight begins your destiny, king of Misthalin."

34

"But what if the prophecy is a fraud?"

Surrounded by piles of ancient books and documents, Reldo muttered his concerns. Some of the books were so fragile that they threatened to crumble at the slightest touch.

Ebenezer stroked his beard gravely.

"Yet the kidnappings cannot be ignored," he said. "It can't be a pure coincidence that the two coincide so completely."

They sat opposite each other in a room on the second floor of the palace. The high leaded-glass window was open, and through it the army of Varrock continued to prepare into the twilight hours.

"But it might not be a coincidence," Reldo said. "Something has been bothering me, ever since the embassy discovered that Tenebra is our enemy." He closed the book, and peered at the alchemist. "No doubt he has planned this for some time—centuries most likely, for the years mean nothing to him. Thus, he could have had agents plant the prophecy itself a hundred years ago or more.

"Then," he continued, "he could have instructed them to renew the frenzy just before he sent the Wyrd here, playing upon our fears of the unknown." Ebenezer nodded.

"It would certainly undermine the confidence of those who fought against him," the old man agreed. "And force the king to face unrest from within."

"Very much so," Reldo acknowledged. "Weakening us to the point where his victory would be a certainty." He sighed. "It may not matter whether or not the legends are true. Suspicion and fear will be what destroy us in the coming fight."

The alchemist nodded again.

"Even within the ranks of our soldiers and recruits, where many claim our cause is hopeless," he said, "They are doing the Black Prince's work for him…"

Silence fell for a moment. Finally Ebenezer sighed.

"Papelford's knowledge would be particularly helpful along this line of inquiry," he said. "Has he been of any help at all?"

Reldo grimaced.

"Not a bit," he said. "When he deigns to be present at all, he just drinks and taunts me." His face fell. "I think he hates me. I think he would kill me, if he could."

Ebenezer leaned forward and put his hand on Reldo's shoulder.

"That's just your nerves playing on you, my young friend. Papelford is a grizzly old man made more so by the fact that his use is not what it was." He smiled in sympathy. "It comes to us all, I am afraid. To tell you the truth, I have felt it myself."

Before Reldo could respond the door was thrust open. An anxious young guard entered.

"Pardon, master alchemist, and you, Master Reldo, but both of you are needed at once in the throne room. We have…" He gulped. "It seems we are to have a visitor."

Reldo helped Ebenezer struggle to his feet. Together they left the library and descended the great staircase. A crowd waited fearfully below, outside the entrance to the throne room. Pia and Jack stood with pale faces, alongside a muted Sally. Lady Anne and Lady Caroline watched nervously from behind a cordon of armed men.

"This way."

The guard guided them through the expectant gathering and toward the door. They entered the narrow end of the long chamber and found several guards standing near the throne, their weapons drawn. Theodore was among them, his sword and shield ready, and nearby stood Doric, stone-faced and tense.

King Roald was at the center of the room, Captain Rovin to his right and Aubury to his left. Papelford leaned on his stick and gazed malevolently toward the throne. Karnac and Gideon were there, too, both staring, their faces grim.

Archbishop Raispher trembled.

"May Saradomin protect us!"

Ebenezer gazed toward the throne. The light there was unnaturally dim, and he had the vague sense of a great cavern that stretched away behind the seat of the kingdom.

His skin chilled and he wanted to run.

"W-what is it?" Reldo stammered.

Nearby, Papelford sneered.

"You've read the books, haven't you?" he challenged. "Don't you know the Gaunt Herald when he appears?"

A fearful utterance passed among the onlookers.

Clip-clop, clip-clop...

The sound echoed down the long room. A chill wind with a sickening smell wafted toward them. A torch was blown out.

Clip-clop, clip-clop, clip-clop...

A black horse and rider appeared out of the gloom. It halted before the throne.

"Speak," King Roald commanded. "*Speak.* I command it!"

Several breaths of silence followed.

"I speak for the true king," the rider hissed. Ebenezer felt rather than heard the words, and they lingered long in his mind, like an echo without sound. "The heir has taken innocent blood. The one who will be king has embraced Zamorak."

Theodore turned his head away in disgust. Doric groaned.

So it's true, then, Ebenezer thought. *Gar'rth has done it.* He staggered on his feet and hid his face in his hand to mask his sorrow.

"Oh, Gar'rth... what have you done?" he whispered to himself.

"The Black Prince's army is marching," the Herald relayed. "Soon he shall reach Paterdomus, an ancient site near where he once fell as a man.

"There he will wait for you."

The Gaunt Herald rode forward. As he came into the light Ebenezer removed his hand to see clearer.

He was a tall creature, manlike, but thin. His arms and legs seemed impossibly long. He possessed no hair on his head or face, and his skin was drawn across his skull as tight as a bowstring.

"There is only one way of preventing a war you will lose." The Herald lifted his finger and pointed to King Roald. "You must die.

"Only you."

King Roald stared for a moment, then spoke.

"You would break the Edicts of Guthix, and condemn us all to unending war?" he answered stiffly. "That would be the consequence of your actions."

"The Edicts will *not* be broken," the Herald replied. "He who comes is simply returning to his homeland. He was once a man— the greatest of men, the best of your race." The Herald's raised hand clenched into a fist.

"Now, will you offer your life to me," he asked, "to spare your kingdom?"

Ebenezer saw sweat appear on the monarch's face as he paled.

"My-my people won't allow it!" he roared. "They won't stand for

having one of the undead upon the throne." Roald pushed himself
forward and brushed past Theodore. Gleeman followed closely, his
hands clenched.

The Herald lowered his hand and tilted his sallow head.

"You refuse to sacrifice one life for many?" he intoned. "Is this
truly how weak the line of my blood has become?"

"*Your blood*?" King Roald said. "Then you speak *through* the
Herald." He laughed savagely. "And you should know we are not
so weak as you presume. We know the importance of the children
you took. We *know* you need seven, and only possess six. We *know*
how to protect the Salve from your plans.

"Even now, those loyal to me—to humanity—are gathering."

The Herald leaned forward.

"You… know… *nothing*," he countered. "The girl Felicity will
soon be mine. A deal with me would save much blood."

"We are not so foolish as to deal with you," Theodore shouted.
"We have all heard the tale of Lord Ruthven's wife and child, and
their fate at your hands."

The Gaunt Herald laughed. It was a rattling sound of death.

"I spared your life, Knight of Falador. And *hers* also. Kara-Meir!"
The Herald sneered. "But as for Lord Ruthven, he broke his word
to me, and he paid the price."

"You killed his wife and took his daughter," Theodore replied.

"A daughter I put to good use." The Herald hissed in anger.
"Whose shriveled head do you think stands impaled upon your
battlement? She became the Wyrd, and since she was not a creature
of Morytania, she possessed the power to cross the Salve. Tasked
with spying, and later with locating seven of the heirs."

Without warning, the Herald snarled, clenched his fist, and
punched the air toward King Roald. The air shimmered.

"Down!" Aubury's voice carried over the shocked cries. Theodore
pushed the king to the ground, as the invisible force passed over

their prostrate bodies. A guard took the full force of the spell. His yellow tunic erupted in flame and the flesh melted from his bones as he opened his mouth to scream.

But no sound came.

The Herald drew his arm back again, angling once more toward Roald. This time Gideon Gleeman stood in his way.

"Do it, Gideon!" Aubury yelled.

The jester ripped off a pattern sewn into his costume, then threw his hand forward. Fire appeared and leapt in a burning arc to consume the horseman. The Herald screamed, falling, as a second torrent of flame engulfed him—this one from Aubury.

As the black figure burned on the pyre of his horse, the two men circled, each pouring fire into the disintegrating corpse.

It's where he stores his runes, Ebenezer realized. *They are sewn into Gideon's costume.*

"You're a wizard!" Doric said, as the Herald ceased moving. Gleeman sighed deeply. "Why didn't you tell us that in Morytania?" the dwarf demanded.

"Albertus found out, when I saved him in Canifis. And I used my magic again during our escape on the airship." Gleeman shook his head. "But mine is a sacred duty, Doric. I am close to the king most of the time, in a position I can play without arousing suspicion. It makes me the perfect bodyguard."

King Roald stood and took Theodore's hand in gratitude, nodding to Gleeman and Aubury, as well. Then he turned to Captain Rovin.

"We must depart for Paterdomus as soon as possible," he said. "Duke Horacio and his bowmen will march at first light tomorrow. Theodore, time and again you have proved yourself to me," he added. "Will you lead the vanguard out tonight?"

The knight bowed his head and sheathed his sword.

"I shall go with my men, sire," he said. The king nodded. Then he turned, and held up his hand for silence.

"None shall know what happened here this night," he said. "I would have the oaths of each of you. Is that clear?"

Heads nodded. Some knees were bent in acknowledgment. No one protested. Even Ebenezer dipped his head to signal his consent.

Suddenly, Reldo raised his hand. The king nodded to him to speak.

"Sire, I believe our enemy has given himself away," he said excitedly. "The birthmark on each of the children is identical to a corresponding one on the altar at Paterdomus, where the seven priests blessed the Salve, and Saradomin granted us His protection. It might be, sire, that these seven 'heirs' are truly that—the descendants of those great men."

A murmur of doubt filled the room. Papelford frowned dismissively. But King Roald's face was set.

"It would make sense," he said, "and it means that Felicity is as important as we supposed her to be, should all seven descendants be needed for the Black Prince's plan." The king clapped his hands in urgency. "Come on, let us proceed. We must ready the army for a march."

Without another word, he left the throne room and the gathering broke up. Theodore disappeared on the monarch's heels, while several guards—under Aubury's direction—picked up the yellow carpet that ran before the throne, and used it to cover the smoldering remains of the Herald.

Ebenezer shuffled from the room. Outside, as messengers and guards hastened to carry out their orders, he found Sally waiting for him. Pia and Jack were with her.

"We heard shouts and fire," she said fearfully. "What happened in there?"

"Nothing to speak of," he said. "Just some theatrics—but things are moving now. All we have done, all the efforts we have made will be weighed in the days to come, Sally." Despite his best efforts, he heard his voice break. "I-I just hope it will be enough, for all our sakes."

Sally reached out and squeezed his hand.

"We must have faith, Ebenezer. We must."

He blinked away a tear and through his misty vision he noted Lady Caroline. She looked very pale and worn, and she gave him a desperate stare.

"Lady Caroline?" he asked as she approached. "Is anything amiss?"

She took his arm and leaned closer to whisper.

"I am frightened," she said. "I am so, so, frightened." Ebenezer took her aside to where they were in no danger of being overheard.

"There's no need," he said. "You are safer in the palace than anywhere—"

"No!" she snapped. Her voice quavered. "It is *not* safe here. Something is... something is wrong—terribly wrong." She gasped. "And no one will even talk about it!"

Sally appeared at her side.

"I think I know what you mean, my lady," she said softly. Ebenezer frowned. Sally turned to him and whispered. "People have gone missing, Ebenezer. Here, in the palace. Lucretia has vanished—" Caroline moaned, "—and there have been others." Sally's face darkened.

"At least five others that I know of, mostly young girls or women. The servants and maids no longer walk alone—not at night. At first we thought it might be the work of the soldiers, conscripted from the dales, but there have been no signs of violence, and no bodies have been found." She looked grimly back over her shoulder to where Pia waited with Jack.

Ebenezer saw how the young girl was straining to hear, and he perceived her fear.

Caroline breathed deeply to calm herself enough to speak.

"Captain Rovin has promised an investigation once the immediate crisis is over," she said. "But with everyone preparing to leave for Paterdomus, all the guards will be with Felicity."

Ebenezer gave her an encouraging smile.

"Which is where they should be, Lady Caroline. If you are worried, then help watch over her." He leaned forward and spoke to both in a low voice. "And stay close to Gideon. He can protect you. Tell Pia and Jack to do the same."

"Gideon?" Caroline mouthed the word in surprise. Sally, he was glad to see, looked genuinely shocked, as well.

"He is a loyal subject of the king, and a capable one." He winked at Caroline. "Did he not, after all, go with the embassy into Morytania—and come out again?"

Caroline nodded slowly. When she looked up she glanced over Sally's shoulder and groaned anxiously. Ebenezer followed her gaze to where a well-dressed man stood imperiously. He noticed their attention and his jowly face puffed itself up more than usual.

"Lord Mews." Caroline gritted her teeth. Her eyes blazed furiously. "That man—that *blasted* man! He had the gall to search my rooms yesterday evening, an hour after midnight. And he watches me always."

Ebenezer sighed.

"No doubt he thinks you can lead him to Lord William, my lady," he said. "It seems as if he is the Inquisition's most wanted man."

"Poor William," Caroline muttered. "The crown has seized his estates. I don't know where he is, but wherever he has gone, I hope he is safe."

"We must hope so, until all this madness has died off," Ebenezer said. He turned to Sally suddenly, his determination drawing her attention. "I am returning to my home, Sally. I need to retrieve a few items from our laboratory—things that might be useful in the nights ahead, as we guard Felicity." Sally grinned.

"You mean *scientific* items, Ebenezer?"

He flashed her a smile and staggered forward on his walking stick, gesturing to Pia and Jack. Both ran over.

"And I shall need help. You two shall both accompany me. Come, if we hurry we might be back in time to see the vanguard leave."

35

Theodore was first from the throne room. He felt a hundred pairs of eyes fasten on him as he left the chamber, heard whispered questions, and saw the fear on the faces of those who waited.

He ignored them all, looking for one face in particular.

Hamel.

The boy stood at the forefront of Theodore's men. Darnley and Philip were there, too, poised behind him.

"Hamel, gather the others," he instructed. "Every man who is able to ride and capable of fighting must be ready to leave in one hour. We depart with the van tonight, and make our way to Paterdomus."

"Please sir, let me come—"

"No, Hamel. You must do as I say," he replied. "There is no place in war for you. I am sorry, but my word is final. Now, gather the men." His tone permitted no argument. Hamel hastened away, his clubbed foot limping slightly.

Darnley dared to frown.

"But what of our dead, sir? The brave men who fell to the

insurgents? They were to be honored tomorrow in Father Lawrence's church."

Theodore glowered. Darnley's face fell.

But he's right to speak on their behalf, Theodore thought.

"Father Lawrence can carry out that duty," he said. "I have already written to each of the parents of those who died." *And every word was a torment,* he recalled. *A judgment of failure on my leadership.*

"Sir?" Philip muttered. He nodded to the throne room. "What happened in there?" Theodore shook his head.

"I am sworn to silence," he replied. "Now go, for we must ready ourselves." The two bowed and turned away, vanishing into the excited crowd.

A perfect white hand took his wrist.

"You go tonight?" Instantly he recognized the voice. "So soon?"

"I have to, Anne," he said, turning to face her. "The king has commanded it." Her face fell. She removed her hand and hid her mouth. Her blue eyes moistened.

Quickly he led her away from the crowded hall and down a passage, holding her wrist tightly. He emerged at the foot of the great staircase just in time to hear her first sob.

"Please, Anne," he said. "Please don't make this any harder than it has to be."

She shook her head and her tears fell.

Theodore felt his anger grow. His grip tightened.

"What's the matter with you?" he said harshly. "You have avoided me for days, and yet I know you keep watching for me. I've seen you at the gallery windows as I train my men in the bailey. I've had reports from Hamel, whom you have questioned to learn my whereabouts." He pulled her closer. Her face grimaced in pain.

"And yet you told me to go, that night! *You* told *me*, Anne." She nodded vigorously, and breathed in deeply.

"I don't w-want you to go, Theodore." She stepped closer and he let go of her wrist. She put her arms around him and pressed her face into his shoulder. "There is so much I want to say to you, Theo. So much." She looked up into his face.

"I love you, Theodore. You know that."

He nodded.

"I do, Anne."

She stepped back.

"I shall be at your quarters, waiting for you," she said. "Come to me before you go."

"Anne, I don't know—" But she ran up the staircase, leaving Theodore alone and breathless.

"You should go to her, squire," Doric's voice sounded from across the hall. He emerged from a doorway, carrying a backpack over his shoulder and holding his double-headed axe in his hand.

Embarrassment made bitter by anger surged inside the knight.

"How long have you been there?" he asked harshly.

Doric ignored his tone.

"Only long enough to see her run off up the stairs." He walked forward and propped his axe up against the wall. "Go to her, Theodore. Your lads are more than capable of readying themselves."

Theodore sighed.

"I know what you think, lad," Doric said. "You think she's made you vulnerable." He squirmed his arm through the strap of his backpack and drew it up across both shoulders. "Didn't you think the same about Kara?"

"Kara was different," he said sharply. Then, with a wooden grin, he continued. "Kara was an infatuation, Doric, one that my promise to Gar'rth has laid to rest. But Anne is, well, I used to think she was a fool." He tightened his jaw. "Now I think I love her."

Doric grinned.

"Then you should go to her tonight, squire." The dwarf punched him lightly on the arm.

Then his face darkened.

"Don't live this life in anticipation of the next, Theodore. You are young, but you've seen far more than most. Take the gifts that life offers, but don't toy with her heart."

The knight nodded slowly.

"Thank you, Doric," he said. He turned to leave, then stopped. "I'm sorry for my rudeness." He took the dwarf's shoulder and squeezed it, before making his way up the stairs.

As she had promised, he found her waiting in his quarters. At first neither of them spoke. No words were needed.

Later on, when they lay together, Anne whispered in his ear.

"I will be waiting for you, when you return, my love," she said. "We can be married before the winter, and you can take a job for the king." Her words were so simple, so honest, and Theodore— more relaxed than he had ever been, more at ease with himself than he ever could recall—simply nodded.

"Yes," he murmured drowsily, truthfully. "That would be nice." He leaned over and kissed her forehead. Anne smiled.

Soon she slept.

Outside, from the bailey, a gong sounded. Reluctantly he pushed the sheet aside and stood. Then he tucked her up in it, tightly, as if it could protect her from the days ahead.

I am afraid, he thought. *Not for myself, but for you. If I should die out there, you will be left alone against the world.* The gong sounded again. It did so twice more before Theodore was dressed and ready.

But as he rode from Varrock, leading the king's vanguard, with a silent Doric at his side, he could not forget her beautiful face.

It is for you I fight, Anne, he promised. *A person. Not an ideal. Not a god. It is for you, and for us.*

• • •

Sally could not sleep. The palace was quieter now since Sir Theodore had led the vanguard away. At dawn, King Roald himself would follow with the main force.

She tossed off her blankets and looked through her window. The moon had gone, and a pink band hung across the eastern sky.

Dawn, she thought. *Will this be one of the last I will see?* She shivered and thought of Felicity, upstairs in the tower, guarded by the best men the king could find.

And Ebenezer.

So much depends on the babe.

She dressed, mindful of the aches in her aged bones. A sudden memory of Albertus made her sad, for her dream of the three of them, together at the alchemist's home in their final years, could never be realized. Nevertheless, it was a dream of which she was fond.

With an aching heart she left her small room and made her way toward the palace's chapel. Since Albertus's death she had felt a greater need for spiritual solace. She hoped it wasn't a weakening of her scientific convictions.

The corridors and stairs were dark. The palace seemed deserted. Once, she thought she saw a figure in the corner of her eye, but when she looked again, there was nothing. Even so, Sally gripped the hilt of her dagger tighter.

Lucretia was nearly as old as I am, she thought. *She has vanished. Along with a few other, far younger women.*

She gritted her teeth, angry with herself for making herself scared. The palace had seen hundreds of newcomers in the previous days. Most likely the missing girls had simply run off with their latest paramours.

But not Lucretia, she knew. *She wouldn't have deserted Lady Caroline.*

"Fools. They are all fools…"

At the sound of the voice, Sally stopped sharp. The chapel was near, but so was the door to the old library in which Reldo had worked. The voice came from there.

"I'll show them yet, I'll... I'll..." Papelford appeared at the entrance, illuminated by a torch. He saw her and froze.

Fear rose inside Sally, for the old man looked demonic. His eyes burned in his narrow face, and when she looked down she gasped.

In his right hand was a dripping object. His wrist was stained red. A foul smell assailed her.

"W-what is that?" she asked, her grip on the dagger tighter than before. "What do you have there?" She backed away as the old man advanced, leaning on his stick.

"It will make me strong," he said. He grinned at her manically and Sally saw for the first time that his chin was stained with a brownish liquid. "Like the master."

Sally turned to run. She had only taken a few strides when a black object shot past her shoulder. She felt her feet being whipped from under her.

But she never hit the floor. A powerful figure grabbed her by the back of her collar with one hand. Its other hand seized her wrist, and she was held up like a puppet.

Sally tried to crane her head back, and to bring the dagger up with her free hand. When she found that she could not do so, she tried to scream.

Crraaack!

The bones in her wrist were crushed. The pain fired through her and killed the scream she had mustered, for she could only gasp at the shock of the agony.

Sally stabbed backward again with the knife in her free hand. This time she felt it hit something, but it seemed like a stone wall.

The thing that gripped her laughed slowly.

"Not what I was hoping for," its voice hissed in her ear. "I wanted Pia—something young—" The creature let go and Sally fell to the floor. Her broken wrist fell under her body and she cried wordlessly in pain.

The next thing she heard was Papelford's voice.

"Do it, master. Join me in my feast of flesh," he sneered. The old man stood in front of her, glaring down in triumph. He bit into the moist object he was holding. It was raw flesh—*human* flesh. He pulled it away from his mouth, and grinned as he chewed.

She tried to scream in horror, but a powerful hand snaked around again from behind, and covered her mouth.

"It will not be long now," he said. "Not long at all."

The hand tightened. Her head twisted backward, and finally she saw the face of the thing that stood above her.

It cannot be, she thought, her mind racing uncontrollably. *This must be a nightmare, for it can't possibly be true.*

It can't!

The last thing she heard was a snap that was both close, and far away.

36

They rode all day, and when they stopped, after dark, it was only to let the horses rest. Nevertheless, Castimir grabbed what sleep he could.

By dawn the following day they were already three hours in the saddle.

The Wilderness was a barren land. From morning to afternoon Castimir could count on one hand all the trees he had seen.

And every one of them was dead.

The Kinshra had prepared for their journey, however, and had brought with them enough forage to last their animals a few days. And since they had lost a dozen warhorses to the Untainted in their fateful charge of the morning before, there certainly would be enough to go round.

Perhaps the Untainted won't have prepared so well, he thought hopefully. *They won't be expecting us to be allied with the Kinshra, so they will plan for a short pursuit.* He sighed bitterly, however. Men like Holdbodi and Einarr—warriors whose names were legend—would not let a few days' hunger worry them.

"Cas...?" Arisha murmured from alongside. "You are scowling again."

He forced a smile that lost its veracity when he looked into her face. Her lips remained cracked and sore, despite the fact that she was drinking regularly. Her eyes were sheened with a filmy yellow, and around their rims, globs of yellow mucus gathered. Even her cheeks were drawn tightly around bone.

On her throat, above the injured shoulder, the black taint was spreading. Her vein seemed swollen, and it was a bright, hideous red.

"We should stop," he said. "You must be in agony." But she just smiled.

"I feel no pain, Cas," she said. "In fact, I feel nothing. The reins in my hands, the saddle beneath me... nothing." She lowered her head. "Guthix doesn't even answer my prayers, Cas. He no longer heeds me. I used my gifts in Morytania to help Albertus, but I cannot do the same for myself. Perhaps Guthix thinks we have wronged Him." Arisha gasped harshly, as if she had been stabbed. Then she sobbed.

"What if I die, Cas?" she said despairingly. "What if I die out here, and He won't give me peace?" She looked up and stared into his eyes. "What have I done?"

She reached over and squeezed his wrist with a pathetic strength. Castimir gritted his teeth and then summoned his voice.

"Lord Daquarius?" he called. "We must rest for a moment, for Haba's sake." The Kinshra lord turned in his saddle and stared.

"Not yet, my friend, but Haba shall rest soon." He pointed to the east where a hill stood marked before the afternoon light. "We make our next stop there, and if our outriders and scouts say there is no sign of pursuit, then it will be a decent rest."

Castimir caught the worried look on his face.

Daquarius has sixteen fighting men under his command, and one cartographer, the wizard mused. *Einarr has near one hundred—a hundred men who believe they have a sacred duty. A hundred men who have lived with unimaginable pain for near on a century.*

Arisha moaned at his side. Castimir took the reins of her horse and rode quickly forward.

Kuhn rode beside him. He said nothing, but his eyes were fastened on Arisha.

At the summit of the hill they dismounted. Daquarius posted lookouts facing in all four directions. The horses were fed with hay, while Arisha slept fitfully. Her fidgets prevented Castimir—still exhausted himself—from sleeping at all.

Twilight fell, and they lit fires, digging the pits deep so the glow would be obscured. Once, Arisha gave a cry in her sleep and her body shook.

"She is dying," Kuhn said. There was emotion in his voice, but Castimir could not tell what it was. He just gritted his teeth.

"She'll survive," he said flatly.

Suddenly Kuhn bared his teeth.

"Riders!" the southernmost lookout shouted. Castimir followed the man's outstretched arm. A cloud of dust appeared, then grew larger. At its base he could see them.

"How many?" Daquarius asked.

"They are too far away, sire," the lookout replied, "but it's a sizeable body of horses."

"Douse the fires," Daquarius said. "Ready the horses."

"Get the maps," Daquarius commanded. The cartographer, Leander, stood up. His face was ashen and his stance spoke of some recent abuse. Frequently he would grasp at his right arm and massage it. He nodded and ran to his saddlebags.

Kuhn looked skyward.

"It will be dark very soon," he said. "If we go now we will be seen. If we wait till dark then we can slip away."

"Slip away?" Castimir said angrily. "They can track in the dark as well as they can in the day. I have watched them." But Kuhn grinned.

"Hear me out, outlander," he said, and Cas didn't like his tone. "Do you love the girl?"

Castimir sneered at him.

"What do you think?"

Leander returned with a rolled parchment. Daquarius rolled it out and leaned closer, following the cartographer's pointed finger.

"Then wait here for them, wizard," Kuhn continued. "You still wear the rags I gave you, save for those around your head, which we could copy for you. You still ride one of their horses. You could buy us time." His eyes blazed. "You could buy *her* time."

"I can't hold off fifty warriors!" he protested.

Daquarius looked up, his interest drawn.

"You wouldn't have to, Cas," he said. "Hide and let them find this camp, then join them on the hunt." He nodded to the map and then stared east. "There is a range of rugged hills a few leagues from here. We call them the Labyrinth. There is only one way through, via a narrow passage, and that's hard to find if you don't know it." His gloved hand flicked the map. "If we lure them into here, you will be well placed to strike when we launch our ambush."

Leander nodded at his master's side.

"You could trap them," he said quietly. "At points the passage is barely wide enough for a horse to make its way. For two horses abreast, it's impossible."

"And once we are there, we have a chance," Daquarius added.

Castimir fell silent, and walked back to where Arisha slept. Sweat coated her entire body. Her hands were clenched in fists, her knuckles white. Her veins seemed to glow in the fading light.

I have no choice, he knew. So he returned to where Daquarius waited, and handed over his backpack full of essence.

"It is wiser if I don't have these," he said. "Just make sure they get to Paterdomus somehow." Daquarius nodded grimly. He opened his mouth to reply, when Hazlard called a warning.

A single man—one of the Untainted—had already reached them. The growing cloud of dust had distracted from his movements. When he reached the bottom of the hill he raised his wrapped hands, palms outward.

"I ride ahead of my kin!" he cried. "I have a message for you. We only want the priestess, and what she took from us. Nothing more."

No one spoke. The man rode closer.

"She will be dead soon, of her wound," he yelled. "You all know it. Only Magnus can save her. So she either dies with you, or takes her chances with us—at her trial."

Kuhn swore and glanced back to Arisha.

"He's right," he said quietly. He looked at Castimir coldly. "We cannot save her here, Cas."

"I won't hand her over to be killed."

"They *won't* kill her!" Kuhn shot back. "They mean to take her for trial, to the highest authority they can find. And that means all the way to Rellekka."

"Rellekka?" Castimir repeated. "That's half a world away!"

"But to get her there, they would have to save her. She would *live*, boy," the barbarian said. "She would live."

"Well?" the emissary shouted. "I'll have your answer!"

Castimir ran to the edge of the hill and gazed down, making certain he couldn't be seen.

"She stays with us!" he replied. "There is more at stake here than your precious duty. Don't you understand that?"

The man didn't reply. Instead he turned his horse and rode away.

When Castimir again joined the Kinshra, he saw that a ragged hood was waiting for him.

"Good luck, wizard of Saradomin," Daquarius whispered as

Castimir pulled the hood over his head.

"Just keep her safe, my lord," he replied. "Can you promise me that?" Daquarius just looked him in the eye.

"I'll do all any man can do, Castimir. That is all anyone can promise."

It came an hour later.

Even Castimir's horse fell still and silent. Its eyes glared in terror. He had never known a horse to hold its breath before.

Then he *felt* it. His skin chilled. A white hoar frost settled over his ragged disguise.

What is it? he said to himself, over and over. *What is it?* He willed his heart to stop beating, fearful that its hammering would give him away.

The darkness grew. Something passed overhead and blotted out the first of the night's stars. They reappeared an instant later as the darkness made its way to the summit of the hill.

C-a-c-k-a, c-a-c-k-a

The strange cry sounded like a bird in distress.

C-a-n-k-a, c-a-n-k-a, came the answer, from the opposite direction. Suddenly the rumble of hooves was deafening. It grew quickly, from both sides, as the riders attempted to prevent any from escaping.

He peered up from the edge of his hollow.

Untainted, Castimir realized with an excited relief. *The waiting is over. Now there is only the doing.*

As he readied himself, the two lines of riders converged on the summit. Men shouted and screamed, swords and axes drawn in anticipation. Torches were lit. But their quarry had already gone.

Castimir rose as the shouts turned into cries of frustration.

Then someone on the summit screamed. It was different from the others. It was the sound of fear. Another joined him, and another. By the time Castimir mounted his horse, the summit was in uproar.

"Revani!" someone shouted. "Revani!"

He rode up the gradient. He *had* to see.

The Untainted were breaking in all directions. In between the panicking horses, however, he saw an impossible sight.

A translucent shadow dragged a screaming man *into* itself. The shadow was shaped like a creature, with an immense maw and two great horns. The maw bit down and the Untainted screamed as his legs were severed. Then the shadow lunged forward and took his head off in a single bite. Finally the riderless horse was heaved into the air, spinning. Its back was broken as the creature pushed it to the ground and ripped its belly.

The shadow darkened and grew denser. A rider charged and stabbed it from behind with the point of his spear. Another man, on foot, brought his axe over his head with both his hands in a blow that would have easily taken the head off a horse. Three more mastered their surprise and joined the fray from afar, aiming their arrows with deliberate caution. Each one hit the creature squarely.

It gave a hideous screech as it seemed to crouch and face the bowmen. Then it bucked forward slightly, a round shape firing from its head. The round shadow smashed into the three bowmen and blew apart as if it were water. Shards of the missile felled their horses instantly. The men screamed as they died, splinters of the stuff penetrating their bodies.

The spearman drew his arm back and rammed his point in a second time.

"Guthix!" he screamed. The creature lashed its limb toward him. He fell beneath an arc of blood. The axe man turned to run then, only to be slashed across the back and tossed into the air.

Somewhere nearby, a horn blew.

Arroooo...

The Untainted abandoned the hill. Castimir followed quickly, watchful of the summit and the creature that had waited there.

Revani? Could that be the peoples' word for revenant? Some believed The Wilderness had once been a great empire, governed by the gods themselves and devastated when the deities fought one another. In that war, all manner of monsters had been pressed into service. According to the legends, even in death their service was not ended.

What manner of beast must it have been in life? he pondered fearfully. He had never seen or read of anything like it.

The Untainted called a halt a few minutes from the hill. They continued to look back nervously, but whatever the dark beast had been, it didn't follow. So they dismounted, and Castimir did the same, following their actions.

When they knelt, he knelt. When they called upon Guthix, he pretended to do the same. And when they leaned forward and kissed the earth, he followed their example.

Once their prayers were ended, Holdbodi stood, raised his hammer, and pointed east. The rest of the Untainted stood and mounted their horses, silently following his lead.

Always east.

To the dawn, he thought. *And to Arisha.*

37

There were thirty-three of them, and Einarr was not among them.

Holdbodi halted some distance from the Labyrinth. In the gloom Castimir could make out a series of vertical cliff faces. Nature herself had built an impassable wall, much as any mortal king might build a wall to protect his keep. Jagged passages disappeared into the rock, and the Kinshra had taken one of them. He peered intently, but found no trail.

The Untainted will find one, he mused with certainty. Behind him, someone spoke.

"Hydig?" Holdbodi said abruptly.

No one answered.

"Hydig!" Holdbodi repeated.

Castimir turned in his saddle.

They were looking at him. All of them. His stomach froze and beneath his hood he swore silently.

Through a slit in the rags, he reached for his belt pouch.

"Who are you?" Holdbodi demanded angrily. "You are not familiar to me. Tell me your name!"

Castimir withdrew a clenched fist and summoned his concentration. His other hand grasped the reins firmly.

Then streams of fire arced from his outstretched hand. His horse reared up, but he was prepared for it. The ground between him and the Untainted leapt with magical flames. Through the flush of heated air, he saw Holdbodi pitch out of his saddle as his horse bucked and fled. Others fell, too, taken by surprise. Those who didn't fall tried vainly to master their animals' fear.

He allowed himself a grin as he reached for the belt.

Suddenly his horse reared again and bucked, too quickly for him to counter. He pitched to the side and fell with a cry, his runes forgotten as he pushed his hands out to break his fall.

"Ooof!" He rolled as he landed, the right arm and shoulder and knee taking the brunt of the impact. When he looked up, his horse galloped away into the darkness. He stood and reached for his satchel this time.

Across the diminishing flames, several of the Untainted had returned. Three of them readied their bows, battling to keep their horses under control as they tried to string their arrows.

Panic their horses, he thought. *Drive them off!*

The first man got an arrow to his bow. He raised it to aim and Castimir crouched, ready to jump. But the horse neighed and turned in a quick circle, upsetting the archer's chance.

He needed a spell, and quickly, though his need for haste would necessitate a weaker magic. He conjured another bolt of flame, but it sailed between two of the riders, dissipating harmlessly.

Arrooo…

The call of the horn sounded above the chaos.

Beyond the fire, the Untainted hesitated.

Arrooo…

But Castimir didn't slow. His hand came away from his satchel's side pocket with six of his precious rune stones.

From the corner of his eye he saw a bow lifted and aimed, the arrow strung. Instinctively he threw himself to one side, and the arrow clattered behind him. But his grip loosened. He felt a single rune stone fall from his grasp.

No! I need the right combination.

A rider leapt the fire, his sword angled down.

Arrooo...

Castimir concentrated on the runes in his hand, trying for a different spell, a lesser one that would only work if he still held the correct combination. He felt the runes respond as the horseman drew his arm back, yelling an incoherent battle cry.

The wizard thrust his right hand forward, palm outward as all but two of the runes evaporated.

Whooshh.

The bolt of air crushed the man's face, pitching him back from the saddle. The horse turned aside at the last instant and galloped away.

The flames were dying now, and two of the Untainted remained. One strung his bow.

Castimir reached for his satchel. Yet he knew there wouldn't be time.

"Wait!" he shouted. "Wait!"

The archer took aim. His companion raced forward over the flames, careful not to obstruct the line of fire.

Castimir froze. He looked at the oncoming rider again and tried to jump aside. The man's sword swept down and tore open his satchel, and runes fell from his bag like blood from a pierced artery. The blade's impact thrust him back, but he kept his feet.

"Wait!" he screamed again as the man raised his sword.

"Hold!" The cry came from nearby, and was accompanied by the clatter of hooves on the rocky ground.

A horse with a Varrock guard charged into the archer, his sword piercing forward in a killing thrust. The archer screamed as he pitched forward from his saddle.

The Untainted who waited above Castimir let out a curse as he urged his own steed about to deal with the greater threat.

Castimir backed himself against the rock face that formed the nearest of the entrances to the Labyrinth. The yellow-clad rider clashed with the Untainted, using the advantage of his speed to turn the man's sword aside and stab home. The Untainted fell from his horse without a scream, the assailant's sword still protruding from his ribs.

Castimir knew he had to identify himself.

"You are from Varrock!" he shouted. Quickly he tore aside his hood. "How many of you are there?"

The man peered down in the darkness.

"Who are you?" he called. The voice was strangely familiar.

"I am Castimir! Castimir who went with the embassy—"

Arrooo...

"Castimir! I know you! I am Captain Hardinge."

"Hardinge! Thank the gods." Castimir couldn't hold back his relief—only to have it turn to fear an instant later.

Hardinge, among whose men was Arisha's failed assassin, he thought. *Has he come to finish the job?*

"Watch out!" Hardinge screamed.

A shadow leapt from the ground. It was the Untainted, still with Hardinge's sword in his abdomen. The man screamed ferociously as he stabbed upward with a long knife. Hardinge reacted immediately.

He threw himself backward as the tip of the blade rattled on his mail shirt, cutting the yellow tunic. As he fell from his horse, Castimir grabbed at his own satchel, finding nothing in the first pocket he tried.

The steed reared to face their attacker. Its forelegs kicked up, driving the Untainted back.

Hardinge staggered to his knees. He drew a knife from his belt.

The Untainted leapt away from the horse, and turned on Castimir.

With no magic to defend himself, the wizard drew one of the two knives he kept at his belt. It felt heavy in his hand, unwieldy, and he wondered if it were blunt.

As his attacker advanced, he was sure he could see the man smile beneath his hood.

"Why aren't you dead?" Castimir gasped, hoping to gain a few seconds for Hardinge to close. But the Untainted didn't hesitate or reply. He came in, his knife thrusting forward in short, fast stabs.

Castimir tried to parry with the edge of his blade. The rock wall at his back hindered his movement. Each time he completed a parry, his elbow bashed against the unforgiving stone.

"Hardinge!" he called out. "Help!"

The Untainted screamed as he jumped forward, still with Hardinge's sword in his body. The wizard lashed out with a cry of his own. Their blades clashed, and Castimir felt his wrist turn. His grip loosened and the knife fell from his hand.

The Untainted angled his arm and stabbed upward. Castimir grabbed the man's wrist, screaming. They fell together, the wizard on the bottom, his knees thrashing upward to strike wherever they could.

A kick connected, and the Untainted weakened. Castimir kicked again, and this time he felt the hilt of Hardinge's sword wobble against his thigh.

With his left hand, Castimir reached down and grabbed the hilt. The Untainted flailed with his free hand, trying to keep him away. His hand seized the hilt. With a sharp intake of breath, he thrust it forward and sideways, doing all he could to widen the wound.

The man released the grip on his knife with an animal yell of pain. Still holding his wrist, Castimir shoved him backward against the rock wall, forcing him to his knees, all the time stabbing and cutting with the embedded blade.

"I don't need magic!" he cried as the Untainted screamed. "I can protect her from you as I am." He pulled the sword back. It came loose with a sickly *squelch*. Castimir raised it above his head as the Untainted reached up from his knees, his hands held to ward off the coming blow.

"No! N—"

Castimir yelled as he brought the edge down. The edge severed the man's hand across the palm.

"No! Nooo!"

"I *can*—" He heaved the blade up again as gore spilt from the sword.

"Pleeease!"

"—protect—" The tip angled down into the Untainted's head. Castimir ignored the man's flailing hand as it grabbed the blade.

"—her!"

Crack!

The sword pierced bone as he drove it forward with all his strength.

The Untainted jerked on the ground, his back against the rock face. Castimir pushed his booted foot against the man's chest and pulled the sword free. Then he turned, and saw Hardinge watching him. The captain looked afraid, he thought.

It made him feel good.

"Castimir," Hardinge said slowly, "it's over. He's dead. The enemy have fled, for now. Did you not hear the horn?"

For some reason Castimir laughed.

"I killed him," he said happily. "With a sword!"

"You did," Hardinge nodded. "But it's over now. Let the sword go."

Horses galloped toward them from the darkness. Castimir found it difficult to focus, and he was aware for the first time of the blood pounding in his head. Now that the excitement was over, his limbs felt strangely loose and his senses muddled.

At the head of the riders came Lord Ruthven, with Kara-Meir by his side. Both wore mail shirts beneath their yellow tabards.

Castimir chortled in relief, for he knew he could trust her.

"Kara! Kara, did you see? I k-killed him. With a sword!"

Arrooo…

"They are gathering again," Lord Ruthven said.

Kara dismounted and ran to Castimir's side.

"Castimir—thank goodness! Are you injured?" She looked around. "Where are the others? Is Arisha with you?" She held him by the shoulders. Suddenly he felt sickened. He dropped the sword and his senses were overwhelmed with mixed feelings of relief and horror.

He pointed behind him, into the entrance of the Labyrinth.

"They are all in there, Kara," he said. "Arisha is very sick. I stayed behind to try and trap them. But Kara, we found it. We have the essence. Not much, but some."

Kara nodded.

"I know, Cas. I know. We met a Kinshra rider that Daquarius had sent to Varrock. He mentioned Kuhn and Haba and the essence, and when we pressed him it was obvious that Haba was actually Arisha." She lowered her face. "He said you were dead, though."

Castimir smiled grimly. Something dry cracked on his face, and he guessed it was the blood of his foe.

"Kuhn would have told them that, before I arrived. He tried to leave me there, at the Mountain of Fire, and take Arisha. She's… she's dying, Kara. An assassin stabbed her with a poisoned blade."

Arrooo. The horn sounded closer now. Much closer.

"Come, we haven't long," Ruthven said, then he spoke to two soldiers. "Gather as many of his runes as we can, for we might well need them." Holding up torches, the soldiers began to search the ground. Ruthven looked anxiously behind him, back to the west. "We must enter the Labyrinth and seek the trail of the Kinshra. If Daquarius goes too far, then he will run into them on the other side."

A horse was brought for Castimir, and he mounted. Several handfuls of runes were returned to him. He put them into his satchel in a secure pocket. He would have to sort them later.

"What do you mean, on the other side?" he asked wearily.

Kara's face was grim.

"We saw at least forty riders heading east earlier today, Cas," she explained as she mounted at his side. "There is a very good chance they will circumvent the Labyrinth to the south."

Castimir swore.

"Then we'll be…"

Kara nodded.

"Trapped," she finished for him. "With no way out. But we have no choice, do we? The essence is in these hills."

They surged forward. Castimir looked behind to count. They numbered less than twenty.

He saw Kara's grim stare.

"We are too few, Kara," he said. "Too few."

38

Kara-Meir fought the weariness. They had ridden for days, trailing the tracks of the Untainted, as Castimir referred to them. What had started as a diplomatic mission had become a desperate rescue.

But who will rescue us? she wondered. *Even if Varrock does send a force out, it won't be soon enough.* Their horses were starving, as were the riders.

She looked sidelong at Castimir. He looked asleep in his saddle. Blood stained his face, and deep lines of worry seemed etched on his brow.

We have risked so much and lost so much in the last few weeks, she thought. *And now, perhaps Arisha. Who will be next?*

She grasped the hilt of her blade. It steadied her nerves. Yet the thought that she might soon be fighting side-by-side with the Kinshra left her feeling curiously empty inside.

They will hate me, she knew, *and I must expect that. Their hate may come with a knife in my back.*

Within an hour of them entering the Labyrinth, a cry sounded ahead.

"Halt!" came the voice. "You are not Untainted. Who are you?"

Kara stared into the night. Figures moved above them on either side of the chasm. One, she saw, was a mage.

"We come from Varrock," Lord Ruthven called. "My name is Lord Ruthven. I am known to Lord Daquarius."

"It's me—it's Cas!" the wizard shouted at Kara's side, his voice exhausted. "The Untainted aren't far behind us!"

"Wait there," the unknown man called down.

They halted in an uneasy silence. Kara strained to hear the expectant sounds of horses behind them. But there was nothing.

Two riders appeared ahead of them in the gloom. Kara recognized their black Kinshra armor. One had his visor up.

"I am Lord Daquarius," a young man said. Kara gazed at him intently. Her hand never left her sword. He noticed her and gave her a puzzled bow.

They all say he is very different to Sulla, she recalled.

"I recognize you, Lord Ruthven," Daquarius murmured. He stretched out his arm and the two men shook hands. Then he looked to Kara. "But who is she?"

"You don't recognize her, then?" Ruthven said. He sighed. "There is no avoiding it—"

"I *know* her!" the warrior at Daquarius's side said, his closed visor giving him a metallic voice. "I *know* you, Kara-Meir." Hearing his words, Daquarius gaped in disbelief. The helmeted man rode closer to her. "She-wolf. Hell-witch. Lord Sulla's Bane."

He lifted his visor to reveal a bearded face dark with anger. His breath was foul, and she turned her head aside to avoid it.

"You are right to look away," the man whispered, mistaking her gesture. "I *saw* you, on the field. I saw what you did." His dark eyes glimmered. "You reveled in your butchery. You *loved* it." He grinned suddenly. "You should worship Zamorak, she-wolf. You would find pleasure in His ways."

LEGACY OF BLOOD   349

"That is all in the past," Kara whispered. "My vendetta against the Kinshra is ended. I swore an oath—"

"To the knight Bhuler? I know." The man drew his sword a finger's length from his scabbard. "This blade helped to cut him down."

Kara drew her own sword then. Instead of straightening her arm to angle the blade up, however, she simply smashed the hilt into his grinning face. She did so with all her strength.

Crack!

Teeth shattered. The man groaned and staggered before falling from the saddle. He made a gurgling noise from the ground as blood poured from his mouth.

"Enough, Hell-witch!" Daquarius shouted. His handsome face was contorted in anger. "My men occupy the spaces above you. If I give the word, they will shoot you—"

"Your men have no bows," Kara said, cutting him off quietly. "You have a wizard up there. He alone poses the danger."

"How could you know that?" Daquarius asked.

"We haven't time for this," Castimir interrupted. "Where is Arisha?"

Daquarius paused, and nodded to her friend.

"Very well," he said, his voice lower. "You are right. Arisha is in the encampment, with the rest of my men." His tone softened. "She won't last long, Castimir."

The young wizard rode forward quickly. Kara sheathed her sword and made to follow, only to have Daquarius seize her arm.

"Guy is one of my most experienced warriors," he said, nodding to the man crouched on the ground. "He served with Sulla, and is cut from the same cloth. But not all of my men are. Most respect what I am trying to do, aware that Sulla was a madman." He gritted his teeth, and his eyes were bright in the gloom. "I will instruct them not to harm you, Hell-witch. But you need to promise me you won't harm them, or provoke them in any way." His grip tightened. "Do I have your word?"

Kara nodded.

"Yes," she responded. "And I will abide by it, as long as they extend me the same courtesy." She stared at him coldly for a long second. His grip faltered and broke. He blinked, and then turned away.

"They say good things about you, Lord Daquarius," she continued. "In this night, if we are to live, then we must work together. For by now the Untainted will have moved to the eastern entrance of the Labyrinth."

His eyes widened in surprise.

"We're trapped here?" he asked. Kara nodded, and he swore angrily. "Make no mistake, Hell-witch, I share the hate my brethren feel for you. If I could, I would kill you, and despite what you have heard of me, I would make you suffer horribly. I would relish your screams. Many men I called friends died because of you. But for now, we shall have our truce."

He turned aside and dismounted to help Guy stand. As Kara rode forward to catch up with Castimir, she was certain she could feel their stares on her back.

The walls of the passage narrowed to where only a single horse could pass through. On either side they slanted outward, thus offering no cover to an assault from above.

I hope none of them up there know me, she thought. *I may have killed a son, or brother, and they might not show restraint.* A tense moment later, however, and the narrow passage widened into a circular space, lit by several small fires. On the opposite side, a similar passage led into the darkness. To her right waited the horses, while to her left she found Arisha, sleeping next to a fire of her own.

Nearby stood a huge barbarian with a white mustache and beard. She felt his eyes appraise her disdainfully. She dismounted and moved to Arisha's side, where she knelt.

Castimir joined her. When he pulled back Arisha's thin blanket, Kara paled.

The priestess's skin had blackened from her throat all the way across her left shoulder and down her arm as far as the elbow. Her veins stood out prominently, glowing with an unnatural light. A yellow hue covered her skin, made more pronounced by the firelight. Her lips were cracked and dry, and her usually thick dark hair was matted.

I cannot heal this, she knew instinctively.

"Oh, Cas… I'm so, so sorry," she said without thinking.

Castimir lowered his head and kissed Arisha's forehead. She didn't stir at all. Kara had to listen carefully for signs of her breath. When he looked up, his face was streaked with tears.

"You can save her though, can't you?" he asked. "Please, Kara, please *try* something. You have herbs in your satchel—" Kara lowered her head, but he continued. "They say you are touched by the gods, Kara…"

Nodding, she took her satchel from across her shoulder and opened it.

"I can try to give her something for her strength." She looked up into his hopeful face. "But it won't cure her, Castimir."

"Try it. Try *anything*." She took out a small wallet and opened it carefully. Inside were dried leaves. Carefully she drew one out and checked it against the light of the fire. The toothed edge of the leaf told her what it was.

"Tarromin?" the big barbarian asked.

Kara nodded but didn't speak. Next she reached into her satchel and pulled out a small glass container with powder inside.

"Get me some water, Cas," she told him as she readied her ingredients. She checked the leaf under the light of the fire, removing the last few flecks of dirt and making sure it was still adequate. Castimir handed her a water pouch. She weighed it carefully before using half of it to wet Arisha's lips.

"There was too much water," she explained. "It would dilute the ingredients and blunt their effectiveness." Then she added the leaf to the pouch, stoppered it, and shook it violently. Then she unsealed it again, opened the glass container, and emptied the powdered brownish substance into the pouch.

"A whole root is better than a powdered one, but with luck this should suffice." Again, she stoppered the pouch and shook it violently for a long moment.

Castimir's eyes never left her.

"Please, Saradomin, let it work," she heard him whisper.

Together they held Arisha's head back and filled her mouth, forcing her to swallow. Arisha took the potion slowly. When it was finished, Kara sat back and waited.

But Arisha did not stir.

Castimir frowned in worry.

"I'm sorry, Cas..."

He didn't reply. Instead he propped the priestess's head up on his lap and stroked her face.

Kara stood and turned away to give them privacy. When she did so, she saw that the Kinshra warriors were watching her. She felt their eyes follow her as she walked to her horse. She heard the whispers and smelled their fear.

"She-wolf."

"Hell-witch."

"*Lord Sulla's Bane.*"

Kara ignored them all.

Lord Ruthven moved close to her.

"The Kinshra are sending men to the west and the east passages," he said. "Daquarius and I have decided that our best option is to hold out here."

She nodded and looked back to Castimir.

I should have given him the potion, she thought. *We will need him if we are to survive.* Her eyes looked upward to the edge of the ravine, where the Kinshra wizard stood. *And him also. Whoever he is, I hope he's good.*

"We will block both passages with stone. It won't keep them out, but it will stop them charging us." He paused, and looked uncertain. "There is, of course, another way."

She peered silently at the sharp-nosed nobleman.

"The Kinshra warriors think Arisha should be handed over," he said. "Daquarius has confided to me that he doubts he will be able to control them, if the Untainted look to prevail." He bowed his head. "I just wanted to tell you myself."

"Thank you. That was kind." She glanced back to her friends. "Soon it won't matter. Arisha won't live to see another sunset." She felt tears come to her eyes, and turned away to hide them. "There is nothing I can do," she muttered. "Not for either of them."

"We will need Castimir's magic, Kara," Ruthven said. "He will need to get his runes ready, and soon. Very soon." She gritted her teeth.

"Just grant them a moment," she said sharply. "For pity's sake!"

A cry went out from above. It was the black-robed wizard.

"A man approaches," he said. "One of them, sire. I think he wishes to speak to us."

"Let him approach, Hazlard," Daquarius shouted back.

A few moments later a solitary figure approached from the west, leading his horse.

"My name is Magnus," he said. "I have come to offer you mercy. There is no escape from here. My people lie ahead and behind, and we outnumber you at least three to one. All we want is what was taken from us, and the priestess who committed such sacrilege."

"The priestess is dying," Ruthven said. "She won't survive another day."

"I thought as much," Magnus replied. "I am a healer, as well as a warrior. I saw her wound. I can save her."

"Save her?" Kara said in disbelief. "You will kill her—"

"We will not!" Magnus snapped. "First I will save her life. Then she will be taken to stand trial at the highest court of our people." He nodded toward the barbarian, who crouched nearby. "Kuhn will vouch for what I say. He knows that when we give our word, it will be our bond."

Kuhn nodded.

"If he can, Magnus will save her."

"You have until dawn to give her up," Magnus said.

"But she might not live until then," Kara fumed. The emissary just shrugged.

"If that is the will of Guthix, then it shall be so," he said. "Nonetheless, at dawn I will return for my answer." With that he turned and vanished among the twists of the passageway.

Daquarius regarded Kara with a hard look. After a moment, he spoke.

"We have no choice," he said. "She has to go. And with her some of the essence. I have those Castimir gave me, and Kuhn has those he took himself. The Untainted won't be looking for two, I suspect. It will leave us with one bagful."

She stared at him coldly and then walked over to Castimir. Arisha was awake, her eyes wide and feverish behind a thin film. She smiled weakly when she saw Kara, and bade her to sit.

"Y-you... you look tired, Kara," she said, wheezing with every word. "Perhaps you should sleep."

Kara smiled. She took Arisha's right hand and caressed it.

"Sleep?" she said. "Sleep makes me uneasy. And I have been having strange dreams recently. About Theodore."

Arisha smiled drowsily.

"Good dreams?"

Kara nodded.

"I suppose so. But very intense. It is similar to the dream we shared at Paterdomus, the one where Gar'rth…" She stopped, and looked down.

I don't want to think about that again, she thought with a shiver.

Castimir nodded.

"I remember it," he said tensely. "He killed us all and then he—" He, too, found it impossible to continue. "I'm sorry, Kara."

She sighed.

"Could these dreams be magically induced?" she asked. "Is such a thing possible?" Castimir tilted his head in thought.

"There were rumors that the Kinshra used a witch in the war, to drive Crown Prince Anlaf mad using such magic." He nodded to Daquarius. "Perhaps he would be able to tell you." But Kara frowned.

"I don't want to talk to them."

Suddenly Arisha gasped. Castimir's eyes widened.

"Please, Cas, could you warm some water for me, over the fire?" The priestess pointed to where several Varrock soldiers stood around a small flame.

"But I don't want to leave you, Arisha," he said, sounding very much like a little boy.

"Please, Cas." She gave him a reassuring look. "I promise to last until you return."

Castimir nodded and gently took her head off his lap, lowering it to the ground. Then he stood up and walked away. Only when he was out of earshot did Arisha speak again.

"Kara, I want you to promise me something," she said. "Can you do that?" The priestess took her hand and squeezed it as hard as she seemed able. It was pathetically weak.

Kara nodded.

"Good," Arisha said. "Then listen…"

39

Ebenezer waited in the round room of King Botolph's Tower. It was long past midnight.

At its center, in her cot, the babe Felicity stirred restlessly. Ellamaria and Lady Anne sat next to each other, above the crib, toying with her to keep her quiet. From a seat near the sealed chimney, Gideon Gleeman watched. Frequently he touched the black patterns stitched into his red uniform, and the alchemist wondered what runes the jester had prepared.

He thought of Sally, and wondered for the hundredth time where she had gone. She had been missing for the whole day. He liked to think that she had left the palace and returned to the city. But he couldn't help doubting it.

Lucretia first, and now Sally. He closed his eyes. *No wonder people are afraid to be alone now.* He moved a hand from his walking stick to his sagging jacket pocket. The hard feel of the round metal object gave him comfort.

Felicity let out a cry. Ellamaria picked her up and held her. Anne watched her.

"You will make the king a very happy man," she said, and Ellamaria blushed. For the first time Ebenezer noticed her tears. He frowned, and she caught his stare.

"Forgive me, master alchemist," she said. She adjusted her hold on Felicity and smiled. "It may not appear so, but I am happy. The king came to see me before he left for Paterdomus." Her smile grew, but the tears continued to flow. "He has asked me to marry him."

"*Shhhh!*" Lady Anne said. "It's supposed to be a secret!" She wore a smile, and Ellamaria laughed.

"I think, in times like this, it is good for us all to have hope for the future," she responded. "And besides, there are none more loyal to the crown than those of us in this room."

Her comment brought a rare smile to the faces of the four guards who stood with their backs to the wall of the tower. They were big men who had proved themselves. Each had a family in Varrock.

"Congratulations, my lady," Gideon said amicably.

"And let me congratulate you as well, Lady Ellamaria," Ebenezer added. He stood awkwardly and bowed. The dark-haired woman repaid his grace with a brilliant smile. Then she returned Felicity to her cot.

From down the spiral stairs, in the guarded anteroom, a grandfather clock chimed the second hour after midnight.

"You look much like her, you know," Anne said after some minutes. She was studying Ellamaria's face intently. "I mean the Lady Elizabeth, the king's previous fiancée."

Ellamaria dared a smile, but behind it Ebenezer detected her discomfort.

And little wonder, he thought. *How strange of Lady Anne to say that.*

"Then I pray I have more fortune than that poor girl," Ellamaria said quietly.

I hope so, too, the alchemist agreed silently. *It would be vile to think of your body lying in the palace crypt, prevented from decaying by some foul magic of Tenebra's.*

"And you, Anne," Ellamaria said, speaking more lightly again. "Have you and Sir Theodore made any such plans?"

Anne glanced around, caught Ebenezer's gaze, and smiled.

"Not yet," she said huskily. "Though when he returns, we have agreed…"

"What?" Ebenezer said loudly. He glanced at the cot, grimaced, and lowered his voice. "You mean you and Theodore are to be *married*?"

She blushed and nodded.

"I would like to hope so."

"But can he do that?" the old man pressed. "Since he is a Knight of Falador, I thought marriage was forbidden."

"Normally it would be so, but he hasn't made his vows yet—not as a knight," Anne replied. "That is something he must do, kneeling before Sir Amik himself. As it is, King Roald was the one who elevated him."

"Then circumstance has indeed smiled on your union," Ebenezer said.

"Circumstance?" A papery voice came from the stairwell. "*Bah*—the belief in good fortune is the hope of fools!" Ebenezer turned as Papelford stepped through the door. The change in the old man startled him. His eyes were red-rimmed and feverish, and his face looked skeletal.

"You shouldn't be here," the alchemist said carefully. He struggled to his feet. He was relieved to see that Gideon had done the same, and that two of the guards had moved to block his way.

"Oh, I know." He waved his hand dismissively. "For *you* have seen to my fall from office—the only thing I ever cared about." Lowering the hand, he craned his neck forward and peered intensely in Ebenezer's direction. "I *hate* you for what you have done." The alchemist saw the truth of it in his red eyes.

"I just wanted to tell you that, before the end," Papelford continued, "for the end must come. Perhaps tonight, or tomorrow. Tenebra will send something soon. He has to, if he wants to retrieve little Felicity."

He gazed toward the crib and licked his lips. He reminded Ebenezer of a hungry dog.

"I am sorry for what I did," Ebenezer said sincerely, "but it was necessary. You blocked our investigation from the outset. Your information was incomplete and at times erroneous, and you denied Reldo access to books that are proving to be of tremendous importance." He stepped closer, and found anger growing within him. "In fact, Papelford, there may be a case for treason, based on your gross incompetence."

To his astonishment, Papelford just laughed.

"Treason?" he said as he cackled. "Who can try me?" He looked to the crib again, and his gaze passed over Ellamaria and Anne. Again he licked his lips hungrily. Then he looked back to Ebenezer and scowled.

"But I am hungry now, so I shall leave you." His eyes blazed. "I must prepare my dinner." He turned on his heel and left the room, shuffling slowly down the stairs.

"I am scared of him," Ellamaria said after a moment. Ebenezer offered her comfort in a reassuring smile.

"He is a bitter old man, my dear." He chuckled, and hoped it sounded convincing. "I should know one when I see one, for I am one myself." He sat back down and sighed contentedly, rejoicing in the hopeful glances of the younger women.

But Papelford is right, he knew. *Tenebra will send something, perhaps even tonight.* He gripped his walking stick all the tighter and bowed his head. His heart beat quicker and sweat gathered on his brow.

But when? he thought. *And what form shall it take?*

He heard steps sounding lightly outside of the room. When he looked up he saw Pia at the top of the stairs. She carried a tray with several steaming mugs. He smiled instinctively when he caught the sweet scent.

"The king left instructions that the watchers should not want for anything," Pia explained. "Apparently, this is coffee. It's very rare and expensive, but it's supposed to keep people awake. I haven't tried any myself, but they tell me it's nice."

She offered a cup to Ebenezer, who took it carefully, to avoid burning himself. When she had finished giving them out, she came and stood at his side.

"Are you sure you haven't tasted it?" he asked with a suspicious look.

Pia frowned.

"No," she said stubbornly. "I thought about it, but I didn't do it."

"Good," he answered, and he rewarded her with a smile. *Perhaps she really is turning over a new leaf,* he thought. He examined her carefully and noticed how pale she looked. "Is anything amiss, my dear?"

Pia glanced quickly at the others, but no one else seemed to be watching her. She moved closer to him.

"I-I am scared, Ebenezer," she whispered. "It's so quiet in the palace now, since the king left with his army. And everyone left has gathered downstairs in the anteroom. They are all afraid, though no one knows of what."

Ebenezer nodded.

"Yes, and so am I, Pia," he confessed. "*He* wants Felicity, and we believe he will try for her tonight. But remember this—the only way here is up the grand stairs. All other doors, on every stair and landing, have been sealed on both sides. The palace is locked shut, and guards watch every entrance.

"Look." He pointed to the window, barred on both sides. Beyond, he could see torches burning along the distant wall that enclosed the palace. Some of the flames moved, carried by unseen guards.

"It feels like a prison," Pia muttered. "It feels so... tense." She shivered suddenly.

"Go back down to the anteroom," he said soothingly. "There is good company there, amid bright fires. You will be safe, I promise you."

She gave an uncertain glance to Gideon, and then nodded before turning toward the stairs. When she was gone, Ebenezer clutched at the heavy object that stretched his jacket pocket.

Whatever you are, you will come tonight, he thought. *And you will not take Felicity. Not while I am alive.*

He tightened his grip on his walking stick, and caught Gideon's anxious stare.

Pia had never been scared of the dark before. As a thief in Ardougne, the darkness had comforted her—hid her from the eyes of her enemies, and kept her safe. But such was not the case in the palace of King Roald. Here, something else had made the darkness its home.

No one had *seen* it, of course, but whispers were rife among the servants. People had gone missing.

Sally and Lucretia, Pia thought as she descended into the dark of the stairwell. *They would not have run away. They were taken.*

"Pia," a voice seemed to whisper in her ear. She froze. The air in the well grew cold, and she shivered.

Did I imagine that? She thought with growing terror. She ran all the way down the stairs until she burst into the anteroom. Startled gazes turned to her instantly.

The hostile eyes of Sir Cecil, King Lathas's ambassador, fell upon her, while those of Master Peregrim, Jack, Karnac, and Lady Caroline gazed at her in concern. The score of assorted guards and nobles fell silent. Lord Mews, sitting with three of his inquisitors, stood.

"Is anything amiss up there?" he asked haughtily. "You can tell me, girl. His grace has charged *me* with ensuring that nothing happens to Felicity."

Pia dipped her head in shame.

"N-no, there is nothing amiss," she said. "I was just scared of being alone."

Lord Mews sneered.

"Stupid girl," he scolded. "We haven't time for your panics. Go and see if the guards at the top of the grand stairs need anything."

Pia cringed.

"It's dark that way—"

"I told you to *go!*"

Pia went.

The corridor that led from the anteroom was the only way out, other than climbing to the tower. It led to the central landing, which in turn led off to a maze of different floors and quarters.

Every door had been bolted on both sides, so the only possible way to reach Felicity would be to ascend the stairs—where a dozen archers stood guard.

But even the presence of the men did little to soothe her nerves. With each hasty step she imagined the voice in her ear.

"Pia," it whispered hungrily, "Pia…" The darkness gave way to the torches that burned on the landing. Armed men turned to stare at her as she emerged from the corridor. She was breathing heavily.

"I-I was sent to see if you needed anything?" she stammered.

The men shook their heads and returned to their duty. Pia moved to the edge of the landing and watched with them. She could sense the tension among them. Some twitched their bowstrings, while others sharpened their knives.

"It's hard," a heavy-set man with a black beard remarked. "The waiting." Pia knew him as Captain Merrick, and he was in command of the landing. Like all the men inside the palace that night, she knew he would have a family in the city.

Her eyes grew accustomed to the gloom. Then she gasped as downstairs, a cloaked figure moved.

"It's just Papelford," Merrick said reassuringly.

"He shouldn't be alone down there," Pia said. Merrick smiled grimly.

"I agree," he said. "But I'm not going to waste my time arguing with the old goat. He's as mean as they come, these days."

"Yet what if he…" Pia's question trailed off as she tried to find the words.

"You're right to worry, girl," he said. "It's not safe to be alone in the palace. People have gone missing, and we don't know how. That's why we have sealed all the doors and windows, and concentrate our strength here." He clenched the hilt of his sword, and moved closer to her.

She turned and stared at him, suddenly fearful. He must have seen it, because he smiled gently.

"I have a daughter your age," Merrick said quietly. "She lives in the city with her mother, and she cried when I reported for duty tonight. She didn't want me to come."

Pia nodded.

"It's like a prison here," she said again, shivering. "We're locked in with *something*."

"And yet there is no safer place, for Felicity at any rate," he murmured. "She is guarded by the best men in Varrock, and Gleeman himself watches over her."

Pia frowned. He saw her puzzlement and smiled again.

"Gleeman plays Varrock's fool," he said. "But it is an act."

"Sir?"

One of his men called out suddenly. Merrick turned and stared down into the gloom. Because of the late hour, some of the torches had gone out, and it was difficult to see. Far below, the white tiles of the hall were just visible.

Something clattered in the murk.

"Blast it!" came a voice. "Would one of you lend a hand to an old man? I am not as strong as I used to be."

Pia gasped as her stomach went cold.

"That voice…" she murmured.

"It's only Papelford!" Merrick said irritably. "You two, come with me—"

Pia grabbed his arm.

"Don't go," she pleaded. "Don't go down there!"

"What?"

"Don't! Please don't!" She felt her lips tremble. "You mustn't!"

Merrick pried her loose.

"Will no one help me?" the voice cried out in anger.

"No!" Pia yelled. "His voice, I've heard that tone before… he's one of them!"

Merrick gave her a gruff look.

"One of them? Girl, he's lived in this palace for longer than I've been alive." Then, as if reconsidering, he stared down into the darkness again. "Master Papelford?" he called. "What is amiss?"

Papelford swore.

"I've tripped, you fool! That is what is amiss. Now, will someone *help* me?"

Merrick motioned to two of his men. One of them lifted a burning torch from the wall, then they strode down the stairs, making no effort to hurry.

"Be careful!" Pia cried. Merrick shot her a look.

"Be quiet!" he hissed.

The two men continued, their light dwindling as they descended.

40

Fifty-two steps, Pia thought. *I have knelt and cleaned them time and again. Just fifty-two...*

"Here I am!" Papelford croaked. "Come here—don't dither!"

The men reached the bottom of the stairs and turned right toward the source of Papelford's voice. Pia searched for him, but wherever he had fallen, it was out of sight.

"Arrrrgh!"

The light of the torch flew across the darkness, as the sounds of a scuffle erupted below them. There was the sound of a sword being drawn, and in the dim light she thought she saw two more shapes appear.

The second soldier screamed, but the sound was quickly cut off. The torch died, and gloom returned to the base of the stairs.

One of the men screamed again.

"What's happening?" Merrick cried. "Papelford!" But no answer came. The captain turned to his men and drew his sword. The dozen bowmen covering the landing aimed down, waiting. Several others gathered at the top of the stairs, forming a shield wall.

Behind them, yet more readied their long pikes.

Try as she might, Pia could see nothing in the shadows. She ran to the nearest torch and pulled it from the wall. No one protested as she hurled it down the stairs, where it rolled toward the bottom.

It came to rest in the crook of a man's arm.

"Larkin, can you hear me?" Merrick called. "Devlin?"

The arm moved, pushing the torch.

"Get him back up here," Merrick ordered. Three men ran through the shield wall and down the steps, their weapons drawn. They gathered up the moving man and dragged him up the stairs. Pia felt ill at the sight, for a line of blood trailed up the stairs behind him.

Will I be fortunate enough to clean them again? she wondered. *Will I live that long?* The shield wall parted to let them through. The man pressed a hand to his throat. It looked as if it had been gnawed by an animal.

"What was it, Devlin?" Merrick asked. "What attacked you?" Devlin shook his head, then grimaced at the pain. His eyes were glazing over.

"I-I d-don't know," he gritted. Blood pumped past the fingers of his gloved hand. Suddenly he exhaled, and his hand dropped.

"Devlin?" Merrick urged. "Devlin!" He leaned down to place his ear over the man's mouth.

"Come on, man," he whispered.

"Sir?" A man called from the shield wall. "Sir!"

Merrick turned his head. Behind him, Devlin stirred.

"What is it?" Merrick asked.

Devlin's eyes flew open. A blue glow burned in his pupils, and his mouth opened wide—unnaturally so. He lurched forward and bit Merrick on the face.

"Arrrrhh!"

"Sir!" A nearby soldier cried out in alarm.

Pia heard the twang of arrows.

Biting and clawing, Devlin—or the thing that had been Devlin—forced Captain Merrick over on his side. A sword was thrust through the undead soldier's back, and a kite shield was rammed into the side of his head.

He staggered as a pikeman charged into him, impaling him upon his long spear. With a massive effort the soldier pitched both Devlin and his weapon out over the balustrade, with Devlin still flailing on its end.

They vanished into the dim light below.

Pia cast a look to the bottom of the stairs. A body of people was creeping forward, some walking, others on all fours. Some had feathered arrows sticking out of their limbs. Each had the same ice-blue stare.

"The dead!" a man on the shield wall screamed. "The dead walk!" As if on command, the archers loosed their arrows again. Several of the things fell, only to stagger back to their feet and continue to march upward, ever closer.

Pia felt a hand fasten around her ankle. She looked down to see Merrick grasping for her.

"Go... get away," he said. "Get G-Gleeman." Pia nodded and pulled her leg from his grasp.

"Gods!" a man shouted from the shield wall. "It's the Lady Elizabeth!"

A stunned silence fell over the men. The nearest of the undead approached the top of the stairs, and she looked so much like Ellamaria that Pia had to look twice.

"B-but she's dead!" Pia moaned. "She's one of them!"

Elizabeth reached forward. With a manic leer she seized the nearest man and dragged his arm within reach of her mouth—of her teeth, which she bared hideously. Her jaw bit down upon his mailed wrist.

With a shout the man punched her backward. Two arrows

hammered into her body, knocking her aside. Then she was lost among those who followed.

"There's no way out!" a young officer shouted. "We're trapped here. Saradomin help us!" A massive soldier—a scarred veteran with one good eye—turned from the shield wall to glare at him.

"This is bigger than us, son," he roared. "We have pledged our lives to Misthalin and to King Roald. Today we see if we are worth our words." With that he hefted his huge shield in front of him and ran down the steps. "Forward!" On either side his fellows followed the example. Behind them came the pikemen, stabbing through deliberate gaps left between the shields.

Quickly the undead were battered aside.

"Back! Back to the top," the veteran roared. "Keep ranks!" Moving together, the men of the shield wall retreated one careful step at a time.

The undead surged up once more.

The young officer knelt by Merrick's side. The bearded man was still, his eyes half-open.

"Sir?" the younger man said, his face deathly pale. "Sir, what are your orders?"

Merrick mouthed a name, but no sound came out. He licked his lips and said it again.

"Grimm," he said. "Grimm will command them." The young man nodded and turned back to the shield wall. The one-eyed giant was again leading an advance, pushing the undead back before retreating.

"Yes," he said. "Grimm is best."

Merrick coughed. Pia noticed with horror a blue shine in his eyes.

"Captain Merrick?" she said, backing away in alarm. Then Merrick *smiled*.

"I told you to get Gideon," he said, his voice unnaturally strong again. "Go on, girl. *Go*."

Pia nodded soundlessly, turned, and ran back to the corridor. She looked one last time to see Merrick stand and draw his sword. With a roar he staggered toward the shield wall, shouting loudly.

Then she turned and ran into the hated darkness.

Ebenezer tightened his jaw and closed his eyes. He pictured Sally in his mind, when they were younger. It could have been her—rather than her sister—whom he married.

Sally, where are you?

He decided he didn't want to know.

Rapid footsteps sounded in the stairwell. He looked up as Pia burst in, out of breath.

"The undead are attacking," she gasped. "Lady Elizabeth is there, and Papelford has vanished, though I am sure it was his voice I heard when—"

"Calm down," he instructed. She nodded and breathed in. Then she turned to Gideon.

"They need you, Gideon," she said. "Captain Merrick has asked for you."

The jester frowned in silence for a moment.

"I cannot go," he said flatly. "Felicity's safety is the most important thing. I must stay to watch her."

"But they are dying!"

"He's right, Pia," Ellamaria said. "No matter what, we must keep the babe safe."

Pia stared.

"W-what are they?" Lady Anne asked hesitantly. "You said it was the Lady Elizabeth." Pia nodded.

"They are zombies, my lady. They can't be killed, I think."

"So it is the bodies from the crypt," Ebenezer observed. "Those who were slain by the Wyrd, and who Papelford kept locked down there. Near a hundred of them." He growled. "Only he and Reldo had the keys to unlock the place. And Reldo is in the anteroom."

"What are you suggesting?" Gideon asked.

"It is Papelford, my friend," the alchemist replied. "Most likely it was his voice Pia heard ordering the attack on the granary. Then no doubt he has been linked to the insurgents from the very start. I'd wager it was he who tried to have Arisha assassinated.

"And it would explain why Reldo was kept away from the books," Ebenezer added. As he did, Lady Anne stood.

"I will go down and help where I may," she said firmly. "If this is true about Papelford, then I fear for us all. So many years so close to the king and our innermost councils…"

Gideon turned to Ebenezer.

"Do you have some skill with runes?" he asked. The alchemist shook his head.

"Not enough. Not nearly enough. Besides," he patted his sagging pocket, "I have my own weapons. But I, too, will remain here— where the future of Misthalin will be decided." Pia's face fell, but the four guards who waited with their weapons drawn all nodded in agreement.

But I shall face the thing that took Sally tonight, he promised. *And I shall burn it.*

Lady Anne vanished down the stairwell, with Pia following. Ebenezer felt Ellamaria's eyes fix on him.

He lowered his gaze and waited.

"You, Mews, get up!" Lady Anne's voice was piercing. "Men are dying out there, and they need your help." Pia skipped past her toward the corridor. The sounds of fighting echoed from the darkness. Suddenly a familiar hand gripped her wrist.

"We should stay together," Jack said. In his other hand her brother held one of the mysterious shards that the spirit lady had gifted him in Morytania.

Shards that she used to conjure a creature from another world, Pia recalled.

"Can you use those at all, Jack?" she asked. But he shook his head sadly. Then his face brightened. "Still, I expect it would hurt if I stabbed someone with them!"

Karnac and Master Peregrim appeared behind her.

"I have fought the undead all my life," the leader of Hope Rock said wearily. "And I will do so again today." He turned to glance at the gnome. Peregrim barely reached his waist. "You are my last comrade from Hope Rock," he said. "Shall we go together, my friend?"

Grimly, Peregrim pulled a short knife from his belt.

"I visited the spirit tree today," he said mournfully. "One stands inside the palace walls in a secret, overgrown place." He smiled. "My prayers gave me hope for tonight, so let us go and do what we can."

Karnac and Peregrim ran down the passage. Pia steeled herself and took Jack's hand. Then she followed them toward the battle on the stairs. The cries sounded terrible as they neared the light of the landing, yet the sight was far worse.

The archers had abandoned their positions. Now they fought in a line with those who held the shield wall. The wall was smaller, for several men had been overwhelmed by the voracious horde. Grimm's voice carried over the fray, but to Pia it seemed strained now, containing an edge of desperation that hadn't been there before.

"We're out of arrows," she heard an archer say as he pushed forward with a bloodstained pike.

"They've done no good, anyway," Grimm yelled, turning. "We must sever the limbs and…" He caught sight of her. "You! Where in the abyss is Gleeman? Captain Merrick commanded you to bring him here." Pia wilted under his gaze.

"He won't come!" Lady Anne called from the corridor. Pia

turned to see her stride forward purposefully. "Felicity is more important." Grimm opened his mouth to speak, but Anne cut him short. "And he's right, too. She's more important than *all* of us."

From the corridor issued a stream of men. Even Lord Mews was armed, though the sword he held trembled in his grasp. Pia caught Sir Cecil's dour look.

"Let's really see how well you kill, little murderess," he said to her as he stepped to the landing's edge. Reldo was next out. The bearded scholar nervously held a dagger.

"Assist with a pike, Reldo," Anne suggested. "Keep them pinned on the stairs. If they make it up to the landing…"

Reldo nodded and ran to obey, adding his weight to a pike held by one of Grimm's remaining men.

"We're trapped here!" Mews whimpered. "Trapped!"

Pia felt a wave of disgust. She turned aside and looked to her right, along the landing. To where Captain Merrick lay slumped against the balustrade.

"Stay here, Jack," she told her brother.

Merrick's eyes were closed. The blood on his face was dry, but the wound had closed up. She wasn't sure a wound as bad as he had sustained could heal so quickly.

"Captain Merrick?" she asked in little more than a whisper.

"Pia! I need you," Lady Anne called. The woman strode over to her. "You know the passageway that leads to the nobles' quarters, don't you?" Pia nodded.

"Of course, my lady. But I can't get to it. The door will be bolted from the other side." In response, Anne smiled.

"Perhaps," she said. "Go and hammer against it as hard and as loud and as long as you can."

"We can't possibly break through in time, Lady Anne," Lord Mews said fearfully.

Anne turned on him.

"I don't plan to *break* anything, you imbecile. Get back to the stairs and help keep them back!" Mews fled to the relative safety of the pikemen and attempted to look busy. "Jack, take a torch to light your way."

"I don't understand, Lady Anne," Pia said as her brother took one of the torches from the wall. "There's no one left in the palace... is there?"

Anne gripped her shoulder.

"We must hope so," she said. Then the uproar from the stairs increased, and she turned to investigate.

Pia turned in the opposite direction and ran past Captain Merrick's still form. Jack in tow, she ran down a short hallway to find the door in question. When she did so, she unbolted the door and battered her clenched fists against it as hard as she could. It hardly made a sound.

She tried again, pounding until her fists were bruised.

"It's useless!"

Jack clutched her arm.

"Use this," he suggested. She looked down to see a small stone statue of some austere man. Grabbing it without a second glance, she smashed it against the wood as hard as she could. The stone broke slightly, causing the man's face to appear even more wrinkled than before.

Twice more she did it, shouting all the time, before the small statue broke in her hands. She gave a cry of resignation.

"Go and tell Lady Anne that we've tried, Jack," she said miserably. She leaned back against the door to catch her breath as Jack turned to obey. Suddenly he froze, and she saw why. "Oh, oh no—"

The slumping form of Captain Merrick appeared around the corner. His sword hung limply in his hand, the tip dragging along the carpet. And his eyes glowed with a blue fire.

"Jack," Pia whispered. "Those shards... can you do anything with them… *anything* at all?" He shook his head. But even so he reached into his pocket and pulled out one of the sharp glass-like objects.

Merrick seemed to see them for the first time.

"Giiirrrrllll," he slurred. She gripped the remains of the statue in her hand.

"Don't let him bite you, Jack," she hissed. "That's what happened to him."

"*Giiirrrrllll…*" Merrick staggered forward, his legs uncertain. He drifted to his right and left, but in the narrow passageway, there was little chance she could get past.

"Grrrlll…"

"Pia," Jack said.

"Hush," she replied, and she moved in front of him, the remains of the statue held out in front.

Jack made a sound behind her.

"Grrrlll…"

Merrick was near now. So close she could see the bloodied froth that surrounded his mouth. His eyes seemed to fix on her.

"Jack?"

"*Move!*" a man's voice said. A hand pushed her aside. Jack's torch leapt up, stabbing forward directly into Merrick's distorted face. His hair was alight in an instant, and a sword swung up to impale the zombie through the belly.

The creature slumped, tearing at its burning head. The sword was withdrawn and then thrust forward again, this time aiming for the heart.

Pia staggered back against the wall. The flames gave a dim light to the dark passage, but it was hard to make out the features of the man who had rescued them. As he withdrew the sword for the second time, however, she realized she knew him.

41

"Y-you! But… you're the traitor!"

Lord William nodded.

"Apparently," he said. He brought the blade back and swung it, two-handed. It caught Merrick in the throat and beheaded him. Then the young lord moaned.

"Never done that before," he said in disgust. He grimaced and stretched his arm awkwardly.

"Is he dead?" Jack asked. William nodded.

"Merrick? Yes, poor man. I've read about these things. Zombies. It's not the first time Varrock's been assaulted by them." He fell silent, and looked back down the passageway. "Now, what is all that noise?" Stepping over Merrick's corpse, he ran to the corner of the landing overlooking the stairs.

Pia ran with him. In the light of the torches he noticed the statue that she had broken. An amused look settled over William's worn face.

"That was my ancestor," he said. "It's good to see my family is still serving Misthalin well, after all these years, no matter what my own failings are." Then he turned. "Gods…"

Pia looked over to the stairs and gasped. The shield wall had broken. Of the soldiers who had stood there, Grimm fought alone, wielding a pike in a sweeping arc that knocked the creatures aside. From behind, others held their pikes to cover him, keeping the dead at a distance.

Grimm gave a heave and smashed one of the things over the edge of the stairs. It vanished into the darkness below.

Lord William shook his head.

"They must cut the heads off, or cave in the skull," he muttered. "That's the only way. Don't these people ever *read*?" He ran forward, shouting wildly. Pia saw Lady Anne turn and smile in relief.

Lord Mews gaped.

"Y-you!" he hissed "Someone—anyone—arrest him!"

"Oh, shut up!" Lady Anne commanded, then she turned. "I am glad to see you, Lord de Adlard. You are far more familiar than I am with the palace. Do we have a way out?"

William nodded.

"We can escape to the galleries, or to the nobles' quarters," he said. "The galleries would be better, though. Through them we can get anywhere in the palace." He approached her and took an arm gently. Pia craned her head to listen. "You were right, Anne—no one could have guessed that I was hiding in your room these days past." Anne smiled broadly. "I owe you a debt of gratitude."

"If you save us today," she replied, "you will have repaid that tenfold, William." She turned and looked toward the melee. "Where is Lady Caroline?"

Pia found her. The dark-haired girl gritted her teeth and held a chair above her head. She hurled it down, just missing Grimm. It crashed into the zombies and tripped the foremost.

Lord William beamed. He ran forward and took her by the arm, planting a kiss on her cheek. Their words were lost in the maelstrom.

"Take off their heads," William shouted a heartbeat later. "That's the only way to halt them. Otherwise they will just rise again!"

Grimm cursed. On the steps below him Pia saw a familiar figure, still with a pike thrust into his abdomen.

"Not you again," Grimm muttered, his great chest heaving. "Third time lucky, hey, Devlin?"

"What is it, in your pocket?" Ellamaria asked, her voice edged with panic. "I've heard stories of your power and science. Can it help us tonight?"

"Only as a last resort," Ebenezer said. *If I set it off in here, the whole tower will be destroyed,* he added silently. *It would take all of us with it, Felicity and Tenebra's new monster. And yet, if we can win downstairs, we might win here, too.*

"It will help them downstairs," he said, reaching a decision. "Here, take it." He reached into his pocket and pulled out a heavy canister. "Light the fuse, here, and then throw it into the midst of the enemy." He managed a slight grin. "But be sure to hide behind something when you do it, and make doubly sure you throw it far. Else it will bring down this entire tower."

Ellamaria licked her lips hesitantly. Then she took the object and, holding it away from her body, ran from the room and down the stairwell.

Gideon sighed.

"Would you really have used it, alchemist? In here?"

Ebenezer snorted.

"I don't know," he said honestly. He returned the jester's stare and smiled coldly. "But I have promised to kill the creature that took Sally and Lucretia, and all those other nameless girls," he added. "I mean to keep my word, one way or the other."

Gideon nodded once, and looked anxiously at the crib.

• • •

Fatigue was taking its toll on the men behind Grimm. That, and panic. More than one looked as if he was on the verge of running.

Lord Mews and his three inquisitors had vanished. Lord William helped where he could, but it was obvious that he was no fighter. He yielded his sword to Karnac, whose own had been lost in the body of one of his foes, and now the nobleman shouted orders and encouragement, pulling some men back for a rest while sending others forward. Never had Pia seen him with such fire. All followed his instructions without question.

Karnac stepped up beside Grimm, hacking furiously at anything that came within reach. His strokes were aimed to decapitate, or if that wasn't possible, to mutilate. He would strike at the arms of his enemies, severing them at the elbows before going for the neck.

"How many of them are there?" Jack asked.

"Ebenezer said there were nearly a hundred," she replied. "Yet we've probably killed no more than twenty."

With a great shout several soldiers charged down the topmost steps, wielding the shields of fallen comrades. The creatures were pushed back, falling atop each other, snowballing down the stairs. For a moment—and a moment only—the staircase was clear.

"Pia!" Lady Anne's commanding voice summoned her attention. "Go back up the tower. Tell Gideon and Ebenezer and their four guards to bring Felicity down here. Tell them we intend to escape through the galleries. We cannot hold them off forever."

"Yes," a new voice said steadily. "We can." Ellamaria appeared from the mouth of the corridor. In her hands she held a heavy black canister with a fuse at its end.

Below, the undead renewed their ascent.

"Light it," Ellamaria ordered. An exhausted archer came forward with a burning torch and did as she commanded. "Now get clear!" she shouted.

Pia ran. She took Jack's arm and bolted around the corner, to where Merrick's body lay still and truly dead. Behind her came Lady Anne and a dozen others.

"Do you think this will be safe—"

The whole palace seemed to leap on its foundations. A raging wind filled with biting stone chips swept over her, tearing at her clothes and scraping her skin raw. Absolute darkness fell. She wasn't aware of any sound, not for what seemed like a long time, for the world was muted and still. Someone pawed at her, the nudges growing in urgency.

A torch appeared. She saw Jack in the haze, beating her, and she wondered if she was on fire.

Only when she sat up did he stop. From far away came the sound of cheering. They peered around what remained of the corner.

In the dust-filled twilight figures emerged. Grimm rose from the ruins of the landing. Blood and white dust covered his face. Ellamaria stood from beneath him, unharmed. Amazingly, the great staircase still stood, though now it was torn with gaping holes. Looking back to the landing, Pia gave a sudden smile, for no one seemed to have been badly hurt. She was even relieved to see Sir Cecil waddle through the fug.

Only Lord William seemed to have suffered. He lay on the ground, and blood flowed from a wound on his face. He was ashen. Lady Caroline wept, holding his head to her breast.

"But it's only a small wound," Pia muttered, unsure if any could hear her words, for her own ears were ringing. William reached inside his cloak and produced a stoppered wooden flask. Greedily he drank from inside. He grinned for the briefest moment, and then lowered his head onto Caroline's lap.

Sound began to return. At the top of the stairs she heard Grimm laugh savagely.

"That must have got most of them," he said.

Crash!

A large piece of masonry smashed onto the floor, falling from the ceiling. Silence followed it until the echoes died.

"We should depart," Anne called. "Someone go and get Felicity and the others. The tower won't be safe anymore." Karnac and an archer ran to obey her orders as the others stood and checked for wounds. Pia walked to the edge of the landing and gazed down.

Suddenly the palace seemed to shake. She lashed out and caught the wrecked balustrade to steady herself. The rubble moved as if with a life of its own, and through the settling dust mutilated shapes once again climbed the remains of the shattered stairs.

"Devlin?" Grimm called in disbelief. "You're one determined corpse, damn you."

The tower shook again. Ebenezer held his breath. Felicity wailed.

"Was that your doing?" Gideon murmured, looking at the roof. Cracks had appeared in the stonework. Fine powder trickled from several points above them.

"We have to get out of here," the alchemist answered. "Right now." Gideon didn't argue.

"You two." The jester pointed to two of the four guards. "Make sure the stairway is clear, and that the anteroom is free of any obstacle. If you can, check the corridor beyond." A piece of the ceiling broke free and shattered on the floor, not a foot from his head.

"We *have* to go," Ebenezer insisted. "The tower's about to fall. It doesn't matter what awaits us below."

The two guards vanished down the stairs. The two who remained made ready. Gideon scooped the screeching Felicity out of her cot.

"Hush, hush, sweet babe," he cooed, bouncing her in his arms. "Hush, hush, or all of Morytania will hear."

Ebenezer staggered forward. He let the guards go first and then Gideon. Only when they had disappeared did he step onto the stairs.

A cry sounded below him.

"Gideon? What's going on?" he demanded.

Snap!

A man made a gurgling sound. Ebenezer held his breath. Then someone screamed for a short second.

"Gideon?" he said again. "Answer me, blast it!" Footsteps sounded from below. Footsteps coming *upward.*

He backed away into the room. The tower shuddered again, as a black-robed figure emerged at the top of the stairs—a short, wizened man with white hair and blood-red eyes. A man who was older than he was. In his arms he held Felicity, now silent.

"You!" Ebenezer choked. "G-gods, how?"

Albertus Black smiled cruelly.

"Did the possibility never occur to you, old friend?" Albertus opened his mouth to reveal his glistening fangs. "I went with our friends to Morytania, in your place. As I lay dying of age and disease and injury, the Lord Tenebra blessed me with his gift. It lived inside me as I lay dying, yet only came to fruition when I finally *did* die— after I crossed the holy river. It was all as he intended. He let our friends escape in order to let me cross."

Ebenezer shook his head in disbelief.

"Did you not wonder why Tenebra's insurgents attacked the refugees from Morytania? Or who gave them the powder they needed to burn the granary under Lord Hyett's direction?" Albertus shook his head. "Your age has made you fallible indeed, old friend. The insurgents recovered my corpse so that I could be freed in this new form and wield its great powers." His grotesque smile grew. "So that I could be fed."

"Please, Albertus," the alchemist said, "please tell me that Sally is alive."

"Would that please you?" he responded softly. "But I cannot, because it would be a lie. She is dead, too, along with Lucretia." He raised an arm and clenched his fist. "You have no idea, no *idea* of the power. I waited in the stairwell for an hour or so, turned to mist, concealed among the stone. I very nearly decided to feed on young Pia. And I killed your two guards by snapping their necks quicker than you could blink.

"As for Gideon, I left him alive. He did, after all, save me from the werewolves. And besides, Tenebra doesn't want to kill everybody. He wants a human race that will serve him."

You're not the man I knew in life, Ebenezer told himself. *He would never have showed so little regard for the lives of others.*

"What is his plan, Albertus?" the alchemist asked, concentrating to keep his voice steady. "Where are the children held?"

The tower shook again. A brick fell from the roof and directly into Felicity's cot.

Albertus laughed.

"It seems as if the fates have ordained her death," he crowed, and his red eyes narrowed. "Yours, too, unless you leave here now. Soon this tower will collapse, and I haven't the time to rescue you."

"Would you, if I asked?" Ebenezer queried.

"I remember the fun we had in life, and I would hope to renew it again in death," Albertus replied, "the two of us together, serving our lord. Think what we could achieve, Ebenezer. Imagine it! Lifetime after lifetime, devoted to science."

"Ebenezer!" Karnac's voice called up the stairs. "Are you there? What's going on?"

"I leave you now, old friend," Albertus said, turning. "Felicity needs to be delivered, and I—"

"No!" Ebenezer leapt forward. His hands fell around Albertus's throat. The vampire watched him with a profound look of amazement.

"Cease your embarrassing scrambling," he demanded. "It's ludicrous, a man of your age behaving like a common brawler." Quicker than the eye could follow, Albertus lashed out with the flat of his hand. The blow caught Ebenezer in the chest and sent him reeling backward, falling onto the remains of Felicity's crib.

Fine stone powder fell onto his face. He felt the tower shake again.

Instinctively he closed his eyes.

"Leave here, old friend," Albertus said. "I beg you. For you don't have long."

An icy wind wafted over his body, numbing his skin. He struggled to sit up, and opened his eyes.

Albertus had gone.

"Ebenezer?" Karnac yelled.

"Get out!" he roared. "Tenebra has her, Karnac—he has Felicity!"

"*What?*"

"Tenebra has her! You must warn them!" He stood cautiously, then grimaced as his old legs wavered. He tottered forward to the stairwell. Behind him, a section of the roof fell.

The alchemist stumbled out, and slipped on the top step, feeling his ankle break.

"Arrrhh!" he gritted, falling again.

"Sir!" A young soldier appeared just a few steps below. "Karnac has Gideon, and I can get you—"

"No, blast it—get clear." He heaved himself into a seated position. "But take this message. Tenebra has Felicity, do you understand? And Albertus Black is a vampire."

The archer frowned.

"Don't worry, sir—"

"Blast you, *get clear*. Delivering this message is the most important thing you will ever accomplish—do you understand? Get it to Paterdomus."

Doubt crossed the young man's face.

"*Do it!*"

"Yes, sir," the soldier replied. He vanished back the way he had come. Ebenezer slid down the stairs, one at a time.

Just a few more minutes, he thought. *King Botolph was a famous builder. Surely it will hold for only a few more—*

Pain burned through his body.

Sally. Eloise. Albertus.

He put his head in his hands, and waited.

Above him the tower shook. This time it didn't stop. The sound grew and grew.

Theodore. Castimir. Arisha. Kara. And you, Gar'rth. May the gods smile on all of you.

Look after them, Doric. All of them.

Please…

42

"*Felicity has been taken!*"

Pia's heart stopped as she saw Karnac drag Gideon Gleeman from the corridor, and heard the shout of the soldier. The whole palace shuddered. Bricks fell from the ceiling.

"*Pia?*" Jack cried at her side.

Lady Anne waved to Karnac.

"Come on!" she called. "You too, Grimm. Now is the time to flee." Grimm jumped back from the stairs and ran toward them.

"Where is Ebenezer?" Ellamaria called. "Where are the guards?" Gideon shook his bloodied head.

"It was the vampire," he said. "Albertus Black killed the men and took Felicity." He gasped. "And Ebenezer is still in the tower."

Ellamaria gasped.

"They took Felicity?" she cried. "Then all is lost!"

The palace wobbled. Pia lost her balance and fell to her knees. From above them came the sound of thunder, impossibly loud. It seemed to her as if the whole world was caving in.

A gush of smoke and debris raced from the mouth of the

corridor with enough force to extinguish the last remaining torch in its sconce. In the darkness, a hand took her shoulder. She was dragged to her feet.

"Come on," Grimm shouted. "They are at the top of the stairs now!"

"They are *still* coming?" Ellamaria groaned.

Grimm smiled.

"Your explosive took out at least three-quarters of them, my lady," he said. "Our chances are much improved."

"Not without Felicity they aren't," Anne said. There was a sound, and Pia looked back toward the stairs. A mutilated corpse stood in the swirling dust, its blue eyes shining. Behind it, other shining orbs appeared.

"Come on!" she shouted, running.

Lord William met them at the very door he had unlocked. The cut on his face was still bleeding, and his cloak was drenched in his blood. He leaned on Caroline's shoulder.

"Go straight through," he said. "To the galleries."

Grimm came last, wheezing from exhaustion. He clapped William on the shoulder.

"I never thought you had such fight in you, boy!" he said. "You have done all of Misthalin proud."

"If I could have told my father," the young lord replied, "that would have been nice." Caroline pulled William along.

"His wound won't stop bleeding," she said fearfully to Anne. "He's bleeding to death, Anne." William shook his head.

"Not yet," he said. "This wound is drying, Caroline, but slowly. I have a potion, but I need to save it. If I'm wounded again, I'll need to have some kept back."

Grimm and Karnac hefted the door shut, and bolted it behind them.

"I will carry him, then," Grimm said. Lord William nodded, and the veteran easily lifted him off his feet.

The group moved through the corridors, the silence violated by the rumblings that were becoming more and more frequent. As they went, they pulled torches from the wall and lit them with those they had taken from the landing. Counting the number of flames, Pia estimated their group at just over twenty.

They entered a gallery and turned a corner. Master Peregrim halted so suddenly that Reldo barreled into him. The gnome gave a shout.

Before them stood Lord Mews and several others who had fled the fight.

"We cannot get out," Mews said. "The doors out of here are sealed on both sides. There's nothing to do but wait for rescue." Grimm nodded his agreement.

Pia slumped down at Jack's side. She was exhausted, and shivered when she remembered her name being whispered to her in the stairwell—knowing now that it must have been the old man, Albertus.

Gideon waited near the entrance to the gallery, groping his costume in the shadows. His hands shook uncontrollably. Looking up, he acknowledged her gaze.

"I'll keep watch here," he said softly. "You should try to sleep." Needing little encouragement, Pia yawned and leaned back against the wall. She listened to the sounds about her.

Caroline wept softly, and between her gasps she told William how she loved him. How she wanted to make a life for them in the future, once his lands were restored. She described in great detail a garden they would make together, and Pia found herself drifting off to sleep in Caroline's fairytale world.

A moment later—or perhaps it was an hour—she awoke with a gasp to the sound of raised voices, and saw Anne confronting Lord Mews.

"Of course I let him in!" he said defensively. "Why wouldn't I? He says it's safe down there now—a way for us to escape."

Pia looked behind him and groaned. Papelford stood near the unbolted door. He grinned horribly in the torchlight.

"No! Oh, no!" Pia cried. "It's him! He's one of them!"

Then a pale figure stepped through the door. A zombie. More followed behind. Papelford laughed.

Grimm stood and yanked an ancient shield from the wall.

"She's not *quite* right," Papelford said, "but I do serve another master. Lord Tenebra is far more powerful than King Roald, and he can reward his followers beyond death itself. Long, indeed, have I labored for him, quietly and diligently. Now the day of his ascension is near." Papelford stepped behind the line of his undead allies. "And now, I bid you all farewell."

Karnac took a step, still holding William's sword. Papelford smirked.

"You can die fighting, if you choose," he said. "But you can't defeat these corpses. You have no magic at all—"

Gideon stepped forward, and Papelford's sneer vanished. The undead charged, and Grimm ran to meet them.

"For Varrock!" he cried. "For Roald!"

His shield smashed into the first of their enemies. Then Karnac's sword darted forward, cutting through the neck of another. Gideon staggered as he held his hand out toward the door. Fire blazed from his clenched fist and torched the creature nearest Papelford.

The old man jumped back with a cry, vanishing through the door.

More of the undead pushed in. Gideon fell to his knees and gasped. The archer who had relayed Ebenezer's message from the tower jumped forward and dragged him to safety.

"There are too many," Anne moaned.

"Caroline?" William said. "Gideon's too weak to hold them. Get the tapestries—the Battle of the Salve, anything that will burn. Light a fire, form a firewall barrier."

Anne ran into the gloom of a nearby gallery. Caroline and Pia followed her.

"This is the biggest," Anne said. She pointed to a heavy tapestry that covered the wall. "It's over two hundred years old." Grabbing it with both hands, she wrenched it down using all her weight. It took all three of them to carry it out.

All the remaining soldiers had formed a desperate line. Some used weapons taken from the walls of the galleries, while others thrust their burning torches forward into the faces of their attackers. Pia saw Captain Merrick's junior officer scream as his hand was bitten. With a curse he hurled himself into the mass of the undead, dragging them down, stabbing with his dagger and screaming as he was torn apart by their tearing claws and biting teeth.

Anne gasped.

"*Come on!*" Caroline urged. She ducked under the tapestry and hefted it over her shoulder. Anne copied her. They ran forward and the men moved to assist them. Ellamaria grabbed a burning torch and thrust it at the creatures, screaming insanely all the while.

With a heave, they hurled the tapestry onto the body of the young officer who—in death—pinned three squirming corpses beneath him. A soldier thrust his torch into the ancient patchwork, and the fragile cloth caught fire immediately.

Pia felt a flicker of hope.

"Pia!" Jack screamed.

The undead Lady Elizabeth jumped forward. Pia froze, but a slender hand pulled her back. She saw Caroline's face form a scream, saw the claws of their attacker rake the noblewoman's body, saw Elizabeth's mouth close toward her savior's arm.

"Caroline!" Pia shrieked as Ellamaria pushed her aside, her torch thrust forward. She stabbed the burning end into Lady Elizabeth's open mouth and forced her back into the growing flames as other men threw their torches onto the tapestry.

"Are you hurt?" Karnac shouted. "Did it bite you?"

Caroline shook her head, and put a hand to her stomach.

"I-I d-don't know." She gathered her wits. "I don't know." A curious expression appeared on her face. She looked at Grimm. The large man gritted his teeth and turned away.

"Oh!" she said, looking down. She stared at her hand. Her palm was soaked in blood.

"Oh…"

A crimson circle soaked her white tunic, spreading outward. Caroline slumped to her knees.

"Oh… oh, goodness," she said.

"Caroline!" Anne grabbed her friend and pulled her back. Karnac took her legs and together they carried her back to Lord William.

Meanwhile Grimm reformed his line, waiting behind the flaming tapestry. From time to time one of the undead tried to attack, but the men just pinned the corpse with their antique spears, and held it in the flames.

Slowly, the tide turned in their favor.

Caroline turned her head to see Lord William.

"William," she said. "Oh, William, I'm sorry, so sorry. I've been so… so dreadfully clumsy."

"Don't speak," Anne urged her. She ripped the girl's clothes to better view the wound. She also checked Caroline's arms.

"D-did it bite you?" William asked. Slowly, he reached forward and stroked her hair.

"I don't think it did," Anne answered in Caroline's place. But her face darkened when she saw the wound. Caroline stared at her friend through pain-filled eyes.

"Will I live, Anne?" she asked. "W-will I?"

Anne remained silent.

"Y-you could never lie, Anne," Caroline observed. "Never."

"I don't know what to do, Caroline," Anne replied. "Th-there's so much blood." Lord William moved to see the wound, and moaned at what he found. He reached inside his cloak and pulled out a small bottle.

"Drink this, Caroline," he said. Then he turned and spoke to Anne. "It'll help stop her bleeding." Anne took the potion from his hand.

"Could it harm her?" she asked. William nodded.

"But she'll die if we don't try something." He looked closely at the bottle. "Too much and it could harden her blood, and her heart will fail. But we have to try. Please, Anne—please give it to her."

Anne nodded and poured the liquid into Caroline's mouth. She held her head back and made sure she swallowed. Caroline's eyes closed.

Pia looked at William. *Something is wrong...* He noticed her and smiled gently. When he moved his hand from his side, it was coated in blood. She stared in horror.

"You're wounded!" she gasped.

Anne heard her, and cursed.

"William!" He waved his hand dismissively.

"It doesn't matter, Anne—only Caroline matters. Besides, I've already taken some—it might be enough."

Caroline moaned. Her eyes opened, and she stared at William.

"Did I tell you about our garden, love?" she asked. She reached down and clasped his hand. William nodded tearfully.

"Tell me again," he said. But Caroline spoke no more, and her eyes fell closed again.

William leaned in to place his head on her shoulder. Moments later he, too, ceased moving.

• • •

"He was a hero," Grimm told Father Lawrence an hour later. He had arrived with a guard of thirty men he had drawn from the palace walls.

"He saved us," Grimm continued. "We'd have been trapped on the landing if it hadn't been for him."

The priest knelt and examined both William and Caroline.

"Take them to my church," he remarked. "We cannot leave them here." He saw Pia's face and gave her an encouraging smile. "Have hope, my girl, and faith, for they both still live. More than anything, you must have faith."

"Without Felicity?" she asked. "Everyone says she was important—more important than anything."

He didn't reply.

"Why didn't you come sooner?" Anne demanded. "You had a garrison at the walls of the palace—a whole garrison!"

"We had orders to hold off," the senior officer protested. "Orders that were sent after the tower's collapse. Signed on the king's own paper."

"Signed by Papelford," Grimm cursed. "Damn him."

Pia stood quickly and addressed the officer.

"You said the tower has collapsed? Is Ebenezer... is there any sign of him?"

The officer shook his head.

"No, child, but no one could have survived."

"And Papelford, where is he?" Grimm asked.

"He's vanished," the officer said, looking chastened. "But we'll find him. I swear to you, we'll find him."

43

Dawn broke from the east. Castimir leaned forward and kissed Arisha's forehead. He felt the hostile eyes of the Kinshra on him.

Even the men under Lord Ruthven were growing impatient.

"It won't be long now," Kara told him.

"I won't let them take her, Kara," he said.

Captain Hardinge approached.

"The pickets report that a man is approaching," he announced. "Probably the same man as last night."

"Magnus," Castimir said, nodding. Arisha stirred for the first time in hours. Kara took Hardinge by the arm and led him away.

"How do you feel?" Castimir asked. She looked dreadful. It was clear she couldn't last.

Arisha smiled sweetly. She held out her hand and he took it as delicately as he would an injured bird.

"I love you, Cas," she sighed. "We are different in so many ways. I like it."

He tried to smile.

"Oh, Cas. Poor Cas. I am—" She swallowed. "I am going to have to go soon, Cas. I must, for all our sakes. For everyone."

"Don't talk like that," he said. He tried to be angry, but his words were whispered.

"Magnus is our only hope for survival, Cas," she said. "Otherwise they'll kill you all."

"I won't allow it," he said. "I have power, too, Arisha. Between Hazlard and me, we might be able to fight them." But Arisha shook her head.

Castimir turned to look at the men who occupied the ravine with him. Few returned his stare. He saw how Kara gritted her teeth and turned away, how Kuhn and Daquarius abruptly ended their conversation. How Guy leered through his broken-toothed mouth.

They are afraid, he realized. *They don't think we can win.* He stood and approached the leaders. Kuhn snarled as he neared, and strode away toward Arisha. He let the big man go.

"We can beat them," he said flatly. "I'm certain of it." Yet Daquarius looked doubtful.

"We haven't time," he said. "Arisha won't live out the day."

In desperation, Castimir turned to Kara.

"Couldn't you fix her another potion?" Her face fell, and he clenched his fists. "Please, Kara, surely you can try?" But she shook her head.

"No, Cas," she said softly. "It won't *heal* her." As he tried to hold back his despair, she put a hand on his shoulder. "Have you said everything you wished to say to her, Cas?"

He nodded. Then he shook his head grimly.

"I don't want to lose her, Kara—" he began.

"Yet you *will* lose her, unless Magnus takes her," she replied. "That is one thing upon which you can count. Would you deny her the only chance she has to live?"

"No," he replied, and he turned back to where Arisha lay. Magnus was already there, and Kuhn was helping her onto a horse. His own stood nearby.

"Wait!" Castimir shouted. He reached for his runes. Suddenly there were arms restraining him, cutting off his air.

"I'm sorry, Cas," Kara said in his ear.

The world began to swim before his eyes.

"K-Kar… agghh." His breath was cut off from his lungs. He clawed for her face in despair, but couldn't twist around.

"Arisha made me promise, Cas," she gritted in his ear. "Promise to stop you. I'm sorry—I had to respect her wishes."

His vision was blocked by swimming black dots. He felt his strength leave him. It felt as if he was falling.

He slid to the ground, still with Kara's arms around his throat.

"You will save her?" Kara said, making it sound more like a demand than a question.

"If I can, yes," Magnus replied.

She watched them ride away, with Kuhn at Arisha's side. As she approached the western path, the priestess gave a feeble wave. Kara nodded in acknowledgment.

A large contingent of the Untainted emerged from the path, and moved to surround them. No doubt they expected some sort of duplicity. But none was forthcoming, and soon they were gone.

She looked down at Castimir, lying where he had fallen. Quickly she took his satchel from him, and searched his robes, locating what she hoped were all of the hiding places he used for his runes. Nearby, Guy smirked maliciously.

"You think your little wizard will be angry when he wakes?" he said with a sneer. "Are you afraid of him, Hell-witch?"

Kara looked up and held his stare.

"I know what he can do," she said. Her eyes narrowed. "So yes, I *am* afraid." She removed his belt pouch as he opened his eyes.

Stowing his possessions on her horse, she returned to where he lay.

"Can you stand?" she asked. "We must make haste for Paterdomus, Cas—"

"Don't call me that," he said coldly. "Don't ever call me that."

Kara felt her face flush.

"I did what *she* asked, Castimir." She locked him with her eyes. "If you cannot understand that—"

"Shut up," he grunted. "Just shut up." Then he stood. "You let Kuhn go with her?"

"It was her decision, Castimir," she replied. "He promised to look after her, and she needed to have someone to turn to."

Castimir laughed foully.

"Turn to? Him? He *wants* her, Kara-Meir." He lowered his head slightly, and looked at her through dark eyes. "And now he's got her. Thanks to you. My friend."

He tapped his belt, and realized the pouch was gone.

"Where are my runes?" he asked.

"I have them," she said. "All of them." Then she waited to see how he would respond.

He laughed.

"You don't trust me, then," he said mirthlessly. "Not enough to let me keep my greatest tools."

"Not until you've calmed down, no." Kara replied. "And without your runes, you won't try to go after her."

"I killed a man with a sword yesterday," he said. "I can do it again."

"Castimir, don't be so blind!" she hissed. "The Untainted think they have all of the essence, yet Daquarius still has what you gave to him for safekeeping. In doing so, you might well have saved Varrock."

"From Gar'rth, you mean," Castimir shot back. She saw his lip twist, and she knew he meant to be cruel. "From your *lover*."

She didn't rise to the challenge.

"I lied then, Castimir. I lied to the king to make him need us, to make him feel as if he didn't dare make any move, conceive any plan, without us." She looked away. "It was ill-conceived on my part, though." She jumped slightly as Castimir spat at her feet.

"You will say anything and do anything to get what *you* want, Kara-Meir. I used to think it was pragmatic, a way for you to get the right things done. Now I know better. I know it's all about you getting your own way. And it's because of *your way* that Arish is gone." Her head snapped up, and she stared at him for a silent moment.

"We haven't time for this, Castimir," she said, and she walked away. But he called after her.

"It was your own way that we fought in the war, for your vengeance," he said. "It was for you that we went to Canifis, to try and save Gar'rth. Well, we've danced to your tune long enough, Hell-witch."

Kara stopped in her tracks. She turned angrily. Behind him she saw Daquarius smirk. Guy leered happily. Castimir shrugged.

"It's a suitable name, I think." She turned and stalked away.

Lord Ruthven came to her side.

"He's angry, Kara-Meir," he said. "But it will blow over. It will have to, when the fighting begins." The old man looked up at the hilltops. "Trust me, I know men. He hates you now, because before he has maintained such a high regard for you. To him, that makes your actions far worse.

"In the end, however, it will give him much-needed perspective."

They mounted their horses and departed along the western path. They had a day's travel ahead of them, before they would reach the Pass of Silvarea. Then another half a day to Paterdomus.

Two days before we reach the Salve, she thought, *and then… Gar'rth.*

44

Even riding at the head of the king's vanguard, among the greatest men in the realm, Theodore could not suppress a shiver, feeling dwarfed by the immensity of the Pass of Silvarea.

When they finally exited to face only a wooded landscape stretching between them and Paterdomus, he breathed a sigh of relief. Off to his right, Darnley bellowed instructions to five hundred men who had to set up a temporary camp.

"I want a palisade here," Darnley announced, "running from one side of the pass to the other. I want it high—as high as a tall man, with walkways along the top and stakes and trenches set before it. *Do you hear me?*"

Theodore watched as they gathered their axes and set off into the trees. Duke Horacio rode up next to him. The bearded man gave a smile.

"Your boys have become men, Sir Theodore," he said. "Good men, too, I might add. Confident and commanding." He cast a look back down the column. Somewhere behind the knights and horsemen marched his bowmen. "Many of my own soldiers are conscripts from the dales. They will need men such as yourself and your knights. Men who will lead by example, and show encouragement." Horacio's eyes narrowed. "Ah!"

A horn sounded behind them. Theodore turned in his saddle, and watched as the yellow standard of King Roald grew nearer.

"The king himself," Horacio murmured approvingly. "No doubt he wants to be at the forefront as his army moves into Paterdomus. A ruler who leads from the front makes a strong gesture."

Theodore agreed, and gazed skyward. The evening was upon them.

"We will be at Paterdomus in an hour," he said.

"Ha!" Horacio laughed. "Have two days on the march been too much for you, Sir Theodore? Do you need a soft bed under your war-weary back?"

Theodore managed a smile.

"I left a softer bed behind," he said wistfully. Horacio's face darkened.

"We all did," he observed.

They waited in silence as King Roald approached, a dozen bodyguards following under Captain Rovin's watchful eye. Among them Theodore recognized the immense Lord Frey, and he remembered the pain the man had caused him after their arm-wrestle at the Midsummer Festival.

He grimaced when he remembered how Gar'rth had actually *beaten* Lord Frey, immediately thereafter.

Such strength, Theodore mused. *Could any of us really stop him?*

King Roald reined his horse to a stop, and gestured to them.

"Come, my friends," he instructed. "Ride with me for the final hour. We shall enter Paterdomus side-by-side, the same way we shall leave it after we have achieved victory." They descended the slope from Silvarea and entered the woods below. Paterdomus occasionally revealed itself above the shivering boughs.

Even from a distance it was immense. Seeing it for the second time, Theodore was still struck by its presence. Carved from black stone, it seemed to grow from the very landscape itself, its great tower higher than any building he had ever seen.

From Morytania, across the River Salve, the temple looked more like a fortress. It stood at the edge of a chasm on the western bank, the waters of the holy river racing past far below. Terraces built into the temple allowed archers to cover the approaches.

As they cleared the woods and came into the open, a bell rang out from high above. The great doors stood open, with a tall stained-glass window on either side—each dominated in the center by a four-pointed star of Saradomin. A body of brown-robed monks waited for their king, standing patiently in a neat line.

At the front, Theodore recognized the worried face of Drezel. As the line knelt, the monk gave him a nod.

"Rise, my friends." The king dismounted ably. "Tell me the news of the enemy."

"Lord Despaard has just returned from beyond the river, sire," Drezel said as he stood. "He reports gatherings of the vampires known as the ravenous, and many thousands of walking corpses. And his group has brought a captive, sire. A foul ghoul—"

"Show me!" Roald commanded. He strode up the stairs into the nave. Drezel hastened after him, directing him as they went. Theodore followed as quickly as he could, anticipation building inside of him.

Drezel ascended a stairwell and threw open a door. Inside, behind a desk, sat Lord Despaard. The dark-haired man stood as soon as he saw the king.

"My liege."

"Well?" Roald demanded. "Where is it?"

Despaard nodded into the darkest corner of the room. Two

black-clad men in leather armor stood with their swords drawn, watching the floor.

Theodore stared hard. *Something* moved.

One of the men leaned down and made a fist with his free hand. The thing moaned in terror and rose onto its knees. Despaard stood and shined his light onto it.

Diseased-looking skin covered the thing's tiny body. Its eyes were huge and red, filled with terror at the shining light.

"Can it speak?" Roald asked.

"Just barely, sire," Despaard answered.

King Roald drew his sword.

"I don't know if you can understand me, ghoul," he said, "but they say that only those with souls can speak. Creatures that can't— such as the horse or the sheep—are soulless, and therefore it is mankind's right to do with them as we see fit." He peered intently, and leveled his shining sword. "Are you soulless, too?" he asked. "Would Saradomin count it against me if I were to slay you?" The tip of the blade hovered above the creature's tiny throat.

"Tell me what you know of the vampires," the king continued. "Of Tenebra, the Black Prince."

Silence.

"He won't yield to threats, sire." Despaard looked uncomfortably to Theodore, and then back to his king. "We've tried that, and made good on them, too." Roald lowered his blade.

"And what have you found?" Despaard shook his head.

"The ghouls are not undead, sire, but they feed on the dead flesh of man or beast. They were once, long ago, as human as you or—" he caught his words, "—as the basest peasant. Therefore they are not a part of the enemy's army. This one was caught to the north of here, on the eastern bank as my scouts retreated. From what he's told us his kin have fled the advancing hordes." Despaard sighed.

"And they are near, sire. You might hear them from the eastern terrace, above the bridge."

"Drezel said there were thousands of them," the king said as he sheathed his sword. Despaard shrugged.

"It's impossible to tell, sire."

"Very well," Roald said. "Attend to your immediate duties, and meet me again in one hour's time." His eyes fell on Drezel. "Then we shall dine, and talk of *essence*."

The room began to empty. As Theodore turned, he heard Despaard ask a question.

"What of the *thing*, sire?"

"Has this one feasted on the flesh of men, Despaard?"

"Yes, sire. It was found doing so—gorging itself on one of our scouts."

"Then let it go," the king said angrily.

"Sire?"

"Let it go from the terrace above the chasm, Despaard. Saradomin will judge it in the waters of the Salve."

The creature screamed as the two men seized it and dragged it from the room, its cries echoing down the stairs to the nave. Theodore followed in a daze, watching the ghoul's pathetic attempt at resistance as it was led away toward the eastern terrace.

"I don't like it," Darnley remarked after finishing a silent prayer before the altar. "Throwing a creature like that to its death—it's not the honorable way to deal with a foe." He shook his head.

"They've entrusted it to Saradomin's judgment," Theodore replied. "Would you do otherwise?" Before the man could answer, another voice spoke up.

"Ah, Sir Theodore!"

It was Aubury, coming down the steps. Behind him strode Sedridor himself. Theodore bowed quickly.

"Has Master Grayzag come with you, sirs?" the knight asked

coldly. "I did not see you on the journey from Varrock."

Aubury risked a smile.

"No," he said, "you wouldn't have. Not unless you had gifts beyond the ken of normal folk. Indeed, we haven't come from Varrock. We have come from the Tower. And as for Grayzag…" Aubury blew out his cheeks. "He will not be joining us here. He has business elsewhere."

Theodore said nothing. He kept his eyes fastened on the wizard.

Sedridor stepped up.

"Your anger is understandable, Sir Theodore," he said in low, even tones. "But soon we shall see if Grayzag's mission was a success. We must all pray for it." He gave a slight bow. "And now, good day."

Darnley smiled broadly.

"Sir, with Master Sedridor here, surely our victory is assured," he said. "He is the greatest wizard in all the world."

Theodore's stare made his face fall.

"Don't trust wizards and what they say," he replied. "In my experience, their powers are overstated, as are their ideals. Today they are here, that is true, but there was only one of them when Falador was betrayed. Master Segainus was found on the walls hacked to death by goblin swords. And if mere goblins can slay a master, then what do you think the vampires will do to them?"

Darnley paled. Theodore breathed in deeply.

"I'm sorry, Darnley," he said. "I don't have much liking for their ways, that is all. But you are right—Sedridor is more than a master. He is *the* master. His presence should give us cause to hope."

As much as the prophecy gives us all cause to despair, he thought silently.

She was as he remembered her. Her silver coat was bright and unmarred, and when she saw him she gave a neigh of recognition

that sounded throughout the stables. She even recognized
Darnley.

"Mare of Falador," Theodore said as he scratched her behind the
ear. "I am pleased to find you well." Quickly he examined her, then
the other animals that had fled from the embassy in Morytania.
Finally, a stable boy guided him to where their saddlebags had
been kept.

"We haven't touched them, sir," the youth explained. "Drezel
ordered us not to when we took the animals in."

Theodore nodded and began his search. The adamant-headed
arrows that Doric had created were the first items he found, but
he cast those aside on the bench and dug deeper. His hand closed
around a metallic canister with a fuse, similar to the one he had
used to destroy Lord Hyett. He smiled grimly as he withdrew it.

"That could cause Tenebra a few problems," he said softly. He
reached in again, searching for a glass vial. When he found it, he
held it more reverently than he had the canister.

"Albertus's phosphorus," he said, holding up the glass and
peering at the powder inside, submerged in water. It would ignite
on contact with the air, he knew.

Doric's voice pierced his reverie.

"Aha! You've found my arrows," he said merrily. Then his voice
turned serious. "And you will be delighted to know that I have
found something of yours." He turned and gestured. "Come here,
lad!"

From around the side of the wooden stall limped Hamel. He was
attired in the costume of one of Duke Horacio's archers. A bow was
slung across his chest. With every step he took, he gave a wince.

Theodore was stunned into silence.

"I-I'm sorry, sir," the boy muttered. "I-I just w-wanted to do my
bit."

Theodore straightened his back and gazed angrily at his aide.

"Have you walked all the way, Hamel?" he demanded. Hamel nodded.

"Every step, sir." The boy winced again, and Theodore sought to hide a smile of pride.

"It must have hurt," he said as flatly as possible. "Have Darnley take you to our lodging, and see what the lads can do for your foot." He raised an eyebrow. "Are you good with a bow?"

Hamel nodded.

"Good enough to kill a spotted kebbit with one arrow, sir." Theodore knew he meant it, for vanity was not one of Hamel's traits. Finally he allowed himself an open smile.

"Despite you disobeying my direct commands, I am glad you are here, Hamel. It is a sore test for any man to be left behind when war threatens. Here—" he lifted Doric's adamant-tipped arrows from the bench, "—take these, and find a position with the archers." He stared hard as his aide accepted them with an expression of wonder. "Make sure you put them to good use."

When Hamel had left, the dwarf's face darkened.

"Is it really that bad, Doric?" he asked. "Do the men speak of defeat?"

Doric cursed.

"I have spent the journey from Varrock listening to as many of them as I could." He shook his head. "This blasted prophecy has them all spooked." He spat. "*More* than spooked, even. They don't think we can win.

"They think that Tenebra's victory has been ordained by fate," he added.

"But will they fight?"

The dwarf shrugged.

"Maybe. Probably. But if Tenebra planted this prophecy a century ago, then he isn't going to waste its power. He might have a way to twist the suspicion enough for them to break and run." He clenched his fist. "I just wish Kara was here, squire. She might have given the men hope. They say she is 'touched by the gods' and, by Guthix's hammer, we need her now. We need her *legend*."

"Paterdomus is strong, Doric," Theodore said, trying to raise his friend's spirits. "It won't fall so easily."

The dwarf shook his head.

"It can be as hard as Dondakan's Rock, squire, but if the men are too fearful to fight, then no fortress can stand."

Suddenly a bell pealed out from the tower. They looked up sharply.

"The warning bell?" Doric suggested. Theodore nodded.

"Come," he said. "We are being called to duty."

Theodore raced into the nave with Doric at his heels. King Roald was sitting in a chair, his head in his hands. Drezel made his way through the throng of people.

"What's happened?" Theodore asked.

"I have received a message, Sir Theodore, from Varrock. The palace was attacked last night. Papelford is a traitor."

"The girl, Felicity, was taken," he said.

Theodore groaned. Doric pushed past him and grabbed the monk by his shirt.

"What else, boy? *What else?*"

Drezel blinked, then continued.

"There were deaths in the palace. Your friend Ebenezer…"

No. It's not possible. Theodore gasped. Doric's fist fell.

"That can't be!" the dwarf raged. "How do you know?"

Not him, the knight thought. *Some trick would have saved him.*

"He died passing on a message of vital import," Drezel said. "He revealed that the attacker was Albertus Black."

"Speak sense, boy," Doric fumed. "Albertus is dead!"

Drezel nodded.

"Yet that was the message we received."

The group was in an uproar. Lord Despaard shouted for calm. The black-clad men of the Society of Owls sealed the door and covered each exit.

"My men and I have pledged our lives to fight the evil that is gathering," Despaard said flatly. There was no fear or passion in his voice, and men listened. "This temple has stood for near a thousand years, and by Saradomin, our generation will not be the one to see it lost." He peered around the room, missing no one. "You are all nobles and men of Misthalin, or priests and monks of the faith. Even if the entire world would stand against us, we *must* fight!"

Silence followed. King Roald stood.

"Lord Despaard is right," he said. "This enemy would have us believe that he is infallible, that he has planned for every move we make. But now Papelford's treachery has been exposed. And we know, thanks to the embassy, that Tenebra will try and cross the Salve via bridges. If those can be destroyed, then we might be able to hold him back.

"And we know also the nature of the weapon he has sent into our lands. A vampire that has apparently taken the form of an old and loyal subject. We must have no mercy."

"We must have hearts of stone!" Doric cried, punching the air. Theodore saw the glistening tears pour down his friend's face.

"Hearts of stone!" others shouted.

"Hearts of stone!" Theodore cried.

But thoughts of Lady Anne killed the lie. He had no heart of stone.

45

Standing outside of his father's tent, Gar'rth heard the temple bell. Paterdomus stood a mile to the west.

Is she there? Gar'rth thought. A part of him hoped she was far away.

On all sides waited the vague shapes of the dead. They were thousands strong, and they had brought the three great bridges Tenebra would use to cross the river.

"There will be a massacre soon," he said.

Georgi stirred behind him.

"Would that please you, my lord?"

"No," he said, and he bowed his head. "It disgusts me, and I don't understand why. Haven't I taken the blood of an innocent? Has Zamorak refused to accept me? I feel the same as I always have."

"You are half-human, my lord. Perhaps it is different for you?"

"Perhaps," he agreed.

"And," Georgi said, "there may be other reasons." He hesitated, looking down.

"Tell me what you mean," Gar'rth demanded.

"Do you remember what you asked of me, my lord? You asked me to protect you from yourself, from what might happen if you were to take an innocent life."

"Georgi? What did you do?"

A moan sounded from the darkness. Gar'rth turned, his hand on the hilt of his sword. A white-faced vampire wearing noble garb stood before him. Gar'rth recognized him immediately. He bowed.

"Master Malak," he said. "Have you come for my father?"

The vampire sneered.

"No, Gar'rth," he answered. "I have come for you. There is somebody who wants to see you." He held out his hand. "Come. It will not take long."

"My lord?" Georgi hissed. "You mustn't—"

"Silence, beast," Malak said. Suddenly he clenched his fist, and Georgi gasped. He clutched his chest and fell to his knees. Black droplets of blood forced their way through the pores of his skin.

"Release him, master." Gar'rth fell to one knee. "Please."

Malak shook his head.

"Still so weak. After all Vanescula has done for you." He unclenched his fist and Georgi moaned with relief. "Come."

Gar'rth patted Georgi's shoulder before following Malak. After several minutes of walking through the wood they came to a small clearing. At its center lay a winged individual. When the figure saw him, it cowered away.

Gar'rth gasped.

"Vanescula?" he said. Gray scales covered her once-flawless skin. Her red eyes looked dim and fear-filled. Her body seemed withered with age. She held up a clawed hand, and looked at Malak with hatred. The vampire nobleman smiled smugly.

"I saved her, Gar'rth," he explained. "And I have brought her here. She hates me for it, for now she is in my debt. But she hates me far more because she knows that I could destroy her now, if I so wished. Her weakness terrifies her."

Vanescula turned her gaze to Gar'rth.

"Do you remember your promise to me, Soft-Heart?" Gar'rth nodded. Vanescula lifted a wing to reveal a hand clasped over her stomach. On the ground next to her lay the Blisterwood knife.

"Take it," she said, and she smiled horribly. The expression was made more grotesque by her current form. "Take it and give it to your father. Give it to him the same way he gave it to me!"

He stepped over her and felt a strange satisfaction watching her cower. He knelt and took the blade.

Suddenly Vanescula's hand shot forward and seized his wrist. Her grip was strong enough to hurt.

"But do it when he is across the river, Soft-Heart. It *must* be then, and not before. Only when he is across the river, for then he will be most vulnerable. Only then can his death be absolute. Do you understand?"

Gar'rth nodded. She let her hand drop, and he stood.

"Fear," she said huskily. "I liked what you did to me, but I have grown tired of being afraid." Her face shimmered and the flawless beauty beneath was revealed. She smiled, then winced in pain.

"Then perhaps you will remember that, before you take another life," Gar'rth said. "Now you know how your prey feels."

Vanescula laughed feebly. Then she coughed violently.

"Sooo good," she mocked as she gasped. "Sooo noble." Gar'rth turned his back on her and made to leave the clearing.

"Your siblings are here too, Gar'rth," she called. He stopped dead and turned to face her. She smiled and then gave a pain-filled laugh before continuing. "Tenebra's other children. Malak will show you, before you return to your father, and then you will see." She coughed into her hand, her eyes never leaving him. When she opened her palm Gar'rth saw it dripped with black spittle. Vanescula moaned bitterly when she noticed it. Then she looked back to Gar'rth.

"Have a look at your brothers, Gar'rth," she said. "And your sisters. See what your father has done to them.

"And then judge me in his light. Only then."

Gar'rth found his way back to his father's tent in a cold daze. The things that Malak had shown him haunted his memory.

Twisted limbs and hungry mouths. Things with three heads and some with none. A raging beast who fought to be free of his ball and chain. A silent girl, chained to a frame on a cart dragged by the undead, her mouth gagged by an iron collar.

Abominations, all of them. Freaks! My siblings!

He entered his tent to find that Tenebra was waiting for him. A frown creased his white brow, and his eyes burned fiercely.

"My meditations are complete," he said. "More important is the fact that Felicity is now in my hands." He stared for a long moment. "And the first of your friends has fallen."

Gar'rth exhaled.

"Who?" he demanded.

"The alchemist. He was killed when Botolph's Tower collapsed." Tenebra shook his head. "That king prided himself on being a builder. He governed his nation well, for much of his life—before he locked himself away as madness descended."

Gar'rth no longer heard him. He felt an unstoppable pressure build behind his eyes. When the tears came, his father looked on in mild disgust.

"Zamorak hasn't taken you as completely as I had hoped. I suspect that Georgi has played a part in it." Gar'rth glanced around, and did not see the servant.

"Where is Georgi?" he asked.

"He has been given the reward he deserves," Tenebra said menacingly. His red eyes narrowed. "And once we take Varrock, we will complete the process properly. This time Kara-Meir will be your cellmate. I promise you that."

Gar'rth growled. Unseen, he reached under his cloak. The power of the Blisterwood knife thrummed up his arm in anticipation.

"After he crosses the river, Gar'rth." He remembered Vanescula's words. *"Only then."*

"I demand Kara as my wife," he said after a moment. His father just stared, then shook his head.

"No, my son," he replied. "She is nothing more than a cheap adventuress. When you sit on the throne, you will marry one of the foremost daughters of Kandarin or Asgarnia. Your children will be the first in a line of rulers that will rule for centuries."

Gar'rth growled again. Tenebra sighed.

"You *will* change, Gar'rth," he said. "Zamorak *will* embrace you, and you will be a different man for it. A stronger, better one. A born ruler." He turned, and gestured west. "Now, it is time. Come."

Tenebra stood at the narrow bridge that crossed the Salve at Paterdomus. Far below, the waters raged. At his father's suggestion, Gar'rth watched from a position where he could not be seen.

Tenebra's voice carried over the fading daylight.

"Come forth, King Roald Remanis, under the flag of truce." He paused, then continued. "But come forth in the knowledge that if you lay down your crown and your life for the rightful king, as the prophecy of the High Priest of Entrana dictates, then no one else need die. No one.

"Come forth!"

After several minutes the door opened, granting access directly to the bridge. Through a sliver of light a man appeared.

King Roald! Gar'rth recognized him immediately. His anger grew.

The man walked steadily until he was nearly all the way across.

"Your terms are unacceptable, Tenebra," Roald said slowly. "The people of my kingdom would never serve you, with what you've become." The two faced each other less than an arm's length apart.

"I could burn the flesh from your bones right now," Tenebra said. Roald nodded.

"As the Herald attempted," he replied. "But here we are under a truce, and were you to break that truce, you would lose all hope of ruling my people."

"Hope?" Tenebra answered with malice. "Hope has nothing to do with it. Your army has no hope. The prophecies of the High Priest of Entrana already have convinced them that their defeat is inevitable, and that your rule is at an end." He sneered, then stepped forward and spoke in little more than a whisper.

"Which is exactly what I intended when I planted that fiction a century ago. And knowing the truth will do you no good. Attempt to reveal it, and you will be seen as grasping at straws. None will believe you."

Roald gaped. His hand closed around the hilt of his sword.

"Your people would do far better with me as their king," Tenebra said. "You are nothing—a mere man, unfit to lead. Scared. Weak. Mortal." He stepped forward, until he was on the bridge.

Gar'rth heard Roald gasp.

"The holy barrier," he said. "How? How have you done this, Tenebra?"

His father laughed at the monarch's confusion.

"Felicity was brought here—to Paterdomus—by my creature," he said. "She and the other children are dead, their sacred blood mixed into the River Salve from an underground chamber a short distance from here. Close, but forgotten by all but a few." He turned his hands palm up, to reveal a wound on each wrist. "My own blood has been mixed into the polluted waters as well, so that I— and all who are bound to me by blood—can no longer be barred."

Gar'rth could smell Roald's fear.

"Who are these children you have so vilely butchered?" the king demanded.

"The children are—were—the heirs of Ivandis and his followers," Tenebra explained. "The children of Varrock, their innocence and purity, those are what inspired Saradomin's protection." Tenebra clenched tight his fist. "And I have *murdered* that innocence. The Salve is just a river now—to me and my creatures—and nothing more."

"Murder and witchcraft," Roald said in disgust. He shook with anger.

"Whatever means are necessary," Tenebra replied. "What I seek is worth any cost—and you have not even begun to see the final tally." The vampire turned his back, and stepped away from the bridge.

Roald screamed with rage. He drew his sword in a single stroke. Gar'rth started forward, unable to stop himself.

"No!"

The blade entered Tenebra's back. The vampire grimaced.

"Fool!" he hissed, turning. Roald let go of the sword, his hands trembling. "Are you so very desperate that you would break a truce? Have my descendants sunk so low?" Tenebra reached over his shoulder and grasped the edge of the sword. Slowly, inexorably, he withdrew it. Then he hurled it at Roald's feet.

"You have no honor," Tenebra murmured. "Go back. Return to your men and explain to them that they will die because of your actions—and your actions alone."

Then Tenebra smiled.

"In one hour, when darkness falls, we come."

The vampire strode into the shadows of Morytania, passing Gar'rth without a look. Roald glared at him in hatred.

"You, Gar'rth!" the king shouted. "You have made your pact with this monster! You sought to protect this murderer of children. I promise you that you will die, even as I draw my last breath! Do you hear?"

Gar'rth looked up at the temple's terrace. It was lined with men. He saw Theodore in his white armor. Beside him stood Doric.

Their stares burned into him.

46

"Archers—loose!"

At Duke Horacio's command, two hundred archers let their arrows fly. Theodore watched from the terrace as two hundred flaming points arched over the Salve, easily visible in the dusk.

And died. By the time they landed, they were simple projectiles. Their fires had been extinguished. Doric growled and Hamel grunted bitterly.

"Magic," Master Sedridor observed drily. "He's keeping his bridges secure."

The first of Tenebra's three great spans crashed into place to the north of Paterdomus. A wave of hungry corpses surged across, while the shield wall under Lord Frey's command braced to stop them. Horacio's archers prepared a second volley.

To the south of Paterdomus, the second bridge was being raised, hauled on chains by undead hands that would pivot the bridge, and then lower it again. Farther south still, the third and last bridge was being positioned, deliberately far enough away to spread the defenders' forces thin, Theodore knew.

Ominously, he noted that the thin stone bridge below remained uncannily empty.

"There are too many of them," Doric growled. The dwarf gripped the haft of his double-headed axe. "Why doesn't King Roald unleash his catapults, to destroy the bridges? What's he waiting for?"

At his side, Lord Despaard grunted.

"His majesty seeks to divide the enemy, my friend. We will allow as many as our men can cope with to cross, and then destroy the bridges. If we can." He frowned. "I have my doubts. Somehow I doubt Tenebra has overlooked the presence of our artillery."

Theodore nodded grimly.

"We have to buy time for Drezel and his monks," he said. "If they can find the chamber Tenebra mentioned, then perhaps they can undo what Albertus has set in motion."

"Not Albertus," Doric said, and he shook his head. "The thing that replaced him.

"And it's too late, regardless. The only thing that might have worked is this essence, and there's no sign of Castimir or Arisha yet. Face it, squire, magic and the occult ain't our business. A sharp edge, guided by a strong arm—that's what we do. We should be down there with the men."

The dwarf spat over the terrace's edge. He grunted as a second wave of arrows fell onto the north bridge beyond Lord Frey's shield wall. Many of Tenebra's zombies fell, only to struggle to their feet again. Those arrows with burning tips had their flames extinguished as they passed midway across the river.

Doric cursed. A dreadful silence descended, only to be pierced by a shout.

"Sir Theodore," Hamel yelled, "the southern bridge! The enemy are massing on the other side of the river." Theodore looked as the bridge in question heaved upward.

"We cannot spread our forces enough to counter that," Lord Despaard warned.

Theodore gritted his teeth.

"Then I'll have to destroy it," he said.

"How?" Despaard remarked. "Our fires are being dowsed by Tenebra's magic. And that one is too far south for the catapults."

Theodore smiled.

"Albertus Black conjured a new form of magic. Remember his sodium tubes and black powder canisters?" He shook his shoulder bag. "I have one left. It might be enough to disable the bridge. Doric, I will need your assistance."

The dwarf nodded. Quickly they ran down the stairs, through the nave, and down the steps to the temple entrance. Doric snatched a burning torch from the wall.

Several hundred men-at-arms waited outside, ready to reinforce the banks when needed. Without a word Theodore mounted his mare and lifted Doric to sit in front of him. Darnley and twelve of his fellow men gathered behind him, the flag of Saradomin held high.

They rounded the corner of Paterdomus, and galloped southward in time to see the bridge rise up against the night. Theodore cursed.

"If they let it fall, we'll be too late!"

"They won't, squire. They have to do it carefully enough that they don't damage it. We should still have time!"

As they drew near, Theodore waved his men back. Darnley and Philip reined in their horses and halted the rest. As the bridge was lowered, Theodore stopped at the bank's edge. With a metallic creaking the ribbed structure landed before them, heavy enough to settle deeply in the soft earth.

Across the river, vague human shapes staggered forward.

"Hurry, squire, hurry!" Doric urged, holding the torch close. Theodore reached into his bag and wrenched out the canister. He held the fuse to Doric's flame.

"Your hand's shaking, squire," Doric said.

"So is yours," the knight replied. He looked up.

The corpses had reached the midpoint of the bridge. They were at least forty abreast, and an unknown number were packed behind—at the very least ten deep. They had stopped suddenly. As Theodore watched, they parted.

"Gods!" Theodore hissed.

A woman bound to a wooden frame was dragged forward on a wheeled cart. Her mouth was stoppered by a metallic collar. As he watched, an undead hand unfastened the iron ring and it fell to the bottom of the wagon.

He felt her gaze upon him.

"Squire!" Doric's voice urged him to action.

The fuse of the canister caught and sizzled.

Theodore waited, breathing deeply.

Counting his heartbeats.

Watching as the fuse burned down.

"*Squire?*"

Theodore drew his arm back and hurled the canister far onto the bridge. It rolled to the foot of an undead man in the foremost rank.

As it did so, the woman chained to the frame shrieked.

Theodore turned the mare and shouted. Instantly she took flight, leaping forward. Behind him the air shimmered as a wave of sound split stone and cracked bark. He turned in the saddle to see the woman draw breath again, her head following him.

"Squire?" Doric shouted again.

CROOOOMMM!

Doric screamed and fell from the saddle. An invisible force knocked Theodore and his mare forward. Hot wind and echoing thunder rolled from the river, accompanied by the splinter of breaking wood.

When he looked back, the end of the bridge sagged and slid from the riverbank, leaving huge grooves in the earth as it collapsed into the water. A cloud of white smoke hid the opposite bank, dissipating on the breeze. There was no sign of the shrieking woman. Nor even of her cart.

Theodore laughed triumphantly.

"Useful stuff, that," Doric said, standing up and brushing himself off. "Do you have any more?" The knight shook his head ruefully.

"We're never that lucky, Doric," he answered. "Still, they can't outflank us now." He hefted the dwarf up as Despaard galloped over to him. The usually dour noble gave him a smile.

"Well done, Sir Theodore," he said. "That will make Tenebra balk. He probably thinks it's some new magic we've got. Might make him more cautious from now on."

"I'm afraid not, Despaard," Theodore responded. "Gar'rth will have told him about the explosives. They will hold no mystery."

Screaming voices from the terrace drew their attention. Roaring flames erupted from the temple, shooting across the river, only to be smothered in an onrushing cloud of darkness.

"The wizards!" Despaard shouted, and they rode back to the temple. Before they could reach it, however, the darkness swept across the Salve and broke upon the terrace like a fist. People screamed. Torches died. Glass shattered and stone shook.

"Master Sedridor? Aubury?" Despaard yelled, charging into the nave.

"I am here," came a weak voice from the stairwell. Sedridor appeared, his face blanched and his gait unsteady. Hamel appeared behind him, holding a dying torch. His face too was white and bloodied, but he managed a faint smile.

"Hamel?" Theodore shouted. "Are there fatalities? Where's Aubury?"

"As yet we have no dead," Hamel called down. "Only injured.

Aubury's unconscious, and I feel like I've been rode over by a horse, sirs!" Theodore laughed in relief.

"Ridden over, Hamel. Not rode."

"Aye, sir. Ridden, then. Still feels the same."

"Can you fight, Master Sedridor?" Doric shouted.

"I'm afraid not, dwarf," the old man gasped. Then, he sank to his knees in a faint. Hamel lifted him to the nearest bench.

"He's out of it," Despaard moaned. "Our best assets are gone."

Doric snarled.

"Best assets? They haven't *done* anything, Despaard. Give me a sharp edge, and I'll give you a blasted bridge and headless corpses. Not moaning old men!"

A king's messenger raced toward them from the main entrance.

"Drezel has found the chamber," he announced. "It's a half-mile to the north." He fell silent for an instant, then added, "The Black Prince spoke the truth. The children are dead."

Doric cursed and spat.

"Can they undo what was done to the river?" Despaard asked.

"They haven't yet tried, my lord," he answered. "There is a creature there, a vampire." The messenger lowered his gaze. "They told me no name, but said the creature was known to you."

Doric looked up and mouthed a single word.

Albertus.

Theodore nodded.

"Then we must remove this creature," Despaard said. "Come, Sir Theodore, let us see if our luck still holds." He gestured at the messenger. "Lead us to Drezel."

Gar'rth's father collapsed into his seat. His face was haggard and grim. He breathed deeply. The werewolf raised an eyebrow.

"I didn't know the dead breathed," he said.

Tenebra smiled grimly.

"The habit of a lifetime—one that I never forgot, even in death," he answered wearily. He looked toward the temple in anger. "Sedridor's resistance was stronger than I anticipated," he said.

Hope flickered inside of Gar'rth.

"Did you kill those on the terrace?" he asked. "Was Kara there?" As soon as he said it, he regretted doing so.

"Kara? No. But she is near. Very near." He paused, then continued. "As for those on the terrace, I didn't intend to kill them—just take them out of the conflict. When we take the throne, the wizards will be valuable assets—I will seek to come to an… understanding with them.

"But the bridge," he said. "That extraordinary magic!"

He looks afraid, Gar'rth thought. *He has planned for so long that even the slightest upset might be felt tenfold.*

"It wasn't magic," Gar'rth said. "It was science. I recognized the smell from here. It's black powder. The dwarfs use it, and it was used by Sulla in his war against Falador."

"Black powder? I would know more about this 'science.' Perhaps Albertus Black will be more valuable to me than I thought." His eyes narrowed. "Do they have more?"

An opportunity. Gar'rth nodded. "Most likely."

"Then my creatures are vulnerable." He stood and clenched his fist. "I must move off the bridges. The banks must be taken. Your brother, the Rager, will lead the attack across the northern bridge. He will drive Roald's shield wall back with his ball and chain."

Tenebra shut his eyes and concentrated. His creatures moved to reinforce the remaining two bridges. Others charged single-file across the ancient stone bridge that led directly to Paterdomus, where a body of armed men awaited their assault.

"We must break through," Tenebra muttered. "We must!"

He turned to Gar'rth.

"When the shield wall breaks, then you will cross. Seek King

Roald. Kill him, and this war ends. Kill him, and you will rule.

"After all, you gave King Roald your oath—to uphold the true king of Varrock. You are the true heir to the throne. So you owe allegiance to yourself—and to me."

Gar'rth thought of the Blisterwood beneath his cloak.

"Will you come across with me?" he asked his father.

After he crosses. Only then.

Tenebra shook his head. He held Gar'rth's stare with his own.

"Not yet, my son," he replied. "Not just yet."

A horn sounded to Theodore's right. Doric cursed. The knight reined his horse in as he looked across the battlefield to Tenebra's northern bridge.

"Lord Frey has given the signal to back away," Despaard said. "The shield wall is broken."

Lord Frey's men were retreating against the pressing horde of the undead. At the center of the enemy gathering stood an immense figure, unsurpassed by any Theodore had seen in its sheer ugliness. Its head was huge and twisted, its wide mouth large enough to bite a man in two. Its long grotesque limbs seemed bent and dislocated. Across its hunched shoulders was a crude form of beaten armor that was strapped to its body. The only weapon it wielded was a huge ball and chain that swung out from its bound wrists and smashed the men of Misthalin under its lethal weight.

On and on it came, raging against the shield wall as a hundred arrows fell upon it. Under such an assault, the thing staggered with a frustrated yell.

A second wave of arrows arched over the retreating shield wall and hissed down. Some cracked against the metal armor. Others found themselves buried in its demented flesh. It staggered again and collapsed to its knees. Then it moaned in agony.

A third cascade of arrows fell upon it, and it moved no more.

But any triumph was short-lived. Behind it, the mass of zombies thrust forward again. The shield wall gave ground at an alarming rate.

"We must press on," the messenger advised. "The entrance to the chamber is near, not far from the king's standard." Theodore shook his head as the messenger gestured for them to continue.

"Lord Frey's men can't hold for much longer," he said.

Duke Horacio's archers fell back behind the shield wall at a steady pace. Already they were barely a hundred yards from King Roald's battle standard that stood atop a low hill. If they retreated past that, Theodore knew, then their morale would vanish.

"We just need to give them time," he said. "Darnley, Philip, take the men and warn King Roald's cavalry to prepare for a charge. We might be able to buy Lord Frey the time he needs to regroup."

"Very good sir," Darnley said.

A horn sounded, somewhere to the west.

His men left him. With an anxious look at the battle, he turned his horse and followed the king's messenger north, cutting along behind the archers. They rode until, out of the gloom, a large mausoleum took shape.

A monk waited outside.

Again, the strange horn sounded from the west, closer now. Theodore turned to stare curiously into the darkness. At the edge of the woods, dozens of torches were advancing.

"Who are they?" he asked Doric. "There are no men behind us, save those who were tasked with building the palisade. Why would they have left their posts?"

"If I didn't know otherwise, I would swear that was a Kinshra horn," Doric whispered. "They're too far away for me to see any details, though."

The monk at the mausoleum gestured urgently. Theodore recognized him as Martin.

"Sir, we must descend," he said. He pointed to an open trapdoor where a ladder vanished into the darkness. "The power of the Salve is our only hope. We *must* try to cleanse it, or all will be lost!"

Despaard turned to the messenger and nodded to the men advancing from the west.

"Find out who they are, then report to the king." The messenger acknowledged, and galloped away. They dismounted, and Despaard took a satchel from his saddle pack and undid the clasps.

"Have you ever fought a vampire before?" Doric whispered.

"Not an intelligent one," the nobleman replied softly. "Sometimes the ravenous, when we have crossed the river. But never like this."

He reached inside and withdrew several glass bulbs filled with a concentration of garlic. There were enough for all four of them. He checked his satchel again. This time he withdrew a single ash stake and a mallet that he fastened on his belt.

"The creature must be weakened before we finish it with the stake," he explained. "We should really have a wizard with us," he sighed.

To the west, the horn sounded again. The thunder of hooves grew louder.

"We can't wait," Martin urged. "Come!" He led them down the ladder and into a tunnel that curved away into the darkness. They followed, and when he signaled a halt, they drew their weapons.

"Master Drezel?" Martin called quietly. From just round a corner the monk's tonsured head appeared. He put a finger to his lips and pointed across the passage's end.

Theodore crept nearer.

A room lay beyond—a cavernous one with several man-made pillars. He shrugged off his shoulder bag. Struggling to hold it in the same hand as the hilt of his sword, he found the phosphorus vial and withdrew it.

Doric crept past him. His very nature gave him an advantage in the dark.

"What can you see?" Theodore asked.

"There are seven statues in a circle." His voice tensed. "The… the bodies of the children are on each plinth. In the center of the room is a well, I think."

Something laughed hideously from the darkness.

47

"Come. Come forward, Theodore," the voice said.

"Doric, Despaard. Come in and face me, your old friend who journeyed with you into the realm of the dead. Come, I say!" From behind a statue Albertus Black appeared. He still wore the same coat he had worn when Theodore had last seen him, as he lay dead on the bank of the Salve.

The knight stepped forward, his sword held out in front of him.

"How could you, Albertus?" he asked. "How could you have killed Felicity?"

"He's not the same as he was in life, Theodore," Despaard said, following close behind. "All that was good in him is gone."

Albertus giggled and rubbed his bloodstained hands together.

"That is true, Despaard. That's true!" He clapped suddenly. His body shook with laughter. "But I am *better* now. I am cured of my illness. My stomach doesn't burn any longer, and my limbs are strong." His red eyes widened. "Strong enough to tear the head off a man, in fact."

Doric moved to stand between Theodore and Despaard. Behind

him came Drezel and Martin. Albertus saw them and smiled.

"You can't undo what I've done. Don't you understand that?" He gestured all around. "This was so forgotten, even by you monks of Saradomin, that it wasn't even hallowed ground." His head twitched uncontrollably for a moment. "The Salve is polluted now, with the blood of the seven innocents. It cannot be cleansed."

"Then vengeance will have to be enough," Doric said menacingly. "Vengeance for what you did to Ebenezer."

Theodore raised the vial. Albertus's eyes narrowed.

"My phosphorus?" he said. "That *could* burn me, no doubt—if you had the opportunity to use it!"

Theodore drew his hand back, but before he could release it Albertus appeared directly in front of him. The old man's hand batted his sword aside and struck him hard in the chest. He crashed violently against the rock wall.

Doric shouted. The dwarf hurled the garlic toward the vampire. The container shattered, and Albertus hissed, his face an animal snarl. Despaard ran forward, the stake in his right hand, his own garlic bulb in the other. Albertus danced backward fearfully.

"It will wear you down, monster," Despaard said. "You haven't been at this very long—you don't know your own powers, or your weaknesses. Already you are growing weak and dizzy."

"I am… I'm still strong enough to deal with the likes of you," the vampire snarled, crouching. With unexpected speed he knocked his attacker to the side. Despaard landed with a cry, and Albertus moved closer, his teeth bared hideously.

Theodore clambered up, but knew he couldn't reach them in time.

"Strong enough to tear the head off a man, in fact."

Without warning, a burst of fire flew past his shoulder, close enough to singe his hair. He ducked aside as the stream consumed the vampire.

Albertus Black screamed.

Doric turned, and shock became glee.

"Castimir!" the dwarf hollered. "By the gods, boy!"

The vampire flailed as the wizard strode forward. His face was set and his stare ice-cold. Behind him came Kara, her sword drawn, and a man in black armor.

Kinshra armor, Theodore realized.

"This is for the children," Castimir said. He pointed his hand, and a second wave of fire lashed forward. The darkness of the chamber was driven back as Albertus screamed. He leapt upward and rolled across the ceiling, tearing at his burning body as the fires consumed him.

He fell to the ground with a sickening *crunch*. Yet he continued to writhe.

"Hold him down!" Despaard shouted. Doric brought the edge of his axe down on Albertus's neck in a blow that would decapitate a mortal man. It dug deep, but didn't cut through. Drezel hurled his cloak across the burning body and gripped one outstretched arm as Martin, still holding his garlic, jumped upon the vampire's back.

Despaard ran forward, taking the hammer from his belt. He jammed the tip of the stake above the vampire's heart, and brought the hammer down.

Thock!

"Aghhh!"

Thock!

"*Grrraaggghhh!*"

Theodore winced as black blood pumped from Albertus's nose and mouth. Drezel and Martin shifted their positions to secure him and suffocate the fires beneath the cloak. Doric took his other arm and held it tightly.

Thock!

Albertus shuddered.

Thock!

His body went still. His red eyes dimmed.

Theodore watched in muted horror as the vampire's face peeled away in powdery layers. The internal energies that had lent him strength now consumed him. The clothes he was wearing flattened under the weight of his attackers, and a fine dust billowed into the air.

Kara swore and ran to the plinths at the foot of each of the seven statues. She gave a cry of rage above the body of a child.

"Do you have the essence?" Doric asked. Castimir nodded. The man in the black armor strode forward and held out a shoulder bag. Drezel stood and took it, staggering a bit under the weight.

"It's all we could bring," the armored man said. Theodore felt his eyes on him. "I am Daquarius," he explained. "Lord of the Kinshra. I am here with Lord Ruthven's permission. Even now, he consults with King Roald."

"Kara, is this true?" Doric asked. She nodded.

"Without him, we would not be here," she said.

"And none of it would have been possible without Arisha," Castimir murmured bitterly. Theodore frowned. Kara glanced toward him, but said nothing.

"Where is she?" Doric said.

"Later, Doric," Kara answered. "Later. First we need to see if we can cleanse the Salve."

Drezel unpacked the shoulder bag, pulling out one of the plates of essence. His eyes went to the well at the chamber's center. The blood of the children still trickled off the plinths, down the well, and into the darkness, leaving a visible stain.

"What do you intend to do?" Despaard asked.

Drezel stood and took Martin's torch. He dropped it into the well and watched it fall.

"I think it leads straight into the river," he said after a moment.

Then he looked up, confusion etched into his features. "Do you think we just *drop* the essence in? The legends say that kings in ancient times did so, upon their coronations. Perhaps, like the runes, it will liquefy and join with the waters."

"There is only one way to know, Drezel," Kara urged. "Try it with one, and see if anything happens."

Drezel took the first piece of the essence, and kissed it.

"Saradomin, hear our prayer," he whispered. "Help us restore the gift you have so generously given."

He held the round object over the well and looked up. He swallowed anxiously.

"Do it!" Kara hissed.

The monk's fingers relaxed. The essence fell. A moment later, from far below, there came the sound of a very faint splash.

They looked at one another, hardly daring to breathe.

Nothing.

Drezel wiped his face nervously.

"I... I could try another," he offered.

"No!" Despaard said firmly. "Not until we're sure it's working. We cannot waste what little we have." He gestured to the rest. "I shall remain here with Drezel while you return to the surface to see if it has changed anything. Whatever happens, we shall await your word."

The catapults were brought to bear on the northern bridge. At the last possible moment, Tenebra summoned the darkness to stop the boulders, but at a steep cost. Black veins stood out on his pale face.

Like cracks in a marble statue, Gar'rth thought. *About to break.* He watched from the eastern end of the narrow stone bridge. The zombie horde, augmented with dozens of the ravenous, reached Misthalin's artillery. Now, Roald's catapults were useless. Gar'rth silently expected, hoped even, that that might mean the end of the bloodshed, that King Roald would see the futility of further violence and withdraw.

But it was not to be. From the north, Roald's cavalry swept south along the bank, led by the king himself. Trumpets announced his coming. A hundred flags of knights and bannermen rippled behind him. Scores of his father's creatures were crushed under the hooves of their warhorses and cut down by sweeping steel.

Yet Tenebra didn't act. His father pressed his hand against his forehead in sudden stress, and it was a stress that his whole army felt too.

They were mindless. Uncertain of their goals. Hesitant and slow.

Roald's charge gained speed, exploiting Tenebra's indecision. Hundreds of the undead were swept aside by the charge of Misthalin's finest names. Maybe thousands. It was time enough for the shield wall to regroup.

Now the king pressed on, toward the stone bridge that had stood since the temple's foundation had been laid. Hatred radiated from the monarch—and Gar'rth was its focus. Behind the king, farther back, rode Theodore in his white armor. With him were Castimir... and Kara.

Gar'rth held his sword and shield awkwardly. He would much rather have used his teeth and claws. The armor he wore felt restrictive, and the helmet—fashioned into a snarling wolf's head—made him feel trapped.

The king halted before the bridge and dismounted. He drew his sword.

"We can shoot him down, sire," Captain Rovin called.

"No!" Roald barked. "He is the future of the enemy. I myself will cut the heart from his body. I will prove to this pretender that I am not afraid.

"This is my battle to fight." He stepped onto the bridge.

Gar'rth waited.

Lord Ruthven hastened forward to speak.

"It is not too late for you, boy," he called. "Disown your father. Pledge your allegiance to the king. Save your life!"

Gar'rth remained silent.

"Speak, boy!" Ruthven yelled. Gar'rth nodded in acknowledgment.

"I cannot disown the one who gave me life, gracious lords," he answered, his voice steady.

"Then I will take that life away from you," Roald said, and he spat. He readied his shield and stood opposite Gar'rth. The bridge had waist-high rails along either side, leaving no room to maneuver.

Suddenly a familiar nausea swept over the werewolf.

A wolfsbane dagger, he realized. *The king must have one!* Before he could react, however, Roald bellowed and charged. His sword swung down and crashed against Gar'rth's kite shield. The impact shook his arm—he hadn't expected the king to possess such strength.

"Come on!" Roald roared. Twice more he hammered his opponent's shield, striking in lightning succession.

His strength is unnatural, Gar'rth realized. *Impossible for a man of his size.* Through the openings in his helmet he saw an amulet with a ruby center. He saw the ring on Roald's finger and he knew, *knew* that the man who so desperately wanted to kill him had augmented his natural abilities by magical means.

Sweat moistened his brow. He fell to his knees as their swords clashed. From the bank, people yelled encouragement.

"Wait!" he gasped. "You don't understand."

The king sneered with contempt, and did not let up.

Gar'rth's vision blurred. His movement was sluggish and his limbs were heavy. Vaguely he saw King Roald step forward, his silver sword swinging down.

His shield was too heavy to lift. He closed his eyes and turned his head.

Clang!

A sting of pain burned his right cheek. His wolf's-head helm rang like a church bell. He felt his blood flow, and his body relaxed. His sword fell and slipped through the railings to fall unnoticed into the Salve.

I don't mind it, he thought curiously. *It's not so bad.*

"Wait! For the god's sake, *wait!*" A woman's voice yelled.

The anger of the words roused him. He looked to the western bank. Kara ran along the bridge. She wore a cuirass over a green arm-length tunic. Her hands were gloved, and in her left hand was her helm. In her right, she held her green-tinted sword.

"Gar'rth!" Kara yelled.

"Stay back!" Roald shouted. "I will kill you if you intervene." He threw down his shield and lifted his sword with both hands. "The pretender shall die today!"

"I have something for you," Gar'rth gritted. "For both of you." He flicked back his cloak and drew the Blisterwood from his belt. "It is the only thing that can kill him... the *only* thing. And I offer it to you."

King Roald hesitated. Kara sheathed her sword. She pushed past Roald and took the Blisterwood cautiously.

He felt her dark eyes bore into his.

"Has Zamorak claimed you, Gar'rth?" she asked. He shook his head.

"I feel about you as I always have, Kara. My love..."

A frown of disapproval played across her features, then it was gone. But it could not be forgotten.

You were my symbol. The one thing I held on to. He reached up to stroke her hair. Before he could, however, King Roald stepped back.

"Tenebra comes," he muttered. Kara looked up and gasped.

"And he's not alone," she said. "May the gods save us!"

"We must go," Roald said, and he grabbed Kara's arm to draw her back. She stood and looked down. Then she gestured for the king to go ahead. As he moved away, the effects of the wolfsbane weapon were lessened.

"Kara," Gar'rth said. "Don't…"

"Can you stand?" she asked. He struggled to his knees, then used the railing to haul himself up. Kara offered her shoulder to him.

He turned, and saw what had made her so afraid. He had been expecting it. The entire opposing bank was lined with more zombies—at least five times as many as those who had already tested Roald's army. They were too numerous to count.

"He's weakening, Kara," he whispered. "Somehow, he is weakening."

Kara urged him west. At the end of the bridge, King Roald waited, his sword at the ready. As they drew closer, Gar'rth's nausea returned.

"He's a hostage. Nothing more," Kara said. "Tenebra won't dare endanger his only heir."

Roald gritted his teeth, but nodded.

"You've bought your beast some time, Kara-Meir," he answered. "But that is all." Then he raised his voice and gestured with his blade. "Everyone into the temple!" he ordered.

Gar'rth let his head rest on Kara's cheek. He breathed in the smell of her hair.

"I love you, Kara," he said as they climbed toward the doorway. "I always have. You gave me hope in a hopeless life."

Kara grunted as she helped him over the threshold.

"Shush! Save your strength, Gar'rth," she muttered.

"How many runes do you have left?" Theodore asked steadily, looking east from the terrace.

Castimir shook his head.

"Not many. Not many at all," he said. Below them the Salve stretched away to the south. He watched the last of the king's soldiers hasten up the steps below. The great door was slammed shut and bolted. Now the entire eastern bank was lined with the undead. Thousands upon thousands of them.

With Tenebra himself at their head.

Waiting.

"Can't you take any from Sedridor?" Daquarius asked. "It seems unlikely he'll use any of them himself. Or perhaps the other wizard?"

"I daren't go through their belongings," Castimir answered. "It is not permitted, and it would leave them undefended. That is unacceptable."

Hazlard grinned.

"Well, I have no such compunctions—"

"Enough, wizard," Daquarius ordered. "You will respect the laws of our allies today." He looked to Theodore. "And even those of our enemies."

The Knight of Falador didn't respond. He kept his gaze held east.

"What are you thinking?" Castimir asked at his side.

"We were only able to make it through to the temple when Tenebra's horde faltered, Cas." He turned suddenly. "Likewise, it was the only thing that saved the men of the shield wall."

Castimir nodded.

"Do you think the essence is working?" he asked.

"I don't know," Theodore replied. "But as you are near out of runes, you should take this." He unslung his shoulder bag and reached inside to pull out a familiar vial.

"Phosphorus?" Castimir said, taking it. Theodore nodded, and handed him the bag as well.

"It should burn any of the undead," he said. "I will fight to the end with my sword, but if you have no runes—"

Running boots sounded on the stairs. King Roald emerged onto the terrace with Kara. Captain Rovin followed.

"Where's Gar'rth?" Doric asked suspiciously.

"He's been tied, downstairs," Kara said. "I think he's still his own man. And he says Tenebra is weakening."

"Could it be the essence?" Castimir asked. "Should we send word to Despaard and instruct him to have Drezel use the rest of it?"

"We don't know enough to warrant that," Doric cautioned.

"Do it," King Roald spat angrily. "Send a rider to Despaard. Tell Drezel to use it all."

"Are you certain, sire?" Rovin asked.

"I said *do it!*" Desperation soaked the king's words. Rovin bowed and signaled to a messenger, who vanished down the steps. Silence fell on the terrace. All eyes stared east.

Tenebra raised his right arm. To the north and the south, the two bridges rumbled under the surge of the enemy.

"His second wave," Doric mused. "I wonder how many there are."

Daquarius snarled angrily.

"The more pertinent question, dwarf, would be to ask how many more he's got behind that."

"Lord Frey and his shield wall will hold them as long as they can," Rovin informed them. "Then they might have to withdraw to the Pass of Silvarea."

"Living muscle against dead limbs?" Doric queried. "The living will tire first."

Castimir peered to the north. So great was the chaos, he found it impossible to see any details. Sounds of the conflict reached him, however—the crash of dead bodies hurling themselves against the ever-more-weary shield wall.

"What can you see?" he asked Kara.

"The shield wall is pulling back. The cavalry are preparing another charge to give them time to regroup." Kara gasped suddenly. "The undead—they've crossed the northern bridge, and turned south. They're coming here!"

"They will encircle us!" Daquarius warned. "We'll be trapped."

"Do we flee, sire?" Rovin asked. "Do we fall back to Silvarea, as did your ancestors of old?"

"There's no time," Kara remarked flatly. "Tenebra's driven a nail between the army and the temple."

"Sirs?" Castimir recognized Hamel. The youth's voice quivered in fear, and he pointed east.

Across the river, Tenebra raised his arms. Above him, the darkness grew blacker.

48

"Down!" Theodore shouted.

Castimir obeyed. From the tower far above, debris cascaded upon them. Theodore held his shield above his head as Kara crouched against him. King Roald was hit by a brick that fell with enough force to make him stagger. Glass and dust covered them all.

"It's not safe up here," Castimir said. "Get off the terrace! Downstairs!" Then he moved to the stairs and descended to the nave. There he took a moment to clean his face, scooping brown water from a bucket.

"Are you hurt, my friend?" a familiar voice said. Castimir opened his eyes cautiously. Before him was Gar'rth. His right cheek was cut open. Black blood dried on his face. His hands were bound behind his back and he was tied in a kneeling position. His head lay on a tabletop.

As if he were about to be beheaded, Castimir realized.

At the sight of his friend, a smile came naturally to him. Quickly he forced it from his face. He wasn't sure he could trust Gar'rth.

"And where is Arisha?" Gar'rth asked.

Castimir lowered his head.

"She was taken, Gar'rth," he answered grimly.

"Is she… is she alive?"

Castimir nodded. At that moment, Captain Rovin stormed over to them.

"You will remain silent," he raged. He drew a wolfsbane dagger. Gar'rth moaned and his eyes grew sluggish. Rovin held it to his throat. "That's right, wolf! If your father enters here, you will be the first to perish. Do you understand?" Then Rovin sheathed his dagger and strode over to his king.

Crashhh!

The chamber door burst open. The undead stormed inside.

"So… so soon," Roald said in astonishment. Then he stood. "Upstairs!" he bellowed.

Yet panic ran among them. Men upended tables to erect rudimentary barriers. Those still coming down from the terrace raced across the aisle, mindful of being cut off. Castimir saw Gar'rth fall under the massed enemy, vanishing from view. Then they advanced toward him.

He gulped and ran toward the stairs, as Roald had commanded. But an overturned table stood before him.

Out of the corner of his eye, he saw a dead face leap toward him. Castimir vaulted the table. A hand took his hindmost leg and he staggered. His shin cracked against the table edge, and he fell. A man stared down at him, hatred in his expression, his sword drawn.

It was Rovin. The captain growled and swung his sword.

Castimir shrank back and screamed.

Slunk!

A shriveled head fell next to him. Rovin heaved him up, and he grinned wickedly.

"Did you think I was going to let you die?" he asked wryly.

"We're in this together!"

The king's men formed a line behind the makeshift barrier. Pikes and swords bristled along its edge. Arrows occasionally flew into the ranks of the gathering enemy.

But the undead just *stopped*. They didn't leap or tear or rush forward.

Instead, they formed a compact group… and waited.

Gar'rth appeared among their ranks, his bonds cut. He stepped forward, and the undead parted around him.

The werewolf noticed Castimir's stare, and his face turned aside in an ugly grimace.

He's done it, the wizard thought. He gathered runes enough for a fire spell. *If he betrays us, then I will destroy him,* he promised himself. *With my last spell I will make Tenebra grieve for all the harm he has done.*

He shifted Theodore's shoulder bag to free his movement.

The phosphorus vial knocked against his back.

He drew a deep breath, and waited.

Kara steadied her sword arm, and never took her eyes off the creatures that milled before her.

One of them shuffled within arm's reach. She stepped forward and thrust the tip of her blade through its forehead. It slumped to its knees as she withdrew her sword and stepped back behind the protection of the outstretched pikes.

The creature fell face-down in silence. The other zombies paid it no notice.

"Evens the odds a bit for later," she said to Daquarius, who stood at her side. "*If* it's actually dead this time."

"Head and the heart," Rovin whispered. "That's the only way to keep them down." He shook his head. "Individually, these zombies are weak enemies, but in numbers they are all but unstoppable.

How can any living army win over enemies who think nothing of an arrow or blade, who feel no pain and know no fear?"

To her left, several positions along the line, Lord Ruthven pointed. Suddenly the zombies stepped back, opening the way.

Tenebra entered.

At first her blood ran cold with fear. She had never seen him before, so close. Now that she did, however, a new thing gripped her.

Curiosity.

"He looks a mess," Doric muttered.

Tenebra staggered forward, coming to rest at the altar to Saradomin. He stood on its raised plinth, and gazed over the heads of his creatures. His strained face widened in a smile, mixed with fatigue.

"Noble men of Varrock," he called, "brave warriors, I propose a truce." He paused, then continued. "The bloodshed can end here. Only one thing is required." Then the smile was gone. "One life for all of yours. Give me your king.

"My descendant."

No one in the line spoke. Kara looked to Roald, but could not read his expression.

"I was the greatest of men in life," Tenebra said. "You cannot conceive of the greatness I can offer the world. True leadership such as you have not seen in many generations."

He paused to wait for an answer. In that instant Theodore cried out.

"The greatest of men?" he shouted. "You have butchered children." Tenebra locked eyes with him, and just stared.

Theodore did not flinch.

"It was a necessary sacrifice," the vampire said, and then his voice rose again. "The children were innocents who bore the symbols of the seven warriors who first blessed this river. Those symbols passed from generation to generation—sometimes by blood, other times not—reflecting Misthalin's link to the Salve. But the time of that link has come to an end.

"They *needed* to die so I could cross." Tenebra's eyes grew hard. "Now, the men of Varrock must make their choice. Give up your king and live, or die by his side. Either way, I will prevail."

No one spoke.

"Gar'rth?" Tenebra said. "Kill King Roald." His son appeared beside him at the altar. But his eyes were focused on Kara's face.

What will you do? she asked silently.

Suddenly the undead surged forward. Kara stabbed and hacked, but the flailing limbs of her enemies pushed her backward, seizing her and disarming her even as her sword impaled the heart of the nearest. To her right she heard Castimir scream as a ball of fire streaked toward the altar.

Toward Gar'rth, she realized.

The vampire lord raised his hands calmly. The ball of fire faded and vanished before it reached his son. But the effort seemed to take its toll. Tenebra sighed wearily and clawed the altar for support.

Kara strained as she was dragged away from the line. She shouted and kicked but undead hands held her fast, tying her hands. None, however, tried to bite or claw her. Instead, she was carried to the altar and forced to kneel.

There she lifted her eyes and saw King Roald in the same situation, at her side.

"I could have my creatures destroy all of you!" Tenebra said angrily. "There are thousands more across the river—*tens* of thousands, waiting for my call. Already your forces are falling back to Silvarea. Paterdomus is surrounded. You *cannot* win today." He looked down the line to Castimir, and grinned. "Your magic is useless against me. I have had countless decades to perfect the art of sorcery. These powers, these skills, are all things I could teach you."

"Just do it!" Roald bellowed angrily. "Just take my head."

Tenebra laughed.

"Not yet," he said. "First there is an important decision to be made—by the one who will take your place upon the throne." He turned. "Gar'rth, you must choose. Whom will you kill today? The girl you believe you love, or the king who has treated you so badly? Like an animal to be put down."

Gar'rth stared. He held King Roald's silver sword in one hand.

"Coward!" Roald spat at his feet. "That is all you will ever be. You *are* an animal." Gar'rth tensed, and took a step in his direction.

No! Kara shouted inwardly.

"Wait, Gar'rth," she said softly. She willed the tears into her eyes. They weren't hard to summon. "You don't have to make this decision," she added. "If you want me, I will be yours."

Gar'rth frowned.

"Not like that, Kara," he said. "This should not be a sacrifice."

"It's not like that," she answered, her voice pleading. "Please…" His eyes narrowed as he studied her face, searching. "Please don't kill me."

Suddenly Tenebra laughed, filling the chamber with echoes.

"Today you will have everything you could want, my son," he said. "Kill the king, and the lives of your people will be yours to use as you see fit." He turned to Roald. "Then we shall see who is the animal." Again he spoke to Gar'rth. "And the woman you want has offered herself willingly, just to save herself," he added. "That is the way of humans, always so desperate to cling to life."

His eyes darkened, and he lowered his head.

"Take her, Gar'rth. She is yours."

Theodore cursed angrily. Doric shouted in incoherent rage.

Kara stared silently, praying he understood.

The knife, Gar'rth, she thought desperately. *Take it from my belt. Use the one weapon that might work.*

Gar'rth knelt before her. His black eyes were sad.

"Please tell me you don't do this from fear, Kara?" he whispered.

"I'm sorry, Gar'rth." She dropped her head, and her eyes flickered toward her belt. Then she raised her face to his.

"Not from fear, Gar'rth," she answered. "But from hope."

Theodore cursed as Gar'rth put his lips to Kara's. At his side Doric shook his head and spat.

Can it be? he thought. *Has Kara offered herself to him to save her own life?*

And Gar'rth—is he still his own man? Or is he truly his father's creature, now?

Theodore closed his eyes. His hate built.

Then he screamed and hurled himself into the zombies that stood before him. The weight of his armor carried him forward, dragging three of them down under him. Doric shouted and leapt forward, as well. Dodging the clawing hands, he reached the place where they had stacked the weapons, and hefted two hand axes.

Along all the line, men shouted in battle rage.

And along all the line, without exception, they charged forward.

Gar'rth dragged her body closer to him and kissed her throat. Beneath her skin he felt the rush of her blood in her jugular. His lust grew.

Then he reached to her belt, where the familiar feel of the Blisterwood knife waited for him.

He kissed her again, and the blood from his wound smeared her face. Somehow he knew his father would approve.

Across the room there was a bellow of hate. He stood to watch

Theodore throw himself from the line in a suicidal fury. Doric followed, and the entire line erupted.

He turned back for an instant.

"Thank you, Kara," Gar'rth said. She nodded, her tears continuing.

He concealed the knife behind his back as he turned to Tenebra. His father gazed in hatred at the suicidal intent of men he believed he had beaten.

The vampire lord's back was to him. Gar'rth gripped the Blisterwood.

He stepped closer to King Roald, to shorten the distance. Roald glared, his eyes widening.

Gar'rth roared and drew his knife hand up.

Thump!

His left shoulder erupted in agony as an arrow appeared just below his face. He dropped King Roald's silver sword. He screamed and staggered, thrusting the Blisterwood forward. He felt it pierce Tenebra's back before his strength deserted him. The edge of the Blisterwood cut his palm as it slipped through his fingers and fell to the floor.

Tenebra screamed and turned. Instantly his eyes fixed on the Blisterwood.

"How...?" He froze, and then raw hatred appeared on his face. "Where does *this* betrayal come from, my son?" He balled his fists in anger and gritted his teeth as though in pain.

Gar'rth struggled to his knees.

"I gave you all a *chance!*" Tenebra shouted. He put his hand on his back and it came away soaked with blood. He snarled. "You had everything you desired, but you are weak—as weak and pitiful as the humans you would have ruled. Instead, you will suffer in ways your siblings could never imagine." He stepped closer. "And your friends, Gar'rth, they will suffer now, suffer for a long, long time."

He struck Gar'rth, causing him to fall and land on the arrow. He screamed in new agony.

Then Tenebra spun and moved to the door. As his foot crossed the threshold he staggered, gave a cry, and then was gone.

Gar'rth stood and leant upon the altar. Pain burned through his body. He pulled the arrow gently. It came out in his hand, and it was tipped with an adamant head.

Out of the corner of his eye, Gar'rth saw Kara sever her bonds on the edge of King Roald's silver sword. His vision blurred.

But the sounds of fighting diminished. When he could see again, the zombies had ceased to fight. They moved aimlessly in all directions, making them easy targets. Kara was loose now. Roald too was free. The king took his sword and stood.

"What is happening?" he asked, but received no answer.

"The Blisterwood," Gar'rth gritted, pointing. Kara scooped it up from the base of the altar. "It's the only thing that can slay Tenebra. Take it, K-Kara."

He felt his strength leave him, and sagged to the floor.

49

Kara felt the *thrum* of the Blisterwood, and ran to the eastern door. Tenebra stood just outside, with his back to her, facing across the river.

"What are you waiting for?" he shouted. "Come on! Come over!"

Kara saw thousands of zombies, waiting on the Morytanian side.

"Obey me!" Tenebra screamed. "To the bridges—before it's too late!"

None moved. Then Tenebra clutched his stomach and gasped. He staggered onto the stone bridge, and fell to his knees.

"The Salve! It's coming back," he cursed. "But that's *impossible*."

Kara moved toward him. Behind her, men poured from the doorway, then stopped in their tracks. Above her she heard people assemble on the terrace.

Across the river, the zombies parted to reveal two figures.

"Malak," Castimir said from behind her. The vampire noble stepped forward. On his shoulder leaned a woman, her face hidden by her red hair.

"What are you doing?" Tenebra seethed. "Send them across!"

The woman pushed back her hair and peered across the waters. Kara felt her anger. Her face was beautiful, but worn.

"Vanescula," Tenebra yelled, his tone turning contrite. "Please! Please send them over!"

The woman stepped carefully away from Malak. She held a hand pressed over her stomach, and walked to the opposite end of the narrow bridge.

"Please, Vanescula!" All that was left was desperation. "We can rule together," Tenebra wailed, "as we were meant to do!"

Vanescula smiled.

"As we were meant to do?" she repeated. She shook her head. "I think not. You were never that important." She looked down into the waters below. "Already the Salve is strengthening, and as it does, so you will weaken, cut off from Morytania.

"Forever," she added.

"No! It's not too late, Vanescula!" Tenebra begged. "Send them over, while there is still time."

The vampire woman licked her lips.

"I *could* do that, couldn't I?" she said, and she looked up at the tower of Paterdomus. "But I don't think I want to."

Tenebra gasped.

"W-what? But why?" he said. "I can conquer all of Misthalin for you."

Vanescula stepped forward. As she reached the stone bridge, her foot was halted by an invisible force.

"I cannot cross," she said bitterly. "Only those you have made— those who are bound to you by blood—were able to do so. But I made you, and thus you are bound to *me*... by blood." She waved her hand to indicate the entire zombie army. "As are these... things." She gave Tenebra a taunting smile. "And I think they will remain here for now."

Tenebra stood—barely.

"No, Vanescula. No!"

She turned back to Malak. She leaned on his shoulder and turned. Suddenly, Kara felt her stare.

You have the Blisterwood, human, a voice sounded in her head. *Use it. And tell the Soft-Heart that Zamorak still waits for him. One day he will take his blessing properly.* Then Vanescula turned her back.

Malak threw a final, victorious look over his shoulder. Tenebra snarled. He clasped his hands together and the darkness before him gathered in a ball. Then he let loose a cry of despair as the darkness unraveled. He fell face-down on the stone.

Kara strode forward, Castimir at her side.

"Do you have runes?" she whispered.

"Didn't you see what happened last time?" he replied coldly.

She saw the phosphorus vial in his hands.

Tenebra looked up at her as she stepped onto the bridge. His face was haggard. He tried to push himself up, only to collapse again.

Pathetic, she thought.

"You!" Tenebra spat, and he sneered at her. "It was *always* you. You kept him from me. You were his shield."

Castimir raised the phosphorus.

"More magic, wizard?" Tenebra asked. He raised his hands. A thin veil of darkness gathered in front of him.

Castimir hurled the vial. It passed through the barrier and broke over the vampire's face and chest.

Tenebra gasped.

"Not this time," Castimir said.

A pale smoke rose from the vampire's cloak. When the first of the flames burst into life Tenebra screamed. He lurched to his feet with the strength of desperation, batting the consuming fires.

Kara jumped forward. Mindful of the flames, she risked a killing blow. The Blisterwood sank handle-deep into the base of Tenebra's skull. She felt it crack.

"*Arrrgh...*"

Tenebra reached to the top of his spine. Kara backed away, leaving the Blisterwood in his skull. The vampire sagged forward. His body slumped on the bridge's railing. The fires continued to burn.

His body went limp, and shifted on the rail, sliding over the edge and down into the chasm, where the holy waters of the Salve waited.

A rider appeared from the north. It was Lord Despaard.

"We did as your messenger commanded, sire," he said as he reined in. "Drezel added what essence we had left to the river. The Black Prince's monsters lost their resolve after that. They simply stood and waited to be cut down. Lord Frey and his shield wall have pushed hundreds back into the river. The day is yours, majesty." King Roald nodded wearily. Then he looked to Kara.

"Then it is time for decisions," he said. "We must decide the fate of the vampire's son."

"Slit his throat and throw him after his father," Rovin said.

"What?" Kara raged. "You saw what he did! He *saved* us. He would have killed Tenebra himself, if not for that archer."

Roald nodded. Then he gestured.

"You speak the truth, yet we must be careful. Place him under arrest," he commanded. "He will return to Varrock with us. But first, we must bury the dead."

They made their way back to the temple. As they did, the bells rang out.

50

The midnight hour had come and gone. Under the dim light of his dying lantern, Sulla balanced a cup of wine to his lips with his artificial hands.

The cup slipped, and a red splash stained his oak desk. He was careful not to spill any on his half-eaten meal.

"Are you drunk?" Jerrod growled, peering in from the next room.

"It's just nerves," Sulla said. "The anticipation of revenge. Nothing more."

They hid in a house the werewolf had rented, unknown to friend and foe alike. Following Simon's death, they laid low for several days. When they remained undiscovered, Jerrod ventured forth. He had returned with their accomplice, Barbec.

And the coded documents.

These simple pieces of paper strike fear in people of influence from here all the way to Kandarin, Sulla mused. *They have already given me a small fortune.*

And that is just the start.

Sulla had sent Barbec south since then, to help plan their

eventual flight from Misthalin.

Downstairs, a door creaked.

"Barbec?" Jerrod whispered.

"No," Sulla hissed. "He won't be coming back. We will meet him in Port Sarim, where Straven will have the documents we need to board the ship."

The thought of Straven made him shudder. The gang-master was an old associate, having carried out work for him when he had been the Kinshra leader. It was a relationship Sulla had called upon to bait his trap.

A footstep sounded. Then another. Someone, slowly, was climbing the stairs.

"Sulla," the werewolf growled tentatively, walking in from the adjoining chamber and taking a position behind the door.

"Let it be," Sulla replied. "I have been expecting this." He again lifted his wine, but his prosthetics shook too much for him to drink.

Nerves, he cursed inwardly.

The footsteps ceased outside the door. Sulla took a deep breath. The handle turned, and a hooded figure entered, dressed in black.

"Sulla?" a muffled voice said.

"Yes," he replied. "Please sit down."

"I represent the Kinshra," the figure said, still standing. "We have been told that you wish to surrender your documents, in return for a pardon from the order. Is this true?"

Sulla swallowed. Then he forced a grin.

"Why don't you come in, Lord William?"

The figure didn't move.

"Well?" Sulla said calmly. "Surely you didn't expect me to be fooled, just because you disguised your voice, did you, boy?"

"Boy?" The figure grunted, then stepped forward into the room. Jerrod shoved the door closed and grabbed the newcomer by the arms.

"Wait!"

A female voice! And one he recognized.

The figure was forced to the floor under Jerrod's strength. The werewolf turned the intruder to face Sulla and pulled back the hood, growling in excitement as he did so.

The woman's terror-filled face was raised to meet his stare. Her blonde hair fell loosely across her cheek, hiding one of her perfect blue eyes.

"Well, well," Sulla remarked. "I would never have expected it."

Jerrod's huge hand covered Lady Anne's mouth.

"But I suppose it makes sense," Sulla continued. "Pretending to love Sir Theodore put you in the perfect position to spy on him. It's classic, but not something I would have expected of you.

"I'm impressed," he added sincerely.

Lady Anne moaned. Sulla nodded and Jerrod's hand relaxed.

"I *do* love him, Sulla." Tears pooled in her eyes. "We aren't all the same as you. Zamorak is not evil. He is not as you would lead people to believe." She faced him contentiously. "And you are assaulting me against the laws of parley. I am a messenger—"

"Huh," Sulla replied derisively. "Was it not you who singled me out and threatened me in the palace? Or did you leave the death mark for others, as well?"

"It was a warning only, Sulla." Doubt crept into her voice. "To persuade you to give up the documents."

"Then consider this a warning, as well," he replied. Sulla gestured, and Jerrod pressed her face into the rug.

Then he leaned in close. She squealed in surprise as the werewolf licked her face.

"Sulla?" she said. "P-please, Sulla. Please..."

A wicked game entered his mind. He smiled and drew his plate closer.

"Does Sir Theodore know about you?" he asked. "About your loyalties?"

Anne shook her head.

"Of course not," she replied. "I'm finished with the Kinshra after this! Theodore and I are to be married—"

Sulla laughed at that, long and loud. When he was finished, he sat and stared at her, letting the malice shine in his eye. He could see the panic it inspired in her, and he relished the feeling.

"P-please, Sulla—I was good to you in the palace. I can *still* be good for you…"

"Silence, woman," he snapped. Jerrod's hand clasped over her mouth. With his other hand the werewolf tore off her cloak. Anne cringed.

Sulla examined his food for a moment.

"You have heard of the Fremennik peoples, of the far north?" he asked slowly. Anne nodded. "They apparently have a tradition there." He scooped up a piece of meat with his prosthetic hand and bit into it greedily, deliberately letting the juices run down his chin. "The men there are messy eaters, wasting their food with abandon, or so the legends say.

"They do this for a reason." His eye stared coldly into Anne's petrified face. Her fear excited him. "It shows that a man can *afford* to waste food. In so doing, it shows that he can provide for his family."

Jerrod ripped Anne's tunic from her shoulder. Her fear ruled her now. She gave a cry and shook her head. Her muffled plea could only be for mercy, he knew.

Yet we haven't even begun, he thought with relish.

He looked to his werewolf friend.

"Jerrod, please join me for dinner."

His eye fell on Anne. She stopped her struggling.

"And Jerrod," he added. "Make it messy."

• • •

Sulla crossed the gangplank uneasily. It was in the cold light of daybreak, and the cries of the gulls and the smell of the sea were new to him. The three-masted ship upon which he stood would be leaving the Asgarnian harbor of Port Sarim within a matter of hours. There were very few people about, and—he noted with satisfaction—no signs of pursuit from Varrock.

A new life in Kandarin, he thought. *Perhaps King Lathas will make use of our services? If he's as ruthless as I suspect, then he won't have any qualms about our methods.*

Jerrod came behind him, crossing the gangplank from the quayside in his human form. Barbec hesitated before taking a single step.

"Nervous?" Sulla called. Barbec bit his lip, and remained on the dock.

A white-bearded man climbed a ladder from someplace in the lower regions of the vessel.

"Get below," he instructed. "Passengers should keep out of the way. Down there." He jabbed a thumb over his shoulder.

Sulla held his tongue. Jerrod went to the ladder the man had indicated, and peered down into the shadows.

"I can't smell anything but fish," the werewolf muttered. "And this sea—it is too changeable, Sulla." He looked around uncomfortably, eyes darting from place to place.

Sulla growled.

"It won't be long now, my friend. Soon we shall leave these shores—and our enemies—far behind. We just have to endure this one voyage, and we will be able to start anew."

Jerrod nodded, and climbed down the ladder. Sulla looked once more to Barbec. He hadn't moved, and his face had grown pale.

"What's wrong?" Sulla shouted over the gangplank. "Are you

afraid of ships?"

Barbec nodded strangely.

Suddenly the white-bearded man pushed Sulla aside roughly. He slipped on the deck and sprawled, unable to balance himself with his prosthetics. When he looked up, he saw the man drop a door into place above the ladder, and slide a bolt across.

"What are you doing?" Sulla shouted as he struggled to his feet. The white-bearded man ignored him.

Below deck, Jerrod howled in fury.

Looking back to the dock, Sulla saw a second figure appear beside Barbec.

Straven, he realized. Panic replaced anger.

"What's the meaning of this?" he shouted.

The gang-master nodded to White-Beard, who pulled a knife from his belt. Sulla backed away, and glanced to the gangplank.

"Straven?" He called. "Barbec!" Both men remained silent. White-Beard was joined by two of his crew. Together they advanced.

"A buyer in Kandarin wants your animal, Sulla," Straven shouted. "He has paid a handsome price for him. You, however—" he shook his head, "—you are not so important. Your precious documents will be handed to King Roald, to soothe his anger at what you did to Lady Anne. Without them, you are of no value at all—at least not while you are breathing."

Sulla tried to hold off White-Beard with his prosthetic right hand, but the strong-looking seaman simply seized him by the wrist and thrust his knife forward.

Slitch.

Pain grew like a fire in Sulla's side. The knife was twisted, and then withdrawn.

Sulla staggered, and moaned. The sound seemed puny compared to the howling of the werewolf.

White-Beard pulled him forward. Both crewmen stabbed him with a glee he could have appreciated, were he not the target. He was dropped to the deck, and his blood ran off the edge.

"Use his corpse to feed his animal," Straven called over. "It's fitting, I think. Though I will need his head."

"Aye," White-Beard replied. He said something else, words that were lost to Sulla as his senses dimmed.

Finally, White-Beard held the edge of his blade to Sulla's throat.

"I can m-make you r-rich," he grated. "Richhh—"

The blade sliced across his throat. Sulla felt his own blood warm his chest. Then all was cold.

51

Pia entered the room quietly. In the bay window of Ebenezer's townhouse, Jack sat playing with his shards. Around the table sat Kara-Meir with the knight Theodore and some of the king's most senior advisors.

Trying to will herself invisible, she moved among them and filled their glasses.

"Lady Anne died very quickly, Sir Theodore," Captain Rovin said sadly. The knight simply stared into his lap, his eyes glazed. Pia had noticed how he barely spoke anymore. She looked to Rovin, and saw him exchange an anxious nod with Kara.

She knew he was lying. She had heard it already. The beautiful Lady Anne had died anything but quickly. According to the gossip she had heard among the palace servants, she had been devoured—still alive—by a werewolf. Some said her tongue had been chewed off, and that the creature had left her eyes for last, so she could see what ruin he had done to her body.

Pia had found a private place, away from everybody, and had wept for the beautiful woman. Even now, she shuddered and fought back tears.

"We will find Jerrod, Theodore," Kara said. "I promise you we will." She put her hand on Theodore's shoulder, and Pia saw her fingers go white due to her firm grip.

Theodore simply nodded, but remained silent.

"Our reports indicate that he was taken to Kandarin aboard a ship," Lord Ruthven said. "Sulla's betrayer—the man who handed over the Kinshra documents—informed us of this. Word will be sent to King Lathas's government."

"And you are sure Sulla is dead?" Doric asked.

Ruthven shared a grim smile with Despaard. The black-clad nobleman left the room for the briefest moment before returning with a wooden box.

"Here is proof, if you care for it," Despaard said. "It will be sent to Falador first, and then on to the Kinshra. Daquarius has earned that much at least."

Kara stood. Despaard opened the box. Her expression was grim, and she kept her dark eyes fastened on the thing inside.

Pia craned her head to see, but she caught only a glance of a shriveled object.

After a moment, Kara nodded.

"Then he really is dead," she said. Despaard nodded, and shut the box.

They sat in silence for several long moments. Then the door opened, and Castimir entered. Quickly he found a seat at the table, and peered from face to face.

"There is still no word of Arisha," he announced. There was an angry edge to his voice. "But I doubt the Untainted would have harmed her. They were not oath breakers."

To Pia, his eyes carried a glint of madness, and when he looked at Mistress Kara she turned away.

"We have no choice," Castimir continued. "We *must* go after her." He frowned and said, "Roald should send an army to rescue her. He would if he had any honor."

Silence fell. Rovin stared at him openly.

"You know that's impossible, boy," he said after a moment. "His majesty's scouts were sent to this Mountain of Fire as soon as we returned to Varrock, but nothing remained there save earth blistered by fire, with the charred remains of these caverns you described. There were none of the Untainted, and there was no essence."

"Aubury knows," Castimir said. "Somehow he knew where I went—the Tower was behind it, for nothing else save magic could have caused such complete destruction. And despite the need for his abilities, Master Grayzag was not at Paterdomus." He fell silent for several long moments, then spoke again.

"If he—if *they* have hurt Arisha, then I will have my revenge."

Theodore looked up from his lap. His eyes were tearful.

"You once told me that revenge is something that needs to be done, Kara. I always thought that it was your anger speaking. Now I know the truth." Kara stepped behind him and put her hands on his shoulders.

"It's wrong of me, I know that," Theodore said. "Revenge is not the way of a Knight of Falador. But still…"

Kara bent down and whispered in his ear. Theodore nodded.

"Perhaps you are right," he said. "But perhaps I am no longer worthy."

"Nonsense, squire," Doric growled. "They are singing songs about you now. How you destroyed the bridge and how you saved Varrock's granary, how Kara slew the Black Prince, how Castimir used his magic to burn a sorcerer who had bested Master Sedridor." He shook his head. "Your reputations have never been greater."

"That's not important, Doric," Theodore said quietly.

"Isn't it?" the dwarf shot back. "People will look to you now, for leadership, for inspiration. Tenebra built his coup on a false prophecy he had fed us a century ago. Yet it was Kara's reputation that rallied the men of Misthalin outside Paterdomus." He turned to face her. "They believed you were 'touched by the gods,' and that gave them strength."

He shook his head again.

"Ebenezer would have agreed with me," he said. "If he's watching us now, he would tell you so."

Theodore nodded and stood. He seemed unsteady on his feet.

"There's truth in what you say, but my thoughts are chaos," he said. "I need to be alone for a while." As he turned to leave, Kara reached out, and he took her hand. She continued to watch him as he departed.

As she moved back to where Jack was sitting, Pia thought of the kindly old alchemist, and a lump appeared in her throat. She had wept at his funeral, too, when they laid his remains beside those of his family.

"Where is Papelford now?" Kara asked. "As the leader of Tenebra's insurgency he should be hanging from the gallows."

"He fled after his undead army was destroyed," Despaard reported. "He tried to hide among the insurgents, but they have lost the will to fight, and scattered. We expect to have him very soon."

"And what will you do with him?" Doric asked. "The public don't know of his treachery."

"It will stay that way, of course," Despaard acknowledged. "The monarchy has suffered greatly, and we cannot allow more damage to be done." Then he brightened. "The king's wedding to Ellamaria will go a long way to curing the distrust that was thrust between the crown and its subjects. That, and the fact that the Inquisition has been shut down, should help a great deal."

"As will the marriage of Lady Caroline and Lord William," Rovin added. "Given his open heroism, he's had his estates returned to him and his place at court has been reinstated."

"But you haven't answered my question, Despaard," Doric grinned. "What will you do with Papelford?" Despaard gave the dwarf a hard look. Pia shuddered at the memory of the horrible old man and his appetites.

"Most treachery is dealt with by execution," Despaard said.

"Will King Roald really do that?" Doric asked. Despaard grinned maliciously.

"I hope so," he said. "The wretch deserves nothing less."

Lord Ruthven put his goblet down with a firm clunk.

"But there is one question none of you has asked," he said. "What about Gar'rth?"

Kara looked up eagerly.

"Has the king made a decision?"

"He has," Ruthven revealed. "Gar'rth will not be executed. However, he is still dangerous as a legitimate claimant to the throne. King Roald's enemies might use him as a figurehead."

Captain Rovin grumbled in agreement.

"So he is to be exiled," Ruthven continued. "He will never enter Varrock again, and he will be barred from Misthalin, as well."

"But where should he go?" Kara asked.

Ruthven shrugged.

"Perhaps Kandarin? King Roald is not without mercy. Gar'rth will be pensioned off by the crown. He will receive a stipend each year—enough to live well." Ruthven's hawk-face grew hard. "That is *more* than generous."

"Then Kandarin it is," Kara said firmly, her voice rising. "For all of us, I think. Theodore wants Jerrod, Castimir wants Arisha, and I wish to clear Pia's name. If Gar'rth is to be sent there as well, then there is no real alternative."

Doric grunted.

"It's a long way away," he said. "And King Lathas isn't King Roald—not by any stretch."

"The man is a tyrant," Despaard said. "A subtle one, though. Be mindful of him, and of his mother. It would be best if you didn't court his attention at all."

Kara-Meir nodded. She turned to Pia and smiled.

"Then it's settled," she said. "We book passage to Kandarin."

EPILOGUE

Arisha shivered in her sleep, and the pain in her abdomen grew. She turned, and the pain eased.

She dreamt of fire, followed by ice. Of a burning mountain with screaming men, and then a long journey into a world of frozen seas, where the sun never set.

The pain in her stomach grew, causing her to wake.

A bearskin blanket covered her naked body, which lay on a mattress of feathers. The small wooden room she was in heaved and yawed. The splash of oars, dipping into water, reached her ears.

I am in a boat, she realized without surprise. She stood and took a thick woolen tunic that lay across the bottom of her blanket. Before dressing, she examined her wounded shoulder.

The black of the poison had gone. There was a healthy scar surrounded by white flesh. She wished she had a mirror to examine herself more fully, but there was none to hand.

She pulled the tunic over her head. When it reached her stomach she paused. The pain was there again. And her belly was swollen.

Oh, Cas, she thought, sitting on the mattress. *Did you realize?*

Did you know?

Part of her wanted to weep from happiness, but a greater part of her kept her silent, reminding her of an uncomfortable truth.

What will they do with the child if they find that he's a mage's baby? the voice said. *What will they do?*

Arisha breathed deeply and flicked her dark hair over her shoulders. She knew what they would do.

Footsteps sounded on the wooden planks outside. The door opened, and Kuhn stood before her. The draft of freezing air made her shiver.

"So, you're finally awake," he said. "I spoke with Magnus. He thinks the poison is all gone."

"Where are we?" she said. Her mouth was terribly dry. It was the first time she had talked aloud in a very long time.

"I'll show you," Kuhn said quietly. His eyes sank to her waist. "You *know*, don't you?"

Arisha's hand covered her belly.

"If they discover the truth…" he ventured, and the look on his face was strange to her. After a moment he continued. "Then it will be mine," he said. "In The Wilderness. That's when it happened."

"Why?" Arisha asked. "Why do this?" Kuhn grinned.

"Better not to ask," he said.

Arisha stood warily. Kuhn came forward and took her hand.

"Many of the Untainted rode ahead to the Mountain of Fire after your capture. They were ambushed there by wizards of the Tower." Kuhn growled angrily. "Very few escaped, and their anger will be great."

"Castimir didn't know, Kuhn," she said. "I can promise that."

Kuhn nodded. He took the bearskin blanket from the bed.

"Come then," he said. "Let me show you where we are."

He helped her through the door and up a short flight of wooden stairs to the deck. The temperature dropped sharply. There was a piercing light, all around her, and it hurt her eyes.

Sun on ice, she realized as she shaded her eyes with the flat of her hand. They were in a longship, with a dragon's head at the prow. There was ice everywhere. A huge wall of it—a cliff that dwarfed even the might of Paterdomus—stretched across the entire horizon.

She shivered, and Kuhn wrapped the bearskin around her shoulders. There was a tenderness in him that hadn't been there before.

"There," he said. "Look." He pointed to a settlement on the shore, with familiar buildings in the style of Gunnarsgrunn. As they drew closer she saw men in furs unloading the catch from their fishing boats. One of them stood, and he was at least twice the size of Kuhn.

Arisha gasped.

"That's not a man," Kuhn observed. "That's a troll, priestess. The people along this shore trade with them."

A troll? she thought with excitement. She had never seen one before, though they featured greatly in the stories of her people. She shivered again, and found that her hand shielded her belly. Kuhn noticed it, too.

"You should go below," he said. "Rellekka is still some days away."

Rellekka, home of my forebears, she thought. *It is likely to be the place of my death.* She closed her eyes as the wind freshened. A cry went up and the sail was raised. The longship picked up speed.

Taking me ever farther from Castimir. She felt her eyes water. Grimly she forced her emotion down. She would not let Kuhn see.

Come soon, my love, she prayed silently. *Come soon.*

About the author

T.S. Church was born and educated in Worcestershire, England. He holds degrees in Information Systems and Business, as well as an MA in Marketing, all from the University of the West of England, Bristol. In his free time, he enjoys playing *RuneScape*. When not spending time in Gielinor, he likes to read and study history. He also participates (reluctantly) in adventure sports, from canoeing the length of the Thames to running half marathons. He is the author of two further *RuneScape* tie-in novels: *Betrayal at Falador* and *Return to Canifis*. To find out more, visit his website, www.tschurch.com.

FOR MORE FANTASTIC FICTION
FROM TITAN BOOKS
CHECK OUT OUR WEBSITE

www.titanbooks.com

WHERE YOU'LL FIND DETAILS
OF ALL OUR EXCITING TITLES